Something Like Regret

The story of a different path
taken by Elizabeth Bennet and Mr. Darcy.

By Kara Louise

D0905955

© 2009 by Kara Louise

Cover image by Kara Louise

ISBN 978-1-4357-5379-2

Published by Heartworks Publication

Printed in the United States of America

Library of Congress Cataloging-in-Publication Data

Kara Louise
Something Like Regret

Note from the author~

I began this novel several years ago, working at it a
little bit at a time, and then putting it aside when I began writing
my modern novel, *Drive and Determination*.
Once that was completed, I decided to go back and finish this one.

Again I had the excellent help of Mary Anne Hinz,
who has helped me edit all my books.
I appreciate her and thank her immensely. She does a great job!

I owe all my inspiration to Jane Austen,
who gave us her original story and all the wonderful characters
that continue to touch the hearts of people today.

As with my other stories, I hope you find this enjoyable.

Kara Louise

Something Like Regret

Prologue

Fitzwilliam Darcy sat stiffly in the carriage as it rambled down the dirt road, uncomfortable from the long ride and restless in his thoughts. His attempt at reading the book he held tightly in his hands had failed miserably. Throughout the day's journey his eyes perused no more than two pages; he comprehended even less. His cousin, Colonel Patrick Fitzwilliam, was in a talkative mood, as was the norm, and Darcy found it markedly aggravating. But that was not the chief foundation for his discomfiture.

The two men were on their way to Rosings. It was enough that this yearly journey meant having to endure three weeks in the company of their aunt, suffering her complaints and outbursts, enduring her deplorable demands and infuriating insinuations, and tolerating her firm conviction that Darcy was to marry her daughter, Anne. On this visit, however, Darcy could not help but reflect on the fact that his aunt's clergyman, William Collins, was Elizabeth Bennet's cousin; his wife, Charlotte, was her best friend; and last year at this time, Miss Bennet had adamantly refused his offer of marriage in this very place.

Darcy stared out the window as they drew near. He had told not a single soul of his offer to Miss Bennet and her subsequent rejection of his suit. He fought hard against the ensuing melancholy and constant self-evaluation that had taken much of the joy out of his life. While others had merely teased him as being out of sorts, it was his sister, Georgiana, who easily perceived that something grave pressed upon him. She inquired about the reasons for his downcast spirits on several occasions, but he did not wish to burden her with his tale of unrequited love.

Soon they would pass the parsonage and then cross the lane over to Rosings. He closed his book and looked out the window, all the while Fitzwilliam carried on about what he had seen and done since the two men had last been together.

Fitzwilliam seemed not to care that Darcy contributed little to the conversation. The Colonel related to his disinterested cousin all the adventures his militia had enjoyed up north. Fitzwilliam was well aware that Darcy was not one who rambled on endlessly, but normally he took a great deal of interest in what he had to say. Today, however, he perceived that his cousin seemed not to be listening; his mind was elsewhere.

"Did you know Darcy, that it can get so cold up north that your breath freezes when you breathe out through your mouth?"

"Is that so?" Darcy responded nonchalantly, his eyes riveted to the window.

"But I tell you truthfully, that the women up there are remarkably affectionate. I can only imagine it is because it gets so cold up there they appreciate the warmth of a man in uniform."

Darcy turned and gave him a scowl.

Fitzwilliam laughed. "I was merely checking to see if you were listening."

"I am, Fitzwilliam, and I am truly not interested in hearing of your mercenary tactics where the fairer sex is concerned."

"Always the proper gentleman," Fitzwilliam teased. "What grave occurrence do you think our aunt will be complaining about during our visit this year?"

"Most likely she has not received her share of abundant adoration, profuse praise, and generous condescension."

"Does she ever?" He shook his head. "As long as we have known her, she has never been content with her lot in life and yet she has so much. She is not happy unless others recognize how much lower they are than she or they verbosely applaud her with accolades that she hardly deserves."

Darcy turned and looked at him with a curious glint in his eyes and then quickly turned away. A sudden tightness in his stomach gave him pause to wonder if he, himself, might have a share of some of those same qualities. Is that what he had expected Elizabeth to appreciate in his offer more so than his love? He looked away as he recollected those things that had held prominence in his words that fateful day.

"Come, Darcy, must you look so glum?" Fitzwilliam slapped him on the shoulder. "We have visited our aunt practically every year at Easter since we were boys. Surely you have learned how to tolerate her eccentricities."

Darcy drew in a deep breath. "Yes, but I do not feel particularly inclined to contend with her this year."

"I am in no doubt you shall find ample opportunity to go on your long walks or vigorous rides on Challiot as you generally do. We can only hope the weather will be accommodating."

"Yes," he answered, barely following his cousin's words as the parsonage came into sight. His breath caught slightly upon seeing it again as a mixture of feelings swarmed over him. Turning away from the window, he clenched his fists, hoping to maintain a modicum of control.

At length, the carriage pulled up to the front of the great edifice that his aunt called home and came to a stop.

"Are you ready, Darcy? Do you need a few moments to gather your fortitude?"

"No, the sooner her generous greeting is over, the better."

The carriage door was opened and the two men stepped out. As if by cue, they both stretched out their arms and shook out the stiffness in their legs due to the length of the ride and the confinement of the compartment. They turned toward each other with mirrored looks that reflected their similar feelings and then began to walk to the house.

When they were ushered into the great hall, a shrill voice pierced their ears.

"My nephews! You have finally arrived! I wondered if I would ever see you!" She rushed towards them in what appeared to be an agitated manner.

6

"How is it that you are so late? Were the roads not satisfactory? I must talk to someone about that!"

Both men walked slowly toward her, each pulling from that source deep within that allowed them to bear up under her excessive attention.

"Good day, Aunt." Patrick Fitzwilliam was the first to receive an embrace from Lady Catherine de Bourgh. He had no need to fear that she would smother him, as her hugs were brief and light and he was able to pull away quickly.

She stepped back and studied his frame. "Patrick, you are too thin. What is the regiment feeding you? I am quite certain not enough. You shall certainly eat like a king here and will lack for nothing. We shall do our best to fatten you up."

Fitzwilliam gritted his teeth and smiled. "Thank you, Aunt. I am most grateful."

"And so you should be. My good brother and his wife are most likely not as attentive to these details as they should be. They wrongly assume you are responsible enough to take care of yourself. Merely by the looks of you, I can see that you do not."

"Yes, Aunt." The Colonel sent a grave look over to his cousin.

"Come here, Fitzwilliam. Let me look at you!" insisted his aunt.

Darcy guardedly approached his aunt as she held out her arms. "It is so good to see you, again!" Her embrace lasted a little longer than his cousin's, but she obliged him by not planting a kiss on his cheek as she often did when he was younger.

"And how does my cousin appear to you, Aunt?" Fitzwilliam asked.

"He is always in fine figure. A good thing for my Anne, too. Unfortunately, her stamina is slowly weakening and she may one day require someone to carry her up and down the stairs at Pemberley."

Fitzwilliam watched his cousin's face cloud over with stifled resentment, and as Darcy began to open his mouth, he quickly interceded. "Aunt, the grounds look wonderful! The flowers are simply grand!"

"Yes, they are." She turned away from the men to look out a window toward the gardens while Fitzwilliam cast his cousin a warning look. "I must admit I pay special attention to all the work my gardeners do."

The three looked out in a brief respite of silence. Darcy could hardly corroborate his cousin's admiration of the gardens, as they were very artificially pruned and tended. He preferred a more natural look and had never felt an affinity for his aunt's style of gardening.

"Come," she said when she felt they had admired enough. "I know Anne looks forward to welcoming you." Her eyes went to Darcy as she said this and as he returned her gaze, he noticed Fitzwilliam's smirk behind her.

They followed her into the drawing room. It was purposely kept dark, and therefore a depressing air hung about the room. Lady Catherine insisted that the drapes be kept drawn when Anne was in the room, believing that too much light might cause her harm. As the three walked in, Darcy readily noticed the look of hopeful longing that barely lit Anne's eyes. He walked over to her and smiled, taking her hand and giving it a light kiss.

"Good day, Anne. It is good to see you."

The young lady smiled. "It is good to see you, as well, Cousin."

Darcy stepped back and watched Fitzwilliam do likewise. It was always the same. They would greet her warmly and then shortly after, she would return to her room, as the excitement of having visitors always wore on her. Darcy watched in disinterested impatience as Fitzwilliam took the young lady's hand. But today he noticed something new. There was actually a spark in her eyes as she looked at the Colonel.

Darcy narrowed his eyes as he saw for the first time that his young cousin, who had supposedly been promised to *him* at birth, seemed to have a bit of a regard for their elder cousin. Now it was *his* turn to smirk as he considered how he would heap on the teasing about his *cousin's* upcoming marriage to Anne.

After their greeting and a few cordial words, Mrs. Jenkinson offered to help Anne back to her room.

"No thank you, Mrs. Jenkinson. I should prefer to remain down here with my cousins if you do not mind."

Lady Catherine looked sternly at her daughter. "Impossible, Anne! You know my sentiments. You require all the rest you can get and this has already been too much excitement for you."

"But they have only just arrived. I should like to visit with them a little longer. Please, Mother."

Lady Catherine grudgingly relented. "For only a few minutes more. Then you must rest. I will hear nothing further from you."

As they visited, Lady Catherine did most of the talking. Darcy watched as Anne stole glances at their cousin, who made every attempt to engage Anne in conversation. Darcy let out a soft chuckle. He could easily see why Anne was so partial to him. Fitzwilliam was most attentive towards their frail cousin, even though he had no romantic inclinations toward her. He had an engaging personality and had nothing to fear in regards to her admiration.

Darcy's thoughts went back to Anne. She was certainly not as fragile as her mother believed her to be. It was true she had been ill as a child and had been greatly weakened because of it. But shielding her from any sort of life, activity, and hardship of any kind had only served to give her the appearance of frailty. Darcy was convinced that all she needed was a bit more freedom to experience the warmth of the sunshine on her face as she walked, the joy of a dance at a ball with a favourite gentleman, or the thrill of going to the theatre or a concert in Town. While he was certain her mother would never allow it, Darcy was convinced it would do nothing but improve her.

In the midst of Darcy's musings, he became aware of his aunt making some sort of reference to Mr. Collins. He turned toward her and caught only the last part of what she was saying.

"So now I must find another clergyman and you know how difficult it is to find one who will be suited for the position. I do not look forward to having to prepare another. Mr. Collins had been so accommodating and he learned to gratify my expectations so well."

"Excuse me, Aunt," Darcy interrupted. "What happened to Mr. Collins?"

"He has quit Hunsford!! He and Mrs. Collins! Three months ago! It has been extremely vexing to find a clergyman who suits me. We have had two come and go already! It is not to be borne!"

Darcy was surprised at the sudden feeling of disappointment he felt upon hearing this news, knowing now there would be no possibility of encountering Miss Elizabeth again. He looked curiously at his aunt as he inquired, "Where did Mr. Collins and his wife go?"

"To that estate that was entailed to him in Hertfordshire, of course. Mr... Mr... whatever his name died late last spring and he and Mrs. Collins claimed their rightful possession of it."

"Mr. Bennet?" Darcy asked abruptly. He then softened his voice in an attempt to hide his piqued interest. "Was it Mr. Bennet who died?"

"Yes, he is the very one. Mr. Bennet. This has been a grave inconvenience." Lady Catherine gave a drawn out huff.

"Yes, I can imagine." Darcy said with noticeable irritation, rubbing his chin as he considered this. "But do you know, Aunt, what happened with the Bennet ladies? Do they remain at Longbourn with Mr. Collins and his wife?"

"The Bennet ladies? Well, how should I know and why should I care about them? They do not concern me. I am solely concerned with finding someone suitable to be Rosings' clergyman." Her grey eyes narrowed into small slits.

Darcy struggled to remain calm. It became a burden even to swallow and although he had determined this past year to put Miss Bennet out of his mind, he had found it increasingly difficult to put her out of his heart. He wanted to know... needed to know... what had become of Miss Elizabeth Bennet.

He struggled for composure, knowing any indication of interest would spark Patrick's curiosity. He could not appear too concerned.

He need not have worried though, because his cousin suddenly asked, "Is that Miss Elizabeth Bennet's family? The one who visited the Collinses last year whilst we were here?"

"The very one," Lady Catherine observed. She shook her head repeatedly. "Impertinent young lady, if I recall. But I really cannot tell you what happened to them. I suppose if they are fortunate, they are still living at Longbourn with the Collinses. After all, he is a clergyman – and they are family – I am quite certain he has had compassion on them and allowed them to remain."

Darcy stood up and walked over to the window, surprised by those thoughts and feelings which had unexpectedly returned. He took in a deep breath to calm himself. Looking out at the grounds, he thought back to the events of a year ago. Miss Bennet's rejection of his suit had hurt and angered him greatly, but judging by the feelings that were presently surfacing, he realized he still cared deeply for her.

As he considered the Bennet ladies' situation, he knew not whether it would be more fortunate for them to still be living at Longbourn with the Collinses or to have been forcibly removed from their home. He could not imagine *her* living in the same household as Collins. *Miss Elizabeth Bennet.* His heart beat rapidly at the mere thought of her, the only woman he had ever loved.

Granted, he had been impulsive in asking for her hand, yet he had reasoned she returned his regard. He had always enjoyed their discussions – he found her wit and intelligence stimulating.

But he discovered too late that while *she* had been relentlessly in *his* thoughts those months since he first made her acquaintance, *he* had certainly not been in *hers*. And those times when he was, it was almost always in a very poor light.

She had lashed out at him in her refusal of his suit. Yet, it had been in the past few months that he finally was able to look back at their last encounter with a measure of equanimity. He had come to the realization that much of what she had said to him that day was true.

"It is my opinion," his aunt continued haughtily, "that if the Bennets had been asked to leave Longbourn, it would serve Miss Bennet right! What insolence she exhibited when she turned down the proposal!"

Stunned, Darcy turned abruptly and drew back as the colour drained from his face.

Fitzwilliam, however, was now interested. "Turned down a proposal? *Whose* proposal?"

Darcy felt a wave of anxiety course through his body and wondered how anyone came to learn of his proposal and her rejection of it.

"Why, Mr. Collins' proposal! Before he asked for the present Mrs. Collins' hand, he had gone to Miss Bennet. I thought you knew. She refused him flatly, she did, without any consideration for his feelings or the welfare of her family."

Darcy swallowed as he contemplated this. That meant when he proposed to her a year ago and was turned down, she had already turned down another proposal. His mind swirled with thoughts as he contemplated the type of woman Miss Bennet was. She had turned down a proposal from the man who would take Longbourn away from her at the death of her father, and then had turned down his proposal; he, who could have provided her with everything she could have ever wanted.

Why?

Deep in his heart he knew why. He could readily understand why she would have turned down Collins. She could never marry a man she did not respect.

Darcy contemplated his own proposal. He had gone to her fairly confident that she would accept his hand. Yet she had turned him down as well. And for the same reason. She did not respect him.

This was all nothing to him now. He spent the last year recovering from his miscalculations. He knew now that he had been wrong in anticipating her acceptance of his suit. As he looked out at the lane that separated Rosings from the parsonage, he was surprised that he could almost hear her voice, "*I might as well enquire why with so evident a design of offending and insulting me, you chose to tell me that you liked me against your will, against your reason, and even against your character.*"

His body involuntarily shuddered at the memory. Combing his fingers through his hair, he turned. "If you will excuse me, I am rather fatigued. I shall be in my room."

As he walked up the grand staircase, he inwardly berated himself for the disappointment he now felt. Had he actually come to Rosings this year with the expectation that he would hear something about her? Possibly even see her again? Was he holding out hope that perhaps the letter he had placed in her hand one year ago may have changed her opinion of him?

Upon reaching his room, he entered and closed the door behind him. He had made such a concerted effort this past year to mend his ways, to examine his prejudices, and lay aside his pride. And even though he told himself it was all done to improve himself as a person, he knew now that he had hoped Miss Elizabeth Bennet might give him a second chance if she saw that he had attended to her criticisms.

She was well aware that he came to Rosings every Easter. He had secretly wished that she would make plans to visit her friend, Charlotte, as well. In the deepest recesses of his being, he hoped that she would be here. But it had been futile and foolish thinking. Even if Collins were still here, she would never have planned a visit knowing there was the possibility that *he* would be here.

He slumped into the chair that faced the desk. It was the same chair and desk where he had written that letter a year ago. He had been hurt and angered by Miss Bennet's words and responded likewise. Now he wondered what she had thought as she first read the missive. What *had* he written? Was his anger so strong in his words of the defence of his character and actions that they rendered her angry as well and reinforced her opinion of him?

He brought his head down into his hands and took in a deep breath. He remained that way for some time before finally lifting his head. Would the Bennet ladies have remained at Longbourn? He absently began shaking his head. He doubted that Miss Elizabeth had. But if not, where would she have gone? What would have become of her?

He knew he would not be able to let this concern drop until he knew for certain that she was in reasonable circumstances. He knew he would do anything to ensure her happiness, although he was convinced that she would never accept any assistance from him. This bit of news – or lack thereof – brought about a very wearisome three weeks for him during his stay at Rosings.

Chapter 1

London

Elizabeth Bennet wrapped the cloak tightly around little Emily, bending down as she straightened it.

"There! I believe you are ready."

"Thank you. I am sorry I dawdled and needed you to help me get ready." She looked up at Elizabeth with pleading eyes. "Will you not join us this morning, Miss Bennet? Why do you never attend church services with us?"

Elizabeth took the little girl's hands in her own and smiled. "You ask me that every week, and every week I tell you. Your mother and father have been so kind to me that on Sundays I am free from my duties so I may visit my family. I accompany my sister, Jane, and my aunt and uncle and little cousins to the church they attend in their neighbourhood."

The little girl pouted. "But today is Easter! I do not know why you cannot spend the day with me and my family."

Elizabeth stood up and patted Emily's head. "You have me for six full days a week. I would think that you would prefer to have one day without me. Besides, when we are in residence at your home in the country this summer, I shall be with you every day. I dare say you will tire of me then and wish to have some time away from me!"

Before the little girl could respond, her mother called from downstairs. "Emily, we are about to leave. Are you ready?"

Emily looked toward the door, then sadly back at Elizabeth. "I think I would enjoy church much better if you were there with me."

"That means a great deal to me, Emily. And one day I shall join you, but not today. Now walk downstairs like the little lady you are. I will be late to my aunt and uncle's if I do not hasten and get myself ready." Elizabeth smiled and shook her head as she watched her ward turn and skip down the stairs.

Each week Emily's plea was the same, but Elizabeth knew that once Emily was with her parents, *she* would be all but forgotten.

As Sunday was her day off, normally Elizabeth did not have any responsibilities with Emily. Today, however, the young girl needed some additional help readying herself, so Elizabeth gladly assisted her. With that task now behind her, Elizabeth could look forward to her day with her family. She would accompany them to church and then visit with them throughout the afternoon and evening. This was the highlight of her week. For the remainder of the week she was governess to six year-old Emily Willstone.

Elizabeth hurried to ready herself. She knew the carriage her uncle would be sending for her would arrive shortly and she did not wish to be late. When she was finished dressing, she looked at herself in the mirror. Her eyes took in the grey dress she wore and how pale her face appeared. It was one of two grey dresses she owned and wore while in half-mourning. She also had two black dresses that had been her complete wardrobe for her days of full-mourning. She still had a little over a month of mourning remaining and she wondered whether she could ever go back to wearing colours again. Her grief was still as fresh and strong as it had been when it happened.

In the waning of spring last year, just as the days were growing in length and warmth, Elizabeth's father unexpectedly died. A trip Elizabeth had planned to take with the Gardiners up north was cancelled. Her youngest sister, Lydia, was sent home from Brighton, where she had been staying as a guest of Colonel Forster and his wife. Jane's loss of Charles Bingley's affections was now swallowed up in the loss of her father. The family grieved together and consoled one another. Elizabeth, being the one who had the strength of character, was the one everyone turned to, yet it was she who suffered the deepest grief in the loss of her father.

While Elizabeth tried to encourage everyone to be strong, there was an underlying uncertainty that each of the Bennet ladies shared. With Longbourn entailed away to their cousin, Mr. Collins, he now had every right to claim it as his own. Whenever Mrs. Bennet brought up the dreaded subject, Elizabeth and Jane would do their best to assuage her fears that they would not be left homeless and destitute.

As was feared, however, several months following Mr. Bennet's death, the Collinses sent notice that they would indeed be moving to Longbourn at the beginning of the new year. Charlotte Collins, Elizabeth's good friend, assured the family that they could remain in their home as long as they required, but Elizabeth knew she could never live at Longbourn when it was no longer theirs, and neither could she live under the same roof as Mr. Collins.

With strong recommendation and urging from Elizabeth, Mrs. Bennet made plans to move into the nearby village of Meryton with her sister and husband, Mr. and Mrs. Phillips. She brought her three youngest daughters to live with them. The Phillips' children were grown and married and the couple was able to take the Bennet ladies into their home, although there was not as much ample space as they had enjoyed at Longbourn.

Elizabeth suggested early on that Jane move in with their mother's brother and wife, Mr. and Mrs. Gardiner, in London, acting as governess for the Gardiners' four children. Jane was delighted when Elizabeth herself secured employment as a governess for a family in London. With this arrangement, they could still visit occasionally.

The Willstones, the family for whom Elizabeth worked, hired her when it became apparent to them in their initial meeting, that she and six year-old Emily seemed to get along quite nicely. Despite Elizabeth's lack of formal education, she impressed them with her knowledge of the basic accomplishments. While explaining she learned much from her own love of reading and self-teaching, she did have access to a few masters who lived in the nearby town of Meryton.

Richard and Lorraine Willstone were exceptionally kind and generous, allowing Elizabeth time off on Sundays to visit the Gardiners and her sister. While Elizabeth was grateful for the employment, it was not a life she had envisioned for herself.

A piercing recollection interrupted her musings of Easter spent in Kent exactly one year ago. She shuddered as she thought how much had changed since then.

What if I had...?

No! She stamped her foot. She would not reproach herself for refusing those two marriage proposals. The first one she could never have agreed to. *The second...*

A knock at the door announced that the carriage had arrived. She pushed away that last thought.

As the carriage drove her through the streets of London from the more fashionable neighbourhood to the less fashionable neighbourhood near Cheapside, Elizabeth looked forward with much anticipation to her day. She would listen with joy to all her aunt and sister had to share about their week and she would recount to them how her own had passed. It would certainly prove to be a more joyous Easter than last year.

When she arrived at the Gardiners' home, she handed off her coat and gloves and eagerly walked into the breakfast room, where a warm meal was being served. She was greeted warmly and profusely.

"Good morning, Lizzy! Happy Easter!" her uncle exclaimed and he rose and walked over to her, wrapping her in his arms.

"Thank you, Uncle. And Happy Easter to all of you." When her uncle released her, she walked over to Jane and gave her a hug. "How are you, Jane?"

"I am well. And how is my dearest sister?" Jane asked.

"Delighted to be here." Elizabeth let out a soft laugh. "As much as I love Emily, the joy of my week is being with all of you."

"And how *is* little Emily?" her aunt asked, as Elizabeth motioned for her to remain seated.

"Her usual self," answered Elizabeth as she walked over and gave her aunt a kiss on the cheek. "She was a little slow this morning getting ready for church, so I gave her some assistance. She went through her usual custom of not wishing to leave without me. I hope I am not late."

"Dearest Lizzy, do not worry about being late. We have plenty of time," her aunt reassured her.

"And plenty of food," added her uncle.

"Now, you must sit down and have something to eat. What would you like?" her aunt asked.

"I must confess I had a muffin at the Willstones', but I do believe the eggs and ham look delicious!"

She joined the others at the table and inquired of the Gardiner children how their week passed. She was anxious to talk with Jane, but knew the children were eager to tell of their activities and so she would wait. Each of the four children was given ample opportunity to tell the highlight of the past week. Jane had taught Laura a new song on the pianoforte; Jonathan finished reading a book; Caleb found a kitten; and little Melissa learned how to tie a bow with the ribbon on her bonnet.

Elizabeth gave much praise to each of her cousins for their wonderful accomplishments. She also applauded Jane for her excellent work as their governess.

"Tell us how your week passed, Lizzy," Mrs. Gardiner requested. "Have you been able to get Emily to practice more on the pianoforte? Has she acquired *your* enjoyment for reading?"

"It is a delicate balance for me to impart the joys of my life to Emily whilst not pushing her so hard that she ends up disliking everything!" Elizabeth looked into her aunt's warm eyes. "I certainly have no difficulty getting her to sing. She loves to sing. And as she would prefer *me* to read her a book than to read one *herself*, she is a little more willing to read a book than to practice on the pianoforte. Unfortunately, playing is still a struggle for her."

Mr. Gardiner chuckled. "Then you must find something Emily enjoys less than playing and give her the choice of the two. Chances are she will pick playing."

Elizabeth laughed. "Such as picking weeds in the garden?" She paused to take a bite from her plate. "I fear she does not have the long, slender fingers that are advantageous in playing, yet her parents would so much love for her to both play and sing."

As the family finished their meal, Elizabeth savoured every bit of conversation as well as every morsel of food. Indeed, she was grateful to be governess to a very sweet little girl with very kind and agreeable parents, but she greatly missed her family the remainder of the week.

Elizabeth's spirits were high at church that morning. She loved the Easter service more than any other during the year. It reinforced the foundation for her faith and gave her reason to joyfully attend services throughout the year.

The message that morning on forgiveness – how God offered up forgiveness to us and how we ought to offer up forgiveness to others – struck within Elizabeth a deep sense of conviction. She realized she had been harbouring resentment toward Mr. Collins and her friend, Charlotte, for taking Longbourn from them. They had every lawful right to claim it as theirs, and after all, they had made the Bennet ladies an offer to remain there as long as needed.

Fortunately, the few months it took for the Collinses to move to Longbourn allowed the Bennets to secure their new living arrangements. Charlotte had a newborn baby and did not think travelling would be wise until he was at least six months old. Elizabeth often wondered if that was Charlotte's way of granting them time to decide what to do. She was grateful that she secured a position as governess for the Willstones and was able to leave before the Collinses arrived.

Elizabeth had written to her friend only once since she had come to London, responding to an inquiry from her as to how she was faring. It was a brief and succinct missive, touched with the hint of resentment that Elizabeth felt. Charlotte had written two more letters that she had never answered, always having a reason to postpone it. Now, she knew she must write Charlotte directly and assure her that she felt no resentment toward her.

In the final prayer that morning, as the reverend asked people to bow their heads, Elizabeth confessed her lack of forgiveness toward the Collinses and promised that she would behave in a forgiving manner toward them henceforth. She did not want bitterness to take hold of her life. At the "Amen," she lifted her head, hoping to feel a great sense of peace. Instead, a restless conviction stirred within her.

She narrowed her eyes as the conviction came in the form of Mr. Darcy. She thought back to his offer of marriage and how it should have been an honour in itself, but she had not been able to view it that way. He had demeaned her and her family. His words had brutally hurt her and she had responded in angry vehemence. Yet the letter he had subsequently written her – and a year of reading and rereading it – had somewhat lessened her animosity. His words to her that day no longer stung and she found that some were indeed true.

It was still difficult, however, to forgive him for his contemptible audacity holding that it was his right – his duty – to convince his friend of the error of his ways in his regard for Jane. Her heart still pounded in anger as she contemplated this. Slowly she turned her head, and catching the serene, resigned look upon Jane's face, she felt that she would never be able to forgive him for *that.*

When the Gardiners and the Bennet sisters returned from church, Jane tended to the four children as they came in, gathering their coats and gloves and ensuring that they were changed out of their church clothes before they came down to play. The spring day was cool, but the sun was shining brightly, giving all it could to warm up the air. The first blossoms of the season were beginning to bloom and the grey, dreary days of winter seemed behind them.

Elizabeth was always grateful for the occasional warmth of a spring Sunday, as the children enjoyed playing outside, allowing her and her sister and aunt to spend some uninterrupted time together. They retired to the sitting room where both Elizabeth and Jane picked up samplers to stitch and their aunt simply sipped a cup of tea, enjoying the presence of her two favourite nieces on this special day.

With the children out of the room, Elizabeth asked the dreaded question she asked each week. "Has there been any news from home?"

Mrs. Gardiner gave Jane a glance alerting Elizabeth to the fact that there had been some news and it most likely was not good. "Yes, Lizzy," Jane replied. "Mother writes about Lydia."

"Lydia! What does she have to say about Lydia?"

Elizabeth's sister and aunt exchanged glances again. "Your mother writes that Lydia has maintained that they have had a sufficient time of mourning and that she should like to rejoin her friends and the regiment, which had been removed from Brighton and is now at stationed at Stratford."

Elizabeth's head went back in exasperation. "And what, pray, does Mother say? Is she at all inclined to forbid this?"

Jane shook her head. "No, in fact, Lydia is most likely gone by now."

Elizabeth took in a deep breath. "Oh, that headstrong girl! It has not even been a full year since Father's death and all she can think about is getting back to her friends and the officers!"

"Be not distressed, Elizabeth," Jane assured her in her characteristically calm voice. "I am sure we can trust that Lydia will be on her best behaviour with the Forsters. They will look after her."

"Her best behaviour will consist of openly flirting with the officers and having no regard for modesty and decorum!"

"Elizabeth, really," her aunt implored. "Have more faith in the Forsters. Have more faith in your sister!"

Elizabeth put her sampler down and folded her arms in front of her. "What else does Mamma say?"

Jane looked down as Mrs. Gardiner gave her another piece of information. "Netherfield has been sold."

"Sold?"

Jane took a deep breath and looked up. Her blue eyes became dim as she continued. "Yes, a family from the north has made an eligible offer and it has been accepted."

"So Mr. Bingley never had an intention of returning."

Jane returned her eyes to her sampler as she slowly shook her head. Elizabeth wondered if she was shielding her tears from her.

"Well, ladies." Mrs. Gardiner thought it was time to change the subject. "Let us turn our attention to something more pleasant. Tell me, Elizabeth, what is new at the Willstone residence?"

Some recent news in that quarter brought a smile to Elizabeth's face. "Mrs. Willstone's sister, Rosalyn Matthews, is coming to London to spend several weeks with the family before we all return to the Willstones' country home in Nottinghamshire."

"And when will that be, dearest?"

"I believe it will be by the end of May or beginning of June."

Jane looked up and sighed. "How we will miss your weekly visits, Lizzy! Is it altogether settled, then?"

"The Willstones are not inclined to spend the summer here."

"Oh, Lizzy, how I wish things were different."

"I know, Jane," Elizabeth said softly. "I know."

"I have heard they have a wonderful estate in the country," her aunt reassured her, a smile revealing some creases that had begun to appear on her face. "I am quite certain you will be much happier there. I can just imagine you taking walks in the beautiful countryside."

"But I shall miss you greatly."

"And we shall miss you, too," her aunt assured her. "And we will look forward to your return to Town!"

For the remainder of the day, the topics of Lydia leaving for Stratford, Netherfield being sold, and her leaving for the country were not discussed. Elizabeth relished the closeness she felt for Jane and her aunt, and envied them for being able to be together when she could not. When she left later that evening, she found herself already looking forward to next week's visit.

Upon arriving back at the Willstones' home, she greeted the family, excused herself, and went up to her room. She was grateful she was not expected to report for her duties until seven o'clock the next morning.

The first thing she did was to go to the desk and pull out a piece of stationery. She sat down and began penning a letter to Charlotte. Whilst she had assured Charlotte that their decision to move out of Longbourn was for the best, she wished now to convey to her how deeply she still treasured her as a friend.

When the letter was complete and addressed, she sat back, looking down at it. It seemed terribly amiss to have the name Collins and Longbourn together. She dropped her hands into her lap and leaned her head back, letting out a long, disheartened sigh.

Elizabeth was normally not one to question providence, but she certainly did not understand all of the events that transpired the previous year. Certainly her father's death had greatly affected and grieved her and her family. As her mother lamented, "His death could not have been more ill-timed! None of our girls married and now we are to be out of Longbourn!"

She thought back with a shake of her head, to the two proposals that she had received and turned down. How ironic that accepting either man would have secured her family's welfare and their ability to remain at Longbourn. Turning them both down put all her family into the situations in which they now found themselves. Accepting the first proposal, from Mr. Collins, would have been an impossibility. Despite being in the esteemed profession of clergyman and the one to benefit from the entail of Longbourn, Elizabeth could never have married such a man.

The one man whose application she *could* have accepted was Mr. Darcy. The passage of a year and his letter had shed new light on certain beliefs she held regarding him, particularly in his dealings with Mr. Wickham. Time had done little, however, to dull those feelings of anger and resentment toward him for his actions in separating Jane and Mr. Bingley. It was very apparent to Elizabeth that Jane still bore the effects of a broken heart.

Elizabeth's anger directed at Mr. Darcy for *those* actions was more potent than her anger at his unfeeling words to her as he declared that he loved her despite the fact that her station in life was so decidedly beneath him.

18

As Elizabeth considered this, she almost laughed. *If only he could see me now! Then he could say with even more conviction that I was decidedly beneath him and he would certainly congratulate himself that I refused him!*

She reflected back on the news she heard today that her youngest sister had been allowed to return to the Forsters as well as the report that Netherfield had been sold. That last piece of news put to rest all hopes that Mr. Bingley would once again return. Both pieces of information left her with a disconcerted ache inside. As far as Lydia was concerned, Elizabeth could only hope that she would show some restraint in her usually unseemly behaviour. And it would make little difference to Jane if Bingley returned to Netherfield, as she was now in London. But it seemed to remove any last ray of hope that Jane may have clung to regarding Mr. Bingley and his affections.

There had always been the hope that they would see each other in London, but that had not come to pass, most likely due to the Gardiners' residence near Cheapside. Mr. Bingley would only be associating with those in superior circles and their paths were unlikely to cross.

Elizabeth brought a slightly unsteady hand up and covered her mouth with her fingertips as she felt her anger against Mr. Darcy rise. Mr. Darcy had made no attempt to put to rights the erroneous information he had given his friend, even when Elizabeth had so adamantly assured him of Jane's love for Mr. Bingley. She shook her head as she realized he would have no reason – no inclination – to do her that favour after she so vehemently refused him. The gnawing thought about forgiveness tried to surface, but she again pushed it down.

She stood up and walked over to her bed, picking up a book from the corner table. She threw herself down on the bed and opened the book, hoping to remove from her mind those intruding thoughts and attend the words on the page. But she could not. If anyone in her family had ever experienced true love, if anyone was deserving of true love, it was Jane, and Elizabeth could not understand why it had been stolen from her. No, she could not forgive Mr. Darcy for that. She did not think she ever could. The gnawing inside grew stronger.

Chapter 2

The next few days brought a flurry of activity to the Willstone residence as everyone readied themselves and the home for the arrival of Mrs. Willstone's sister, Rosalyn. Elizabeth eagerly looked forward to meeting this young lady who was merely a year older than herself. Mrs. Willstone hoped that the two young ladies would enjoy each other's company in the ensuing weeks Rosalyn would be staying with them in London and possibly the whole summer in the country. Elizabeth was certain they would, if she found her to be as affable as Mrs. Willstone.

Rosalyn arrived on Thursday afternoon that week. Elizabeth was sitting in a rocking chair in her room with a light coverlet over her. She had briefly dozed off with a book in her hands while Emily was napping and was awakened by the sound of the bell ringing, announcing the arrival of guests. Knowing that Rosalyn was due to arrive today, she promptly stood up, smoothed her dress, and went to the dresser mirror to readjust her hair.

She slipped into Emily's room and gently nudged the girl. Emily slowly opened her eyes and looked at Elizabeth.

"Did I oversleep, Miss Bennet?"

"No, Emily. I am awakening you because I believe your Aunt Rosalyn is here."

The little girl fisted her hands and rubbed her eyes, yawning as she did. "Do you think she brought me a gift? She oftentimes brings me something."

"We shall see. The sooner we get you ready and go downstairs, the sooner you shall find out." She leaned down and gave her a big smile. "Now, let us dress you in that pretty yellow frock you picked out earlier."

Elizabeth helped Emily dress, brushed out and adorned her hair with ribbons, and escorted her into the drawing room where the Willstones and Miss Matthews were gathered. The younger of the ladies, dressed in a fashionable gown and standing slightly taller than Elizabeth, rose and opened her arms for her niece.

"Emily! I am so delighted to see you! My how you are grown!"

"Do you have a surprise for me?"

"Watch your manners, Emily," Elizabeth whispered.

Miss Matthews looked to Elizabeth and smiled. "You must be Miss Bennet."

Mrs. Willstone brought her hands together in delight. "Miss Bennet, may I introduce you to my sister, Rosalyn Matthews? And Rosalyn, this is Elizabeth Bennet."

I have heard much about you through Lorraine's letters, Miss Bennet. She writes that you are doing a wonderful job."

"And I have heard much about you from your sister's very own words, Miss Matthews. It is a pleasure to finally make your acquaintance."

Rosalyn looked down at Emily with a conspiratorial look. "And if you heard anything from Emily, you know that I always bring her something."

"Did you? Did you?" Emily squealed excitedly.

"Well, let me look in my bag here and see if there is anything you might like." Rosalyn's light blue eyes twinkled; her thin lips pursed in a smile.

Emily clasped her hands together with a burst of anticipation as she anxiously watched her aunt look down into her handbag. "Now, let me see. Do you suppose this could be for you?" She slowly pulled out a lacy embroidered handkerchief.

"Noooo," the little girl laughed.

Elizabeth smiled as she came to suspect that this was the manner which always passed between the two.

"Oh, here is something you might enjoy," Miss Matthews whispered, glancing up at the young girl. She pulled out a small, leather bound book. "Would this be it?"

"Noooo!" Emily cried, standing on her tiptoes trying to look into her aunt's bag herself.

"Hmmm," Miss Matthews continued. She began to pull something out of the bag and peered closely at it. "No, I do not think this could be it."

"What is it?" asked Emily, barely able to control her countenance.

"Just a little doll… but no, this could not be it." Miss Matthews looked over to her niece with a smile teasing the corners of her mouth.

"Yes! I am sure that is it!" Emily reached out her small arms, palms upright, greatly wishing to see it.

Miss Matthews slowly pulled the doll out of the bag and put it in Emily's hands. The girl laughed with unrestrained glee. "How beautiful she is!" the young girl exclaimed. "Does she have a name?"

"I thought you might choose a name for her."

"I shall call her…ummmm…" She tapped her fingers against her lips. "Elizabeth! I shall name her Elizabeth. May I go play with her?"

"Certainly," Miss Matthews said, "if it is agreeable to your mother and Miss Bennet.

"The little girl looked to her mother and then to Elizabeth, who each gave her an assenting nod.

Emily proudly carried her new doll off to the corner of the room and Elizabeth began to follow.

"No, Miss Bennet, please join us," Miss Matthews reached out her arm. "I should like to become better acquainted with you."

Elizabeth sat down, eager to get to know Miss Matthews a little better as well. Elizabeth liked her friendly smile and welcoming demeanour. In addition to being taller than herself, she was fairer in complexion and hair, and she was most graceful in her movements.

"Miss Bennet, that is quite a tribute to you, to have Emily name her doll after you."

"Indeed?"

"She has named every doll she has ever owned after someone special in her life!"

"Well, I must admit I consider *her* very special as well!"

The three ladies visited for quite some time as Emily entertained herself with her new doll. Elizabeth liked Rosalyn. She carried herself well but without any trace of hauteur or condescension. She appeared to be well educated and well read. The two soon found themselves in a spirited discussion comparing the merits of poets Joseph Addison and William Lisle Bowles.

At one point, Rosalyn expressed her condolences for the loss of her father. "I see you are still in mourning. Do you mind me asking what he was like?"

"He was a very good man. Intelligent and kind. Very witty. I am deeply indebted to him for passing on to me the love of reading. He spent a good deal of the day reading, and encouraged me to do likewise. We would often sit in his study discussing one of his books or dissecting a favourite poem." Elizabeth sighed as she felt her eyes tear up. "I do miss him very much."

Rosalyn reached out, taking her hand. "He sounds like a wonderful father. What do you miss most about him?"

Elizabeth pondered this for a moment. "The way he challenged me to be all I could be and to learn all I could. We were without a governess you see, but I had such a desire to learn. I am quite certain it came from my father." She took in a shaky breath. "My favourite pastime spent with him was playing chess. Of my four sisters, I was the only one who enjoyed the strategy of the game and could best him on occasion."

"You play chess?"

"Yes, but it has been a long time since I have played."

"Unfortunately, none of us here play, although my brother, Simon, plays well. He tried to teach me on several occasions, but I simply could not remember how each piece moved. It would be much easier if each piece moved only one direction!"

"But then it would be draughts," Elizabeth said with a smile.

They both laughed at this, and went on to discuss a myriad of other things.

Elizabeth lost all sense of time, as she, Mrs. Willstone, and Miss Matthews spent a good part of the afternoon conversing. Other than her visits with the Gardiners and Jane, Elizabeth could not recall having spent a more enjoyable afternoon in quite a long time.

Elizabeth occasionally glanced toward Mrs. Willstone, who seemed quite pleased that she and her sister were getting on so well. She was more than grateful that these two ladies from wealthy, prominent families did not look down on her due to her current station in life. That she had gone from a landed gentleman's daughter to have to seek employment as a governess did nothing to lower her in their eyes. The rigid line that separated governesses from their employers seemed overlooked by them.

For the remainder of the week, Rosalyn often accompanied Elizabeth as she gave lessons to Emily and worked with her on her manners, singing, and piano playing. Rosalyn enjoyed the friendship that was developing between her and Elizabeth, and as she also took great pleasure in spending time with her niece, she was quite pleased to be able to do both at the same time.

Elizabeth customarily adjourned to her chambers after Emily was settled in bed, feeling strongly that her employment as governess did not allow for her to enjoy the comforts and privileges of the home. Therefore, she rarely visited with the Willstones in the evenings. But with fervent invitations from Rosalyn and consensus from Mrs. Willstone, Elizabeth began to feel as though she had been accepted as almost part of the family.

Shortly after Rosalyn's arrival, it became the expected norm for Elizabeth to return downstairs after seeing Emily off to bed, and the ladies would continue whatever conversations had been struck up during the day. They proceeded to cover every topic of interest imaginable.

Rosalyn gave Elizabeth what she missed most in no longer having Jane around; someone with whom to converse. They challenged each other and encouraged one another, and although their conversations did not take the place of her talks with Jane, Elizabeth found Rosalyn to be almost as amiable.

That following Sunday, when Elizabeth spent the afternoon with the Gardiners and Jane, they noticed immediately the glow in Elizabeth's eyes and the warmth in her cheeks. For the first time since her father's death, she had come to the Gardiners in exceedingly good spirits and they were most grateful. She did not come ravenous for good company and conversation, as she had fed on it all week. Instead, she arrived with contentment and an eagerness to share stories with her family about her new friend.

Elizabeth had never pined for any of the social privileges that those of the first circles enjoyed, but she took great delight in hearing Rosalyn talk about all the engagements she enjoyed over the years whenever she spent time in London.

As Rosalyn described the balls to which she had been invited, the concerts and theatre plays she had attended, and the presentations at Court, Elizabeth delighted in the enchanting way she described them. She could not help but feel just a small bit of envy as she wished that perhaps just once she would like to step into Rosalyn's world and experience it for herself.

"Oh, Elizabeth! The music just fills your ears as hundreds of dancing couples bow and curtsey, swirl and promenade down the endless ballrooms!" Rosalyn's eyes lit up as she described the balls in London, which, although similar to ones that Elizabeth attended in the country, were on a much grander, more prestigious scale.

"And all the fine gentlemen! Oh, sometimes I can barely breathe when one asks for my hand!"

Elizabeth smiled, fully cognizant of the fact that she would never receive an invitation to such a ball or to dance with such gentlemen, being in the position in which she now found herself. She closed her eyes, allowing herself to dream, as

Rosalyn finished her narrative.

At length, Rosalyn softened her voice and her light blue eyes widened.

"Elizabeth, do you think a gentleman would find me attractive?"

Elizabeth opened her eyes and looked at her. She tilted her head and narrowed her eyes, teasing her with her scrutiny.

"Please, Elizabeth! I am serious!"

"I think any man would find you a most handsome young lady!"

"You do not say that merely to appease me?"

"Rosalyn, you have beautiful blue eyes, a fine nose, nicely shaped lips, and a tall, slender figure." Elizabeth smiled. "You have a charming personality and I know that you must certainly turn many a man's head."

"Please do not think me silly, Elizabeth, it is just that sometimes I wonder why…" She took in a deep breath and pursed her lips.

"Rosalyn?"

She shrugged her shoulders. "It is just that *he* never looks my way."

Elizabeth's eyes widened. *"He?"* she asked. "Who is *he*?"

Rosalyn gave her head a firm shake. "Oh, I could never tell!"

"Pray, Rosalyn! Why?"

"He is far above me, above our family. He would never take a second look at me."

"Rosalyn, your family is much esteemed. Why would you say that?"

"To own the truth, Elizabeth, my father married beneath him. My mother had no noticeable connections, and growing up, I felt the disdain of many families who were of more refined and well bred society."

"Oh, Rosalyn, certainly you must be mistaken."

"Whether or not I am mistaken, this gentleman has never acknowledged me and if Lorraine knew that I continued to pine for him, she would scold me ruthlessly!"

Elizabeth laughed. "Pine for him? Can you not tell me more? Now I am most curious."

"I will only say that he is a man who lived near my family when I was growing up. The first time I ever saw him, I just knew he was the one I wished to marry! But I could never tell you his name!"

"And you still pine for him?"

She nodded her head slowly. "My whole family knew of my infatuation with him when I was younger and they laughed and thought me young and silly. Now that I am older…"

"Your feelings are unchanged."

"Yes," she said as she nodded her head.

"If you cannot tell me his name, you must tell me everything else about this man!"

"Well," Rosalyn dropped her eyes and a blush softly coloured her features. "He is terribly handsome. Tall and handsome. And he is wealthy, although I really cannot say that is all that appeals to me." She paused and smiled. "Well, perhaps a little bit. I suppose that is a good thing." She was rambling now, and Elizabeth made a futile attempt to stifle a smirk. "He is a good, principled man, from everything I hear. No one speaks ill of him."

She gave Elizabeth a pointed look. "Should I even allow myself to hope that he would notice me?"

"Rosalyn, if he is such a man as you describe, you have no reason to be ashamed of your feelings. And he would be a fool not to take notice of you."

A satisfied smile graced Rosalyn's lips. "You are too kind, Elizabeth."

That night as Elizabeth lay in her bed, her head swirled with thoughts of balls and dances and being presented to the queen and handsome gentlemen. But it was the image of one particular gentleman that kept intruding, reminding her that any happiness for her sister had been destroyed by his actions.

~~*

It was in the latter part of the following week that Elizabeth began to hear of preparations for visitors that were to come the following Saturday. Mrs. Willstone, who was the epitome of a charming hostess, worked closely with the kitchen staff in planning the refreshments and meal that would be served. She arranged every detail from the time guests would arrive, which was about five o'clock in the afternoon, through to the conclusion of the evening.

Elizabeth was told that they would prefer to visit with their guests without the presence of Emily, but that they would send for her at some time in the evening. Mrs. Willstone instructed Elizabeth to take her dinner with Emily early and then have her ready to come down for a short visit when she was summoned, returning to her chambers afterwards.

She heard little about the guests who were coming; only that there would be a party of eight. Mrs. Willstone and Rosalyn had grown up near one of the young ladies and they were both anxious to meet the young man about whom people had been speculating would soon make her an offer. Rosalyn appeared to be most concerned about making a good impression on this particular couple and repeatedly consulted Elizabeth about what to wear, how to style her hair, and even what song to play if she was asked to perform on the pianoforte.

On Saturday, Elizabeth knew her greatest responsibility was to keep little Emily quiet and out of everyone's way. Mrs. Willstone kept busy with the kitchen staff ensuring everything was coming along as desired. She walked through the house inspecting it for cleanliness and admonished the staff if something was found not up to her expectations.

Elizabeth was grateful for the mildly warm day, which meant that she and Emily could spend a good amount of time outdoors and out of the way. A small play area in the rear of the house afforded Emily with some delightful amusements. Elizabeth obligingly pushed Emily in the swing and helped her build sand castles in the sandbox, making up a story for the young girl about a handsome prince who lived in the very castle they built.

After the noon meal, Elizabeth and Emily took a long walk to a park down the street where they enjoyed the array of beautiful flowers lining the path and listened to the flurry of birds as they sang their cheerful songs. Elizabeth enjoyed teaching Emily all the names of the flowers that grew nearby and the birds that flew overhead. Emily seemed just as eager to learn them.

When they returned to the house, they proceeded upstairs where Emily napped and Elizabeth took the opportunity to read. Per Mrs. Willstone's wish, they ate an early supper, and then returned upstairs to dress for company. Once they were ready, Elizabeth would keep Emily entertained with some books until the young girl was called for.

They were just finishing up their first book when Elizabeth heard the bell announce the arrival of guests. Emily was anxious to go down and meet them, but Elizabeth reminded her that the adults wished to dine, have some time together, and they would call for her when they wanted her to join them.

Finally, after finishing three books and playing with her new doll for a short while, a young servant girl, Lilia, came to the door to summon them. Emily anxiously jumped to her feet, ready to run downstairs, but Elizabeth stopped her.

"Now, Emily, let me have a look at you to make sure you are presentable." Elizabeth turned the girl completely around, readjusting a curl that had fallen out of place. "Remember to be very polite and curtsey, say 'please' and 'thank you' and only speak when spoken to."

"Yes, Miss Elizabeth."

Elizabeth smiled and smoothed out the young girl's dress. "There! I do believe you are ready!"

Emily clasped her hands and then took one of Elizabeth's in her own. "Come, Miss Bennet."

"No, I believe I will stay here." Elizabeth told Emily. "Miss Lilia shall take you down."

Lilia looked at Elizabeth and smiled. "I understand that *you* are expected to come down as well."

"Are you quite sure? I would not wish to impose."

Emily looked to Elizabeth and back to the maid. "She would not impose, would she?"

Lilia laughed. "No, Miss Emily, I do not believe she would be imposing." She turned to Elizabeth. "Come along with us, Miss Bennet."

Elizabeth looked to the little girl. "Come, Emily. We shall both meet the guests, then."

They walked down the stairs, or at least Elizabeth walked. Emily had more of a skip to her gait as she was always eager to meet new people.

They walked in and Elizabeth's gaze drifted across the room. When Mrs. Willstone noticed them at the door, she smiled and beckoned them to come over.

A young lady, who had been seated facing away from the door, turned and

Elizabeth saw that she looked to be rather young. She smiled shyly at Elizabeth.

When the gentleman next to her turned, Elizabeth was rendered motionless for a few moments. A look of shock passed between both of them at first, and then a tentative smile came across the gentleman's face. He stood up abruptly.

"Miss Bennet!" the young man exclaimed. "It is… it is good to see you again!" His features betrayed the awkwardness they both felt and the young lady next to him looked somewhat bewildered, looking from him and back to Elizabeth.

"Mr. Bingley," Elizabeth replied after quickly composing herself. "Is everything well with you?"

"I am… I am quite well, thank you," he answered with a nervous laugh. "And you and your family?" A deep questioning look swept over his face.

"You may not have heard that our father passed away last year."

Mr. Bingley's eyes widened and his jaw dropped. "No…no, I had not heard. Please accept my deepest condolences… to you and all your family. I imagine it must be very difficult."

"Yes," Elizabeth answered. "We are doing the best we can."

An awkward pause took hold of the room as they looked at each other and then each looked away. It was shock enough to be suddenly facing Bingley again, but worsened by the fact that he was standing next to the young lady she supposed had replaced Jane's affections.

"Miss Bennet, you are acquainted with Mr. Bingley?" Mrs. Willstone quickly interjected.

Elizabeth looked to Mrs. Willstone. "Yes… yes I am. He let a residence near Longbourn some time ago."

Elizabeth looked directly at him. "I had heard that Netherfield was purchased."

"Yes, I have not…" Bingley began. "I heard that as well." He seemed at a loss for words. The young lady at his side continued to look from him to Elizabeth, and back to him again.

When the conversation between them ceased, Mrs. Willstone proceeded to make the rest of the introductions.

"May I introduce you all to Emily's governess, Miss Elizabeth Bennet? She then turned to Elizabeth. "Miss Bennet, this is Mr. and Mrs. Estes, Mr. and Mrs. Fountain, Mr. and Mrs. Hampton. You are acquainted with Mr. Bingley, and this fine young lady is Miss Georgiana Darcy."

*draughts is the British name for the game of checkers

Chapter 3

Elizabeth hoped that the initial awkwardness of her encounter with Mr. Bingley had been noticed solely by the two of them, but an occasional glance in Miss Darcy's direction made her wonder about the young girl's uneasy expression. A flush of Elizabeth's cheeks ensued when she thought that perhaps Miss Darcy knew of her refusal to her brother's offer of marriage. More likely, perhaps, was that Miss Darcy's attachment to Mr. Bingley prompted some feelings of jealousy, if she indeed noticed their discomfiture.

Elizabeth was grateful, then, as the others in the party turned their attention to Emily. Emily approached each person and curtseyed, bestowing on each the hope that all things were well with them and that it was a pleasure making their acquaintance.

Fortunately, Emily's visit was relatively short and her parents thanked Elizabeth and excused them. Emily bid each of them a good night, after which Elizabeth ushered her charge upstairs.

As Elizabeth's hand rested upon the little girl's shoulder guiding her up the stairs and she teemed with disappointment as she considered that Jane's hopes would now be hopelessly shattered. When she recalled Rosalyn's words the other day about an announcement forthcoming, she realized it must have been Mr. Bingley and Miss Darcy of whom she spoke. Pausing slightly on the step, she found herself shaking uncontrollably as the disappointment gave rise to an overwhelming anger.

Emily looked up at Elizabeth. "Is there anything wrong, Miss Bennet?"

Elizabeth forced a smile and looked down, suddenly aware that she had to push away these feelings for the moment. "I am well. I only just remembered something."

"What?"

Elizabeth grasped the young girl's hand and patted it. "I forgot to tell you how well-mannered you were down there. You behaved superbly!"

Emily grinned and squeezed Elizabeth's hand, holding it tightly as they went up to her room.

Elizabeth was tired and looked forward to some solitude. Fortunately, as Emily prepared for bed, she picked out one of the shorter storybooks for Elizabeth to read to her. Once she was tucked in and Elizabeth began to read, the little girl's eyes grew heavy. The excitement of visitors this evening must have been too much for her and she fell asleep even before Elizabeth turned to the final page. Elizabeth leaned over and kissed her goodnight and then quietly stepped out of the room.

Letting out a deep sigh of relief as she walked down the long hallway to her chambers, Elizabeth contemplated the time spent downstairs with Mr. Bingley and Miss Darcy. It was quite apparent that Mr. Bingley felt awkward when he saw Elizabeth. At times he appeared to be almost distracted; he looked toward her as though he wished to say something to her, but then abruptly changed his mind.

He was very polite and affable toward Miss Darcy, but Elizabeth clearly noticed the lack of intensity in his attentions to her. And Miss Darcy, although very polite, seemed even less outward in her regard for him than Jane ever had been. Of course, it could be that Elizabeth was only seeing things the way she wished to see them.

She sat down on her bed and stared absently at the wall for a short time as she made an attempt to sort out her feelings. Another wave of disappointment flooded through her, swirling around with her anger. She was greatly disappointed that Mr. Bingley had toyed with Jane's heart and had obviously taken and heeded the advice of his good friend.

Her eyes unwittingly went to the drawer that housed all her personal items. Mr. Darcy's letter remained tucked securely within the pages of a book. It had been several months since she had last perused the missive that he had so meticulously written, laying out the defence of his actions and character. She knew it almost by heart. She had initially read it in anger, but had come, over the course of this past year, to realize the honour she ought to have felt in being singled out by such a man. He unquestionably had his faults; what he had done in separating Bingley from her sister had been callous. But she had come to realize that his dealings with Wickham had not been as ruthless as the latter had made them out to be.

She turned her head briskly to the side, stifling a sob. *No!* She would not allow herself to succumb to tears. How easily her tears fell every time she considered how her father's unexpected death turned her family out of their home, placing a burden upon all of them. She was determined not to feel sorry for herself. How many times she had to push away the thought that if she had only accepted Mr. Darcy's offer, her family now would all be well taken care of and neither she nor Jane would have had to seek out positions as governesses.

She consoled herself with the fact that both she and her sister were in good homes and had pleasant wards. Jane had always enjoyed caring for the Gardiner children when the opportunity rose. Elizabeth could find no fault with the Willstones or Emily, but she was all too aware that it was a step down in society's eyes for both of them. She could only imagine that after tonight's visit, Mr. Darcy would come to know of it from his sister or Bingley. She pulled her feet up onto the bed and lay her head down on the pillow.

She often chided herself that if she had accepted Mr. Darcy's offer and became his wife, she would have had it in her power to undo his one terrible injustice. Certainly, as Mr. Bingley was his best friend and Jane was her sister, those two would have had numerous opportunities to meet again and restore what they once had. Hence, Jane would likely be the one to marry Mr. Bingley instead of Miss Darcy. That was her one true regret in refusing him.

In the short time she was downstairs this evening, Elizabeth had watched

Miss Darcy, out of curiosity and a determination to find fault with her. Wickham had characterized her as proud, yet she saw nothing of that. She had to admit that this misleading information served to reinforce Darcy's claim that Wickham was not to be believed. Miss Darcy seemed a sweet, yet shy girl, and Elizabeth could not, in all honesty, blame Mr. Bingley for forming an attachment with her.

She pounded a fist onto her pillow. "But he loved Jane! I am certain of it!" Her fervent whisper was expelled forcefully from deep within her. She buried her head into the pillow, which acted as a handkerchief, catching the lone tear that slid down her cheek.

She lay there motionless for awhile, and finally, after a few moments, Elizabeth arose and slowly changed into her nightdress. She occasionally heard laughter or an outburst from the party downstairs. It distressed her to hear such joviality, knowing the pain it would instil in Jane once she was informed of their betrothal. It troubled her that she would be the one who would have to tell Jane before she heard it from someone else through some other means.

"Oh, Jane," she whispered to herself. "You are the last person in the world that I would want to hurt with such information."

She climbed into her bed after snuffing out the candle. With her eyes wide open, she stared upward in the darkened room and listened as the voices grew faint. At length, with the sound of a distant door closing, Elizabeth assumed that the guests had finally departed.

She rolled over and hoped that she would be able to put tonight's events out of her mind and get a good night's sleep, but the insistent pounding of her heart and her restless mind did little to aid in her wish.

After a few minutes, there was a soft tap at Elizabeth's door. She opened her eyes and answered, "Yes?"

"Elizabeth, it is Rosalyn. May I come in?"

Elizabeth sat up in her bed, moving a strand of hair that had fallen across her face and wiping any telltale sign of a tear from her cheek.

"Yes, Rosalyn, do come in," Elizabeth answered as cheerfully as she could, but truly wishing to be left alone.

Rosalyn walked in holding a candle and used it to light a candle on the night stand. A soft glow lit both ladies' faces.

"I am so sorry to disturb you, Elizabeth. Were you already asleep?"

"No, no, Rosalyn. I only now just put out the candle. The guests are gone, I presume?"

"Yes," Rosalyn answered and looked down at her hands. She looked up expectantly at Elizabeth as if she wished to say something.

"What is it, Rosalyn?"

"Is it… is it really true, Elizabeth?"

Although Elizabeth had not fallen asleep yet, she found it difficult to comprehend what Rosalyn was asking.

"Is *what* true, Rosalyn?"

"That you are acquainted with Mr. Darcy?"

Elizabeth's eyes widened in surprise. "Mr. Darcy? I... I am... only a little. Why do you ask?"

"After you left, we talked about how both Mr. Bingley and Mr. Darcy had made your acquaintance at Netherfield. Mr. Bingley was more than gracious in his words about you and your family, and from the sound of it, you were in their company a great deal."

"We did see them on occasion. They were present at some dances and we attended a ball that Mr. Bingley hosted at Netherfield."

"Oh, Elizabeth! I am simply beside myself! But you must promise me never to mention a word of this to anyone!" Her blue eyes deepened in intensity.

Elizabeth was now wide awake and most attentive to Rosalyn's words. She watched as Rosalyn took in a deep breath and looked around as if to make sure that there was no one listening.

"*He* is the one, Elizabeth! Mr. Darcy is the one!"

Elizabeth found it difficult to swallow as her mouth became inexplicably dry. "You mean that Mr. Darcy is..."

"Yes! The gentleman of whom I spoke the other day!" Rosalyn clasped her hands together. "I cannot believe I am telling you this!"

Elizabeth looked down and fixed her gaze upon her hands. *I cannot believe I am hearing this*, she thought to herself.

"His family lived on just the other side of a neighbouring village when I was growing up. Because of my mother's poor connections, we only occasionally frequented the elite circles that the Darcys did. From the first moment I saw him, though, I knew he was the one I wished to marry."

Elizabeth could only hope that the shock of hearing this was not displayed prominently across her features. "I thought I understood that your family was from Staffordshire, whereas I believe Mr. Darcy to be from Derbyshire."

Rosalyn sat down on the edge of the bed. "We were in different, but neighbouring counties. Pemberley is situated on the Derbyshire side a few miles from where we lived."

"I see," Elizabeth said, really never expecting Mr. Darcy to be the one of whom Rosalyn spoke. She tried to grasp all that her friend was saying.

"Unfortunately, the manor near Pemberley in which I grew up was only let by my parents. When I was fourteen, my father was able to purchase the home in which they now live, which is in Northamptonshire. I was so disappointed when we moved away. I truly believed I would never see him again. As a young girl, I was quite devastated."

"And have you seen much of him since then?" Elizabeth pensively asked.

"I have seen him on a few occasions in Town; our families have spoken occasionally, but I have always been too nervous to say anything to him." Rosalyn appealed to Elizabeth with wide eyes as she earnestly asked, "Would you please tell me something about him?" Pausing to take a deep breath, she then asked, "What is your opinion of him from the time he spent at Netherfield?"

"What… what would you have me tell you?"

Rosalyn stood up and twirled about, as if she were a ballerina on a stage, her hands clasped tightly together.

"Tell me whether you believe he is not the handsomest man you have ever met… and kind… and generous…"

She stopped twirling and looked intently at Elizabeth. "Well?"

Elizabeth immediately felt the increase in her heartbeat. "I cannot speak on all those things, but yes, Rosalyn. I suppose… he is basically a good man." How could she say otherwise? What could she say to her friend about him that was not in a positive light? Despite her anger at him for separating Jane and Bingley, she had come to recognize over the past year that he was, in essentials, a good man. She could not deny that. She had even come to realize the struggle he must have faced in deciding to ask for her hand. She could not excuse the manner in which he made his offer, but she at least had come to a better understanding of it. Still, in her eyes his greatest fault was his interference between Jane and Bingley, but she could never speak of that to Rosalyn.

Rosalyn collapsed down upon the bed again and looked at Elizabeth with wide, eager eyes. "Tell me everything you remember, please."

Elizabeth knew she could never do that. Those initial impressions she had of him and his subsequent actions could never be disclosed to her. "He is a very intelligent man, somewhat reserved…"

"Oh, yes! That makes him such a mystery to every lady in the ton! They often talk amongst themselves about what he must be thinking when he stands so silently!"

Elizabeth paused to consider how she persistently and quite wrongly assumed he had been quietly assessing her faults when he had his eye upon her. Little did she know then, that he had been admiring her.

Rosalyn leaned in to her. "And for the past year, it is said that he has been most formidable. Almost as if…"

Elizabeth tilted her head and leaned in, waiting for Rosalyn to finish.

Rosalyn whispered fervently. "Almost as if he had suffered a great anguish! Do you believe a man such as himself could have had…" her whisper softened even more, "his heart broken?"

Before Elizabeth could even think through an answer, Rosalyn continued. "I find it highly romantic to consider that his heart *was* broken and that someone… perhaps myself… might be the only one who might be able to bring him comfort."

Rosalyn reached out and took one of Elizabeth's hands in both of hers. Holding it tightly, she whispered, "Tell me the truth, Elizabeth, do you think my regard for him a foolish one? Having known him, do you think he would ever consider forming an attachment with someone like me who does not have the most superior connections?"

Elizabeth was grateful for the dimness of the room as she felt a warmth infuse her cheeks. "I… he would be a fool not to, Rosalyn."

A smile spread across Rosalyn's face and she stood up to walk toward the door, but stopped and turned back before opening it.

"Elizabeth, you *will* keep this a secret, will you not? You will not tell Lorraine, will you?"

"I promise I will not tell a soul!"

Rosalyn cheerfully walked out of the room, leaving Elizabeth somewhat stunned. Of course she could not divulge to Rosalyn all that had transpired between them. She *must* allow her friend to believe it was merely a slight acquaintance. She would not even inform her about Jane and Mr. Bingley's brief, yet fervent, regard for one another. Now that he was practically engaged to Mr. Darcy's sister, it would only serve to arouse more questions.

Elizabeth let out a moan. She could spend the whole of the night trying to ascertain everyone's thoughts and feelings, but she was tired and wanted a respite from her musings.

All was quiet in the house now, except for the pounding of Elizabeth's heart. As she made every attempt to empty her mind from all her thoughts, she could only hope that the acquaintance Mr. Darcy appeared to have with this family would not throw her unexpectedly into his path.

Chapter 4

The following day, Elizabeth poured herself into Emily's lessons. She would not permit herself idle time, which would only serve to allow her mind to recall the events of the prior evening. She had slept restlessly, concern building within as she contemplated having to inform Jane before long of Mr. Bingley's engagement, as well as a deepening alarm that Rosalyn would somehow come to hear of Mr. Darcy's offer to her.

That evening, the Willstones and Rosalyn were to attend a small dinner party. Elizabeth had heard a little bit about it previously in the week, but now there was much speculation on Rosalyn's part whether Mr. Darcy would be there. Since his identity was now known to Elizabeth, Rosalyn was more inclined to express her feelings to Elizabeth, and today they included the hope that he might make an appearance tonight. With every passing between the two young ladies, a look of hopefulness on Rosalyn's face or a brief word spoken to Elizabeth reinforced the much anticipated prospect of seeing him.

Everyone at the Willstones' the previous evening had expressed their plans to attend this dinner party. Rosalyn told Elizabeth that it was all she could do to keep from asking Miss Darcy whether or not her brother would also be accompanying them. She had lofty expectations that since his sister would be there, he would be, as well.

That evening, after Rosalyn spent over an hour with her personal maid insisting she make her as beautiful as she could, she asked for Elizabeth to join her alone in her chambers.

Elizabeth saw to it that Emily was playing contentedly by herself and went to her friend.

"Oh, Elizabeth!" Rosalyn rushed to greet her when Elizabeth appeared at her door. "Come inside, please!" She ushered Elizabeth in and closed the door behind them. Pointing to a chair, she asked Elizabeth to sit down.

Taking the chair across from her, Rosalyn began, "I am beside myself and I just needed to talk to you!" Her eyes were shining and Elizabeth had to admit she had never seen her look lovelier.

"I just have an extraordinarily strong feeling he will be there tonight and being the somewhat small party that it is, there is every possibility that I will have the opportunity to speak with him! I so want him to think well of me, yet I fear I will not know what to say!"

Elizabeth reached over and gently put her hand upon Rosalyn's, which were folded in her lap. "Rosalyn, whatever you do, just be yourself." She bestowed a gentle smile on her friend as she gave Rosalyn words of encouragement that she felt would actually put her in Mr. Darcy's good stead.

"When you saw him in Hertfordshire, was there anything you noticed that he liked or disliked? Did you notice him with women in whose company he seemed to enjoy? What kind of woman do you think he prefers?"

Elizabeth looked down, feeling a most unwelcome blush spread out upon her cheeks. She hoped Rosalyn would not notice. She sympathised with her friend and truly wanted to give her some helpful advice.

Looking back up Elizabeth said, "Do not attempt to flatter him or placate him. I believe him to be a man who sees through any sort of arts that a woman might use to secure his notice."

Rosalyn looked at her intently. "Yes, I believe you are right. What else, Elizabeth? What else can you tell me?"

"If it appears that he wishes to be left alone, by all means do not beleaguer him with petty questions and conversation. You, yourself, mentioned that he is reserved. It is best to make a good impression now and use future opportunities to show him how intelligent you are."

"Yes! That is very wise, Elizabeth. Is there anything else?"

"Mmmm," Elizabeth thought and a sly smile tugged at the corner of her lips. "You might try disagreeing with him on some point."

"Disagree with him! Oh, how you tease me!" Rosalyn laughed as she pulled Elizabeth toward her in a hug. "I could never do that!"

"No," Elizabeth said with a shake of her head. "No, I suppose you could not."

After reassuring Rosalyn that she truly had nothing about which to worry, she sent her off with hopes of securing Mr. Darcy's affections. She could only laugh at the irony of this situation; how she was ensuring this young lady's hopes about the very man who had proposed and been refused by herself. She had been tempted several times to tell Rosalyn that he most likely had many faults, but could not bring herself to do that. When she finally quit Rosalyn's room, she wondered about all she had truly said about the man. She was quite certain none of it reflected poorly on him.

After the Willstones and Rosalyn departed, Elizabeth attempted to ascertain her own feelings as to whether or not she wished Mr. Darcy to be at the dinner tonight. Curiosity prompted her to wonder exactly how he was doing, yet an apprehension of encountering him again gave rise to the wish that he not be present. She knew that Rosalyn would likely pay her a visit in her chambers with any such news when they returned later. Elizabeth would know by morning whether her friend's hopes had been fulfilled or dashed.

Elizabeth found herself unable to sleep that night and propped herself up in her bed with a book. She read into the early hours of the morning and listened with a surprising sense of expectancy for everyone to return, until sleep eventually overtook her.

~~*

Elizabeth's book had fallen down upon her lap and the candle snuffed as it burnt down. Her breathing became heavy and laboured as dreams besieged her in what little time she slept. She dreamt that Mr. Darcy was paying a call and fear gripped her as she heard the sharp rap at the door. Trying to flee from his presence, she found she could not run. The sound of the tapping at the door became louder and more insistent.

She abruptly awakened to see Rosalyn peering into the room through a slightly opened door.

"Elizabeth, I am sorry to awaken you. You must have been in a sound sleep as you did not answer when I knocked, but you must allow me to tell you what transpired tonight!"

Elizabeth slowly lifted her head and gazed at the light in Rosalyn's eyes, reflecting off the flame of the candle she was holding. Elizabeth knew immediately what her friend was about to tell her and she braced herself for it.

"He was there, tonight, Elizabeth! He was there!"

Closing her eyes briefly and pressing her lips tightly together, Elizabeth breathed in slowly to calm her rapidly beating heart. She looked up at Rosalyn. "You mean Mr. Darcy?"

"Yes!" Rosalyn answered slowly as all her breath was expelled. She quickly took Elizabeth's hand and held it tightly in her own. "It was a small party of about twenty and would you believe it? He purposely took the chair next to mine for the dinner! I did not think I would be able to breathe throughout it and the thought of eating was the absolute last thing on my mind!"

Rosalyn laughed and squeezed Elizabeth's hand tighter. "When he spoke to me, I could barely tend to his words!" Her voice gradually rose in intensity and rapidity with each morsel of information she gave to Elizabeth, but in a whisper she concluded with, "I cannot help but think he purposely singled me out!"

Elizabeth made an attempt to smile. "I am very glad to hear that, Rosalyn, but could we wait until morning? I am quite tired!"

"Oh, yes, please forgive me, Elizabeth!" Rosalyn sat still for a moment, seemingly not yet ready to quit the room. "But first, I must tell you! He mentioned you by name, having heard that you are living here as a governess!"

Elizabeth felt her throat constrict as the colour drained from her face. "He did?"

"Yes, and you cannot guess what else!"

Elizabeth shook her head slowly, feeling apprehension rise. "I cannot imagine."

"He indicated a slight curiosity whether you had spoken of him at all. When I said that indeed you had, he said he hoped it had been in a favourable light."

Elizabeth's eyes widened, and looking down at her nervously entwining hands, her face warmed with a blush.

"Elizabeth," Rosalyn leaned it to her. "He is clearly hopeful that I have heard only good things about him from you."

Elizabeth looked up at her through guarded eyes. "Yes, so it would seem." She took in a breath and held it before asking her next question. "Rosalyn, what *did* you tell him that I said about him?"

"I told him you only had the kindest words about him; that you spoke highly of your respect for him and felt that he was a most admirable gentleman; that there was not a finer man that could be found."

Elizabeth eyes widened and she laughed nervously. "Rosalyn, did I truly say all that?"

"Well, you know how I can get carried away at times. He seemed quite pleased with your estimation of him and I said a few more things, only wishing to please him more." She paused for a moment and her eyes widened. "I hope you do not mind! Oh, please forgive me for embellishing your opinion of him. I just knew that you thought highly of him from what little you said."

Elizabeth's mind swirled in turmoil as she wondered what he must think of her now. "Well, it is behind us and Mr. Darcy must be quite convinced that I have spoken of him only in the highest regard and he can be assured of your good opinion of him!"

"Thank you, so much, Elizabeth!" Rosalyn stood up to walk towards the door. "I shall sleep most soundly and contentedly tonight!"

When Rosalyn stepped out and closed the door, Elizabeth leaned her head back down on the pillow, her thoughts warring with her feelings. "And I shall sleep most restlessly!"

~~*

Elizabeth did indeed sleep restlessly for the remainder of the night. Over and over, she pondered why Mr. Darcy had inquired of her opinion of him to Rosalyn. *Was he truly concerned that I spoke favourably of him because he wished for Rosalyn to have a good opinion of him? Does he think so highly of himself that he hopes to learn that I have changed my opinion of him? Or does he merely hope that I am suffering the consequences of refusing him and now realize his worth and the significance of his offer?*

Considering any of those options did little to calm her erratically beating heart. Knowing all that Rosalyn told him – truly more than what she had really said – made her wonder what he now thought of her. *Whatever his opinion of me, he must feel himself quite self-satisfied now!*

"Ohhh!" Elizabeth pounded the pillow. It should not matter what his estimation of her was or why he wanted to know her opinion of him! Elizabeth dove into her pillow face down. But to own the truth, it *did* matter to her, and she could not help but wonder why.

The next morning, Rosalyn came up to Elizabeth several times, recalling some incident from the previous night that she wished to share with her; everything from what Mr. Darcy wore to what foods he seemed to enjoy the most.

"Elizabeth, when I first noticed him, he was standing with his back to me. But I was quite certain it was him because of the manner in which he walked as someone called him over. Have you ever noticed how he appears to glide across the floor? And he had on the most impeccable dark blue attire. When he turned and looked at me, I quite forgot of what I was speaking to Mrs. Remington!"

And then she spoke of the meal. "He took a rather small portion of duck, but seemed to take a rather large portion of potatoes. He had little interest at all in the beet soup, but he did eat a good deal of the bread pudding."

Elizabeth made several futile attempts to change the subject. However much she did not wish to hear about him, she did inquire about Mr. Bingley and Miss Darcy and whether an announcement of their betrothal had been made.

"No, I had very little opportunity to speak to them as they left early. I did hear people whispering and conjecturing about them, though, and they all think an announcement is forthcoming."

Throughout the day, Elizabeth found it exceedingly difficult to concentrate on Emily's lessons. She found herself easily distracted and even little Emily noticed it.

"Miss Bennet," Emily said, reaching out and taking Elizabeth's hand. "Are you feeling unwell this morning? You do not seem yourself."

Elizabeth smiled. "You certainly are an astute child, Emily."

"What is… astute?"

Elizabeth smiled. "Astute means you are smart about things and have good judgment. You can sense things to be a certain way. For example, you say I do not seem to be myself. You are correct, but I had not told you how I was feeling."

"I can see it in your eyes."

"Truly? And as you grow up, you will notice more and more things like that, making you a good studier of character."

"Is that good?"

Elizabeth tilted her head. "It can be in some ways." She thought back to her study of Mr. Darcy. "But we must not always rely on what we first perceive. We may not always be correct."

"How will we know if we are mistaken?"

Elizabeth sighed. "Sometimes we may not know until it is too late. But," Elizabeth clasped her hands together. "A good rule of thumb is to not be too quick to judge someone poorly, but always be willing to judge them well. Then, collect the facts you need to support or disprove your opinion."

Emily smiled. "That does sound like a good idea."

Elizabeth felt a little better after her talk with Emily. She enjoyed sharing lessons she had learned from people, books, and her own experience. Fortunately, the young girl did not ask what it was that was bothering her and Elizabeth did not volunteer the information.

~~*

To Elizabeth's relief and Rosalyn's regret, for several weeks there were no balls, no parties, and no evenings at the theatre that claimed Mr. Darcy, his sister, or Mr. Bingley in attendance. Rosalyn still harboured hopes that Mr.

Darcy had a fondness for her, but kept it between herself and Elizabeth. She had not owned up to her sister what her hopes and dreams concerning him were.

Elizabeth was grateful for his absence at those functions, but that did not prevent Rosalyn from mentioning him at every opportunity in which they found themselves alone. While she dearly enjoyed the friendship they shared, when the subject of Mr. Darcy came up, Elizabeth had to choose her words very carefully so as not to divulge anything she would later regret.

She was also immeasurably grateful that no announcement concerning Miss Darcy and Mr. Bingley had been made. The more time that passed without one, the longer she could withhold causing Jane more pain. She had made a decision early on that she would not burden Jane with the fact that she had seen him again until it was absolutely necessary. She knew it would only be a matter of time.

Chapter 5

Blue skies and mild breezes became increasingly prominent in the ensuing weeks, replacing the grey skies and cold dampness that had plagued London throughout the spring. The promise of summer brought with it the anticipation of colourful gardens, warmer days, and of course, the move to the country. The house was all astir with plans and packing.

While Elizabeth savoured each visit to her aunt and uncle's, more often than not her smiles were forced and she found it difficult to join the others in their laughter. It pained her to know that these visits would shortly be coming to an end when she departed with the Willstones for the north. But just as she was determined to guard what she said to Rosalyn about Mr. Darcy, so she had to be careful not to mention Mr. Bingley to Jane. Until she knew for a certainty that an announcement between him and Miss Darcy had been made, she would not acknowledge to her sister that she had seen him. It was an insufferable thought that lingered continually in the back of her mind.

As the time drew nearer for their departure, arrangements were made for one final party at the Willstones' home and Elizabeth had been asked to practice a song for Emily to sing for the guests. Invitations were sent out to all their closest acquaintances, and Elizabeth pondered quietly whether that would include Mr. Darcy, Miss Darcy, and Mr. Bingley. She could only hope and pray that he would not attend and that they had not yet become betrothed.

Elizabeth diligently tended to her duties over little Emily, working with fervour on a song she would play on the pianoforte and Emily would sing. She did everything to put which guests might attend out of her mind. Rosalyn, however, brought forth that subject to Elizabeth at every opportunity. It was with great disappointment, then, that the day before the party, she came to see Elizabeth.

"He most likely will not be here, Elizabeth," she pouted despondently.

Elizabeth tilted her head at Rosalyn and gave her a sly smile. "Of whom do you speak?"

"Oh, Elizabeth, how you tease me! We have heard from Miss Darcy that she and Mr. Bingley will attend, but nothing from her brother." Rosalyn let out a deep sigh. "It is just as I feared. My sister supposes that he has already left for the country and will not be returning to London until next season."

A great sense of relief flooded Elizabeth, but she felt compassion for her friend's disappointed hopes. "I am sure there will be plenty of opportunities to see him in Town next year."

Rosalyn waved her hand through the air in a dramatic gesture. "Oh, no. I am convinced he will be married by then. Or at least promised to someone."

Curiosity prompted Elizabeth to ask, "Why do you say that?"

Reaching out and grasping Elizabeth's hands, Rosalyn answered, "If his sister is to marry, he will be released from the burden of her guardianship and feel the freedom to take a wife of his own. Some say it may have been due to his devotion and care for his sister that he has not yet married. It only makes sense."

Elizabeth abruptly looked down as her heart began to pound. Slowly looking back up to Rosalyn, she asked apprehensively, "Are they engaged, then? Miss Darcy and Mr. Bingley?"

"I have not heard that there has been an announcement, but everyone believes it will be soon. And if that is the case, if I do not see Mr. Darcy before we leave for the country, it may be too late. I will be gravely disappointed."

"Rosalyn," Elizabeth tried to reassure her. "There are many fine men out there. Certainly someone other than Mr. Darcy would make you a wonderful husband."

"Perhaps," she said as she drew her hands into her lap and wove her fingers nervously together. "But he is so good, and kind, and generous. He is devoted to his sister and does not seem to be impressed with the trappings of society. Besides that, he is so terribly handsome. He is just about the only man in the world I could ever consider marrying!"

Elizabeth let out an unwitting breathy chuckle. Rosalyn looked up abruptly. "Do you think me foolish?"

"No, Rosalyn." Elizabeth answered, chiding herself for her reaction. She recollected the words she lashed out at him when she refused his offer of marriage, that he would be the last man she could ever be prevailed upon to marry. "If he is as good as you say, I cannot think you foolish at all."

~~*

On the day of the Willstones' party, an early morning light rain dampened the grounds. But later in the afternoon the clouds were pushed north by a pleasant southerly breeze, allowing the sun to peek out intermittently. By late afternoon, the blue sky prevailed and the sun poured down its warmth on the Willstone household.

Due to the cool and wet weather, Elizabeth was forced to keep Emily entertained indoors. The excitement the girl felt about the evening gave her an abundance of energy, and it was all Elizabeth could do to keep her out of the way of the servants making final preparations for the evening.

Elizabeth had been given instructions to keep Emily upstairs again until she was called for. Guests would begin arriving in late afternoon and a supper would be served in the early evening. Emily would be asked to sing in the parlour just prior to the supper being served, before everyone proceeded to the dining room.

The two had been working together on their song rather diligently. They had practiced it over and over for the past two weeks until both knew it quite well. Emily had no qualms about singing in front of an audience, so Elizabeth did not have to fear that the young girl would suffer any nerves. She was quite sure her charge would perform splendidly.

Being a larger party, Elizabeth knew she would not be put in a position to have to speak to anyone. She and Emily would come out, perform, and then take their leave and return upstairs. If Miss Darcy and Mr. Bingley were there, she would not be required to converse with them. At least she was prepared this time to see them, and she would bear it admirably, although she still harboured lingering disappointment for her dear Jane.

She readied herself in her dark grey muslin gown, before attending to Emily. The longer the little girl could remain in her everyday dress, the easier it would be. When Elizabeth began to hear voices coming from downstairs, she knew that people had begun to arrive. She went in and tended to Emily.

She took care to curl Emily's long hair and weave it with ribbons. She helped her put on her dress, which was a dark pink satin with lace sleeves and a bow at the neckline, which Emily insisted on tying herself. When they were both finally ready, Elizabeth took Emily by the hand and they sat down in the two chairs in her young ward's room. Elizabeth had Emily pick out a book that she could read quietly to herself as they waited to be called downstairs.

Emily actually read through two books, only asking Elizabeth for assistance three times. Elizabeth was pleased with the girl's progress and her plan was to steer the girl to books that were a little more challenging during the summer months in the country.

At one point, Emily stopped, looking determinedly at Elizabeth. "I think you should put on a more colourful dress. You would look so much prettier!"

Elizabeth smiled softly. "You know, Emily, that I wear only grey or black because I am in mourning. When a year has passed since my father's death, I will go back to wearing my other dresses."

Emily's lips turned down in a pout. "I wish you could look pretty tonight. Everyone downstairs will be dressed so finely."

"Just a little while longer," Elizabeth answered, somewhat surprised by the young girl's comment.

At length, just as Emily was about to begin her third book, there was a tap at the door.

"Yes," Elizabeth answered.

It was Lilia, and she peeked her head in. "They are ready for Miss Emily to sing, now."

Emily quickly stood up and the maid clasped her hands together. "Why, don't you look simply beautiful and all grown up!"

A smile graced Emily's face, and in a very adult manner she said, "Thank you, Mrs. Hutchins," followed by a gracious curtsey. "Miss Bennet cannot look beautiful yet, for she is still in the morning."

Elizabeth and Lilia chuckled at her innocent mistake. Elizabeth took the opportunity to gently correct her. "I am in mourning, Emily, not in the morning."

"Oh." A brief look of confusion passed over Emily's face, but she reached up for Elizabeth's hand and the two walked downstairs.

As they came into the room, people were visiting with each other as they stood or sat around the parlour. This gave Elizabeth a few moments to go over some things with Emily, position her where she ought to stand, and then arrange her music at the piano. While she did so, her gaze swept quickly over the crowd. She let out a brief sigh of relief when she saw neither Miss Darcy nor Mr. Bingley.

Emily's father walked over to his daughter and cleared his voice. Speaking to his guests he said, "Our precious daughter, Emily, loves to sing, and we have asked her to entertain you tonight with one of her favourite songs." He looked at Emily and then at Elizabeth and nodded for them to proceed.

Elizabeth played a short introduction, and then Emily began to sing. Her voice, matured beyond her youthful age, was clear and steady. As Elizabeth occasionally glanced over at her, she was proud to see that the young girl remained poised, had a pleasant countenance, and seemed ever so confident.

Having completed the first verse, Elizabeth adeptly reached up to turn the page of her music. Her gaze was momentarily distracted by the sight of someone walking through the doorway. It was Miss Darcy.

Elizabeth forced her gaze back down to the music score to relocate her place; only a few errant keys brought her back nicely without doing the piece too much harm. But she did not have to look back up to see who had walked in with the young lady. As her eyes scanned the music, she could easily determine that it was not Mr. Bingley. It was Mr. Darcy!

As her gaze drifted unwittingly back up, their eyes met, followed by a slight jarring of the keys and an involuntary lowering of her head. This cannot be! As her heart raced, her eyes blurred, making the reading of notes very difficult. Fortunately for her, she had the song partly memorized, and once she had inwardly chided herself and turned her attention back on Emily, one would hardly know she had not played the piece precisely as written.

A look from Emily, however, displayed the young girl's surprise at the sudden rearrangement of the piece.

When they finished with the song, Elizabeth collected herself and slowly closed the piece of music, taking it in her hands and forcing a smile upon her face before standing. It need not have mattered. The guests were all standing and clapping their hands in appreciation for Emily's song. No one likely noticed Elizabeth's blunder. Except Emily.

Elizabeth remained at the piano while the applause continued, allowing the young girl to receive all the adulation. It also gave Elizabeth a moment to gaze back over the crowd. She had not seen where Mr. Darcy and his sister went after she lowered her head, but she was curious to look upon him now that she was somewhat more composed.

Her eyes turned toward the left, sensing a pair of eyes upon her. Standing taller than those around him, Mr. Darcy stood out. She lifted her head, took in a deep breath, and acknowledged him with a brief, polite smile, as if she was merely seeing an old acquaintance. He was an old acquaintance! The fact that she had mercilessly refused his offer of marriage the last time she had seen him was another matter.

Mr. Darcy nodded slightly, causing Elizabeth to blush faintly. His eyes held hers and she could only guess as to the meaning in his intense stare. She finally was able to look away and turned back to Emily.

The young girl ran into her arms, thrilled for the response of the crowd. Elizabeth leaned down to give the girl a hug, and then the two hurriedly returned upstairs.

Once up in Emily's room, the young girl turned to Elizabeth. "What happened? You played the song differently than we had practiced!"

Elizabeth drew her hand over the young girl's head, combing her fingers down her long hair. "I am so sorry, Emily. I lost my place for a moment, but I do not think anyone noticed. You did a fine job disguising my mistake."

A satisfied smile graced Emily's face. "I did, did I not?"

"You certainly did."

After readying Emily for bed and allowing her to read a few more books, Elizabeth returned to her room. She was grateful for the solitude as she thought back to that moment when she saw Mr. Darcy walk in. While she had prepared herself for seeing Miss Darcy and Mr. Bingley, she was certainly not expecting to encounter Mr. Darcy. She was surprised that it was not anger she felt when she first saw him. Perhaps all of Rosalyn's words of praise about the man had begun to soften her prejudice against him. Certainly she knew, both from his letter and a year of reflection, that he was basically a good man, just as she had affirmed to Rosalyn.

As she thought about the moment she saw him walk in, she realized that she had been struck by the intensity of his eyes. When his gaze met hers, every thought about where she was and what she was doing vanished. While knowing the song well, it took her a moment to compose herself. She could only do that by averting her eyes and lowering her head so as not to see him.

She thought back to her acknowledgement of him after the song. She knew that she could have taken no notice of him, but something compelled her to look at him and smile.

She turned and saw a reflection of herself in her mirror. Confusing emotions began to swirl within as she noticed the grey dress. She recalled Emily's words earlier, wishing she could have been prettier tonight. She was suddenly gripped with distress that Mr. Darcy had seen her that way. Perhaps that was the reason for the look in his eyes. He was appalled at how much she was altered.

She shook her head and pounded her fists against her dress. She must not allow herself to think this way. "I have no reason to fret about what he thinks of me," she whispered to her reflection, "whether he thinks I am altered or not!"

While she had justified to herself every good reason to refuse his proposal, and while he may not be as horrid as she thought he was, she had no reason to consider that he would ever renew his address. Not, of course, that she would want him to.

When she finally crawled into bed, after listening for some time to the gaiety coming from downstairs, she could not help but wonder who Mr. Darcy would talk to, what he would say, and how Rosalyn would behave around him.

She closed her eyes as she thought how desperately Rosalyn might conduct herself if indeed she felt this would be her only opportunity to secure his notice. Elizabeth knew Mr. Darcy well enough to know that he would not look kindly upon any behaviour displayed to attract his notice. She could only hope Rosalyn would behave in a most prudent manner.

She found it difficult to fall asleep, even after voices became subdued and guests began to depart. She found herself waiting for Rosalyn to come bursting into the room to give her an account of the evening. While she dreaded it, she was surprised to realize that a small part of her hoped to hear all that transpired over the course of the evening.

In the early hours of the morning the house was dark and quiet. Rosalyn never came to Elizabeth's room, and Elizabeth lay in bed wide awake. Images of Mr. Darcy's face, his nod, and his tall, handsome demeanour flooded her thoughts. She knew that even if she were spared these thoughts by sleep coming upon her, he would invade her dreams. And when she did fall asleep just before dawn, he was there just as she had expected.

~~*

A spattering of raindrops against the window woke Elizabeth. Pulling her coverlet up over her shoulders, she curled up, grateful that it was Sunday. She could sleep in a little longer before setting out for her aunt and uncle's.

Her mind swirled with thoughts of last night and the dream that had been so vivid. It did not surprise her that Mr. Darcy was prominent in her dream, but the nature of it came as a surprise to her. She was at his wedding. He was standing up front waiting for his bride to come down the aisle. Rosalyn was sitting next to Elizabeth crying inconsolably.

Suddenly the doors to the back of the church opened wide and everyone turned to see the bride come down the aisle. Elizabeth did not know who the bride was, and was just as anxious as everyone to see who would step out and walk down the aisle to him.

For several moments everyone waited, but no one came. Turning toward the people in the church, Mr. Darcy demanded, "Where is my bride?"

His eyes searched the crowded church as young ladies called out asking, "Is it me? Is it me?"

He grew impatient, and finally turned and noticed Elizabeth; his eyes glaring out at her. "What are you doing over there, Elizabeth?" he demanded to know.

She looked down, and to her dismay, saw that she was wearing a wedding gown. She did not understand why she was dressed as a bride, and all the while Rosalyn continued to sob next to her.

She awoke suddenly; her heart beating wildly. His gaze, looking out at her in her dream, was just as real to her as his gaze last evening. She shook her head as she tried to rid her mind of thoughts of him. Her hand went up and covered her mouth as she realized with a start that in truth she had begun to think differently about him. Yet she knew now nothing could ever come of it.

Elizabeth wondered why Rosalyn had not come to her last evening to enlighten her about all the events from the previous night. Could, or should, Elizabeth hope that Rosalyn's hopes were dashed? Perhaps there was something she discovered about him that made her realize he was not her ideal. Could she have realized that her belief – her hope – that he had formed an attachment to her, was erroneous?

Elizabeth took her time getting ready, and just as she was about to leave her room to go downstairs, there was a knock at the door.

"Elizabeth, it is Rosalyn. May I come in?"

Just anticipating the purpose of the visit prompted Elizabeth to feel somewhat anxious, but she cheerfully answered, "Do come in, Rosalyn."

A sombre faced young lady walked in. She lacked all the cheerfulness and sparkle that her other visits had. Elizabeth could only imagine what prompted this and hoped that whatever it was, Rosalyn would soon recover from it.

Rosalyn walked away from Elizabeth toward the window, and then abruptly turned back toward her. "You did not tell me of all your dealings with Mr. Darcy. I cannot believe you kept it from me."

Elizabeth's eyes widened and her mouth went dry. Before she was able to answer, Rosalyn continued, "He told us everything. How could you not have told me?"

Feeling her hands begin to shake, Elizabeth clasped them together tightly. She could not imagine Mr. Darcy informing them of his proposal and her refusal, and did not know what to say. "Rosalyn, I am sorry that I did not tell you. I am truly surprised that Mr. Darcy did. You must think me completely devoid of reason and a fool!"

Rosalyn stepped forward and reached out to Elizabeth. "Certainly not," she said as she smiled softly. "It is not your fault that Mr. Bingley prefers your sister to Miss Darcy. Poor Miss Darcy. I hope she does not take this too hard."

Trying to comprehend all that Rosalyn was saying, Elizabeth simply asked, "What? What about Miss Darcy and Mr. Bingley?"

"Oh, I am sorry. I jumped ahead of myself. Mr. Darcy confidentially informed us that he was here last night in Mr. Bingley's place, as there was no longer any attachment between Mr. Bingley and his sister. He went on to say that Mr. Bingley had realized that he still had strong feelings for a young lady he knew previously… and that young lady was your sister, Jane!"

Great relief flooded Elizabeth mingled with a profusion of joy! Mr. Bingley had every intention of calling on Jane. He still loved her! Elizabeth could not have been happier and she knew her sister would be elated and would dearly welcome him.

Elizabeth leaned over and hugged Rosalyn. "You do not know how happy this makes me! I must confess that I was surprised when I saw Mr. Bingley with Miss Darcy when they came to the house, and was so disheartened when I heard that an engagement between them was expected by all. I felt that all hope was gone for my sister. I was so in despair for Jane that I did not have the heart to even tell her that I had seen him and I still have not."

"Then you and your sister shall have much to talk about today, shall you not?" Rosalyn asked.

"Oh, yes, especially if Mr. Bingley has already called." Elizabeth suddenly thought of Miss Darcy. "But how did Miss Darcy appear? Do you think she is very upset?"

Rosalyn shrugged her shoulders. "She is a very quiet girl; perhaps she was a bit more subdued last night than on the few other times I saw her. When we first inquired about Mr. Bingley, she merely replied that he could not attend due to other plans that arose. It was only when we mentioned him to Mr. Darcy that he informed us what had truly happened."

Elizabeth tilted her head at Rosalyn, wondering whether Mr. Bingley's decision to return to Jane was sanctioned by Mr. Darcy or not. "And Mr. Darcy, how did he seem with the news? Did it appear that he harboured any anger or resentment toward Mr. Bingley for his actions regarding his sister?"

"He seemed only to have concern for her. He acted a bit protective of her throughout the evening. But he definitely made a point of informing us that it was your sister for whom Mr. Bingley still harboured an attachment."

This bit of news surprised Elizabeth, for certainly Bingley's actions most likely cost him Mr. Darcy's friendship. "I am certain that Mr. Darcy must be gravely concerned for his sister," Elizabeth answered, convinced that now, with his sister's loss, he would have more reason to think ill of her – and her family.

"It is sad for her," Rosalyn let out a sympathetic sigh. "But only think that this means she is not to marry and therefore Mr. Darcy will not be so inclined to find a wife for himself directly. It gives me a little more time."

Elizabeth let out a resigned chuckle. "Yes, Rosalyn. It may just do that."

Chapter 6

After the Willstones departed for church, Elizabeth hurried to get herself ready for her weekly visit to see Jane and the Gardiners. While she had earlier felt great sorrow anticipating this day – it being their last visit for several months – she could now look forward to it with great joy. Knowing that Mr. Bingley may have already paid Jane a call and that there was every hope of them being restored in their love and affection for one another brought her much elation. The mere hope of that would carry her through those months in the North Country far away from her family.

When Elizabeth arrived, the vibrant smiles with which her aunt and sister welcomed her caused her to hope that Mr. Bingley had indeed paid a call. Jane's first words out of her mouth confirmed it.

"He came, Lizzy! He came!"

Elizabeth immediately went up to Jane and wrapped her arms about her. "Just by seeing your rapturous face, dear Jane, I have no need to ask of whom you speak. Mr. Bingley paid a call." It was more of an affirmation than a question.

Jane nodded as tears of joy pooled in her eyes. "Just yesterday. I was so anxious for you to come today to tell you."

"I am so pleased, Jane." Elizabeth drew back and tilted her head at her sister. "And did you find him well? Is he just as you remember him to be?"

"Yes." Jane laughed softly. "He has been in good health. He told me that he saw you at the Willstones. How could you not have told me? He was so grieved to hear about Father. He expressed tremendous regret in our loss and offered heartfelt consolation. He also assured us how sorry he was that he never returned to Netherfield."

Elizabeth smiled as Jane spoke animatedly, quite unlike her normal manner. "And did he make plans to call on you again?"

Jane let out a contented sigh. "Yes. He is meeting us at church this morning and will be returning to spend the afternoon here. I hope you do not mind, Elizabeth. I know this is your last visit for several months and…"

"You must know that I welcome Mr. Bingley's company more than anyone's," she fervently assured her sister. "Nothing could make me happier!"

As they ate breakfast together before leaving for services, Jane and Mrs. Gardiner related all that happened during Mr. Bingley's visit; how he stayed for more than an hour, how it appeared he could not take his eyes off Jane, and how he repeatedly told them how good it was to see her again and to make the Gardiners' acquaintance.

Elizabeth enlightened them about how surprised she was when she saw Mr. Bingley at the Willstones'. She confessed to Jane that she had not told her of it because she did not want to raise Jane's hopes that anything would come of it. She did not mention Miss Darcy, and knew not whether he mentioned her during his visit the day before. Most likely he had not.

~~*

Elizabeth sat in the services that morning seated next to Jane. She knew from Jane's serene countenance that the elation she felt permeated the very depths of her being. Mr. Bingley, seated on the other side of Jane, exhibited his feelings of abundant joy in the expression on his face and the enthusiasm with which he sang the hymns. Elizabeth could see by the manner in which both Jane and Mr. Bingley looked at each other that their feelings were still very much the same. She knew not whether he had been forced to sever his friendship with Mr. Darcy in reuniting with her, but she knew there would likely be ill will between the two men if only due to his abandoning Miss Darcy. The young girl must feel the loss greatly and her brother was likely never to forgive his friend. But she also knew that the smile Mr. Bingley wore now, was not such a one as she had seen at all when he had been with Miss Darcy.

When they returned to the house, Elizabeth was grateful to see that neither Jane nor Bingley displayed any signs of awkwardness. It almost appeared to Elizabeth as if there had only been a few days since they had last met at Netherfield, instead of more than the year it had been, and that no uncertainty had ever arisen about his regard. Whatever Bingley sacrificed in order to return to Jane, he seemed not to be overly wrought by it. He was content to be with her, and she returned the sentiment.

While she was confident Jane and Mr. Bingley would fare well and that their love seemed as strong as ever, she could not help but wonder what this decision had actually cost him. Several times during the course of the afternoon she had to purse her lips tightly together to prevent from asking him, "What does Mr. Darcy think of this?" or "Is Miss Darcy terribly hurt?" She had never divulged information to Jane about Mr. Darcy's actions in convincing his friend to doubt her affections. She had also never enlightened her that she had seen Mr. Bingley in the company of Miss Darcy and that everyone had expected an engagement between the two. No, she would do nothing to lessen the joy that Jane felt now having been reunited with the man she had continued to love since he departed Netherfield.

Elizabeth prolonged her stay as long as possible, knowing that when she said goodbye to Jane, it would be for several months. As they hugged one last time, Elizabeth whispered into her sister's ear, being able to honestly say, "I leave you in good hands, my dearest sister. If not for this most pleasant circumstance, I would be distraught, knowing we are to be separated by so many miles and so many months. But I leave content, knowing that you are truly happy again."

Elizabeth felt a shudder course through Jane, knowing her parting words had wrought mixed feelings in her sister and evoked some tears. But she knew that while there were a few tears for her departure, they were mingled with many more tears of joy for Mr. Bingley's return.

After saying their final, lengthy, and very emotional goodbyes, Elizabeth left, knowing that the only thing that might bring her back sooner would be a wedding. Elizabeth's heart filled with joyous anticipation of that thought.

She smiled almost all the way back, her mind and heart more at ease than they had been in a long time. She was not only leaving her sister in a good situation, but she was returning to the country, where the fresh air and miles of good walking would leave her refreshed. Now that Jane was happy, she could look forward to leaving London and all that had transpired here the past several weeks.

She had greatly missed Longbourn and life in the country since coming to London. While she had enjoyed it at first, she had come to long for her lengthy walks across fields and up Oakham Mount. She knew not what the Willstones' manor or surrounding area would be like, but she looked forward to having some time to explore it.

~~*

When Elizabeth returned to the Willstones', she was met with about as much joy as she had left at her aunt and uncle's home. Rosalyn and Mr. and Mrs. Willstone were in a very animated conversation in the sitting room when she walked in.

Not wishing to disturb them, Elizabeth peeked her head in and wished them a good evening, then proceeded toward the stairs to go up to her room. Rosalyn rushed out and asked Elizabeth to join them for a moment.

With eyes as bright as her smile was wide, she said, "Come, we have some very exciting news."

Elizabeth knew that whatever the news was, it could not surpass in excellence all that had come to pass this day. She walked in and joined them eager nevertheless, to hear what it was that had Rosalyn so vibrant.

Mr. Willstone greeted Elizabeth and then nodded to Rosalyn with a teasing twinkle in his eye. "So are you going to tell her or should I?"

The way Rosalyn clasped her hands and looked at her with such joy on her face, Elizabeth was quite sure what… or at least who… this was all about. "You will not believe what happened, today. I am sure you will be just as amazed as we all were."

"I cannot imagine, Rosalyn. What happened?"

Looking first to her sister, then to Mr. Willstone, Rosalyn then turned to Elizabeth. "The Darcys were at services this morning. Mr. Darcy and his sister joined us directly afterwards and we talked about our journey to the country in a few days and their departure on the morrow."

Elizabeth nodded, feeling somewhat apprehensive, but encouraging her to continue.

"You will not believe this! I cannot believe this!" Her face grew flushed and she fanned herself demurely with her hand. "Mr. Darcy and his sister have invited us to come to Pemberley!"

Elizabeth was stunned into silence. "Your family will be going to Pemberley?" she finally asked.

"All of us! For a fortnight! You included, of course."

"No!" Elizabeth exclaimed abruptly, her brows furrowing in astonishment as she attempted to make out what this meant. "I mean, surely you are jesting, are you not?"

"She is not jesting. It is true," Mrs. Willstone answered as she looked at her sister and smiled. "Rosalyn could not be happier."

Rosalyn leaned toward Elizabeth with a conspiratorial glint in her eyes. "They know the regard I have for him. They had guessed all along." She let out a slight giggle as she said, "And here we thought we were keeping such a good secret between ourselves!"

"Hmmm," Elizabeth said with a compulsory smile, still wondering how all this transpired and why.

"Mr. Darcy has invited some men to join him for several days of hunting," Mr. Willstone explained. "Miss Darcy is going to entertain the ladies. I dare say I have always wanted to see Pemberley. I have heard so much about it over the years from Lorraine's family."

Rosalyn reached over and touched Elizabeth's arm. "Is this not the most exciting news?"

"I cannot find the words to express my feelings," Elizabeth said honestly. "It is all quite… astonishing."

Mr. Willstone leaned back in his chair, planting both arms firmly on the armrests. "I do not believe Mr. Darcy customarily invites people to Pemberley that he does not know intimately. This comes as quite a surprise – and an honour – to us!"

"And Miss Darcy," chimed in Mrs. Willstone, "is so quiet and shy. We were quite pleasantly surprised by her wish to entertain the ladies while the men are out. This may perhaps be her introduction to hosting a small party."

Mr. Willstone nodded. "Now, we have cautioned our Rosalyn not to look upon this with too much expectation." He looked over at her and winked. "But with the attention Mr. Darcy has paid toward her recently, we cannot help but hope that he has formed an attachment to her and wishes to further their acquaintance."

Elizabeth glanced over at Rosalyn. She was indeed very pretty. Her manners were pleasing and she had a very engaging personality. Pushing down a myriad of feelings that were beginning to rise, she answered, "I know of no reason why he should not."

Elizabeth's words could not have made Rosalyn more happy and herself feel more confused.

After allowing Rosalyn sufficient time to express how this might just be the opportunity for all her hopes and dreams to be fulfilled, Elizabeth looked at Mrs. Willstone. "Under the circumstances, I feel somewhat awkward trespassing upon

Pemberley. After all, Mr. Bingley forsook Miss Darcy for my very own sister. I cannot believe that she or her brother would wish me there. Do you suppose they are under the misapprehension that I will not be accompanying you?"

The Willstones looked at each other. "We had not thought of that, dear," began Mrs. Willstone.

With her hands folded in her lap, Elizabeth began to nervously intertwine her fingers together and suggested, "Perhaps it would be best if Emily and I went on directly to your country home, instead."

"If I recall correctly, Miss Darcy seemed most pleased to extend the invitation and Mr. Darcy assured us that we were all invited," Mrs. Willstone continued. "I believe he may have even mentioned your name. I would not fret, my dear, as you will most likely be tending to Emily most of the time. Why, you may hardly see Miss Darcy or her brother at all!"

For some reason, those words of assurance left Elizabeth even more unsettled. She knew, and rightfully so, that her position of governess would prevent her from socializing with the family at Pemberley as she had recently become accustomed to doing here.

"I understand your meaning, Mrs. Willstone."

"Elizabeth," Mrs. Willstone looked at her with compassion. "You know we dearly love you and have been thoroughly elated at the friendship you and Rosalyn have developed, but... taking into consideration the stature of the Darcys and Pemberley... well, we must act in a way that is expected."

"Certainly." The smile that formed on Elizabeth's face was forced, and not one that came from her heart.

The subject of conversation then turned to the logistics of their travels. They would depart in two days for Northamptonshire, where Rosalyn and Lorraine's brother now resided. After spending two weeks there, they would take their greatly anticipated detour to Derbyshire and Pemberley, where they would stay an additional two weeks. From there they would finally, and for Rosalyn most reluctantly, depart Mr. Darcy and Pemberley and travel to the Willstones' manor in Nottinghamshire.

Later that evening, after discussing the details – and all the possibilities – of their stay at Pemberley, Elizabeth went to bed with her head in a whirl. She truly wondered why Mr. Darcy would have extended this invitation to the Willstones knowing it would likely include her.

Even if she did not see much of her, Miss Darcy certainly would not want her there as a constant reminder of Mr. Bingley forsaking her for Jane. This scheme that everyone in this household looked upon with great anticipation was for Elizabeth a most disconcerting prospect.

A stray thought played around Elizabeth's mind that perhaps Mr. Darcy had some vengeful plan to punish her for her refusal. Perhaps he did wish to pursue Rosalyn, and he would do it all before Elizabeth's eyes. He would make sure she knew exactly all that she had turned down in refusing his offer. He would ensure that she would come to regret the very words she uttered against him.

She could also possibly become the recipient of Mr. Darcy's resentful temper because of Mr. Bingley's inconstancy in his regard for his sister in favour of her sister. She recollected his words, "My good opinion once lost is lost forever." He could hardly have a good opinion of her after all she had done and said, but probably even more so was the hurt that had been inflicted upon his sister, for which he might choose to blame her.

Is his sole intent to punish me? Does he truly intend to make sure I come to regret my refusing him and the humiliation I so willingly bestowed upon him?

"No," she said aloud softly. "I do not believe him to be that sort of man." She did not know why, but she felt for a certainty that it was not in his nature to resort to that manner of behaviour. At least she hoped that he was not.

~~*

The last two days in Town provided continued speculation and every expressed hope and dream that Rosalyn had ever hidden in her heart. There could be no other reason for this invitation than Mr. Darcy's implicit intent to further his acquaintance with her for reasons of an affection he must hold toward her. What greater opportunity could there be for him to get to know her, and her to get to know him, his sister, and Pemberley, than a stay of a fortnight? To Rosalyn, it was most apparent.

To Elizabeth, however, things did not seem as clear. She often found herself reflecting on his character and what she thought she knew of him. Again and again she came to the conclusion that Rosalyn did not seem to be the type of woman with whom he would have formed an attachment. Yet just as often she chided herself, for what did she really know of his character? She had been blind, so completely mistaken, when it came to realizing he had such a strong affection for her that he wanted to ask for her hand. When he came to her to make her an offer, it had been the last thing she had ever expected from him.

No, he was not a man who was easily understood.

She knew not what to expect once they arrived at Pemberley and could only hope that she would be able to stay sequestered away with Emily as the remainder of the Willstone family enjoyed the hospitality of Mr. Darcy and his sister.

Chapter 7

Elizabeth was seated beside Rosalyn and across from little Emily as the carriage rambled down the dirt road, full of ruts and pits from recent rains. The travellers were tossed by the swaying of the carriage, much like Elizabeth's thoughts. Their last few days in Town and their recent stay at the Matthews' home in Northamptonshire had passed far too quickly for her spirits to remain calm. They were now on their way to Pemberley.

She had endeavoured time and again to view this as judiciously as she could. She had, after all, been acknowledged in the invitation to Pemberley and therefore should have nothing to prompt the feelings of awkwardness and confusion that she was experiencing. She should be able to view Mr. Darcy as the gentleman that he was, not solely as the man whose proposal she had refused.

The mere thought caused a tightening in her chest and a quickening in her pulse. How she wished she could easily push down those feelings that arose with every reminder of their destination; with every word from Rosalyn of her hopes and expectations; with every recollection of those harsh words she spewed at Mr. Darcy in her refusal.

The man whom Rosalyn fervently admired and esteemed, Elizabeth had profoundly despised and condemned. He certainly could not feel benevolently toward her being in his home. Yet... Mr. Darcy had purposely mentioned her in extending his invitation for the Willstone party to come to Pemberley.

Elizabeth let out a frustrated sigh.

Rosalyn turned to her. "Elizabeth, is the trip too much?"

Elizabeth forced a smile. "I am well. Perhaps a little tired."

Emily looked at Elizabeth and tilted her head as she asked, "Are you not pleased to be going to... where are we going?"

Elizabeth lifted her eyes to the perceptive little girl; so much like herself when she was younger.

"It is Pemberley, and why would you say such a thing, Emily?" Rosalyn inquired of her niece. "I am certain Miss Bennet is quite pleased at the prospect of seeing it, as much as I am."

Emily looked to her aunt with an air of youthful self-assurance. "Perhaps, but every time we talk about going to Pemberley, her eyebrows pinch together." She turned back to Elizabeth. "Like that."

Elizabeth nervously laughed, bringing her fingers up absently to smooth the crease between her brows. She was able to honestly say to her young ward, "Emily, I have indeed been out of sorts recently. But it is due to having left my sister in Town." She reached over to take Emily's hand and said, "Forgive me if I have appeared troubled." She hoped that would answer Emily's concerns.

A jolt in the carriage turned their thoughts back to the conditions of the road. "This road is certainly not allowing for a smooth ride," Rosalyn grumbled. "I am sure the recent rains have only served to make them in dire need of repair. I do hope the weather will be cooperative and allow us to see all there is to see."

Rosalyn let out a giggle. "On the other hand, perhaps if it does rain, the men's days of sport will have to be abandoned and we will just have to tolerate Mr. Darcy's company inside. Do you think we shall be able to endure being in his presence all that time?" Another giggle followed and she turned to Elizabeth. "I must confess that perhaps a little rain might be the very thing we need!"

Elizabeth turned her head abruptly and looked out the window. She wanted nothing more than for this to be all over. Perhaps the two weeks at Pemberley would pass quickly and before she knew it they would be on their way to Staffordshire; away from Pemberley and Mr. Darcy. He, however, would continue to be with Rosalyn, even if only in her dreams. Elizabeth knew that after spending a fortnight at Pemberley, when they finally departed, things would likely not be the same for either one of them.

The three carriages conveying the Willstones, Elizabeth and her travelling companions, and the servants and luggage stopped for a short time at an inn. They all eagerly stepped out, grateful to be able to stretch their legs, eat, and freshen themselves. As Elizabeth took a short walk to calm her ever rising nerves, she breathed in the country air that had been cleansed by the rains and thought ahead to their next stop.

The next time she stepped out of the carriage, she would be stepping onto Pemberley's soil; the place where Mr. Darcy was born and now bore the title Master; the home she could have called her own.

~~*

Upon returning to their carriages, it was mid-afternoon and after a short while, Emily grew tired and put her head across Elizabeth's lap. She fell asleep quickly. Elizabeth closed her eyes as well, but her thoughts prevented her from attaining any rest.

She tried to direct her thoughts to the previous two weeks spent at the Matthews' country home instead of the two weeks that were to come. Elizabeth found the Matthews' home comfortable and spacious and the hospitality delightfully warm. She had enjoyed the company of Rosalyn and Lorraine's brother, Simon, and his family. They were most attentive to her and welcomed her into their home as much as if she had been a dear friend.

When they had been there a few days, Elizabeth was surprised to realize how much she missed being in the country since coming to London. Once again she was able to ramble over hill and dale; sometimes with Emily during the day, and sometimes without her early in the morning. On the two Sundays they were there, when she was free from her duties, she took longer walks as she explored the diverse countryside. She followed path or stream, or forded her own way through the sparsely wooded areas. She could not have been happier.

Unfortunately, the rain had moved in the past three days, and she had not been able to walk at all. They were all left to entertain themselves with indoor amusements. Elizabeth was pleased that Simon Matthews was as avid a chess player as she and she enjoyed a few challenging sets with him.

Emily was occupied much of the time with her little cousins, both of whom were just a little younger than herself. She loved helping their nanny care for them, and Elizabeth oftentimes found that her duties as governess and regularly scheduled times of teaching were not expected as much as when they had been in Town. That frequently put her in the company of the Willstone and Matthews families. While Elizabeth enjoyed their company, Rosalyn seemed disposed to speak only on the subject of which she could now openly discuss, and which solely would satisfy her – Mr. Darcy.

Elizabeth opened her eyes when she noticed that the inside of the carriage had grown dim. Looking out the window, she saw that they were riding through a dense thicket of trees. The sun, approaching close to the horizon, sent diffused streaks of light through the thick cluster of foliage, little of which was reaching them. She shuddered as a coolness suddenly pervaded the carriage.

She pulled up a blanket to cover both her and Emily, who was still sleeping, and she noticed that Rosalyn was gazing out the window with wide eyes.

"We have entered Pemberley Woods," Rosalyn uttered softly when she saw that Elizabeth had stirred. "It is even more beautiful than I remember."

Elizabeth intertwined her fingers together and her heart began to pound violently at those words. It seemed to be as loud as the rumble of the carriage travelling down the road. She took in a few slow breaths in a vain attempt to compose herself. Her own gaze turned to look out her window as she felt a blush creep upon her face – or perhaps it was turning white with alarm – so as not to let Rosalyn see the effect her words had on her.

Her eyes took in everything around her. She noticed a wide, briskly moving stream that seemed to dictate to the road its curves and turns, and when to proceed straight ahead. Sometimes it disappeared behind the trees and at other times it burst forth from them as it continued on its way.

"I had no idea…" Elizabeth whispered, as she drew the blanket more tightly about her.

"The woods will become less dense as we draw nearer the home." Rosalyn spoke with a fervent hush, her eyes sparkling with anticipation. "I believe we shall see it first out your window, and then a turn in the road will bring it around to my side."

Upon hearing voices, Emily stirred. As she stretched out her arms she asked, "Are we there yet?"

"Almost," Rosalyn replied. "Look outside Miss Bennet's window and watch for a magnificent home. We shall see it soon."

Elizabeth kept her head turned toward the window. She dared not look at Emily for fear of what the young girl might read on her face.

They continued on for some time, expectation rising within each young lady in the carriage to catch the first glimpse of Pemberley. Elizabeth expected to see the home at every bend in the road, at the crest of every hill, but it was kept from their view. What she did see was delightfully beckoning mounds and valleys, a myriad of flora and fauna, and the ever present stream urging them along.

The carriage began to slow, and Elizabeth and Rosalyn looked at each other curiously. When Elizabeth turned back to the window, she gasped, for there in all its splendour was Pemberley. Situated majestically across a small crystal blue lake, it rose in stature and breadth in glorious prominence.

Emily squealed with excitement, and Rosalyn silently brought both hands up and covered her rapidly beating heart. A knock at the carriage door startled them all out of their reverie.

"Come, girls," Mr. Willstone called. "Step out and take a look at the grand Pemberley before we make our way down the road to it."

He helped each one out, and they joined Mrs. Willstone, who was already taking in its beauty.

"Look, Rosalyn," she said, as her sister drew to her side. "I am as much in awe of it today as I was when I was younger."

"It is beautiful."

They watched as the setting sun cast an ethereal golden hue across the stone edifice. The deepening oranges and reds of the clouds painted a rainbow palette of colours as it reflected down on the lake at the front. A slight breeze stirred small white caps on the lake, distorting the mirrored image of Pemberley that extended down into the depths of the water.

Emily ran over to join her mother, who took her hand. Mrs. Willstone then leaned over and looked at Elizabeth. "What do you think of it, my dear? Is it not grand?"

Having seen nothing as magnificent in all her life, she nodded her head slowly. "Yes, Mrs. Willstone. It is beyond anything I have ever seen."

Mrs. Willstone smiled and let out a contented sigh. "What an honour for us and our Rosalyn. Such an opportunity as this does not often come along."

"Now, now," cautioned Mr. Willstone. "It is not as if he has made our Rosalyn an offer or even stated his intentions toward her. We have to remember that Mr. and Miss Darcy merely extended an invitation to all of us to spend two weeks here. I believe there will be a few other guests and it may be nothing more than that." A sly grin on his face revealed that he was teasing his sister-in-law.

"Oh, Richard, how you love to provoke me!" laughed Rosalyn. "You, yourself, told me you thought his invitation was on my behalf."

"True, but I am only being cautious. We would not want to have our hopes dashed, now, would we?"

As they talked amongst themselves, Elizabeth continued to watch as the waning sunlight deepened the hue of the stone and marble that graced the front. The grass and flowers surrounding the home intensified in colour. Oblivious to the conversation around her, the only thought that played through her mind was that this could have been her home. Of this, she could have been mistress.

"Well, let us hurry and proceed to the house before darkness settles upon us!"

Mr. Willstone's cheery voice alerted Elizabeth to the fact that they were all returning to their carriages. She took one last glance at Pemberley before turning to follow. From here she could view it and appreciate it for all its beauty. She could admire it and esteem it for all that it was. Once she stepped inside its doors, her open admiration... and any burgeoning longing for what might have been hers... could never be openly shown.

Once inside the carriage, Elizabeth shivered, and pulled her shawl tightly about her. She then noticed Emily looking at her with a very discerning eye. Elizabeth attempted to smile, for she did not wish for her to think that she was not pleased with coming here.

Leaning down to her she said, "We shall be there shortly, Emily. Is this not exciting?"

Emily slowly nodded, and then Rosalyn let out a squeal. "Look, we are now coming upon it! Come, Emily, look out my side. We are finally at Pemberley!"

All three ladies strained to look out and they watched as the carriage approached the sizeable manor. As it grew in stature as they drew near, Elizabeth felt as though her heart would burst. The magnificence of the home was one thing, but to know that in only a matter of moments, she would be face to face with Mr. Darcy and his sister was almost too much to bear. Neither could possibly want her there.

Rosalyn suddenly reached out for Elizabeth's hand and turned to her. "Oh, Elizabeth, how am I to endure these two weeks? You must help me! If you see me do anything that appears to displease Mr. Darcy, you must enlighten me. I will leave it to you to be my secret informer, for I fear this might be a trial of sorts, to see if I meet his exceedingly high standards."

"Exceedingly high standards?" Elizabeth asked curiously.

"Oh, yes. A man of his standing certainly has expectations to marry only an exceptional woman. I may not have the highest connections, but I certainly have the qualifications to be Mistress of a place such as this." She let out a long, drawn-out sigh as she strained to look ahead. "We are almost there. I can see the other two carriages have stopped and the servants are helping Lorraine and Richard out."

Turning back to Elizabeth, she said softly, "I know your association with him was not particularly intimate, but if there is anything you can recall that either pleased or displeased him, I would be eternally grateful for any advice."

Even if Elizabeth had any advice for the young lady, Rosalyn did not wait to hear, for she turned back to the window and began to comment on how close they were – how soon it would be – before they pulled up and stopped.

Elizabeth distracted herself by helping Emily get ready. She smoothed the young girl's hair and retied the bow at the neckline of her dress. The two were startled when Rosalyn let out a muffled shriek.

"He is coming outside!" Pulling herself upright as the carriage slowed down, she turned her head slightly to the window. "He is greeting Lorraine and Richard. How kind of him. Miss Darcy has now come out and joined them!"

A slight gasp followed and Rosalyn turned to them. With hushed excitement she exclaimed, "He is coming over! He is going to open the door for us himself!" Clasping her hands together, she whispered, "This is such an honour!"

At the sound of the handle being turned, Rosalyn turned back. A graceful calm swept over her as she smiled warmly at the gentleman opening the door. Elizabeth watched, her heart pulsating wildly, but could only see his hand reaching in. She then heard his voice, "Miss Matthews, welcome to Pemberley."

His voice was much warmer than she remembered, and the sound of it caused an unwitting shiver to course through her. Her heart pounded as she knew the moment had arrived when she would be forced to face him.

"Thank you, Mr. Darcy," Rosalyn said warmly, as she took his hand and stepped out with the cool elegance of someone completely at ease.

Elizabeth gave Emily a gentle nudge toward the door as his hand reached in once more. Emily took it and happily jumped down. Elizabeth looked down to gather her things and then slowly slid across the seat to the door. She expected Mr. Darcy to escort her two travelling companions to the others and allow a servant to help her step out of the carriage.

Elizabeth clasped her small parcel tightly, looking around her for anything that may have been left. Once assured that she had everything, she took in a slow breath and closed her eyes to still her erratically beating heart. Upon opening her eyes, she became aware of a figure at the door. She slowly turned her head, at precisely the moment Mr. Darcy lowered his head to peer in.

As their eyes met, he drew back slightly. He pursed his lips and briefly looked down, taking a quick breath and letting it out.

When he looked up again, he asked, "May I?" and reached out his hand.

"Thank you," she said, her voice soft and quivering slightly. Her mind was in such upheaval that she had to remind herself to move. She tentatively extended her hand toward him and he reached out to take it. His hand was warm to the touch and Elizabeth was not prepared for the jolt of feeling that surged through her as his fingers clasped around hers. A tremor passed through her that travelled through her fingers all the way to her toes.

Her eyes turned down as she hoped he was not able to readily discern in her expression the feelings he evoked in her.

Confusion swept over her. He seemed different. His eyes seemed softer than she had remembered; his voice more gentle. Yet there was something of surprise in his response when he first looked in and saw her, and Elizabeth wondered whether he had truly not expected her to come.

Once Elizabeth stepped out, she waited for Darcy to release her hand. She stood for a moment facing him, feeling all the awkwardness that their meeting again prompted, while at the same time experiencing a plethora of thoughts and emotions that were foreign to her.

He seemed to catch himself and released her hand abruptly, silently extending his arm toward the others. She walked ahead of him, grateful that he was behind her, but fully aware of his presence there. She inwardly chided herself for those unexpected and startling feelings that arose when she first beheld his face peering into the carriage. She would have to maintain a bit more presence of mind in his company. She must remember her place, and most of all, who she now was.

Darcy's long strides drew him up alongside of her and she was flooded again with all the awkwardness of their last meeting. It was not due solely to the fact that she had refused his offer of marriage, but in the realization that she had been wrong about so many things concerning his character. She had made flagrant accusations against him that had been based on incorrect assumptions. When she saw him that last day at Rosings, encountering him out in the grove, he had been solemn, abrupt, and spoke only what was necessary as he handed her the letter.

She walked in his shadow, yet there was something more that alerted her to his presence beside her. There was something that she could not define – could not describe – that caused flutters deep within. That was what disconcerted her. She once had been able to look upon him with disdain, but now her feelings were tangled with a most problematic sense of regard toward him. She wished to let out a huff and stomp her foot and pound her fists in the air to rid herself of them. This was most inconvenient and definitely ill-timed, and she would be forced to conceal these feelings from everyone!

They came upon the rest of the party who stood in a circle conversing. Rosalyn had secured Miss Darcy's attention, for which Elizabeth was grateful. Miss Darcy and Rosalyn were talking about their travels, Rosalyn conversing in a most animated, unnatural manner. Fortunately, the energetic conversations around her caused those earlier feelings she experienced to diminish.

Miss Darcy looked over at Elizabeth. With a polite smile, she said, "It is good to see you again, Miss Bennet. Welcome to Pemberley."

"Thank you, Miss Darcy. It is a pleasure."

Elizabeth's heart calmed adequately, having both initial meetings over, but at present she was at a loss to know what to do, where to fix her gaze. Mr. Darcy was situated behind her again, and she did not feel the freedom to look out over the park or up to the house, for fear he would suspect admiration on her part.

She could not deny that the woods and park were beautiful and the house magnificent, but she reasoned that if she gazed with admiration upon any of them, he might believe her to feel something like regret for turning this all down. She contemplated looking down at her feet, but felt that would only make the likelihood of those feelings even greater. No, the only place she felt she could look without any speculation on his part was up at the sky, for certainly Mr. Darcy could not rightfully claim any of it as his own.

Chapter 8

After receiving profuse words of admiration for the park along with gratitude to the Darcys for extending the invitation to Pemberley from the Willstones, the party was invited inside. With each step Elizabeth took up the marble steps toward the great door of the house, she felt an increasing sense of eagerness to see the interior. She had certainly been captivated by the woods and grounds that surrounded Pemberley. The exterior of the home itself was truly magnificent. She was now fervent to view the home itself.

Putting away all thought of who the owner was – and to whom it had once been offered – she stepped inside with the others.

Elizabeth stifled the gasp, but could not conceal her look of admiration as they stepped into the entryway. It was truly majestic, in a way that gave honour to those who built it centuries before, as well as its heritage through the years. She could not deny that it was everything agreeable to her sensibilities.

It took barely a moment for her mind to be settled on the subject. She could not – she would not – keep her views of the place to herself. It was far too beautiful for her to remain silent. Straightening her shoulders and taking a deep breath, she joined the others in their warm approbation.

"You have a beautiful home, Miss Darcy," she said softly. Turning her head slightly, she met Mr. Darcy's eyes and acknowledged him, as well, with a demure nod. "Mr. Darcy."

He returned her compliment with a nod of his own, his eyes never leaving her face. Feeling an uncharacteristic blush threatening to spread across her features, she quickly turned back to face Miss Darcy. Unfortunately, Rosalyn had now garnered the young lady's attention and was uttering unending words of admiration. Again Elizabeth did not know where to look, upon what to settle her eyes. It was all too grand in its aspect… too humbling in the realization that it could all have been hers.

"Thank you, Miss Bennet," Miss Darcy replied after a moment, acknowledging her words of appreciation in the midst of Rosalyn's effusive praise. "That is very kind of you." Elizabeth smiled, but readily noticed the look of discomfiture written across her features. Certainly her presence there reminded Miss Darcy of Mr. Bingley and her recent loss.

The servants lined up with the luggage, and Mr. Darcy issued instructions regarding the rooms in which each member of the party was to reside. Turning back to the party, he clasped his hands together. "The servants will take each of you to your rooms where you may freshen up. We shall dine in two hours, so please take whatever time you need. Feel free to rest, or you may tour the house if you are so inclined. See Mrs. Reynolds if that is your wish. Presently my other guests – a long-time family friend and his family and my cousin – are relaxing after a rather full day. You shall meet them at supper. I am quite certain you shall enjoy their company."

"The Colonel is here?" Elizabeth asked as she turned to him, a smile highlighting her features.

"No," Mr. Darcy answered softly. "It is not the Colonel."

"Oh," she replied, her smile disappearing as she unwittingly bit her lower lip. She would have enjoyed the Colonel's diverting company. Her eyes narrowed at the sudden thought that it might be Anne to whom he referred. If it was Anne, Rosalyn might hear of their "expected" marriage. She would be devastated. An unwitting look of concern swept across her features.

Darcy's jaw clenched as he studied Elizabeth's demeanour. "It is another cousin, Peter Hamilton, the son of my father's sister."

"I see," Elizabeth replied.

"Well, unless you have any questions, I shall allow you to proceed to your rooms. The servants will show each of you the way," Darcy said, giving a quick sharp bow. "I shall see you at supper." With that, he turned to walk away.

As they followed the servants up the stairs, Elizabeth felt her elbow being grasped somewhat violently. She turned to see that Rosalyn was the culprit.

"You are acquainted with one of his cousins?" Rosalyn asked in a hushed voice. "Why did you not tell me?"

Elizabeth looked at her with more than a little amazement, but answered quickly. "I did not know you were interested in Mr. Darcy's cousin, as well." She gave her a teasing smile.

"Of course not!" she said in a fervent whisper, squeezing her arm to bring her to a stop. "I have never met the man. Oh, Elizabeth, I do not mean to beleaguer you…" She let out a breathy huff. "I must confess, though, that there have been occasions when I have felt somewhat jealous of you and your earlier acquaintance with Mr. Darcy."

"It was nothing, Rosalyn." Elizabeth looked back to the stairs ahead of her as she began again to climb. She felt a tightening in her stomach as she repeated, "It was nothing."

Upon reaching the top of the stairs everyone was led down a hall and shown to their rooms. Their rooms were all situated closely; Elizabeth being in a room adjacent to Rosalyn, and Emily and her parents in separate rooms across the hall from them.

She followed the servant who carried her luggage into her chambers. Absent from Mr. Darcy she felt the freedom to sweep her eyes throughout the room, a smile revealing the admiration she felt in what she saw. She was in a corner room of the house, with large windows hugging each other where the walls met.

It was decorated with a slight feminine touch. Tiny flowers dotted the sheer window coverings and the thick coverlet on the bed. A sampler was hung prominently on one wall and a painting on another. A vase of fresh flowers displayed its array of colours atop a chest of drawers.

Stepping further inside, she could almost imagine it being one of the finest rooms in the house; it was certainly finer than anything she had ever seen. When she took into consideration all she had seen of the house, however, she knew that there were most likely rooms of much greater consequence, particularly those of Mr. Darcy and his sister. This room was in all probability typical of what the others would be like.

The servant, having laid down her bags, bowed and stepped from the room. A maid then entered and walked over to a closet, opening the doors. When she disappeared within, Elizabeth could not stop herself from walking over and peeking inside. She almost bumped into the maid walking out.

"Is there any particular way you want me to unpack and put away your belongings, Miss?" the maid asked.

"No," answered Elizabeth, still gazing inside the closet. Her mind went back to Rosings and how Mr. Collins commented on the astonishing shelves in the little closet. This closet had not only shelves, but beautifully stained wood drawers and was about as big inside as her room was back home.

Her stomach tightened as she considered home. What was her home now? It certainly was no longer Longbourn. She could not consider the Willstones' home as hers. Her hand went up to her heart as the thought that this could have been hers pushed itself forward again.

"Is there anything not to your liking, Miss Bennet?" the maid asked as she looked over at her.

"No… no, it is more than suitable. I could not ask for anything more. Thank you."

The maid smiled. "Have you seen the prospect outside your windows? Those two windows have the nicest views."

Walking over to the two corner windows, she pulled back one of the sheer window coverings and looked down at the lake in front. Even in the muted light of day, with the sun set beyond the horizon, it glistened. She could see the darkness of the dense trees in the woods beyond from which they came. She felt a flutter of excitement in the anticipation of walking through those woods.

She then peered out the other window. She looked out at what appeared to be a flower garden. "It is too dark to see, but am I looking down on a garden?" she asked the maid.

"It certainly is… and it is blossoming with summer flowers of every hue. It has several natural paths that wind their way throughout. Tomorrow you will be able to see just how beautiful it is!"

Beyond the garden, coming from the area behind the home, she noticed the silhouette of a ridge. It did not seem terribly high and she thought momentarily about how she might like to climb to the top.

As Elizabeth turned away, she caught a glimpse of herself in the mirror. She was grateful that she was no longer in mourning and had begun to wear colours again. For some reason that she could not articulate, the mere thought of walking through Pemberley and being in Mr. Darcy's presence while dressed in drab blacks and greys was not something she wished to do, despite still missing her father exceedingly.

Elizabeth excused herself from the maid and walked across the wide hall to check on Emily. She peeked in and saw Emily pulling out a doll and her toys from a small bag. "Do you like your room, Emily?" she asked, walking in.

"Oh, yes," Emily answered. "But I am glad to be in a room so close to Mama and Papa and you and Aunt Rosalyn. I think it is a very big house."

Elizabeth laughed. "Yes it is," she said as she walked over to the window and peered out. Emily's room looked out over the back courtyard, and she could easily see both wings at either side that extended back. She could not even imagine how many rooms Pemberley had with its three stories and considerable length. She noticed once again the ridge and wondered what the view was from the top. She smiled as she considered that there would be much to explore here!

~~*

Elizabeth thought it was prudent that she take a tour of the house so she would become familiar with its layout and learn what areas there might be that were not open to her and Emily. But more than that, she was simply curious to see it. Rosalyn was more than happy to accompany her. Emily remained back in her room to rest.

They encountered Mrs. Reynolds in the hallway, on her way to see if anyone wished to do that very thing. The Willstones declined, also wanting to rest, leaving only Rosalyn and Elizabeth to participate in Mrs. Reynolds' tour. She began by giving them a brief history of the home, telling how it had been in the Darcy family for over 200 years and had regularly provided a source of steady income for the villages nearby. She seemed more than pleased to tell them how the Darcys have always been greatly esteemed by the tenants and local villagers.

She brought her hands together with a clap. "Well, enough of that. You wanted to see the house, so see the house we shall!"

As they walked down the hall, the housekeeper explained that most of the rooms in that wing of the house were guest apartments. "But here," she said, as she came to a stop, "is Miss Darcy's favourite sitting room. Come in, please." They stepped into a spacious room that occupied the opposite corner of the house from Elizabeth's room. Instead of a window on each wall at the corner, there were two sets. From Elizabeth's perception, it was two or almost three times as large as her room.

There were several plush chairs and sofas placed around the room. A writing desk and a number of tables occupied the space.

"We have another sitting room downstairs, as well," began Mrs. Reynolds, "but Miss Darcy is especially partial to this room. Most likely it is due to the large windows and the beautiful prospect overlooking the south and east." As they glanced about, she continued. "Miss Darcy spends much time here and often took her studies in here."

"I can see why she enjoys this room so much," effused Rosalyn. "It must be the finest room in the house."

"It suits Miss Darcy, but it has had very little done to it over the years. I do believe her brother is planning to make some improvements on it for her… he dotes on her endlessly. But oh, it is to be a surprise, so please do not mention it to her."

"We would not spoil Mr. Darcy's surprise for anything!" exclaimed Rosalyn. "He is certainly a wonderful brother!"

"Most attentive to his sister, yes. And to all his servants and tenants, as well. I have never heard one complaint uttered against him."

Rosalyn caught Elizabeth's eye, and with a slight nod of her head and a smile gave Elizabeth all the assurance she needed that Rosalyn had determined there was no man finer.

It is going to be a very long two weeks, Elizabeth thought to herself.

As they walked out, Rosalyn asked, "Is this room used solely by Miss Darcy? Does she consider it her private sitting room?"

"Oh, no. It is frequently used by our guests. Feel free to come in at your leisure. If Miss Darcy requires time alone, which she often does, she has a private room off her chambers that gives her all the privacy she needs. They are located just down the hall in the opposite direction from your rooms."

Mrs. Reynolds extended her hand down the hallway. "In addition to Miss Darcy's chambers, Mr. Darcy's chambers are also located down this hall, as well as a beautiful suite that will one day belong to the Mistress of Pemberley, when he takes a wife. I have never seen a grander suite, but unfortunately, that wing is private."

Mrs. Reynolds walked ahead. "Follow me, please."

Elizabeth was not surprised when Rosalyn leaned in to whisper, "How I would love to see that suite!"

Elizabeth looked to her with a resigned smile. "Perhaps some day you shall." Those words could not have made Rosalyn happier. Unfortunately for Elizabeth, they seemed to leave her mouth with a bad taste.

From there they went down the stairs. "You will see several of these rooms tonight, so I shall only point them out." Turning at the bottom of the stairs, she showed them where the dining room and the parlour room were.

She then came to a stop in front of an open door.

"This is Pemberley's greatest distinction. The library at Pemberley is one of the largest and most complete in the whole of Derbyshire. It is the Master's determination and love of reading that keeps it growing and up to date. Shall we?" she asked as she allowed the two ladies to enter.

Elizabeth stepped in. Her gaze travelled down the length of the library in one direction and then the other. It was unlike anything she had ever seen.

"I could lock myself up in here for a month and never come out!" she exclaimed as she spun back around. "It is beaut…" she stopped when she saw Mr. Darcy step out from a row of books.

"Hello, Mrs. Reynolds. Ladies." He held a leather-bound book loosely in one hand, tapping it lightly with the fingers on his other hand. He looked to Elizabeth with a small smile tugging at one corner of his mouth. "I fear, Miss Bennet, you would grow quite hungry locked in here for a month. Unless, that is, you made arrangements with the staff to slip your food under the door. I cannot say I have ever heard of anyone surviving solely on a diet of books."

Rosalyn's laugh seemed to Elizabeth to be just a little artificial as she said, "You are so right, Mr. Darcy, but as Miss Bennet would most likely choose reading over any activity, including eating, she might determine to prove you wrong."

"Well, then, it is settled. Arrange for Miss Bennet's belongings to be brought down here, Mrs. Reynolds, as well as her meals."

Elizabeth arched an eyebrow. She was more grateful than she was surprised by Mr. Darcy's light teasing. It at least removed the mortification she felt knowing he overheard her comment. "I thank you, sir, but my chambers are more than sufficient."

"You are pleased with Pemberley, then?"

She understood his question all too well. Nodding her head, she answered, "I am very well pleased."

As if suddenly having an afterthought, he looked to Rosalyn. "And you, Miss Matthews, are your accommodations to your liking?"

A smile flashed across her face. "Oh! They are superb! Everything is positively splendid! I could not have asked for anything more!"

Darcy nodded his head. "I am glad to hear that. Now, if you will excuse me… unless, Miss Bennet you are quite certain you do not wish to move in here. I can certainly make the arrangements."

Elizabeth laughed. "As great a temptation as that might be, I must decline, for my duties as governess would prohibit that."

His eyes narrowed for a brief moment, and then he replied, "Yes. Your duties."

He gave a polite bow and then stepped out of the library as the ladies stepped further in. "Feel free to take some time to look around," Mrs. Reynolds told them. "This is quite a collection. You are more than welcome to borrow any of the books to read while you are here. Just leave them on the desk when you are finished so they can be returned to their proper place."

Elizabeth stepped one direction and Rosalyn the other. As Elizabeth walked deeper into the library, the smell of leather and the dark, rich wood of the shelves made her think of her father. Her eyes glistened with tears as she thought just how much he would have loved spending time in here. It was her father who had passed the love of reading on to her. She walked to the far end, passed a row of shelves, and ran her fingers along the spine of the books, reading the array of authors and titles.

As she perused the books, her mind raced between thoughts of her father and also how Mr. Darcy had eased her discomfort just now. She had a sudden recollection of the look that had crossed his face when he questioned her about moving her belongings into here as being the same look as when they had been at Netherfield. It was in the drawing room as she and Miss Bingley took a turn about the room.

Her eyes widened at the thought that he had been teasing – or had he in truth been *flirting* – when he told them he could observe their figures better from where he sat. Her fingers continued to brush against the books as her mind raced in a turmoil. She had never before considered that his words had been directed toward her in *that* manner.

As she continued to turn all these thoughts over in her mind, her hand absently went from the books to a door at the far end. She reached down to the handle, and at only a light touch, the door opened. To her dismay, she found herself looking into a study.

Darcy was sitting at his desk, leaning back in his chair with his hands cradling the back of his head; his feet were stretched out and resting on top of the desk. At the sound of the door opening, he scrambled to right himself, pulling his feet down, standing up, and turning around.

Elizabeth froze and could not step back and close the door soon enough. "I am so…so… sorry," Elizabeth stuttered. "I did not know…"

Darcy reached for his coat, which he had taken off and had tossed onto the corner of his desk. He struggled to put his arm into its sleeve as he said, "No… no, it was my fault. I thought I had locked it."

Elizabeth was finally able to take some steps backward, her face flushed with embarrassment. She did not even attempt to close the door, but quickly turned to remove herself as swiftly as possible. *What was I thinking?* she asked herself. What must *he* be thinking?

"Come, Elizabeth. We are moving on!" Rosalyn's voice broke into her assaulting accusations against herself.

"Coming," Elizabeth answered in a rather shaky voice, more than grateful to leave. As she quickly walked out of the library, she refrained from stomping her foot in frustration. *He must think I am so impertinent… so imprudent… so …* "Ohhh!" she let out in a huff.

"Here we are, Miss Bennet. Is anything amiss?"

Elizabeth smiled. "No, nothing at all."

Mrs. Reynolds and Rosalyn were standing next to a closed door. "This is Mr. Darcy's study," she told them. As he is now in here, we would not think of disturbing him. This is one place where he can come when he wishes to be alone. It is the one place where guests cannot go unless invited. Now, follow me."

Elizabeth's insides tightened as they walked past and she felt that even to take a breath was a monumental chore. Yes, this was going to be a long two weeks, indeed!

Chapter 9

As they continued down the hall, they came to a pair of closed double doors. Mrs. Reynolds turned to the two ladies before opening them. "This is Pemberley's ballroom. Throughout the years, many guests have been in awe of its splendour and grandeur when they step in. Unfortunately it has been a very long time since a ball was held here."

She turned to open the doors, and as they swung open Elizabeth and Rosalyn followed Mrs. Reynolds in. They both gasped as they gazed around the room. It was unlike anything Elizabeth had ever seen; certainly nothing in her neighbourhood in Hertfordshire even came close to being its equal. Stepping in, Elizabeth could almost hear the music, see the women in their fashionable gowns dancing under the candlelit chandeliers, and feel the delight of the guests.

Rosalyn walked aimlessly about the room, her eyes bright, her jaw dropped. She took a step out toward the centre of the room and spun around with arms stretched out wide, as if taking a step in a dance and being twirled by her partner. "If only we could have a ball while we are here," she whispered to Elizabeth, tucking her hand through her arm. "It would be quite heavenly."

With great reluctance they left the ballroom. Mrs. Reynolds then pointed out the downstairs sitting room, and indicated to Elizabeth where the children's playroom and nursery were located. Elizabeth's heart and mind were seized with the realization that those rooms were now her world much more so than a ballroom. She doubted, in her current position, that she would ever attend a ball in such a place as this.

They came to another set of stairs with two hallways going in separate directions from it. She described one wing as being the servants' quarters, and the other wing as being additional apartments that were rarely used. She advised them that the sickroom was the first room down the servant's hallway.

"We shall take these stairs back up. They will take us through the Portrait Hall, past the Music Room, and then to the hallway that goes back to your rooms. Very nicely planned, Pemberley is."

They ascended the grand staircase, and Mrs. Reynolds described in detail how the exquisite woodwork and tile had come from different places around England and Europe, and the paintings that lined the walls were acquired by the late Mr. Darcy on his journeys.

Elizabeth was surprised she was able to attend to Mrs. Reynolds' words, as her mind still raced with the mortification she felt in walking into Mr. Darcy's study unexpectedly... unannounced. She unwittingly let out a sigh of frustration.

Upon hearing her, Rosalyn leaned in close and whispered, "It is all breathtaking, is it not?"

Elizabeth merely nodded an accord, being content to allow Rosalyn to believe it was her admiration of the place that prompted her sigh. As she looked around her, however, she had to agree with Rosalyn's estimation of Pemberley.

Breathtaking.

Upon reaching the top of the stairs, they found themselves in the Portrait Hall. Mrs. Reynolds began by explaining that the portraits at this end of the hall were the oldest, and at the far end hung the more recent paintings. She pointed out names and ancestral connection to the present Mr. and Miss Darcy as they walked between the myriad of faces looking down at them.

As Elizabeth glanced up at each face, she found herself searching for any similarity between the person in the painting and that person she just so rudely walked in on. She did, on occasion, see a crook of the mouth, the shape of the nose, or the deep set brown eyes that belonged to Mr. Darcy. She wondered if Rosalyn was doing the same. A furtive glance at her friend revealed an interest solely in a portrait at the far end of the hall. Mr. Darcy's.

As they drew closer to that portrait, Elizabeth felt Rosalyn's hand grip her arm. As if prodding her because she was not walking briskly enough, they soon found themselves looking up at the larger than life portrait. Mr. Darcy was standing outside. A large tree trunk framed him on one side, and the leafy branches arched over him. He stood atop a hill, and it looked like the peaks of Derbyshire were spread out behind him in the distance. He looked particularly content in his surroundings. Dressed immaculately, he had an air of distinction about him.

"It is a wonderful likeness of him!" gushed Rosalyn. "He is such a distinguished man!"

"Oh, indeed, he is," agreed Mrs. Reynolds. "Quite fastidious about being proper in all things."

A small smile began to form on Elizabeth's face as she reflected upon her recent encounter with him. While she was deeply embarrassed by her injudicious manners, she realized he must have been just as mortified being caught in such an undignified posture. His look of surprise was not merely due to her walking in on him, but by being seen in such a fashion, leaning casually back in his chair, with his feet propped up on the desk, his coat tossed casually over the corner of it.

She could not prevent a giggle from escaping as she contemplated this, all the while Rosalyn and Mrs. Reynolds affirmed each other in their noble opinion of the man. The both stopped and looked questioningly at her.

"Elizabeth?" Rosalyn asked, her eyes displaying her displeasure. "What do you find so humorous?"

Pressing her fingers up to her mouth to conceal any further laughter, she shook her head as tears of repressed laughter filled her eyes. That she could feel so mortified one moment and laugh about it the next, she could not comprehend. She certainly did not know how to answer Rosalyn.

"I am sorry," she said, as she again thought of the disparity between the man in the study and the fastidious man he wished for all to see. "My mind was on other things. Pray, forgive me, for I was not being particularly attentive." She suddenly wondered who the real man was.

Rosalyn smiled a reluctant acceptance and turned back to Mrs. Reynolds, who seemed eager to talk about the final portrait.

"This is Miss Darcy, painted just a year ago. Her brother arranged for the sitting and we are all pleased with the results. Do you not think it a remarkable likeness?"

"Yes," both ladies answered.

"She is certainly handsome," added Rosalyn. "A very fine young lady, indeed."

"And her brother has had such a hand in that. He is so good to her and has always been there for her. It was very difficult when their father passed, but Mr. Darcy stepped into the role of guardian admirably."

"Such uncommon devotion," sighed Rosalyn.

"Yes, one would be hard pressed to find a brother who has taken care of his sister as well as he has Miss Darcy." Mrs. Reynolds clasped her hands together. "Up ahead is the Music Room. Follow me, please."

Before continuing on, the two ladies both looked up again at the portrait of the Master of Pemberley. Each had a whirlwind of thoughts concerning the man whose likeness they scrutinized one last time.

Elizabeth thought there was something different about him in this portrait, but she could not readily define it. It was the manner of his posture, the expression on his face, which entirely conflicted with what she knew of him – with what she thought she knew of him.

Turning together, the two young ladies caught up with Mrs. Reynolds, who had entered a room at one end of the hall.

They both gasped when they stepped inside. A beautiful pianoforte had prominence in the centre of the room. Surrounding it were chairs and sofas. A harp was in the corner.

Mrs. Reynolds turned to face them. "This pianoforte was given to Miss Darcy last year on her sixteenth birthday from her brother. She practices several times a day, so you most likely will hear the young lady play while you are here. I am quite certain you will appreciate how proficient she is."

"Will she perform for us?" Rosalyn asked.

"She may, although she is somewhat shy about performing before others. You will be especially honoured if she does."

"And the harp?" asked Elizabeth.

"The harp was the late Mrs. Darcy's instrument. She played beautifully. Now it is only played by guests with that talent. Mr. Darcy loves to listen to the harp. Do either of you play?"

Both ladies shook their head. Rosalyn looked most disappointed, and Elizabeth believed her to be chiding herself for never learning the instrument.

Mrs. Reynolds clasped her hands together. "This is the wing where your chambers are located. It appears we have less than an hour before the meal. That should give you enough time to freshen up."

She then excused herself, leaving the two ladies to return to their chambers. Elizabeth stopped to check on Emily, and upon finding her asleep, she quietly closed the door and returned to her chambers. She was grateful for some time to be alone before she returned to Emily's room to ready her. It allowed her to ponder all that had happened, all that she had seen, and all that might happen in these next two weeks. She assumed Rosalyn could only be contemplating the same.

~~*

Just before the supper hour, Elizabeth awakened and dressed Emily for the meal. As she readied her, Elizabeth talked with her about the importance of displaying good manners. Despite her own awkward display of ill-manners earlier, she could only hope that Emily would be a model of all that Elizabeth had taught her.

"Remember, Emily, that you do not interrupt conversation. Only speak to the adults if you are spoken to. If no one talks during the course of the meal, you must remain silent yourself. We are guests, after all, and must observe Mr. and Miss Darcy and follow their example."

"I will remember," Emily said in a melancholy voice. "But what if no one talks? I must remain silent the whole time?"

Elizabeth recalled the meals she took when Mr. Darcy was present. He was not an avid talker. From what she had seen of his sister, she was even less. "If no one is talking, we must assume they prefer to eat in silence and we will abide by their wishes."

Emily pursed her lips in a brief pout, but it was soon forgotten.

As the dinner hour approached, they joined the others in the hallway before walking down to the dining room. Taking their place behind the others, Elizabeth paused briefly as she wondered whether she and Emily would even dine with them. She told herself not to be disappointed if they did not.

As they drew near the dining room, they could hear voices and laughter. Mrs. Willstone turned to Rosalyn with a wide smile and said, "This sounds like a lively group!" She reached over and tucked in a wayward lock of her sister's hair. "Remember to be gracious and friendly to Mr. Darcy's guests. It will be to your benefit to gain their good opinion."

"You know I will. You are beginning to sound more like Mama every day!"

"Since she is not here, I rightly assume that responsibility." Both ladies softly laughed.

The party walked in and as they were noticed, faces turned to them with welcoming smiles. Mr. Darcy promptly joined them and after a short bow, he greeted them.

"Good evening. I trust that all of you have had a restful afternoon after your travels and that you have found your rooms equally comfortable and accommodating." He gave a quick glance in Elizabeth's direction and with a slightly raised brow said, "I hope you have not encountered anything too indecorous."

"Of course not!" exclaimed Rosalyn exuberantly as Elizabeth's cheeks took on a deepened hue and her heart pounded erratically.

Quickly turning to his other guests, Mr. Darcy made the introductions. "May I introduce Mr. and Mrs. Richard Willstone, their daughter Miss Emily Willstone, and Mrs. Willstone's sister, Miss Rosalyn Matthews." After pausing slightly, he looked hesitantly over to Elizabeth, an inexplicable glint in his eyes. "And this is Miss Elizabeth Bennet, Miss Emily Willstone's governess." As all eyes had now turned to her, she hoped the blush upon her cheeks had paled.

He followed with introductions of his other guests. "These are my good friends, Mr. and Mrs. Benjamin Goldsmith, their children Misses Gladys and Harriet Goldsmith, and their governess Miss Ellen Bartley."

Looking over at a gentleman who stood off by himself, he continued, "This is my cousin, Mr. Peter Hamilton. He is the son of my late father's sister." He looked over to Georgiana and nodded, encouraging her to continue.

Stepping forward at her brother's prompting, she softly said, "Shall we all be seated? I believe supper is ready to be served." The young girl gestured toward the table, and everyone walked in.

Since there was no indication where anyone was to sit, Elizabeth watched Miss Bartley to see where she and her two wards seated themselves. Both of the girls looked to be a little older than Emily. She was pleased that Emily would have some companions with whom to play while here. Miss Bartley appeared to be close to the age of her mother and Elizabeth was suddenly gripped with the dreadful thought that perhaps she, too, might remain an unmarried governess for the duration of her life.

When Miss Bartley and the girls took seats at the far end of the table, Elizabeth and Emily joined them.

Miss Darcy took her place at the centre of the table, leaving two seats between her and her brother, who sat down at the head of the table.

Elizabeth could see the struggle Rosalyn faced deciding where to sit, and finally, she took the chair next to Miss Darcy. Elizabeth wondered how difficult a decision that must have been for her to show preference to the young girl over the one with whom she was so enamoured.

As the servants brought out the food, conversations began. Taking note of this, and being a little more forthcoming than the other two girls, Emily struck up conversations with them, doing most of the talking herself. Elizabeth had to hush her several times when she became a little too loud.

Elizabeth took the opportunity to get to know Miss Bartley. She seemed a pleasant lady and had been with the girls for four years. Gladys was eight and Harriet was seven. Prior to this employment, she had been governess of a family of seven children for a total of eighteen years.

As Elizabeth directed her gaze down the table, she could see that Rosalyn was doing everything in her power to engage Miss Darcy in conversation. The young girl politely answered, but it was quite evident by the look on her face, that she felt a bit of discomfiture. Elizabeth believed it to be due to Rosalyn's resolute attention. Elizabeth's eyes narrowed as it appeared that Rosalyn was completely unaware of the effect she was having on her. Certainly anyone could see that Miss Darcy was uncomfortable, yet she bore up admirably, being singled out in such a way.

Elizabeth's eyes drifted to Mr. Darcy, who was also watching this interaction. He was carrying on a conversation with the Willstones, but Elizabeth could see in his features, as he repeatedly glanced at his sister and Rosalyn, that he noticed her unease as well. Rosalyn turned to look at him several times and smiled, believing, Elizabeth supposed, that he was most appreciative of her efforts at befriending his sister.

As Elizabeth contemplated all this, she heard her name spoken.

"Miss Bennet?"

She looked over to see Mr. Darcy's cousin had repeated her name.

"I am sorry, Mr. Hamilton," she answered as she drew her napkin up and dabbed at the corners of her mouth.

"It is quite all right," he answered, leaning back casually. "I understand that you come originally from Hertfordshire."

"That is correct. I lived there until about eight months ago, at which time I took the position of Emily's governess."

"I have only been through there once. Were you fond of it?"

Elizabeth felt a rush of emotion threaten to spill over and took a sip of water to quell them. "I enjoyed my life there, yes. It suited me perfectly."

"Do you prefer country life to living in Town?" He leaned toward her as he asked softly. "You have spent these past eight months in London and I believe you will be spending the summer at the Willstones' country home. Which do you think you will prefer?"

Elizabeth smiled at his engaging manner. "If I had all the amenities of London at my disposal, I suppose I would enjoy it very much. As it is, I have looked forward to these summer months where I can amble about the countryside."

"Ah! You are an explorer, then!" He paused to take a bite. "You will find much to enjoy and explore here around Pemberley."

"I am sure I shall," Elizabeth returned softly.

"I never tire of coming here, although..." he paused and looked at Darcy. "...I fear *he* may grow tired of me showing up when least expected."

"Were you not expected on this visit?"

Hamilton shook his head. Speaking in a hushed tone, he continued, "I understood that he and Georgiana were returning to Pemberley for a quiet summer, and when I came in from the sea, I journeyed here, expecting to find only my two cousins."

"You are in the navy?" Elizabeth asked.

Hamilton nodded. "I have leave for a month and decided to spend some of it here. How was I to know that he had invited guests? The man rarely does that. Family yes, but this is quite unusual for him. It is good, but unusual."

Elizabeth turned her eyes toward Darcy. His attention was directed at the Goldsmiths, and he laughed at something Mrs. Goldsmith said. Elizabeth suddenly thought it odd that she had never really seen him laugh before. The smile reached his eyes and it seemed to display contentment. *That was it!* That was what the portrait of him suggested – a contentment that she had never before seen in him. A contentment he never experienced while visiting in their little country neighbourhood.

"I understand you and my cousin knew each other in Hertfordshire."

Elizabeth's eyes widened, wondering exactly what else he knew. "Uh, yes. We had a… brief acquaintance… through his friend, Mr. Bingley." Her hand determinedly reached out for the glass of water again, and she took another sip, grateful this time for the moisture that filled her suddenly dry mouth.

"Ahh, yes, Bingley." Mr. Hamilton sat upright in his chair. "I have not yet made his acquaintance, but I know he and my cousin are good friends."

Elizabeth forced a smile, wondering whether Mr. Bingley and Mr. Darcy were indeed *still* friends, after his actions regarding Miss Darcy. "What position do you hold in the navy, Mr. Hamilton?"

He leaned forward now, his arms crossed on the table in front of him. "I anticipate a promotion forthcoming. I was a second lieutenant on the frigate I just returned from, but hope soon to become a captain."

"Have you always wished to be in the navy?" Elizabeth asked.

Hamilton gave a sly glance at Mr. Darcy and then turned back to Elizabeth. "I do not have the means by which I can be as idle as my cousin. I have the unfortunate distinction of being the third son born to my parents and I was forced to make a decision early on whether to join the navy or go into the church."

With a teasing smile, Elizabeth asked, "So when did you discover you preferred climbing the scaffoldings to furl and unfurl the sails to guide the course of a ship over the preaching of sermons and making visits to guide the course of its villagers?"

Mr. Hamilton smiled. "One does sound more adventurous than the other, but I would be untruthful if I told you my early years on board a ship were anything but dreadful. It would be most ill-mannered of me to give you an accurate account of my experiences."

"But you are the better man for it, so they say!" Elizabeth laughed softly.

"Perhaps. Suffice it to say, food and accommodations, as well as the treatment we midshipmen received, often tempted me to forego that for the relatively easy life of a clergyman."

"Or the idle life of a gentleman," Elizabeth said as she looked up at Darcy,

74

who met her glance. An awkward blush coloured her cheeks when she saw his dark eyes flash back down to the meal in front of him. She surmised he knew they were talking about him.

"I think it best we finish our meal," Mr. Hamilton whispered, "as we are getting a rather scowling look from my cousin at that end of the table."

Elizabeth turned her attention back to her meal. She enjoyed her repartee with Mr. Hamilton and felt she had an ally in him. He had no reason to feel ill towards her, and she rather enjoyed his conversation. Mr. Darcy, however, would most likely not look kindly upon his cousin associating with a woman of such lowly position, who also happened to have the distinction of refusing his offer of marriage.

As everyone was enjoying the last course, an elegant fruit cobbler topped with cream, Miss Darcy addressed the party. Her voice was hushed and unsteady, and there were several times she looked to her brother for reassurance, but she seemed determined to make this announcement on her own.

"We would like to invite everyone to a picnic tomorrow afternoon at one o'clock. Since the men have made plans to fish in the morning, that ought to give them ample time to catch a sufficient amount."

"Or give up trying," laughed Hamilton.

The party joined him in laughter, and Georgiana nervously continued. "We decided to have the picnic tomorrow because the grounds have finally dried out after all the rains we have had, and since we know not when the next rains will come, we thought it best to do it as soon as possible."

Everyone seemed pleased with the idea of a picnic, and even more so when she mentioned there would be games to play, kites to fly, and an elaborate treasure hunt, designed by her brother.

After the meal was over, the men were invited by Mr. Darcy to join him in his study and Georgiana invited Mrs. Goldsmith, Mrs. Willstone, and Miss Matthews to join her in the parlour. Elizabeth and Miss Bartley were expected to take their wards to the children's playroom for the remainder of the evening.

As Elizabeth held Emily's hand as they walked, the two could not feel more differently. Emily took each step eagerly, looking forward to her new friends and the new playthings she would discover. Elizabeth, on the other hand, fought back feelings of regret. She could not help but consider that despite her upbringing, despite her years as the daughter of a gentleman, despite the offer of marriage she received from Mr. Darcy himself, she was now beneath him... beneath them all. It was something she would have to get used to. But she knew it would be extremely difficult here in this beautiful place called Pemberley.

Chapter 10

When Elizabeth awoke the next morning, a muted ray of sunlight penetrated the darkness of the room, announcing the dawn of a new day. As her eyes grew accustomed to the dimness, she looked about her, feeling anew a great sense of admiration for her room, this house, and its grounds. Much to her dismay, she was feeling an ever increasing appreciation for its Master, which wrought in her a real sense of disappointment now that she would be considered significantly beneath him.

While in the playroom the previous evening, in between conversing with Miss Bartley, reading a story to Emily, and listening to her read a story aloud, Elizabeth spent a good amount of time contemplating her first day at Pemberley. Truth be told, her contemplations dwelt mostly on Mr. Darcy and his conduct toward her. She had to admit he had treated her with kind civility, generous respect, and even playful teasing on occasion. She warmed at the thought.

Fisting both hands, she brought them down forcefully onto the coverlet. "What has come over me?" she whispered to herself. "I am no longer in a position to even consider this!"

She threw off the coverlet and sat up, swinging her legs over the side of the bed. Raising both arms, she stretched and took in a deep breath, letting it out in a yawn. Elizabeth walked over to the windows and pulled back the sheer window coverings, looking first toward the front and then at the hill behind the house.

Elizabeth smiled as she gazed out at the early morning dawn, strangely beckoning her to take that walk to the top of the hill. Propelled by this thought, she quickly changed into one of her day dresses, and readied herself to go outside.

She quietly opened her door and stepped out, stopping as she did to listen for others who might be awake. Hearing only the distant clanging of pans from the kitchen, and the subsequent aroma from the baking being done there, she quietly made her way downstairs.

Elizabeth inhaled deeply as the aroma, most likely breads being baked, wafted stronger as she proceeded down the stairs. She pondered whether to inform one of the servants that she would be going out, but reasoned that since it was still early, she would likely return before most of the others came out of their rooms. Breakfast, they had been told, would be served at eight o'clock.

As she stepped outside the door, she came to a halt. Her senses were pleasantly assaulted with a myriad of birds singing their songs to the rising sun. A light breeze played with the ribbons on her bonnet and a few loose strands of her hair. Looking out across the grounds, her eyes soaked in the glistening waters of the lake and the stream that fed it. Drawing her eyes upward, she marvelled at the blue sky that was dotted with just a few clouds, pink and orange in the morning sky. The dense green woods on the other side of the lake tempted her to come hither and explore.

But not this morning. They had travelled through the woods in their approach yesterday. The woody ridge behind the home might take a little exertion on her part, but she was determined to look for some path that might take her to the top.

Walking towards the back of the great house, she was delighted to find a footpath that looked well travelled. She eagerly began her ascent. The path curved effortlessly up the hillside, and she turned occasionally to see the prospect below. The house stood majestically before her, so immense in stature and breadth, that it blocked most of her view of the lake and some of the woods beyond from this lower height.

As she neared the summit, Elizabeth stopped to regain her breath and she turned again to look down at the house and grounds. She was now able to see the depth of the woods, the winding stream that they had followed coming in, and the house. Her heart fluttered at the sight of it, standing tall and proud, situated prominently upon a sloping rise.

As her eyes swept the panorama before her, she let out a soft sigh. If indeed Mr. Darcy had feelings of affection for Rosalyn, her own presence here was an unfortunate thorn he had to endure for the sake of their acquaintance. She gave a swift kick to a stone in front of her, sending it off into a nearby thicket.

She glanced one more time at Pemberley below and then continued on her way. When at last she reached the top, she was greeted with a breathtaking view across the valley of the distant peaks of Derbyshire. Little villages dotted the countryside, and she was able to see a rather large river winding hither and thither, sending off little streams in various directions or taking the waters from some that flowed into it.

The sun had already crested up over the peaks and she felt the promising warmth of the day as it beat down on her. She felt a greater sense of admiration for the sight than she did exertion from the walk, but upon noticing a small bench, she walked over to it and sat down. Her eyes took in every pleasing scene below. She enjoyed this temporary respite from her duties as governess and the grief that still stung in the loss of her father.

A noise from further along the ridge drew Elizabeth's attention. She turned her head sharply in its direction, expecting to see an animal. Instead, she was startled to see Mr. Darcy emerge from around a clump of trees. He halted in his stride as he met her gaze.

A small smile emerged on his face. "Miss Bennet, I see that you have… again… discovered my favourite place of retreat."

Elizabeth abruptly stood up as he continued to walk toward her. "Pray, forgive me, Mr. Darcy. I did not mean to intrude. Please excuse me."

She turned to leave, but just as suddenly Mr. Darcy reached out and his hand briefly touched her arm to stay her. Even after he had removed it, she could still feel the warmth of its imprint.

"Do not feel as though you must leave," he said as he turned to look out over the valley. "The panorama is here for anyone to enjoy as long as they are inclined to take the short climb up. Unfortunately, not many do."

"It is beautiful," she said, tilting her head and letting out a soft sigh. "It reminds me of Cowper's poems. The ones in which he is so descriptive of the land."

"Ah, you enjoy Cowper?" he asked. His voice softened, as he turned his gaze to the view. "*While far beyond, and overthwart the stream that, as with molten glass, inlays the vale, the sloping land recedes into the clouds; displaying on its varied side the grace of hedge-row beauties numberless…*"

"Yes, much like that one," Elizabeth replied, her heart pounding so violently she was quite certain, in that hushed moment, that Mr. Darcy could hear it.

"I believe Cowper wrote that verse inspired by this view."

Elizabeth turned her head toward him in surprise. "No! Surely you jest, Mr. Darcy. Besides, in that same poem he mentions the River Ouse, and that is definitely not the River Ouse we see down there!"

Mr. Darcy smiled, sharply raising his brow, "Perhaps he did not write the full poem inspired by this view, but I do speak the truth when I say he was once a guest at Pemberley, Miss Bennet, and I like to think that this view contributed to his imagery he painted with words."

"He truly stood in this spot?"

Mr. Darcy nodded.

Elizabeth smiled and bowed her head in acquiescence. "I shall grant you then, that it may have inspired him in part, but it could have just as easily been from the view atop Oakham Mount near Longbourn, as Mr. Cowper lived in Hertfordshire, you know."

Mr. Darcy gave a mock bow. "And so I shall grant you that, Miss Bennet." After a moment of silence Darcy asked, "Did you arrive up here this morning in time to see the sunrise?"

"I am afraid I did not."

"Then you must promise me you will come up here early enough some morning to see it. It is usually quite stunning. Will you do that?"

"I most certainly will try." The quiver in Elizabeth's voice betrayed her confusion and she quickly added, "I must go. Emily will be waking soon."

Mr. Darcy reached out and touched her arm again, this time letting his hand linger a moment longer. "Miss Bennet."

Elizabeth's heart pounded and she slowly looked up into his face. "Yes?"

He took in a deep breath as his eyes met hers. He studied her face for a moment and then said, "I would not wish for your stay at Pemberley to be awkward. I want to assure you that you are welcome here. When I invited the Willstones and Miss Matthews to Pemberley, I was well aware that you would be included in their party and I want you to know that I harbour no ill feelings regarding what transpired between us. It is, I hope, all forgotten."

Elizabeth moistened her lips as she heard his words. They were comforting, and yet at the same time, not. "Thank you, Mr. Darcy. I understand. If you will excuse me…" She gave a slight curtsey as Mr. Darcy bowed, and turned to return down the path.

She did not look back to see if he followed. Her feelings swirled with confusion. She was grateful for his attempt to alleviate her discomfiture, yet wondered if his words were another indication of his fondness for Rosalyn. Certainly he did not want her to inform Rosalyn about his offer of marriage. *"It is, I hope, all forgotten."*

Elizabeth kept her eyes on the path on the way down, rarely turning her gaze to Pemberley. She kicked a rock that lay in her path as she tried to drive the intruding thought that now, when she was finally beginning to see the good man that he was, she was no longer his equal, and he had now turned his affections toward Rosalyn.

When she returned to the house, she went to her room to freshen up, and then helped Emily get ready for breakfast, all the while pondering the Master of this home.

~~*

When Elizabeth brought Emily downstairs, they were met by Rosalyn, who greeted the pair enthusiastically. "Elizabeth, I am about to burst with my thoughts and feelings. We must get ourselves away some time today so we can talk. I must tell you all that happened last evening."

Elizabeth forced a smile. "We shall have the whole morning before the picnic. Perhaps we can meet some time after breakfast?"

"Yes! That would be wonderful. Shall we meet in the sitting room Mrs. Reynolds showed us yesterday? We should be out of the way of others in there."

Elizabeth could only nod an agreement to this scheme, for Mr. Darcy approached. "Good morning, ladies."

The three ladies curtsied and wished him a good morning as Rosalyn suddenly grasped Elizabeth's arm for support. Elizabeth was grateful that he did not make any reference to seeing her out while walking this morning. Extending his arm toward the dining room, he invited the ladies to join him.

"Miss Willstone," he said, as he looked down at Emily. "Would you do me the honour of taking my arm?"

Squealing with happiness, the young child rushed to take his arm. Rosalyn did not miss the opportunity and exclaimed, "And may I be so fortunate to take the other?" Without waiting for his response, she wrapped her hand gently around his arm, giving Elizabeth a backward glance of evident contentment. Elizabeth offered her another forced smile and followed behind.

This is where I now belong, she told herself. *I cannot expect to be placed as an equal with the others. Particularly with Mr. Darcy.*

The prospect of the picnic again dominated the conversation around the table that morning. While they were eating and engaged in this joyous conversation, a servant entered. Walking up to the head of the table, he said, "Two letters for you, Mr. Darcy, and one for you, Mr. Hamilton." He then approached Elizabeth. "And a letter for you, Miss Bennet."

Elizabeth looked down and recognized Jane's handwriting immediately. A smile spread across her face as she broke the seal.

Hamilton looked at her. "Did you receive a letter from your family, Miss Bennet?" he asked.

"Yes! It is from…" Elizabeth stopped herself, knowing that to mention Jane might cause Miss Darcy distress. "It is from my family." Slipping it into her pocket, she said, "I shall read it later."

After breakfast, Elizabeth took advantage of a few spare moments before meeting Rosalyn to read Jane's letter. Emily had joined the other two girls in the playroom with Miss Bartley, and Elizabeth made arrangements with her that if she watched the girls in the morning, Elizabeth would return the favour and watch them for her in the afternoon.

In her room, Elizabeth sat down in a large wooden rocking chair and reached into her pocket for the letter. She leaned back on an embroidered pillow which gave her much comfort as she sat and rocked. She opened the letter and began reading.

My dearest sister,

You must know how much I miss you! It has been two weeks and I already long for our Sunday meetings. But I must also confess that I am truly happy. I will delay no longer and I shall tell you! Mr. Bingley has made me an offer of marriage!

Elizabeth's heart began pounding as she read those words. Her heart burst with happiness for Jane. She was also well pleased that Mr. Bingley stood strong in defiance of Mr. Darcy, who had been so instrumental in separating the two of them initially. She continued reading,

Lizzy, I cannot even believe it has happened; I pinch myself often to make certain I am not dreaming. He spoke first to our uncle to get his permission. We went for a walk one afternoon and he asked me as we sat on a bench in the park down the road. We shall marry in September. I do hope you make arrangements to be in Town and will stand up with me.

You might be surprised, Lizzy, by our guest the day after you departed for the country. Mr. Bingley arrived with Mr. Darcy! He spent the whole afternoon and then remained to dine with us, and was exceptionally cordial to us all. He left soon after, but I must admit that he seemed to enjoy talking with our aunt about Lambton, while she enjoyed talking with him about Pemberley. We both commented to each other later that evening that he was quite amiable. It was certainly a surprise to us that he did not have that way about him that he did in Hertfordshire, although I never truly believed him to be as proud as so many others did. I hope that you have found him to be just as amiable as we did and are enjoying your stay at his Pemberley!

Elizabeth's hands dropped into her lap. Could it be that he no longer felt his friend's actions were foolish and he now supported his decision? Did he even know that Mr. Bingley was going to ask for her hand? She closed her eyes as she rocked in the chair, her smile never leaving her face. She rejoiced in her sister's happiness until suddenly, her smile departed as she thought of Miss Darcy. What would this mean when *she* heard the news?

Tapping the letter in her hand, she decided that she would not allow concern for Miss Darcy to rob her of her delight. Miss Darcy need not know. In fact, no one needed to know until they left Pemberley. She would not even tell Rosalyn or the Willstones.

She finished reading the letter; Jane informed her she had no news from their family in Hertfordshire, and their aunt made a special request that she visit a close friend of hers, a Mrs. Ketterling, in Lambton. Elizabeth thought she might be able to do that on Sunday, which was two days away, and quickly penned a note to have sent to her, asking if she would be available for Elizabeth to pay her a call in the afternoon.

Elizabeth read Jane's letter one more time, and she then proceeded down the hall to the sitting room, where she knew Rosalyn would be waiting. Just before she stepped through the door, she fisted her hands tightly for a second and drew in a breath, letting it out slowly. She could only imagine the things Rosalyn wished to talk about with her. And those things would all centre around one man – Mr. Darcy.

When she walked in, Rosalyn was standing at the window looking out. Her hands were clasped together and tucked under her chin, almost as if in prayer.

When she heard Elizabeth walk in, she spun around and rushed over to her. "Come, sit, Elizabeth. I have so much to tell you."

When Rosalyn had finished, it was all Elizabeth could have expected. Rosalyn was more and more certain that Mr. Darcy was singling her out and acquainted Elizabeth with all that occurred after she left with Emily last evening.

"When the men finally returned," Rosalyn spoke most spiritedly, "Mr. Darcy came and sat by his sister and me. We talked for a good part of the next hour." Rosalyn let out a breathy sigh. "I am quite of the opinion that he is pleased with my attentions to his sister."

"Truly?" Elizabeth wondered whether it was more that he was protecting his sister from Rosalyn's attentions.

She told Elizabeth how they played cards and Mr. Darcy and his cousin played chess, and then the evening concluded with Mrs. Goldsmith playing and singing for them.

"So what do you think?" Rosalyn asked as she folded her hands and placed them demurely in her lap.

Elizabeth shook her head. "Hmmm?"

"Are you of the opinion we have been invited here for my benefit?"

Elizabeth pursed her lips tightly together and then said very carefully, "He is a very eligible, handsome, and good man …"

"And rich," added Rosalyn.

"Yes, so he is, and being such a man, he most likely wants to be certain he knows a woman quite well before he makes any kind of offer to her."

"Oh, I hope I have pleased him. I know I am not as intelligent or witty as some women, but I do so want his good opinion."

The breath caught in Elizabeth's throat as she heard the words spoken that were quite opposite of the words she had lashed out at him. *I have never desired your good opinion.* Those had been her very own words to him, and yet now she realized that she, too, wished for his good opinion. She was quite certain it was too late.

The sound of heavy footsteps coming down the hall drew their attention, and Rosalyn looked at Elizabeth in surprise. "Could the men already be done with fishing? Have we been here that long?"

They both looked toward the door and saw that it was Mr. Darcy. He looked in and upon seeing them, he stopped.

"Hello, ladies."

"Hello, Mr. Darcy," both ladies replied.

"How was fishing?" Rosalyn asked.

Darcy chuckled. "It is likely the other men will be at it all morning. I made certain they were all set up and then I had to leave them to meet with my steward, Mr. Barstow." He stepped into the room. "Are you enjoying this sitting room?"

"Oh, yes!" gushed Rosalyn. "It is very nice."

"It is Georgiana's favourite room. For the past year it has been my intention of surprising her and having it redecorated for her."

"I think that would be such a wonderful surprise!"

"My only dilemma is how to decorate it and what colours and fabrics to use that would please her. That is not something about which I normally make decisions and I have continually postponed it."

He looked at both of them as he said this, but he looked back at Rosalyn as she said, "Mr. Darcy, I would be more than happy to give you some advice." She then began telling him how he ought to decorate his sister's sitting room. Elizabeth was almost embarrassed as her friend went into detail about colour, fabrics, and even the amount of lace he should have in the curtains.

When she finished, Mr. Darcy looked at her oddly. "Thank you, Miss Matthews. I appreciate your recommendation." With an awkward bow, he turned and walked out of the room.

Elizabeth was certain his comment had not been one to which he expected an answer.

When they heard him enter through a door down the hall, Rosalyn grasped Elizabeth's hands. "Do you realize what just happened?"

Elizabeth's eyebrows pinched together as she said, "No, I am afraid I do not."

"He wished to know how I wanted the room decorated, so that when Pemberley becomes mine, this room will be exactly as I want it to be."

Elizabeth's jaw dropped as she heard her words. "Rosalyn, are you quite certain?"

"Yes! This is just the assurance I have been waiting for. I must go tell my sister!" Rosalyn left the room quickly, leaving Elizabeth stunned.

Elizabeth kept her eyes toward the empty doorway and shook her head. They had not even been at Pemberley one full day, and Rosalyn was already imagining herself as its Mistress.

Chapter 11

At precisely one o'clock, the guests made their way out to the front grounds of Pemberley and saw that a canopy had been erected on the north side of the lake. Mr. Darcy and his sister welcomed everyone as they arrived and they were invited to sit down on the chairs that were placed under the canopy or on blankets that were spread out on the lawn.

Elizabeth followed Emily over to a blanket and sat beside her and the Goldsmith girls.

Once everyone was seated, Miss Darcy gave a few instructions. "The picnic lunch is ready to be served, and once you have your plate, you may return to the chairs here, sit on the blanket, or walk around and eat. We urge you to enjoy the day any way you choose."

Servants were lined up on one side of a large table filled with food, ready to fill the guests' plates. After receiving hers, Emily skipped back to the blanket, holding her plate out from her as she tried to keep it from tipping. Elizabeth watched, hoping she would not take a spill.

Taking her own plate, Elizabeth glanced around her. Mr. Darcy was conversing with the Goldsmiths and his sister. Rosalyn, shaded from the sun with a parasol, kept a vigilant eye on the group, waiting, Elizabeth mused disparagingly, for the first opportunity to claim her place next to Mr. Darcy.

Elizabeth grimaced briefly at her increasingly critical thoughts. Her lips pursed tightly together as she considered whether her view of Rosalyn's behaviour was sound or due to her own increasing feelings for Mr. Darcy.

She did not yet see Mr. Hamilton, Emily was enjoying her two friends' company, everyone else was engaged in conversation with another, and as she wished for a few moments alone to ponder her sister's good news, she decided to walk down to the water's edge and eat there.

She was equally enjoying her repast and the view when she heard her name called. She looked up, surprised to see Miss Darcy walking toward her.

"Hello, Miss Darcy."

"Hello, Miss Bennet. I hope you find everything to your satisfaction."

"Very much so," Elizabeth replied.

"I understand congratulations are in order. My brother has informed me that your sister and Mr. Bingley are engaged."

Elizabeth's jaw dropped slowly as she studied the young girl. She noted nothing in Miss Darcy's demeanour that indicated regret or lingering affection toward Mr. Bingley. Elizabeth slowly smiled. "Thank you. But how is it your brother came to hear of it?"

"He received a letter today from Mr. Bingley."

Elizabeth smiled hesitantly. "His letter was from Mr. Bingley?"

"Yes."

Elizabeth looked at the young girl, wishing very much to know what she was thinking – how she truly felt about this news.

After a brief silence, Miss Darcy obliged her. "I would not wish you to be under any misapprehension concerning Mr. Bingley and myself, Miss Bennet. He is a friend, and that is all. I have no ill feelings toward him or your sister."

Elizabeth tilted her head at the young girl. "I am truly glad to hear that your heart is safe from being broken. I was unsure how you felt toward me even being here."

Georgiana slowly shook her head. "I know there was much speculation about Mr. Bingley and me. Truth be told, I did seek him out." She looked down at her hands, as her fingers nervously intertwined. "My brother, you see, had often teasingly hinted to both of us how much it would please him if we were to marry. Last year my brother became extremely downcast and I was under the mistaken belief that it was because he had been earnest in that wish and he was disappointed in me. I felt the only way to bring him out of his gloom was to abide by his wishes."

"That was why you sought Mr. Bingley out?"

Georgiana nodded. "It was when we first saw you at the Willstones that I realized neither Mr. Bingley nor I had strong feelings of affection for each other."

"When you saw me?"

"Yes. I had heard about Mr. Bingley and Miss Bennet over a year ago. I knew he had been very fond of her and that his heart had been broken because she did not love him."

"But she did…"

"Yes, I know that now, but I had been given the impression she did not. When we saw you at the Willstones, I wrongly assumed you were that Miss Bennet. I could see by Mr. Bingley's behaviour that he still had strong feelings for her. It was in the way his face lit up that caught my attention. And his smile was unlike any I had ever seen. When I found out that you were but her sister, I realized how much he still must love her. I could not help but wonder how much more his countenance would have brightened if it had been her that he had seen."

Elizabeth smiled. "You are a wise and discerning young lady."

"It would have been wrong for me to insist Mr. Bingley do the honourable thing and ignore the regard he had for Miss Bennet because people expected an engagement between us. Besides, in all that time I had spent in Mr. Bingley's company, my brother's deportment had not improved in the slightest."

Elizabeth's hand went to her neck and she nervously fingered the cross on her necklace. "Did you ever discover the reason why he became despondent?"

"No. It was after his return from Kent last year at Easter that it evidenced itself." Georgiana turned and gazed at the lake. "The only hint I received was when he told me he thought he knew himself and he had been clearly mistaken."

Georgiana let out a soft sigh and looked over to where her brother stood. "While I still know nothing of what prompted him to grow so gravely despondent, he now seems much recovered."

Georgiana's eyebrows pinched together and her lips quivered slightly as she said, "I may never know what caused his sudden despair, but I can make a guess what has brought him out of it." She gestured toward him and Rosalyn.

Elizabeth's heart unexpectedly lurched as she glanced at Mr. Darcy, who was flanked on one side by Rosalyn and the other by Mrs. Willstone. He looked her way and their eyes briefly met. He then turned his head abruptly away.

"Do you mean Miss Matthews?" Elizabeth asked tentatively, her fingers again nervously playing with the cross on her necklace.

Georgiana nodded.

Elizabeth took in a deep breath and thought through very carefully what she wanted to say. "Miss Darcy, certainly you know what it is like to be on the receiving end of this type of speculation. Are you quite certain?"

Georgiana looked to the ground and then back up to Elizabeth. "I would never speak what is merely gossip. While my brother has never divulged much to me over the years about any woman he has had affection for, I know him very well. Inviting the Willstones and Miss Matthews to Pemberley was quite out of character for him. His disposition improved dramatically in London after we began frequenting the same circles as her and her family."

Now Georgiana took Elizabeth's hand in hers. "I would not speak so openly if it was merely my own speculation, but I overheard Miss Mathews and her sister speaking earlier today of a very much expected offer of marriage."

Elizabeth pursed her lips together, knowing perfectly well what she overheard… and why. "Miss Darcy, how do you know that their conversation was not merely mutual hopes being expressed?"

"It may be, but…" Georgiana stopped herself. "You are correct," she expelled a soft chuckle. "We ought not speculate." Looking back toward her brother and guests she said, "I have enjoyed speaking with you, Miss Bennet. Shall we go back now and rejoin the others?"

The two walked back as Elizabeth's thoughts whirled with her own speculations about whether Mr. Darcy indeed was singling out Rosalyn, and her fervent hope that he was not.

Elizabeth sat down on the blanket next to Emily, who was playing a game with the two other girls. Miss Bartley had stepped away and was talking to Mrs. Goldsmith.

A shadow came over her as someone approached and stood behind her – a gentleman she could see – and she turned around and glanced up. It was Mr. Hamilton.

"I see you have finally decided to join us, Mr. Hamilton. I wondered if you had something of greater import keeping you away. Perhaps your captain orders came through."

"I would hope not yet, for I would not want to miss this picnic for anything, but unfortunately I was precluded from arriving on time by a misfortune."

"Nothing serious, I hope."

He took a seat beside her as he explained. "Merely a tumble into the river, which required quite a bit of cleaning up on my part."

Elizabeth threw her head back in a laugh. "I hope it was all in a battle with a great fish. Who won? You or the fish? Are we to feast on it tonight?"

Mr. Hamilton lowered his head, shaking it slowly. "I wish it had been that noble. But to own the truth, Miss Bennet, I stepped on a rock which gave way, causing me to slip and I landed fully in the water."

Elizabeth covered her smile with her fingers as she put on her most sympathetic expression. "How unfortunate! I hope the other men did not observe your tumble and make sport of you!"

"Ah, but they did. Merciless men! Not one of them helped me out, either!"

Elizabeth chuckled. "I am grateful you came through it unscathed."

"Except for my pride, yes, I came through it unscathed. Besides, what is a little water to a sea captain?" Mr. Hamilton laughed as he spoke, his eyes twinkling with mirth.

They continued to talk about the food, the weather, and as he asked about her family, Mr. Darcy came and stood before them. "I understand you took a spill, Hamilton," he said.

"I did, but as you can see, I clean up quite well!" Hamilton laughed, and then invited his cousin to sit down and join them.

"Do you mind if I join you?" Mr. Darcy directed his question to Elizabeth.

"Please do," she replied, and upon feeling a warmth of colour upon her face, she looked away and busied her hands with straightening out her dress. Her heart began to pound as she felt his presence near, and she took a deep breath in an attempt to calm her rising feelings.

"Miss Bennet, may I extend my congratulations to you on the engagement of your sister and Mr. Bingley."

She turned toward him, surprised by his words, but she said with a smile. "Thank you, sir. I appreciate your thoughtful sentiment. They both have a fervent, equal regard for one another and I am quite certain they shall be blissfully happy." A raised eyebrow was the only indication that there was a deeper meaning in her reply.

Darcy stared at her for a few moments as he contemplated the import of her words. He had fervently, yet erroneously, believed that Miss Bennet was indifferent to his friend. A quick nod acknowledged her words.

Emily's excitement interrupted their conversation. "Look at that bird, Miss Bennet!" She pointed to a black and white bird flying around them catching bugs in the air. "What kind is it?"

"It is a pied flycatcher!" Both Elizabeth and Darcy answered at once, then turned their eyes to the other.

Keeping his eyes fixed on Elizabeth, he asked, "Is Miss Bennet a bird enthusiast?" The question was almost as much to Elizabeth as to Emily.

"Oh, yes!" the young girl cheerfully exclaimed. "She teaches me all the names of the birds, and the flowers, and the trees. I even know some of the birds by their sounds and I have learned some of the trees by their leaves!"

"You might be interested then, Miss Bennet, in some books I have in my library. They contain beautiful drawings of birds, their names, and a description. I have other books, as well, of the flowers you will see around here. You might wish to take them out with you and Emily some day while you are here. You are more than welcome to them." He turned and looked at Emily. "Would you like that Miss Willstone?"

"Oh, yes!"

He looked back at Elizabeth. "And you, Miss Bennet. Would you like that?"

"I would not wish to damage the books, sir, by bringing them outside."

"Have no fear; they have smudges enough from my own handling of them. When we return, I shall procure them for you."

"Thank you, Mr. Darcy," Elizabeth said softly, pondering his attention.

He continued with a soft smile, "You may also have a slight advantage in the treasure hunt, Miss Bennet, if indeed you do know your birds, flowers, and trees well. That will likely help on a few of the clues."

"Then she is to be on my team!" exclaimed Hamilton. "It is fixed. Miss Bennet and I are a team!

"We shall see," Mr. Darcy sternly replied.

"So your friend Bingley is finally to be married is he?" asked Mr. Hamilton. "What say you, Darcy? In no short time, you and I shall be the only remaining eligible men around!"

"You know that is absurd," he answered with a small smile. "As a sea captain, you shall be the most sought out man around. You shall have a bride in no time."

"Ah," Elizabeth interjected, with a hint of laughter in her voice. "But surely he must find one soon, for if not, he certainly cannot expect to find a woman once out on the great ocean!"

"The lady speaks the truth!" exclaimed Mr. Hamilton. "I must find a suitable woman before I venture back out to sea." A glance at Elizabeth and a smile did not go unnoticed by Darcy, who pursed his lips tightly together.

"The difficulty is that there are so many ladies of so varied temperaments and qualities!" Hamilton turned to Elizabeth. "What type of woman ought I be looking for?"

"You must find a most suitable wife; one who has a strength of disposition, for she shall either have to remain home raising her brood of children while you are out at sea, or when you have a ship of your own, she may be required to be at sea alongside you." She then let out a soft chuckle. "And she must be exceptionally plain!"

Hamilton threw his head back in laughter. "Pray, tell me why!"

Elizabeth smiled. "She shall be the only woman on board that ship full of men!"

Mr. Hamilton shook his head fervently as he continued to laugh. "Miss Bennet, you have truly done some thinking about the matter." His face grew solemn as he said, "But I do not fear finding a wife; my greater fear is that I shall be turned down if I make her an offer. What have I to contribute to a marriage but a meagre fortune?" He cast a mocking glance at Darcy. "Now my good cousin here shall never have worries in that matter. He has no fear of ever being turned down."

Hamilton's words evoked a tightening in Elizabeth's chest that made it difficult to even take a breath. She saw Darcy's hands clench tightly together before she turned away in discomfiture, not wishing to look upon his face and see what was written on his expression.

Hamilton continued, completely oblivious to the reactions of the two with whom he conversed. He then turned to Miss Bennet. "You are not the type that breaks hearts are you, Miss Bennet? Have you ever broken the heart of a man and turned down his offer?"

Confusion swept over Elizabeth. She drew in a shaky breath and looked at Mr. Hamilton in despair. "I… I…" she could say no more and looked down as she felt her face hot with mortification.

"You have!" exclaimed Hamilton teasingly. "Can we hear about the brute? Do you have any regrets?"

Shaking her head, she mumbled, "It… I…"

"Hamilton!" Darcy said firmly. "It is not yours or anyone's business!"

Elizabeth cautiously lifted her eyes up to Mr. Darcy and saw him glaring at his cousin, his face set with disgust. When he turned and looked at her, she gave a slight nod of her head in thanks.

Darcy stood up abruptly, making the claim that he was required to take care of some things before the treasure hunt began. As he stood before them, he admonished his cousin to join him with such a stern demeanour that would brook no hesitation.

The two walked away, and Elizabeth's heart beat wildly as she heard Mr. Darcy's hushed, but intense voice directed at his cousin. She kept her eyes cast down as she was filled with regret that he had been subjected to a reminder of her refusal in such a callous manner. She closed her eyes and took in several deep breaths, willing her heart to be still.

Chapter 12

Elizabeth kept her eyes on Mr. Darcy and his cousin as they walked some distance away engaged in a highly spirited discussion. Her heart still pounded from the incident, both from her discomfiture over Mr. Hamilton's remarks and the proximity of Mr. Darcy's presence. As she attempted to collect herself, she glanced over toward Rosalyn, who was speaking with Mrs. Goldsmith. She took in a deep, grateful breath that her friend had not been near enough to hear that prior conversation; she did not need to have Rosalyn pressing her for information about whose offer she had refused.

Later, Elizabeth sat and watched as kites were brought out for the young girls. With the help of some of the men, they all greatly enjoyed this diversion. The wind was such that the kites easily soared high above the trees. Elizabeth treasured the glimpses she caught of Mr. Darcy as he took the time with Emily and her friends to show them how to keep the kite aloft. She had to admit to herself that she found his attentiveness to them rather appealing.

When the wind died down and the girls tired of this activity, Mr. Darcy summoned everyone together. He called up Mr. Goldsmith, Mr. Willstone, and Mr. Hamilton, and then asked his sister to explain the rules of the treasure hunt.

Looking nervous, but fulfilling her duties as hostess, she began. "We have divided you all into three teams, headed by these fine gentlemen. Mr. Goldsmith's team consists of me, Mrs. Willstone, and Miss Harriet. Mr. Willstone will have Miss Matthews, Miss Bartley, and Miss Emily on his team. On Mr. Hamilton's team are Mrs. Goldsmith, Miss Bennet, and Miss Gladys."

She continued to explain that each team was required to decipher ten clues and that each clue would tell where to find the next one. Her brother would be available if assistance was needed and the winner would be the first team back with the least amount of help from him.

Georgiana smiled softly and looked with admiration at Mr. Darcy. "I want you all to be assured that my good brother came up with all the clues and I have not seen even one, so our team does not have an advantage!"

Mr. Darcy then stepped forward. "Are there any questions?"

When no one answered, Darcy held up some pieces of paper. These are your team's first clue. They are all different, so you will likely be heading off in different directions. The men have been given information regarding the boundaries of the search, how a clue might or might not be hidden, and what you can and cannot do in searching for it. The more spirited ones can rush ahead of the others to retrieve the clues, and if anyone gets fatigued, you may return here and wait for the others. They may come ask for your help in deciphering the clues while you rest. Your team will not be penalized unless I am consulted. Are you all ready?"

Mr. Darcy could not have had a more captive audience, as everyone was excited to begin. He passed out each clue, admonishing everyone not to look at it until the hunt began. He then stepped back. Standing erect with his hands clasped behind him, he announced with all the dignity of the Master of a great estate, "Ladies and gentlemen, the treasure hunt has begun!"

The teams tore open their clue, gathering together to read and decipher it.

Mr. Hamilton looked at his team's clue and then looked up, his mouth askew. "It is a verse from Cowper's *The Poplar Field*. Is anyone here familiar with it?"

"I am, to some extent," exclaimed Elizabeth. "What does it say?"

Everyone listened expectantly while Hamilton read the clue.

"Cowper's 'The Poplar Field' will tell all;
If the third verse you can recall;
It begins with 'Twelve years have elapsed since I first took a view;'
and ends with the place where you'll find the next clue."

As Hamilton finished reading, all heads turned toward Elizabeth, hope radiating from their eyes.

"Oh, my!" she said, as she began to recall how that verse went. "Let me see... Twelve years have elapsed since I first took a view... of my favourite field... and the bank where they grew, And now in the grass behold they are laid, And the tree is my seat that once lent me a shade."

"A field?" asked Mrs. Goldsmith.

"No, the bank of the lake... or the stream," interjected Hamilton.

Elizabeth shook her head firmly, "No, no! The very last line talks about the tree that is now my seat but once gave me shade." She looked at Mr. Hamilton. "Do you know if there is a tree that has fallen, leaving only a stump?"

He thought for a moment, and then his eyes lit up in recollection.

"Yes! The old elm, down by the stables! Come, this way!"

He pointed the way, and Gladys skipped hurriedly ahead of the others, wishing to be the first one there to begin looking for the next clue. Mrs. Goldsmith walked briskly behind her bolstered by her enthusiasm.

Mr. Hamilton put his hand on Elizabeth's arm to slow her pace. Her thoughts immediately went to this morning and how warm Mr. Darcy's hand felt on her arm. Mr. Hamilton's hand left no similar effect.

"Please, allow me to ask for your forgiveness, Miss Bennet. I was most insolent earlier and I am deeply sorry for causing you unease. It was unpardonable and I can only hope you will forgive me." He rubbed his hands together nervously and let out a slow breath.

"Thank you, Mr. Hamilton. I accept your apology and you are very much forgiven."

"I am wholly relieved!" he said, a broad smile appearing. "Darcy gave me quite the tongue lashing that I thoroughly deserved. Initially, he was adamant that you not even be on my team, believing you to be so visibly distressed by my words, but I insisted. I needed to have an opportunity to express my deepest regrets."

They walked a little farther and he continued, "One of my greatest faults, Miss Bennet, is teasing and not knowing when to stop. You must think me completely devoid of civility."

"Mr. Hamilton, I have often found myself in trouble as well because of my own teasing. Let us forgive and forget."

"Gladly!" he said, just as they reached Mrs. Goldsmith, who had slowed down.

"I lost sight of Gladys," she said. "But I see the stables and I assume she is looking for the next clue."

They all turned to look up the path when they heard Gladys' excited squeal. "I have it! I have it!" She came running toward them holding the clue up over her head as if she were flying one of the kites again.

The treasure hunt was entertaining; the clues being diverse enough so that each member of the team could work at least one. On more than one occasion in the midst of the hunt, Elizabeth's thoughts went to the gentleman who would put so much effort into providing this type of diversion for his guests. She would have never imagined the man she knew in Hertfordshire to be capable of something like this.

There were puzzles, clues from literature and poems, as their first one was, and a few simple ones for the children that merely had a word written that was missing several letters. Gladys was easily able to decipher "sandbox" and "carriage house."

When they found their last clue, they quickly made their way back to the canopy, hoping to be the first team back. They only sought out Mr. Darcy's help on one clue. They affirmed each other with confident expectation that they may, indeed, be the winning team.

Rosalyn sat underneath the canopy next to Mr. Darcy, having returned early due to fatigue. Elizabeth watched her friend laugh gaily at something he said, yet she noticed a look of anxiety etched upon her features. She was quite certain that Mr. Darcy had not expressed his intentions as Rosalyn had so hoped.

As the other teams returned, refreshing drinks and tea cakes were offered. Everyone laughed amongst themselves as they recollected their different adventures and how they either did or did not decipher the clues readily. Mr. Darcy seemed satisfied that everyone enjoyed themselves.

He drew their attention once they had all returned to announce the winners. As it turned out, Mr. Hamilton's team came in first, Mr. Goldsmith's team came in second, and Mr. Willstone's team came in third.

Georgiana did the honours and handed out the prizes. All the men received fishing rods, the ladies received beautiful lace handkerchiefs, and the young girls received a kite of their own, which pleased them immensely. Georgiana explained that while the treasure hunt did indeed have winners, the hope was that everyone enjoyed it, and so she and her brother decided all would receive a prize of equal worth.

The remainder of the afternoon was spent playing games. Elizabeth remained with the girls and later, when they wanted a bit more activity, she walked with them over to the children's play area, where they had earlier found several amusements. It was in a slightly sheltered area in the back courtyard of the house.

Elizabeth sat on a bench that faced an open area to the west; a view of the woods beyond. She could relax here, away from Mr. Hamilton's curious looks and Mr. Darcy's unsettling presence. She no longer felt awkward in his presence. Instead, it was his accommodating behaviour toward her, the way in which he ensured her comfort, the very nearness of him, and seeing the good in him that prompted within her a discomfiture of a very different kind.

Despite the warmth of the afternoon, she shivered as a chill coursed through her. She twirled a ringlet of hair around a finger as she pondered what had brought about such thoughts and feelings. She slowly shook her head as the realization came unbidden to her. *Could she have fallen in love with him?*

Her head leant back abruptly against the wall of the house behind her and she dropped the ringlet of hair, slowly bringing her hand down and placing it over her heart. She could feel its steady, but very strong and erratic pulsing. Perhaps this was what he had intended all along – for her to fall in love with him and to experience what he suffered when she refused him. She was now a governess! He could never love her again; would never make her another offer. What man of his standing in society would?

She closed her eyes and took in a deep breath, staving off the tears that threatened to spill down her face. With her eyes closed, she could feel the slight breeze tease her face just as it whipped around the building; she could hear the leaves rustling in the great trees, and smell the fragrance of the flowers that grew in the gardens. She could not escape the fact that she was at Pemberley. While all this could have been hers, it was more the realization that its Master was a good, honourable, and respectable man who would now have been her husband if she had only accepted his proposal.

~~*

The Goldsmith girls soon grew tired and departed. Emily no longer found it to be as diverting without them, so she and Elizabeth also returned indoors. As they walked past the library, Emily remembered Mr. Darcy's words about the books.

"Miss Bennet, may we go in and find those books Mr. Darcy told us about?"

"Perhaps it would be best to wait for him. He has far too many books in there and I would have no idea where to find them."

"We can at least look." Emily looked up with pleading eyes.

"Very well," laughed Elizabeth. "We can try."

They walked in and Elizabeth closed her eyes as she breathed in the scent of the leather bound books. Again, memories of her father's library swept over her, and she steeled herself for the grief that often and unexpectedly consumed her.

Tears began to pool in her eyes, and she chided herself for her sentimentality. She reached into her pocket for the handkerchief she had just been given. Before dabbing it to her eyes, she fingered the silky material and perused the intricate lace. She had never owned something so beautiful.

"Miss Bennet, have you found it yet?" Emily called out from behind one of the rows of books.

"No, no," Elizabeth replied, pocketing her handkerchief.

"Do you ladies need some assistance?"

At the sound of Mr. Darcy's voice, Elizabeth's heart lurched. She was grateful when Emily answered.

"We are looking for the book on birds you told us about."

"Ahh! It is over here, quite close to where Miss Bennet is."

The two walked over to her and she watched him glance up and down the bookshelves. He stood so close to her that she felt as though her heart would burst from beating so violently.

Emily, so enthusiastic for the prospect of this book, leaned into him, which in turn caused him to bump into Elizabeth, sending her slightly off balance.

"Pardon me, Miss Bennet," he said as he quickly reached out and placed his hands on her shoulders to set her aright. Her eyes met and held his for the short duration he kept his hands there steadying her.

Elizabeth tried to appear calm, indifferent even, as his eyes searched hers, but she felt he could see all that she wished to hide from him. He finally released her shoulders and turned his attention back to the shelf, knowing exactly where to locate the book.

He cleared his throat and said, "Here it is, Miss Willstone. I daresay you will not find a book with finer drawings."

She opened the book, and after looking at several of the drawings said, "May I go show it to my mother?"

Mr. Darcy nodded. "Certainly. I believe she is in the drawing room."

Emily began to skip out of the library, and Elizabeth gave her a soft reminder. "Emily, remember to walk inside the house and take care with that book."

She stopped and turned around. "Yes, Miss Bennet."

Elizabeth and Mr. Darcy watched Emily disappear from the library. He turned slightly toward her, and then looked away, as if wishing to say something, but sensing her unease. He absently reached up to a row of books and straightened them. His eyes remained straight ahead on the bookshelf in front of him.

"I understand Hamilton apologized to you earlier for his remarks."

Elizabeth suddenly felt as though her mouth had lost all its moisture. In vain, she licked her lips before answering. "Yes, he did. I accepted his apology and forgave him."

Darcy nodded, still fingering the books on the shelf. "He had no right to press you as he did!"

Elizabeth lowered her head and said softly, "He had no way of knowing..." Her voice trailed off.

Darcy dropped his hands to his side. "He is young and often speaks without thinking. He has much to learn."

Elizabeth nodded silently.

Darcy turned his head and looked down at Elizabeth. Her head was still lowered away from him. "Please excuse me. My steward is waiting to see me in my study."

As he began to walk away, Elizabeth put a hand on his arm. He stopped and looked down at her hand, prompting her to quickly pull it away.

"I would like to thank you, Mr. Darcy, for a very enjoyable afternoon." The smile on her face conveyed a hope that she could be in his presence with a degree of equanimity.

"I am pleased you enjoyed it."

Elizabeth let out a breathy chuckle. "I would not have supposed you interested in planning such a thing as a treasure hunt."

He raised an eyebrow and he allowed a very slight smile to grace his face. "My father often used a treasure hunt to help me in my studies. The enticement of finding a treasure prompted me on more than one occasion to learn my lessons well. Truth be told, many of the clues we used today were ones that my father used."

"I believe your father must have been very wise." Elizabeth let out a genial laugh.

Darcy's eyes met hers and he smiled. "Yes, he was. I can only hope to be half as wise as he was."

Emily suddenly appeared at the door. "Miss Bennet, may we go for a walk and take this book? I want to see if I can find some of these birds."

Darcy raised an eyebrow at Elizabeth. "It sounds as if someone desires your presence."

"Hmm, yes. Duty calls." She turned to her charge. "Emily, that sounds like a splendid idea!"

They walked toward the door, Emily holding protectively onto the book, and Elizabeth hearing Darcy let out a sharp breath.

~~*

They returned to the house after spending a good hour out on the grounds discovering the names of several birds. Elizabeth told Emily she would keep the book in her room for safe keeping and to let her know when she wished to look through it.

They were met in the hall by one of the servants, who held a letter in his hand. "A letter was just delivered for you, Miss Bennet."

"Thank you," Elizabeth replied as she looked at the unfamiliar handwriting. She quickly tore it open, discovering it to be from her aunt's friend, Mrs. Ketterling.

Her eyes skimmed the brief missive.

Dear Miss Bennet,

We were overjoyed to hear that the niece of my good friend is so close – and staying at Pemberley, at that! We would be delighted to have you join us on Sunday afternoon. I look with great anticipation to showing you around our pleasant village, pointing out places that were so special to your aunt and me in our younger years.

Please plan to stay for dinner, as I am inviting some others who were acquainted with Madeline, as well. My husband and I would be pleased to come for you in our carriage. Look for us to be at Pemberley around one o'clock.

Yours, Mrs. Adele Ketterling

Elizabeth folded the letter. It appeared her plans for Sunday, with church in the morning, were settled.

During the evening meal that night, there was just as much joyous reflection on the treasure hunt as there had been eager expectation of it the previous night. Everyone laughed at their attempts to decipher the clues and how Mr. Goldsmith's team, on more than one occasion, erred greatly in their conjectures and lost precious time making up for it.

Mr. Darcy received much praise for his excellent scheme, receiving it humbly. It appeared to Elizabeth, noticing his pinched brow and tightly pursed lips, that he felt awkward receiving such accolades. She brought her napkin up to her lips to cover an appreciative smile that appeared, realizing he was not a man who did things for the admiration of others, but because he wanted to do them.

Chapter 13

The next morning, Elizabeth awoke with the sun already sending forth its dawning rays. She sat up in bed and stretched, surprised that she slept in as late as she had. She stood up and went to the window. Looking back up toward the ridge, she wondered whether Mr. Darcy had been up there this morning watching the sunrise.

Later, when she and Emily joined the others in the morning room for breakfast, she masked her disappointment when she learned that the men had already set out for a day of hunting. Rosalyn, however, gave Elizabeth a very pointed look of distress upon hearing the news.

Elizabeth was grateful that she had the excuse of needing time with Emily to go over her lessons, so she was not so much in Rosalyn's company that day. With every word her friend uttered about Mr. Darcy, Elizabeth had to fight thoughts of corresponding denial – either of her own feelings toward him or of what Rosalyn was expecting of him. She was gradually being worn down by it.

Miss Darcy had given them permission to play the pianoforte in the music room, and Emily enjoyed the benefit of receiving lessons along with Gladys and Harriet. By the end of the day, Elizabeth believed they had accomplished much.

The men returned in late afternoon; Elizabeth heard their jovial boasting as they entered through the back courtyard. Their hunt must have been successful and enjoyable, judging by their thunderous banter.

Everyone heard about the men's day during the evening meal. Mr. Hamilton claimed he had never shot so well, and Mr. Willstone was quite of the opinion that he had never seen so many birds. There was some teasing about missed shots, but they all seemed quite pleased with the day. Elizabeth readily noticed that same look of satisfaction and contentment in Mr. Darcy's expression, similar to his portrait in the Gallery.

That night, once Elizabeth and Miss Bartley had taken the girls to the nursery, it was apparent they all seemed a little more tired than usual. Perhaps the diligence of study proved more fatiguing than the rigorous activity the day before. Before long, Miss Bartley thought it would be wise to take her two wards upstairs and ready them for bed. Emily wished to remain up a little longer to complete a picture she had been drawing with crayons.

When she had finished the drawing and proudly shown it to Elizabeth, Elizabeth suggested they retire to their chambers. Emily protested only by asking to go in to her mother and father to show them her picture and say goodnight.

"They are with the adults, now, Emily. You know she will come up later."

"But I know I shall be asleep by then. May I please?"

Elizabeth considered whether or not it would be appropriate, but since the two of them had been treated so kindly, she knew of no reason why they should not. They returned to the sitting room.

When Elizabeth and Emily stepped in, there was a game of whist in progress at one table, and Mr. Darcy and Mr. Hamilton were engaged in a game of chess at another. The Willstones were seated next to the Goldsmiths, and the two ladies were talking. Mrs. Willstone looked up when they walked in.

"Is anything amiss, Emily? Miss Bennet?" she asked.

"No," Elizabeth replied. "Emily wished to come in and show you her drawing and say goodnight."

Emily held out her drawing to her mother and Elizabeth heard her name called out.

"Miss Bennet! Come hither!" It was Mr. Hamilton.

As Emily continued visiting with her parents, Elizabeth walked over to the table where the two men were engaged in a match. At first glance, her eyes took in the beauty of the chessboard. Rather than a simple painted piece of wood, the lighter squares appeared to be made of marble with mostly blue veins. The black squares appeared to be onyx. It glistened in the light of the candles. The pieces were carved in the same marble and onyx. It was a beautiful set.

She next glanced at the pieces on the board, taking a quick survey of the progress of the game. "May I ask who is winning?" she inquired.

"I am, of course," boasted Mr. Hamilton. "I believe Darcy has lost his touch. I have won three matches to his one, and he usually bests me every game!"

Rosalyn came and stood next to Elizabeth, laughing. "Mr. Hamilton has complained these past two nights that he might as well be playing a novice, and wishes for a more challenging opponent. Of course, I cannot oblige him, but, Elizabeth, you play!"

Elizabeth shook her head firmly and laughed. "Oh, no, I am sure I will not be much of a challenge to Mr. Hamilton, either."

"Come! You must agree to play!" Hamilton's face brightened. "Darcy, I insist that whoever wins this game will play Miss Bennet!"

"I am sorry," she said. "I must take Emily upstairs and put her to bed."

At that moment, Mrs. Willstone came over. "If you do not mind, I am rather fatigued and I believe I shall retire for the night. Miss Bennet, I shall take Emily upstairs and put her to bed."

"There you have it!" exclaimed Hamilton. "I shall finally have a more challenging opponent!"

"I do wish I could learn to play!" Rosalyn lamented. "Elizabeth, you must teach me. Perhaps whilst you and Mr. Hamilton play, you could explain the game to me."

Elizabeth shrugged. "I doubt it will be an ideal match. Mr. Hamilton thinks me a proficient. I fear he shall be greatly disappointed."

"Well at least you shall be better than my cous… Darcy! What did you just do there?"

"You are blabbering about and obviously not concentrating," he answered wryly.

Hamilton studied the board. "But I have had no need to concentrate!" He studied the board for some time, and finally, after moving his hand above each piece trying to decide which one to move, he finally settled on one. "There!"

Darcy shook his head. "Do you really want to do that?"

Hamilton placed his palms firmly on the table, leaning over the board to give it a better scrutinizing. Without much conviction, he answered, "Yes, I do!"

Arching an eyebrow and looking up at Elizabeth, Darcy asked, "What is your opinion, Miss Bennet?"

"I shall hold my opinion for a few more moves," she answered him, giving him a knowing smile.

It took only those few moves for Darcy to win the match. A brooding Hamilton shook his head. "You tricked me, Darcy. You allowed me to think I had finally learned how to out-play and out-strategize you!"

"I did no such thing," Darcy answered smoothly, as he returned the pieces to their starting places.

"Hamilton, please allow Miss Bennet to have a seat."

When she sat down, Darcy said, "You may begin, Miss Bennet."

"So how do you decide what piece to play? How to begin?" Rosalyn asked eagerly, having taken a seat at the table. She watched as Elizabeth reached out and moved one of her pieces.

"The object is to capture the king," began Darcy as he pointed out the king to her. "He is the most vital piece of all, for once he is trapped, the game is over."

"True," said Elizabeth, "but he is also one of the weakest pieces…"

"Vulnerable…" interjected Darcy. He made a move and then looked up. "Not weak. Rules are such that he can only move one square at a time. He is not at liberty to move as one might wish. What he can do is greatly limited."

Elizabeth gave a slight nod of agreement. "Now the queen," she said, pointing it out with a smile, "is without doubt the most powerful piece, being able to move in any direction as many squares as she wishes." She looked at Mr. Darcy to see whether he had a differing opinion on that.

Darcy cradled his jaw with his hand and studied Elizabeth with careful deliberation. "Barring any obstruction, of course."

"Of course," conceded Elizabeth.

They each made several moves in silence until Darcy offered, "Sometimes she must be sacrificed to save the king."

Elizabeth looked at him oddly. "Yes, but that is not often wise!" she said with a nervous laugh, noticing the intensity of his gaze.

Rosalyn let out a groan. "This is no help to me at all!"

"As you develop your strategy, it is wise to study your partner to help you anticipate what he might do," Elizabeth said as she moved one of her pawns and then looked back up to Mr. Darcy. "You must think several moves ahead, but then your partner may surprise you."

Darcy rubbed his jaw as he heard her words. "Very true. It is extremely risky to make a move without considering all possibilities." Suddenly his voice changed. "I once made a move based on what I thought would prompt a particular response, having foolishly considered no other option. I was… gravely mistaken."

Elizabeth fixed her eyes on the board, unwilling to look up as she felt her head spin. *Was he speaking of me just now? Is he referring to his offer and my refusal?* What had previously been light banter about the game had evolved into something else. *Or had their conversation all along been about them?* He spoke with more gentleness than animosity, however, and she suddenly realized how confident he must have felt coming to her and expecting her to accept his suit. *Of course he would have!* How much more she comprehended now, and how much more ashamed she felt for the cruel words she lashed out at him.

"It took me quite a while to recover from that miscalculation," Darcy added, as he made his move. "It is always wise to be ready with another strategy if you find yourself faced with that situation." Elizabeth found the courage to lift her eyes to him and noticed that he was now looking at Rosalyn.

Elizabeth quickly dropped her eyes back down to the board. Her heart beat wildly as she contemplated his meaning. *Is his pursuit of Rosalyn a new strategy of his?* She felt her cheeks warm and stared down at the board absently, finally taking her turn. Her insides tightened as she considered that he had every right to turn his affection toward Rosalyn.

Darcy quickly made another move. When she did glance up at him again, his eyes were back upon her. She wanted to look away, but she could not, feeling as though his eyes were communicating something more than words could do.

"So what are you going to do next, Elizabeth?" asked Rosalyn, who was, by good fortune, looking down at the board instead of up at them.

"Well… um… that is a good question, Rosalyn," Elizabeth said, a tremble in her voice. She attempted to turn her full attention to the match, but her mind staunchly forbid her to think of anything save for the meaning of his words. She reached out and her fingers hovered over a knight. She drew it back when she saw it was shaking.

Elizabeth stared at the board a long time, her hands gripped tightly together under the table. She saw nothing but the individual pieces that were now scattered around the board. His words had so unsettled her that she could formulate no strategy in defence.

She finally moved another pawn, taking in a deep breath and letting it out slowly as she attempted to rein in her thoughts. She needed to say something to Mr. Darcy, but was unsure how to say it and whether he would even understand her meaning.

Very softly and slowly she said, "I recall a time when I, too, greatly misjudged a partner, and due to that misapprehension, I made a very grievous, thoughtless error." She quickly lifted her eyes to Darcy and then looked back down. "I have only of late come to regard my response as insulting and offensive…" She swallowed hard, as her mouth was now dry. "…and I am very remorseful for my actions."

Elizabeth's heart pounded and she could barely breathe, but she had admitted to him that she had realized how wrong she had been! Had he recognized it?

Darcy's eyes remained fixed on the board, his chin resting on his fisted hand. She saw his jaw tighten and an eyebrow lift ever so slightly. He raised his eyes slowly, his face following shortly thereafter. A slight nod of his head gave Elizabeth the impression that he understood.

"This is proving to be quite an interesting game," Hamilton spoke up; quite certain something of great import was being communicated between his cousin and Miss Bennet that had nothing to do with the game of chess. He looked over at Miss Matthews to see whether she had any expression of similar comprehension on her face. She did not.

"Watch out, Miss Bennet," Hamilton exclaimed. Both Elizabeth and Darcy turned to face him. "He is getting ready to strike the final blow!"

"You underestimate Miss Bennet, Hamilton," Darcy said softly. "I am sure she has some strategic moves planned."

This time, when Elizabeth looked down at the board, she saw it. In four moves, one of her pawns had reached Mr. Darcy's side of the board.

"Good for you!" exclaimed Hamilton. "Now we can be hopeful for at least a stalemate."

"What happened?" asked Rosalyn. "What just happened?"

Darcy looked over at her, picking up a pawn. "The pawn is the most common of all the pieces on the chess board. As you can see, there are eight of them. But occasionally, one pawn, through some exceptional merit and proficiency, makes its way across the board and then can take on the higher qualities of another piece, for instance..." his eyes turned to Elizabeth as he said, "the queen."

He slowly clasped his hands together, resting his elbows on the table. He then acknowledged her with a slight smile.

Elizabeth's head swirled with a myriad of thoughts, and feelings of hope coursed through her that this time his words were meant as a compliment to her. While she was certainly not a commoner, she was considerably lower than he.

Within two moves, Darcy took her real queen with his rook. "You have sacrificed your queen, Miss Bennet."

"Sometimes that must be done."

Within two moves, Elizabeth had trapped Darcy's king.

"It appears you have me, Miss Bennet. Congratulations."

Elizabeth could not move, wondering again at the meaning of his words. "Thank you," she said as she slowly took in a breath to calm herself. She stood up from the table, her heart pounding violently.

"You do not wish to play another? Give me another chance?" Elizabeth thought she heard a slight quaver in his voice.

"No, I fear not tonight." She did not trust herself to remain in his presence one more moment.

Rosalyn, who had been looking curiously back and forth between Elizabeth and Mr. Darcy as they conversed, felt a slight stab of envy at their friendly banter. She determined that she must learn to play this game!

"Shall we play again tomorrow night then?" he asked, looking up with an expectant glimmer in his eyes.

"I am not altogether certain," she said, feeling as though her knees might crumble at any moment. "I have plans to visit some friends of my aunt who live in Lambton and I will be staying for dinner. I fear I might be returning late."

Darcy skewed his mouth. "I see." He turned to his cousin as his fingers drummed the table. "Hamilton? Shall we go at another match?"

"Oh, no! I shall not be made a fool of again. I see that even Miss Bennet is more proficient than I. Come, Miss Mathews, allow me to teach you the game, then perhaps I might have a slight chance to win."

"I should like that very much!" she replied with enthusiasm.

Elizabeth stood up and bid everyone a good night. By now, the Goldsmiths had both returned to their room, leaving only Miss Darcy, who was reading.

Elizabeth walked over to her. "Good night, Miss Darcy."

"Miss Bennet," Georgiana said with a smile. "I do believe that my brother enjoyed his match with you. Our cousin does not play as well or as often, and when he visits, my brother does not feel as though he can play as strategically as he would like. His matches the past few nights could be described as fairly half-hearted, to say the least. Until yours tonight."

"I am quite certain he was not playing his best. I know he allowed me some moves."

"Perhaps," replied Georgiana softly, "But I know he was enjoying himself for he was smiling."

"Smiling?" Elizabeth laughed nervously and turned her eyes toward him. She saw that he had taken up a book, but had not yet opened it. His eyes were turned toward them. Looking quickly back at Miss Darcy, she said, "Good night, Miss Darcy. Have a pleasant evening."

As she walked to her room, she passed the library. She knew that sleep would not come any time soon, so she walked in, hoping to find something suitable to read. She returned to the area where earlier she had seen books of poetry. Her fingers trailed up and down the spines, reading the names of the authors until she found it. Cowper! She pulled it from the shelf and returned to her room holding the book tightly to her heart.

Chapter 14

Once in her room and dressed in her nightdress, Elizabeth settled herself comfortably in the rocking chair in the corner of the room and draped a coverlet over her lap. She picked up the large volume of Cowper's poems and opened it to the first page. She began to read, but found it difficult, for her heart still pounded and her mind still reeled from the recent events of the evening.

Looking over to the small table next to her bed, she stood up and walked over to it, opening its one small drawer. She pulled out a book, and from underneath, she picked up several pieces of folded paper. Her recent letter from Jane was on one sheet, and the letter Mr. Darcy had written to her over a year ago consisted of two sheets of paper on both sides.

She brought the two letters over to her bed, propped up the pillow and reclined against it. Carefully unfolding them, she reread Jane's letter first, going over the portion about Mr. Darcy's visit and how amiable she and the Gardiners found him. She could now read her sister's words with nary a concern for Miss Darcy's heartache, since hearing her account of what had transpired between the two. She also no longer held onto the concern that Mr. Darcy's friendship with Mr. Bingley was jeopardized by his and Jane's engagement, as he had appeared truly happy for them when he offered her his congratulations the day of the treasure hunt.

When she finished reading Jane's letter, she slowly turned to the other. She looked at the meticulous handwriting, and knowing who it was from and all that had transpired between them brought about a wave of fluttering deep within her.

Elizabeth read his letter again. She knew not how many times she had read his missive since the day he first handed it to her, but she truly believed that every reading had been done in a different state of mind. She found it rather unbelievable that she could now read his justification for separating Jane and Mr. Bingley with a modicum of understanding.

She placed the letter in her lap and lifted her eyes toward the ceiling. He had truly been looking out for his friend's best interest. Elizabeth could readily concur that Jane did not overtly display her feelings of affection for Mr. Bingley, and Mr. Darcy did not believe her to be in love with him.

She closed her eyes and clutched the letters to her heart. She had been so angry at Mr. Darcy that she had not even considered that the success he had in separating them should have reflected even more on Mr. Bingley's weakness of character than any power of persuasion he had over him.

She took in a deep breath. Well, she would give Mr. Bingley the benefit of the doubt. He trusted his friend implicitly. He trusted his judgment, his opinion, and his guidance. She had seen the respect that others had for Mr. Darcy and now understood that he was a man who earned and deserved it. Mr. Bingley had not been carelessly following the advice of someone who was foolish and thoughtless, or even unjust, as she once accused Mr. Darcy of being. She could at least credit Mr. Bingley with the good sense to put his implicit trust in someone of noble repute.

She smiled as she thought of her sister. Yes, she would allow Jane to love Mr. Bingley, despite the fact that she, herself, would find it difficult to love a man so easily swayed. While Jane had a generous and forgiving demeanour, she need not ever know all the reasons behind those months of separation, longing, and wondering.

She ran her fingers over his signature at the bottom of the second page. *Fitzwilliam Darcy.* She could not prevent a sigh from escaping.

A light tap at the door startled her out of her reverie. It slowly opened as Elizabeth quickly shoved the letters under her pillow. Rosalyn poked her head in. Hands shaking, Elizabeth quickly reached for the book of Cowper's poems and she attempted to display a calm demeanour despite the alarm she felt instead.

"Elizabeth!" Rosalyn greeted her cheerily. "I am so pleased you are still awake. May I come in?"

Elizabeth nodded, her heart still pounding.

Rosalyn came over and sat on the edge of the bed. Elizabeth glanced down at her pillow to make sure the letters were not protruding, giving them an unobserved little shove to make sure.

She leaned in to Elizabeth and said in a whisper, "Miss Darcy just informed us that she has some special plans for us tomorrow!"

"Special plans? Did she say what they were?" asked Elizabeth, feeling somewhat disappointed that she already had plans to visit the Ketterlings.

Rosalyn shook her head. "She is to tell us in the morning, but I think we are to go on a journey! Is this not the best news?"

"It ought to be very nice," Elizabeth assured her.

"This is the perfect opportunity for me. While we are out on our little excursion, I intend to make Mr. Darcy notice me and to convince Miss Darcy that she absolutely cannot abide anyone else becoming her sister in the near future!"

"Convince Miss Darcy?" Elizabeth asked, wariness colouring her features.

Rosalyn tossed her head casually and smiled a rather artful smile. "Perhaps, once we become inseparable friends, a bit of persuasion on her part to her brother will help my cause."

Elizabeth smiled weakly. "How do you intend to do this?"

Rosalyn clasped her hands in her lap and tilted her head. "I shall divide my time tomorrow between Mr. Darcy and his sister. While I am with the one or the other, I shall be gracious, attentive, and be most deferential in my words to them."

Elizabeth bit her lower lip as she listened to Rosalyn. Her brows furrowed as she considered poor Miss Darcy in the midst of Rosalyn's undivided attention, and Mr. Darcy as he endured Rosalyn's scheme to secure his affection.

"Rosalyn," Elizabeth was surprised to hear her voice, and when her friend looked toward her, she took in a deep breath. "Please remember to be your natural self. I believe Mr. Darcy can easily detect artifice. I do not believe he is a man who wants to be incessantly and carelessly flattered."

Rosalyn waved a hand at her. "Elizabeth, every man appreciates a little flattery! Besides, I have been nothing but myself here. I merely believe he needs to see another side of me."

"Perhaps," was Elizabeth's only reply. Changing the subject, she asked, "Did you learn anything tonight from Mr. Hamilton about chess?"

Rosalyn shrugged her shoulders. "Mr. Hamilton. He is a lively, friendly sort. I would be pretty much taken by him if he had at least some fortune. I wish Mr. Darcy was as witty as he was. Sometimes Mr. Darcy can be so very serious. But I cannot forget his fortune – this Pemberley." She sighed. "Oh, to be Mistress of it!"

Before leaving, Rosalyn grasped Elizabeth's two hands. "Remember to pray for me tomorrow that I will have success. Will you?"

When Rosalyn danced out of her room, Elizabeth bit her lip. She knew she could not pray for such a thing, and hoped fervently that Mr. Darcy would not succumb to Rosalyn's attentions. She no more loved him than Elizabeth had loved him at Rosings.

With much agitation, she reached under the pillow and grabbed the letters, quickly placing them back under the book in the drawer in case Rosalyn suddenly returned.

Elizabeth opened Cowper's book again. She read late into the night, delighting in his poems that were descriptive of scenery, his faith, and even his distress. Several pages seemed smudged, as if someone opened them often to read the verses on the pages over and over. She found herself studying portions that had been underlined and wondered if it had been done by Mr. Darcy himself.

Later that night, after reading many pages of poems, she slowly closed the book. She placed her hand upon it, absently stroking it, as if it were the very heart of Mr. Darcy.

~~*

The next morning when she awoke, she sat up in bed, at first wondering whether the previous evening's time spent in the sitting room had been a dream. When she had at last convinced herself it was not, she began recollecting all that had been spoken between her and Mr. Darcy.

Certainly she had not been of a rational mind to hear his words as he meant them to be understood. Having earlier that day contemplated that she might possibly love him, she certainly must have misinterpreted what was, most likely, a simple explanation of the game of chess.

She slipped the coverlet off and stood up, walking over to the window. It was grey and misty outside, certainly not the type of weather in which to go walking.

105

She sat down on the rocking chair and again picked up Cowper's book of poems. In a way she was grateful for the excuse not to go out this morning. She did not feel up to encountering Mr. Darcy. She did not wish to misinterpret more of his conversation and consequently betray her own feelings for him – if she had not already. It was scandalous for her to even consider that he might still have feelings for her. Even if he did, her current situation would prohibit any alliance between them.

After reading through several poems, she readied herself and walked across the hall to Emily's room.

She tapped on the door as she slowly opened it. "Good morning, Emily. Did you sleep well?"

"Yes," she replied, stretching out her arms. "It is a most comfortable bed. Do not tell Mama and Papa, but it is far more comfortable than my own!"

Elizabeth smiled. "Mine is most comfortable, as well." Even with all her thoughts and feelings that were stirred last night, she had barely a thought once she placed her head down upon the pillow. "Why do you suppose that is?"

Emily looked up at Elizabeth with a broad smile. "I heard Mama and Papa say that Mr. Darcy is very fast... fast... fastid..."

"Fastidious?" Elizabeth asked with a smile.

"Yes, that is what Mama said. What does that mean?"

"Well," Elizabeth thought before she answered. "To be fastidious means that you have a decided opinion about things and will not settle for anything less."

"Is that good?" Emily asked.

"It can be good if the person's opinion is reasonable and just."

"Do you think Mr. Darcy's opinion is reasonable and just?"

Elizabeth's heart stirred as she contemplated Emily's innocent question. She lifted her gaze from the girl to the window as if looking out to the hill where she and Mr. Darcy had met the other morning. "Yes," she answered slowly. "I believe it is."

~~*

At breakfast that morning, everyone arrived dressed for church. Miss Darcy announced the plans for the afternoon, once they returned from services. Everyone seemed pleased with the prospect of a carriage ride through the peaks. The early morning fog was beginning to burn away, and the hope was that by early afternoon it would be a beautiful day.

Mr. Darcy made a most agreeable declaration that he had two fairly large carriages for occasions such as this that would hold everyone comfortably. The kitchen staff was even now preparing a meal that would be sent along with them, and plans were to enjoy it at one of Georgiana's favourite lookouts, an easy ride up the peaks.

Elizabeth admitted to herself a twinge of envy as she heard their plans and for but only a short moment considered cancelling her visit with the Ketterlings. She would not disappoint her aunt, however, and quickly dismissed that idea.

Later that morning, when they arrived at Pemberley Church, Elizabeth watched as Mr. Darcy walked briskly through the churchgoers, greeting many with a simple hello and bow. Georgiana appeared to be more attentive to them, asking about their families and answering their enquiries.

Mr. Darcy seemed intent on moving past these people and getting inside. She chuckled to herself as she recalled his comment when they were at Rosings that he did not feel comfortable amongst people with whom he was not familiar. She wondered how well he truly knew his neighbours.

As they approached the doors of the church, however, he stopped abruptly. The rector greeted him with a fervent handshake and the two spoke briefly. He then turned, waiting for everyone to join him and made introductions.

Elizabeth guessed the rector to be close to fifty years old. He had a genuine smile that reached all the way to his eyes. As he acknowledged and welcomed each person, he looked intently at them, as if truly caring for them. She liked him already.

They stepped inside and Elizabeth stifled a gasp as she gazed at the beauty around her. There were three stained glass windows along each wall, and one in the front. The rays of the sun shone brilliantly through the window at the front, sending beams of coloured light throughout.

Mr. Darcy led the party to his private section off to the side at the front of the church. He and Georgiana took their seats at one end of the pew and the others then took theirs. Elizabeth glanced up, and from this vantage alone, they had the view of another stained glass. It was set deeply in the wall, so it had not been visible from the other parts of the church.

As she was admiring its beauty, Reverend Grierson began the service, welcoming everyone, especially Mr. and Miss Darcy and their esteemed guests. After singing a few hymns, Reverend Grierson began his sermon, teaching on the joy one ought to have if they put their trust in God, when life is going our way as well as when one goes through valleys in life.

As Elizabeth listened to his words, she truly believed he was speaking from experience, not merely extolling the virtues from the Scriptures. She often stole a glance at Mr. Darcy, who was seated in the row ahead of her and at the other end. She wondered whether he had a preference for sermons that prompted self-examination or induced slumber.

He seemed engaged in the sermon, unlike others who were fighting to keep their eyes open and their head upright. He sat slightly askew, leaning toward the end of the pew, his fingers slowly massaging his jaw in contemplation of the words. An occasional nod and a slight smile gave Elizabeth the impression he was truly listening, agreeing with all the reverend had to say.

After the services, they returned to Pemberley and everyone hurried to change out of their church clothes into attire more suitable for an outing. Elizabeth, choosing to remain in her nicer dress, helped Emily change and then proceeded to the sitting room to wait for the Ketterlings to arrive.

As she waited, the sound of a carriage approaching brought her to her feet and she went to the window. Instead of seeing one carriage, she watched as two huge, beautiful carriages, each emblazoned with an emblem, stopped in front. She noticed that Mr. Darcy was out there speaking to the drivers. It was apparent these were the two carriages he had spoken of earlier.

As she stood at the window, Mr. Darcy happened to look toward it, causing her to draw back quickly. She shook her head in frustration, feeling wholly like a young girl with a secret affection. She returned to her chair to wait, reminding herself that indeed, it was a secret, and she could not – would not – tell a soul.

As the others began making their way to the front, she stepped out into the hall and wished them all a pleasant day. She had a great desire to join them, but knew she could not disappoint her aunt or the Ketterlings. It was when Rosalyn approached with a cunning glint in her eye that Elizabeth truly wished she could go along.

Rosalyn grasped Elizabeth's two hands. "Do not forget to say a prayer for me today, Elizabeth." Leaning in, she gave Elizabeth's hands a squeeze, and released them. "It is a very important day!"

Elizabeth smiled weakly as Rosalyn turned and scurried off determinedly. She let out a long breath and shook her head. She almost felt more pity for Miss Darcy than she did for Mr. Darcy. He could – and would – politely excuse himself if he felt Rosalyn's presence bothersome. Miss Darcy, however, was still too young and unsure of herself. She would feel that she must endure Rosalyn's attentions if only because she was her guest and it was her duty.

Elizabeth returned to the sitting room and to the window that overlooked the front. She saw Rosalyn step out and walk toward the carriages. Mr. Darcy helped her step up into one and Rosalyn playfully tilted her head back, saying something to him with a broad smile. It appeared to her that Mr. Darcy smiled back, but shook his head in answer to her. He then stepped out of Elizabeth's view, but she was quite certain he was not riding in the same carriage as Rosalyn. That gave her a sense of satisfaction. The two carriages then proceeded to pull away and slowly made their way around the long circular drive. Elizabeth kept her eyes on them until she could see them no longer.

Placing her hand over her heart, she slowly turned and let out a long sigh. Looking up, she found herself face to face with Mr. Darcy, who was standing in the doorway!

So stunned was she to see him there, that she cried out, "Mr. Darcy! The carriages have left without you!"

"I had something I needed to attend to. I shall ride and easily catch up with them shortly." His tall frame filled the door frame and he leant casually against it. "I doubt that anyone even knows that I am not with them."

Elizabeth could not prevent the arching of a brow as she considered that most likely *one* lady observed him return to the house.

"When are your friends to arrive, Miss Bennet?" he asked, as he began to walk toward her. She felt her pulse race as he slowly narrowed the distance between them.

"They should be here shortly," she said with deliberate calmness in an attempt to veil her clamouring heart.

Darcy walked up to the window and stood next to her, gazing out. "I will wait until they have arrived to see you safely away." He shifted his weight from one foot to another.

She allowed a playful smile to permeate her face. "Do you anticipate some harm coming upon me here at Pemberley, sir?"

A sly glance up at his profile was met by a slight upturn of his mouth.

"Certainly not," he replied. "Nonetheless…"

"Mr. Darcy, truly, you have no need to do that," Elizabeth protested, turning her gaze out, as well. "It is apparent you have things to do."

"I should like to meet the Ketterlings all the same."

Elizabeth was surprised at his words; surprised that he would wish to make the acquaintance of this simple couple from Lambton. Her heart stirred at his expressed wish, but also because there was the possibility he would find them common folk and very much beneath him. Very softly she said, "I am quite certain they will be most honoured to make your acquaintance."

They stood silently for a moment, and then Mr. Darcy asked, "What did you think of the service this morning?"

Elizabeth turned to him, quite flattered that he would wish to know her opinion. "I enjoyed it immensely. Reverend Grierson gave a very inspiring sermon."

Darcy turned his face toward hers; his brow pinched, emulating the fervour of his words. "He speaks from his heart, and he knows of what he speaks. When he speaks of joy in the midst of the valleys of life, he knows it all too well. He lost his wife and only child fifteen years ago. Watching him go through that and how his faith remained steadfast spoke volumes to me."

"That is a grievous burden to bear."

Darcy exhaled forcefully. "After having a man such as Mr. Grierson as Pemberley's rector for most of my life, you can see, Miss Bennet, why I was so adamantly opposed to Wickham in his decision to go into that profession." His voice softened. "I am also grateful that Hamilton did not go into the profession for that same reason. While a good man, he often speaks without first thinking. The navy is better suited for him."

Elizabeth knew of what he spoke. Hamilton did provoke a very uncomfortable moment at the picnic with his teasing.

It was silent for a moment until Elizabeth added very softly, "And then there is Mr. Collins."

It was not a question, but he replied, shaking his head fiercely, "Yes, Mr. Collins. Unfortunately, my aunt's idea of a good clergyman is one who exalts her over the good Lord." He let out a disgusted breath. "You had every right…"

He stopped abruptly, running his hand through his hair. "Do your mother and three younger sisters remain at Longbourn?"

"No" she replied, her heart pounding as she contemplated what he was about to say. She turned to face the window and gazed out. With a somewhat shaky voice she replied, "I fear my mother despises Mr. Collins more than she loves Longbourn. They have moved in with my Aunt and Uncle Phillips in Meryton."

Mr. Darcy's voice softened and he turned and faced her. "I will say that I am glad he is no longer in the profession of clergyman, however, it does pain me the consequence of that."

Elizabeth looked up at him and whispered, "Thank you."

Their eyes locked for a moment and he studied her face, as if searching for some clue to an unanswered question.

The sound of a carriage approaching drew them both to look out the window.

"My friends are here. I must go."

"Would you allow me to walk out with you so I can make their acquaintance?"

Elizabeth nodded her head slowly, a myriad of feelings that she could not identify welling up inside of her. She was appreciative of his particular attention, even though he was under no obligation to pay such to her and she was totally undeserving of it. "It would be my pleasure."

Chapter 15

As Elizabeth and Darcy made their way out of the sitting room, she walked slightly ahead of him. For a brief moment she felt his hand press lightly against her back, guiding her along. That slight touch evoked a dizzying shiver that swept through her, and she felt her face warm with an annoying blush. It took every ounce of effort to remain poised and calm.

They came to the front hall to see that the butler had answered the bell and had invited the couple in. Upon first glance, Elizabeth was pleased to see a very nicely dressed couple. She saw their eyes sweep the hall, taking in everything around them, and their faces exhibited an appreciation for all they beheld.

When Mrs. Ketterling noticed the two approaching, including the Master of Pemberley himself, she grasped her husband's arm tightly as if requiring it to keep her upright. A stiff, nervous bow from Mr. Ketterling and an awkward curtsey from his wife were acknowledged by more formal ones given in return by Mr. Darcy and Elizabeth.

"Mr. and Mrs. Ketterling," Elizabeth said as she approached the couple. "It is such a pleasure to meet you both. I am Elizabeth Bennet."

"It is a pleasure to make your acquaintance," Mrs. Ketterling responded, stepping forward with outstretched hands. Taking Elizabeth's hands in hers, she said, "We have been so looking forward to this visit."

Elizabeth smiled and then introduced them both to Mr. Darcy.

"It is good to finally make your acquaintance, sir," Mr. Ketterling said, extending his hand out. As the men shook hands, he continued, "We have always appreciated yours and your good father's prodigious goodwill and generosity to Lambton and the neighbourhood. Your late father was a good man."

A pinched brow and a slight crease in Mr. Darcy's forehead again betrayed his discomfiture at such overt praise. "Thank you. He was a good example. I believe we both merely do what ought to be done," he replied. "It benefits all."

The couple continued to smile and heap praises upon the man quite profusely, obviously in awe of him. Elizabeth pursed her lips tightly together to keep herself from smiling at the scene, but she was quite certain at least part of her lips were curling up. She could not, however, mask the astonishment on her face at Mr. Darcy's next remark.

"Please feel at liberty to come by Pemberley any time while Miss Bennet is here. You are most welcome."

The Ketterlings' eyes widened in unison, and they seemed to be struck speechless. At length, Mr. Ketterling found his voice. "Thank you, Mr. Darcy. How very kind of you!"

Mrs. Ketterling gushed, "This is such an honour! Two of our sons work at Landerfield Manor, and I do not believe we have ever received an invitation from the Grudermans."

"You have sons?" Darcy asked, his interest suddenly piqued. "How many?"

"Three sons," Mrs. Ketterling answered proudly. "All are in their twenties."

"Are any of them still at home?" Mr. Darcy asked, a noticeable twitch seizing his mouth.

"Our eldest is married," Mrs. Ketterling said proudly. "The other two have their own quarters at Landerfield."

Elizabeth watched their exchange in wonder. He truly seemed interested in this couple, and she felt a sensation of satisfaction that he extended an invitation to them to return to Pemberley.

They walked out, and the coachman opened the door to the carriage. Darcy stepped up. "May I?" he asked, extending his hand.

Elizabeth tentatively reached out, allowing him to wrap his hand around her fingers, bringing her up to the carriage. His grip was firm and warm, and he held on a few moments longer than was needed. Elizabeth was startled by the depth of feeling this simple act of courtesy evoked. She took her seat, hoping that when the Ketterlings stepped in, the flush on her cheeks and her shortness of breath would not be noticed.

When the three were settled in, the coachman closed the door. Mr. Darcy ducked his head to look in the window. "Shall we send someone for Miss Bennet later this evening?"

Mr. Ketterling put up his hand. "No, no. We shall bring her back ourselves."

Mr. Darcy looked down toward his feet, and then back up. "And when can we expect her return?"

"We shall have her back by dusk, sir," laughed Mr. Ketterling.

"Good... good. I hope you have a very enjoyable visit." He stole a glance at Elizabeth before stepping away from the window. He then turned and walked away.

Elizabeth fought hard to hide the look of confusion that swept through her. His remarks to the Ketterlings reminded her of a father making inquiries of a young man who has designs on his daughter. She was both flattered and at the same time wondered whether he was merely looking out for one of his guests. Considering she was a guest who at one time ruthlessly refused his marriage proposal, she did not deserve such kind behaviour.

Mr. and Mrs. Ketterling's continued admiration for Mr. Darcy assured Elizabeth that they were oblivious to anything she was feeling. Fortunately for her, they soon began talking about Lambton, and how much they enjoyed living there.

She nodded absently, wishing she could tend to their words, but found her thoughts straying back to Darcy's words.

She wondered whether earlier he was going to say that she had every right to turn down Mr. Collins' proposal. *Did he know?* Inwardly she shuddered. *Of course, he did*, reasoned Elizabeth. His aunt would certainly have informed him and his cousin just how foolhardy she had been in refusing him. She could only imagine what her response would be if she was aware she had also turned down her illustrious nephew!

She turned her head abruptly to look out the window, feigning an interest in the scenery, but more so hoping to conceal from the Ketterlings the feelings of dismay she was experiencing. As she considered the two men who had both proposed and been refused by her, she reflected on how different each was from the other. *One* had been so much more worthy of her consent, in character, generosity, and goodness. Unfortunately, her words to *him* that day in refusing him had been spiteful and spoken with unforgivable vehemence.

Chiding herself for her wayward thoughts and inattention, she turned back to the Ketterlings and smiled. "It is certainly lovely here."

They rode into the small village of Lambton, and Mrs. Ketterling pointed out what had changed and what had not since hers and her aunt's childhood. She pointed out the park where they played, the store that sold the very best candy, and the assembly room, where they both attended their first ball.

They took a turn down a small winding dirt road, and after passing several small homes, the carriage stopped.

"Is this your home?" Elizabeth asked.

Mrs. Ketterling shook her head. "No, my dear. This was your aunt's home."

She smiled as she reached out for Mrs. Ketterling's hand. "This is where she grew up?"

Both Mr. and Mrs. Ketterling nodded. "Unfortunately, we only just discovered the owners are away," Mrs. Ketterling told Elizabeth. "We had so wished to inquire about a tour of the inside."

"But we can certainly walk about the grounds if you like," Mr. Ketterling offered.

"I would like that very much."

A cobblestone path made its way up to the front door. Ivy clung to the brick home, winding up and over the doorpost. It was a simple two story home, but very well kept.

"Come around here," Mrs. Ketterling said as she pointed to the back of the home. "You must see this."

They walked around the back and Elizabeth immediately heard the sound of water. She saw a bench situated out in the midst of trees, which appeared to be where they were headed. As they drew nearer, Elizabeth saw that a stream ran just beyond.

"This is lovely!" Elizabeth exclaimed. "My aunt had a stream behind her house."

"Yes," Mrs. Ketterling clasped her hands together. "And this bench is where the two of us often sat dreaming our dreams." She looked over at her husband, who had gone on down toward the water's edge.

"Truth be told, Miss Bennet," her fervent whisper was coupled with a slight giggle. "Our dreams often consisted of meeting – and marrying – someone like Mr. Darcy!"

Elizabeth drew her head back. "Mr. Darcy?"

"Well, the late Mr. Darcy, of course. So handsome and kind he was." She let out a long sigh.

Elizabeth pursed her lips together in a smile. Nodding toward Mr. Ketterling, she said, "Your husband seems very kind."

"Oh, yes, he is, as is Mr. Gardiner. I was so pleased when your aunt married him. Do you know that your uncle proposed right here on this bench?"

"Did he?" Elizabeth asked, smiling as she pictured that in her mind.

"Oh, yes, he did. While I was very happy that they were marrying, I was not too happy with him for taking her from me. We were such good friends." With a shake of her head she said, "Well, enough of that. There is much more to see."

They spent another hour riding about and walking the streets of Lambton, sometimes stopping to look into a shop window or paying a call at a friend's home. After the Ketterlings had shown Elizabeth everything she could possibly have wished to see, they made their way to their home.

It was a modest sized home with what looked like two rooms upstairs. She thought it must have been quite noisy raising a family with three boys in such small confines. But it was well kept and decorated simply, but nicely.

Elizabeth visited with Mrs. Ketterling for most of the afternoon, and later in the day, guests began arriving. Four other couples had been invited for dinner, all of whom had been a close acquaintance of her aunt.

She delighted in the stories they told about her aunt, some of the things she had done when she was young seemed so unlike her. She looked forward to the next time she saw her aunt so she could tease her mercilessly.

At one point, the subject turned to the Darcys. They were very much in awe that Elizabeth was a guest at Pemberley.

"Well, not quite a guest," she corrected them. "The family I work for as governess was invited by Mr. Darcy. It has just been fortunate that I was included."

"Oh, yes!" praised Mrs. Ketterling. "But such courtesy he extended to you, today!" She turned to the others. "He escorted Miss Bennet out when we arrived and ensured her prodigious care."

"Not something just any Master would do!" exclaimed one of the guests. "He is certainly exceptional!"

Elizabeth was tempted to inform them that they had once been acquainted, but decided against it, for she did not wish to incite any questions. She listened with interest as they began to tell stories of Mr. Darcy, his late father, and Pemberley.

There was one, in particular, that captured her notice.

"You remember the Danville picnic?"

Everyone chuckled. "Poor, young Mr. Darcy. He must have been in his early twenties, was he not?"

"Yes, we all felt sorry for the young man."

"Why did you feel sorry for him?" asked Elizabeth.

They began to relate the tale, everyone contributing what they recollected.

She was told that the Danvilles had a very nice estate about ten miles away. The young Mr. Darcy was recently home from school and he and his father and sister had been invited to the picnic. It was quite a lavish affair and the Danvilles had to hire a great deal of extra help. Several people from Lambton were hired for the occasion, a few who were dining with her that very evening.

"This was one of the first gatherings that the young Mr. Darcy attended since returning from Oxford," one of the ladies, Mrs. Stanfield, said. "He had left a young man of medium stature, rather scrawny and shy, and returned a tall, muscular, handsome young man. He turned many a ladies' head, he did."

Another added, "His father, who had begun at that time to tire easily, had gone to sit with his friends, while his son held Miss Darcy's hand to take her over to some children's games and amusements that were taking place. She could have been no more than ten years old. As he walked through the crowd, the heads were turning and the tongues were wagging about how much he was worth, how well he looked, and what a privilege it would be to be Mistress of Pemberley!"

Mrs. Ketterling looked at Elizabeth and exclaimed, "The poor young man looked as though he wanted to be anywhere but there!"

Mrs. Stanfield continued, "Before long, he found himself surrounded by an array of very fashionably dressed ladies who were doing all they could to garner his attention and seek an introduction. It was actually quite comical to see what antics these ladies would do to ensure his notice. They made fools of themselves before his very eyes."

Mrs. Ketterling finished the story. "But that was not the worst of it! In the midst of all this shameless self-promotion, Miss Darcy slipped from his fingers. He could not pull himself away quick enough, but when he did, she was nowhere in sight!

"Disappeared right from his side! Mr. Darcy searched the game of tag that was being played nearby, but she was not amongst the children. He grew quite frantic, wondering where she went. He looked about him in every direction calling her name.

"Eventually, she was found hiding in some bushes. She had been too shy to join in the children's activities on her own, and had become fearful in the midst of the overbearing ladies.

"It has been a story widely circulated in Lambton that he always very much disliked being the centre of attention likely because of that incident. And that he watched out prodigiously for his young sister.

After hearing that story, Elizabeth thought back to her first impressions of him. At the Meryton Assembly, he stood off to the side, either by a window or door, or by the fireplace. She thought with regret how tongues were wagging that night about his worth. All she saw was a man who wanted to be anywhere but there. Now she knew why!

After dinner, they gathered in the small sitting room for games. It seemed to Elizabeth that most everyone had plans to spend a good part of the evening there.

It was close to nine o'clock when the sound of rain could be heard. Everyone quickly finished the games they were playing and readied themselves to take their leave. They all expressed great appreciation in getting to know Mrs. Gardiner's niece, and hoped to see her again soon.

Once all the guests had departed, Mr. Ketterling said, "It is best we go before the roads are too muddied." They donned their coats and set out for the carriage.

Despite the rain, it was mild outside. Often the summer rains came through briefly, cooling the air only slightly. Elizabeth hoped that by morning the skies would be clear and the air freshened in the way that only a rain can do.

The ride back to Pemberley took longer than the one to Lambton. Elizabeth could readily perceive that the road was getting muddier as the carriage dipped and rocked. She hoped the Ketterlings would be all right in their journey home.

When at last they pulled up in front of Pemberley, there was only a slight mist coming down. The coachman jumped down off the front and opened the door, as a servant from Pemberley came out to escort Elizabeth into the house.

"Thank you so very much," Elizabeth said as she took their hands in hers, giving them a gentle squeeze. "I truly enjoyed myself, your hospitality, your friends, and hearing all those stories about my aunt."

"It was our pleasure," replied Mrs. Ketterling. "If you have the opportunity to come again before you leave, or if you need anything, our home is open. You are always welcome."

"Thank you. And do not forget Mr. Darcy's invitation." She smiled. "Good night." Elizabeth stepped out and hurried into the house.

As she entered, she heard sounds of laughter coming from the direction of the drawing room. Mrs. Reynolds approached her, clasping her hands together. "Good! You have returned. Did you have an enjoyable day, Miss Bennet?"

"Yes, thank you."

"Did you wish to join the others in the drawing room?"

Elizabeth pondered for a moment. "I… perhaps I ought to go check on Emily, and then I shall return to my room."

"Yes, ma'am," nodded Mrs. Reynolds. "I shall inform Mr. Darcy that you have returned."

"There is no need for that," Elizabeth protested with a warm laugh.

"Oh, but there is. As soon as it began to rain, he asked to be notified when you returned."

Mrs. Reynolds curtseyed and walked away, leaving Elizabeth to wonder whether he wished to be notified because she was merely his guest, or was it concern for her. Her heart beat loudly as she took the stairs up to her room, feeling a greater admiration for the man – whether he wished her to or not.

Chapter 16

Elizabeth was awakened in the night by the sound of a hard, driving rain lashing against the window pane. With a sigh of resignation, she realized her hopes for a sunny, rain freshened morning were doubtful. She curled up underneath the blankets, pulling them up over her shoulders, grateful for the warm and dry sanctuary that Pemberley offered.

A flash of lightning lit the room, followed a few seconds later by a deep rumbling. She swung her legs over the side of the bed and stood up, reaching for her robe. She knew that Emily would likely be awakened by the thunder, frightened as she always was by it, and she would be ready to go to her if her parents did not.

She walked over to her window and peered out, unable to distinguish anything, even when the flashes of light lit the sky. The rain was so fierce; it ran down the window in torrents. Another boom, this time louder, shook the room. Elizabeth knew immediately that she would soon hear Emily call for her, so she walked across the hall to her room, taking a quilted coverlet with her.

She opened Emily's door quietly and stepped in. She did not hear the girl stirring, so she tiptoed over to a chair and sat down, draping the coverlet over her. She leant her head back and closed her eyes, but only for a moment. With the next flash of light and deafening thunder, Emily awakened and let out a whimper.

Elizabeth immediately rose from the chair and walked over to the bed. She stroked the little girl's head. "I am here, Emily. There is nothing to fear."

"Why does it have to be so loud?" she asked as she buried her head against Elizabeth.

"It must be fairly close," Elizabeth said soothingly. "But remember, the thunder cannot hurt you."

"Gladys told me it is so loud because God is angry," she said fretfully.

Elizabeth chuckled softly. "Perhaps not angry," she assured her. "He may just be reminding us how powerful He is. If the thunder were only a whimpering rumble, we would not think Him powerful at all."

"Is it good that He is powerful?" Emily asked.

"Oh, yes," answered Elizabeth. "For then we know He can answer our prayers."

"Does He answer all our prayers?"

Elizabeth thought back to Rosalyn asking Elizabeth to pray for success in her scheme to attract Mr. Darcy's attention. Shaking her head she said, "If He does not think it best for us, He will not. We have to trust Him for His answer, whether it is what we want or not." She knew that perhaps any prayer she prayed seeking Mr. Darcy's affection may not be answered as she desired, as well.

She stayed with the young girl for the remainder the night, falling asleep on the edge of her bed as the thunder and lightening gradually diminished. The rain, however, kept up its steady deluge.

At dawn, as a muted light crept into Emily's room, Elizabeth awakened. She sat up on the edge of the bed and rubbed her shoulder, which ached due to the awkward position in which she had slept.

She walked over to the window and looked out. Just looking down at the flooded courtyard sent a shiver through her and she pulled her robe tightly about her. She doubted there would be any outdoor amusements today.

Later that morning, as they gathered for breakfast, Miss Darcy informed the party that due to all the rain, Mr. Darcy, along with his cousin, had gone out early with his steward to survey the land. She hoped they would return shortly. Her demeanour reflected a slight reticence at having the responsibility of everyone's comfort without her brother by her side and a storm outside.

Rosalyn's face displayed her great disappointment for the same reason. In watching her, Elizabeth wondered about their excursion the previous day. There had been no Rosalyn coming to her room last night or this morning to confide in her whether her hopes and expectations had been met – or dashed.

Elizabeth listened with a more than curious ear for talk about their tour the previous day; however, everyone was more apt to express concern about the rain and their hopes that it would end soon.

Elizabeth decided to spend the day with Emily going over her studies. Their time in the country had only allowed for their lessons to be sporadic

Emily had enjoyed the recent respite from memorizing the dates and reigns of the Kings of England and identifying the countries and their capitols on a map. She had hoped today would be another day of leisure without those lessons, and was disappointed when Elizabeth remained firm.

As somewhat of an enticement to Emily, it was proposed that she and the Goldsmith girls would have some of their lessons together. This produced much excitement amongst the three young girls, and they happily endured their lessons for most of the morning.

Later, Emily had her lesson in the music room playing and singing. It was apparent to Elizabeth that Emily needed a great deal more practice and she was grateful for the opportunity to refresh her skills. With the stay at Pemberley being two weeks, she felt strongly that there would be an evening of music that might allow Emily the occasion to perform. She wanted to ensure her young ward would perform adeptly.

They sat at the pianoforte practicing a duet, Elizabeth playing the more difficult lower part, and Emily the easier higher part. As they played, Miss Darcy walked in quietly and sat down.

When Elizabeth noticed her, she abruptly stopped. "Miss Darcy, you must wish to play. Emily is looking for any excuse to begin reciting her kings." She looked at Emily with a teasing smile.

"No, I heard you play and thought I would come in and listen. It sounded very nice."

"Thank you," Elizabeth said, and then turned to Emily. "What do you say, Emily?"

"Thank you, Miss Darcy," she dutifully replied.

"I shall sit here quietly and read, if it is no bother." She sat down in a chair and opened her book.

Elizabeth turned her attention back to Emily, but silently wondered why Miss Darcy would have come in here, knowing how much she enjoyed the other sitting room. She had suspected that she felt somewhat overwhelmed by the unexpected departure of her brother with all the guests looking to her for some sort of diversion. She must have given everyone leave to spend the morning at their own leisure.

At one point, Elizabeth glanced up and noticed Miss Darcy watching. She suddenly had an idea. "Miss Darcy, I understand that you are quite proficient at the pianoforte. Would you have some advice for Emily?"

Georgiana's face brightened. "I would be honoured to give her advice." She arose swiftly and walked over. Sitting down on the bench on the other side of Emily, she quietly watched her play, and then gave her a few helpful suggestions on finger placement, touch, and rhythm.

Georgiana worked with Emily for close to an hour. At length, Emily began to practice on her own while Elizabeth and Georgiana walked over to some chairs and sat down. "Miss Darcy, you have a natural gift not only of playing, but of teaching," smiled Elizabeth.

Georgiana's face lit up. "Do you really think so?"

"I do. Have you taught anyone to play before?"

A slight blush crept across Georgiana's face. "No, I merely taught Miss Willstone in the manner in which I remember learning."

Elizabeth smiled at her. "You not only give very helpful instruction, but your manner is very gentle and patient."

"Thank you," Georgiana appeared to greatly appreciate this compliment. "I think I would enjoy imparting my love for music to someone else, although it is truly something I have never really considered doing. I believe I am expected to perform, not teach. Perhaps someday, however, I will teach my own children."

Elizabeth let out an appreciative laugh. "Yes, perhaps you shall."

"You must feel a great sense of fulfilment in teaching Emily."

"It is something *I* never really considered, either, until about a year ago."

"Was that when your father died?"

Elizabeth nodded, fighting back the threat of tears. She let out a soft laugh, "But to answer your question, Miss Darcy, I do enjoy teaching Emily. I am not proficient at all things – such as drawing and painting – she will, therefore, receive instructions from masters as she gets older. I confess that I enjoy reading and learning on my own, and I can only hope that Emily will see that she, too, can take opportunities herself to continue to read and learn, even when her studies are completed."

"There you are!" The voice pierced through the room, causing Georgiana to flinch. Both ladies looked up to see Rosalyn standing in the doorway. "I have been in the sitting room waiting for you, Miss Darcy." Her eyebrows pinched in confusion. "I was hoping to talk with you."

"I am sorry," Georgiana offered. "I heard the music coming from in here and wandered in. I was not aware you were expecting me in the sitting room."

"I understood you to say you were going to spend some time in there."

Elizabeth heard Georgiana let out a very soft sigh. "I shall be there shortly." Turning to Elizabeth, she said, "I enjoyed our time in here, Miss Bennet." She then joined Rosalyn and the two walked out.

Elizabeth brought a finger up to her lips and tapped them thoughtfully as she watched them leave. She was not altogether certain, but it seemed to her that Miss Darcy did *not* wish to spend time with Rosalyn. If she knew Rosalyn as well as she had come to know her, her fervent aspirations for Mr. Darcy were such that they were causing Miss Darcy more than a little disquiet. Emily, who had stopped playing, confirmed her suspicions.

"I do not think Miss Darcy likes Rosalyn."

"Emily!" Elizabeth exclaimed. "Why would you say such a thing?"

"Because of yesterday. I could see it on her face while we were out looking at the peaks. Whenever Rosalyn came up to her, I noticed her eyebrows pinch." Emily mimicked on her own face the appearance of pinched eyebrows. She then turned back to her playing.

Elizabeth had to laugh at her imitation. "Did you see her make that face very often?"

Emily nodded. "Whenever Rosalyn was with her *or* with her brother. I noticed a definite frown when Rosalyn was out walking with Mr. Darcy."

Elizabeth smiled and patted the young girl's head as she considered how discerning little Emily was. "Was Rosalyn often with Mr. Darcy... or Miss Darcy?"

"The only time she was not with Mr. Darcy or Miss Darcy, she was with Mr. Hamilton. He frequently joined them." She stopped and looked at Elizabeth. "I think Mr. Darcy was most pleased whenever he came by."

Elizabeth shook her head as she contemplated Rosalyn's scheme. From Emily's description of the events, Rosalyn had succeeded in achieving the *exact opposite* of that which she so greatly desired.

~~*

Elizabeth returned to the music room after getting Emily settled in her room to take her afternoon nap. She brought a book to read and hoped she could remain there undetected by Rosalyn. Elizabeth let out a long sigh. She had so enjoyed Rosalyn's company when she first came to the Willstones' home in London. Yet now she had come to dread her very presence. Had Rosalyn changed? Or was it due solely to both of them having feelings for Mr. Darcy?

The sound of footsteps coming down the hall caused Elizabeth to tense. She looked up to see Mrs. Goldsmith enter. She had not really spent much time with the lady, and now actually welcomed the opportunity. She thought it might be interesting to see how an acquaintance of Mr. Darcy treated her... as a governess.

"Hello, Mrs. Goldsmith," Elizabeth said softly.

"Oh!" Mrs. Goldsmith said as she turned. "I did not see you."

"Do you play the piano?" Elizabeth asked her.

"I play a little. When Gladys and Harriet began learning, it helped me recall what little I learned when I was younger. I must confess that I had been rather neglectful of practicing through the years. I actually find now that I enjoy it more than I did when I was younger."

Elizabeth smiled. "You can play if you like. It will not disturb me. I am only reading."

Mrs. Goldsmith waved her hand in the air. "Oh, I am quite sure it will disturb you. I said I can play a little," she laughed. "But not well, at all!"

She came in and sat down next to Elizabeth. "I have always enjoyed this room," she said softly. "I often thought that by just sitting in here, my music skills would improve."

Elizabeth laughed. "How nice that would be if improvement came without all the practice!"

"Yes." Mrs. Goldsmith leaned back in the chair. Elizabeth could see in the manner she was resting that she was quite comfortable.

"How long have you been acquainted with Mr. Darcy?" Elizabeth asked.

"My husband, Benjamin, and Mr. Darcy went to Oxford together. From the moment they met, they became the closest of friends."

"Hmmm," Elizabeth replied.

"I used to be quite intimidated by him," Mrs. Goldsmith continued. "And quite resentful."

Elizabeth's eyes widened. "Truly? Of Mr. Darcy?"

Mrs. Goldsmith nodded her head. "I feared he would not think well of me. I had neither the connections nor the fortune that Benjamin's family expected, and I believed he felt the same. I resented him because my husband always sought his advice. I felt as though he had some sort of control over Benjamin."

"And now?" Elizabeth's curiosity was piqued.

Mrs. Goldsmith smiled. "Now I am indebted to him."

"Indebted?" Elizabeth's surprise was evident.

With a smile lighting up her face, she went on to explain, "Benjamin's family did indeed consider that an alliance with me would be disgraceful, foolish, and dishonourable. They could not... would not... consider that the love we had for each other was sufficient grounds for marriage."

"What about Mr. Darcy?" Elizabeth asked softly.

"Believe it or not, Miss Bennet, Mr. Darcy is a man who believes strongly in

121

a marriage based on love. He not only encouraged my Benjamin to make me an offer of marriage, but he also helped smooth things over with his family." Her eyes lit up as she said, "Needless to say, I was pleasantly surprised to discover Mr. Darcy was a very honourable man, who liberally gave very wise advice, and who also happens to believe in love." She looked at Elizabeth and laughed. "You cannot find fault with a man like that."

"No, no." Elizabeth laughed nervously.

The two talked for a length of time, eventually moving on to the subject of Mr. Bingley.

"Did you know him?" Elizabeth inquired.

"Barely. He studied quite a few years after my husband, and he and Mr. Darcy became good friends after my husband graduated."

Elizabeth then told her that he was now engaged to her sister.

"I am very happy for him," Mrs. Goldsmith said. "I know Benjamin always hoped for the opportunity to get to know him better, but our paths have simply not crossed all that often." She took Elizabeth's hand and smiled, "Perhaps with his upcoming marriage, we will find ourselves frequenting the same circles."

Just as quickly, though, her face shaded. "I only wish we could find someone suitable for Mr. Darcy. He has spent so much time making sure his friends marry for love, that he has had little time to find it himself." She let out a downhearted sigh. "I do not think…" She stopped suddenly. "We can only hope he is waiting for just the right person!"

Elizabeth enjoyed her talk with Mrs. Goldsmith; she very much enjoyed her company. But she was eager to be left alone, because of a nagging thought. There was something she needed to think more on, and she required solitude to do it. Mrs. Goldsmith finally left, and once she had the music room to herself, she thought back over their conversation. Mrs. Goldsmith had said much, but what was it that had her so unsettled?

She sat at the pianoforte and played aimlessly until it suddenly came to her. Mrs. Goldsmith said that Mr. Darcy made sure his friends married for love, and that he seemed to have had little time to find it himself. He was a man who strongly believed in marrying for love. Elizabeth knew he loved her when he first proposed. He was a man violently in love! He admitted it to her himself! But did he actually believe *her* to be in love with *him*? Would he have asked for her hand if he did not believe that?

She rubbed her hands nervously together as she thought about his comment to her as they had played chess the other evening. He said he once made a move without considering all the possibilities.

She took in a deep breath. He *had* to have believed she loved him! He not only believed she would accept him, as she had already realized, he believed she would have accepted him because she *loved* him!

~~*

Elizabeth heard later in the day that Mr. Darcy had finally returned to the

122

house. The rain had swollen some creeks and the roads were quite muddied and difficult to manoeuvre, but other than that, there was nothing of immediate concern. She heard the news from Rosalyn, who came up and found Elizabeth still in the music room waiting for Emily to wake up from her nap. She had been downstairs when the men returned.

She sat down next to Elizabeth quite perturbed. "I do not see why he has to go out in such dreadful conditions," she lamented. "Let others do that. Why must he go?"

Elizabeth raised her eyes at Rosalyn's passionate complaint. "Perhaps it is something he has always done, and his father before him."

Rosalyn shook her head. "He is Master here, Elizabeth, and can send servants to do that sort of thing. He has been gone all day!"

I know, Elizabeth thought to herself. "How was the outing yesterday?" she asked, eager to change the subject, although bracing herself for what she might hear.

A smile suddenly appeared. "It was wonderful. It is truly unfortunate you were not able to go. The peaks were magnificent, and we had the most delightful tour. Our picnic was in a beautifully situated spot overlooking the valley. As we walked around after our meal, Mr. Darcy took my arm as we had to climb a little incline." She paused to let out a breathy sigh. "I truly felt as though I were in heaven. We had such a pleasant conversation."

Elizabeth tilted her head. "What did you talk about?"

Rosalyn shrugged her shoulders and shook her head. "Oh, all kinds of things."

Elizabeth turned to her, waiting for Rosalyn to elaborate. When she did not, she said quietly, "Sounds interesting."

Rosalyn relayed to her that she had at first been disappointed that Mr. Darcy had not ridden in the carriage with her. Apparently he had something to tend to and rode his horse out to meet them. But it gave Rosalyn much pleasure as she informed Elizabeth just how fine he looked on a horse and what an excellent rider he was.

Elizabeth thought back to the one time she remembered seeing Mr. Darcy on his horse – at least up close. He and Mr. Bingley had ridden into Meryton and encountered her and her sisters just after they had met Mr. Wickham. The only thing she remembered from that incident was noticing the scowl on Mr. Darcy's face as he most rudely and unexpectedly rode off, leaving Mr. Bingley behind. She had no recollection of thinking to herself how fine he looked. She had been too prejudiced against him to notice *anything* good about him!

It caused a sharp pain deep within as she realized what all her misjudgement – of his character and behaviour – had cost her.

As her thoughts took her one direction and Rosalyn's discourse continued unabated, the Master himself stepped in, very nicely cleaned up after being out all day in the mud and rain.

They exchanged greetings and then Darcy addressed Elizabeth. "Did you go out walking today, Miss Bennet?"

She had to laugh as he had the most earnest look on his face save for a slight twinkle in his eyes. "No, sir. Unfortunately I neglected to pack a pair of mud boots, so I was quite confined to the house."

He chuckled. "It is unfortunately quite muddy out there. Did you enjoy your visit yesterday? How did you find the Ketterlings?"

"They are quite amiable and I enjoyed myself immensely." She told him of her tour of Lambton, seeing her aunt's home, and meeting some of her friends. She conveniently left out all the stories she heard about the Darcy family.

"I am glad you found them to your liking. Will you join us this evening and allow me another opportunity to redeem myself at chess?"

Elizabeth laughed. "If you wish."

He departed with a soft, "Good. I shall see you both later." Rosalyn looked at Elizabeth oddly, but said nothing. Elizabeth excused herself, telling Rosalyn she needed to go see if Emily had awakened from her nap.

Rosalyn only replied that she needed to speak with her sister.

Chapter 17

Elizabeth left Rosalyn and walked to Emily's room, her feelings whirling within her. She shook her head as she considered how much she now treasured and appreciated *any* notice Mr. Darcy paid to her. How unlike their acquaintance in Hertfordshire when she surmised that the notice he gave her was solely to find fault with her.

When Elizabeth came to Emily's room, she found her awake and quietly drawing with crayons. Elizabeth allowed her to entertain herself in this manner until it was time to prepare Emily for dinner.

When they walked down for dinner, Emily squealed with delight when she noticed her parents waiting at the bottom of the staircase. With a hearty greeting, Mr. Willstone picked up his daughter and swung her around. He then carried her toward the dining room. Elizabeth started to follow, but Mrs. Willstone put up a hand to halt her.

"If you please, Miss Bennet, I wish to have a word with you."

"Certainly," Elizabeth replied, noting the look of displeasure on Mrs. Willstone's face. "Is anything wrong?"

"Well, yes and no." She reached for Elizabeth's hand and took her aside. In a whisper, she said, "Miss Bennet, I regret having to bring up this matter, but I fear I must. There have been far too many occasions recently when you have shown a little too much familiarity with Mr. Darcy and his sister. I suggest you remember your position."

Elizabeth's eyebrows arched high at Mrs. Willstone's words. Never before had she ever referred to her as being in a lower station.

"If you recall, Mrs. Willstone, I was acquainted with Mr. Darcy before I ever took the position of governess. At the time of our acquaintance, I do believe he considered me his equal."

"Tsk. Tsk." She patted Elizabeth's hand. "Perhaps it appeared that way. You must remember who he is, my dear. Certainly you understand that he cannot afford to have associations that might tarnish the Darcy name!" She gave her a condescending smile. "I am sure you will understand when I beseech you to refrain from speaking to him… or his sister… in such a familiar manner." Her lips pursed tightly. "And we must insist that you do not come to the drawing room in the evenings ever again."

Elizabeth bit her lower lip as she fought an increasing sense of insult and personal disappointment. "Earlier, Mr. Darcy himself invited me to join the others in the drawing room this evening for another game of chess."

Mrs. Willstone shook her head abruptly. "He is only being polite to you and does not truly expect you to do such a thing. No doubt you have noticed that Miss Bartley does not come to the drawing room. She knows her place. And consider Miss Darcy. The poor girl is so very young and unsure of herself, attempting to learn her duties as Mistress. Do not tempt her with associations that are unsuitable."

Elizabeth felt her chest tighten so much that she could barely breathe. Certainly Rosalyn was instrumental in prompting this discourse. Elizabeth had readily noticed that Rosalyn had seemed somewhat perturbed during the conversation earlier between herself and Mr. Darcy. Moreover, when Rosalyn came upon Miss Darcy with Elizabeth in the music room, there were traces of jealousy in her demeanour.

A myriad of thoughts assaulted Elizabeth, especially when Mrs. Willstone gently patted her hand and continued, "We would not want Mr. Darcy to think ill of Rosalyn because of unbefitting behaviour tolerated by her family."

"You think my behaviour unbefitting?" Elizabeth asked incredulously.

Mrs. Willstone glanced briefly toward the ground in an unwitting gesture of discomfiture. "Unbefitting a governess, yes. Miss Bennet, you must know we grieve with you over your change of circumstances. It must be terribly difficult, but Mr. Darcy may be watching Rosalyn carefully for any signs of improper behaviour from her or her family..." Her eyes slowly looked up. "...or the family's governess."

Elizabeth wished to defend her actions with everything inside of her, but she knew her only defence was that Mr. Darcy had once made her an offer of marriage, and he was treating her with kindness and courtesy... much more than she ever deserved. "Yes, Mrs. Willstone," she replied softly.

Elizabeth was grateful at least, that Mrs. Willstone had not banished her from eating with the others in the dining room. She could easily have requested her to eat with Emily elsewhere. Perhaps if it were not for the presence of the Goldsmiths' governess, she would have been. She entered the dining room behind the Willstones and uttered a short and succinct greeting to Mr. and Miss Darcy, walked around to the far side of the table and took the seat next to Emily. As much as she would have liked to converse with the others, she resisted and kept her attention on Emily for the duration of the meal. She did not think she could feel the disparity between her and the others more than at this moment.

~~*

After finishing the meal, Elizabeth and Miss Bartley took the young girls to the children's nursery and allowed them to play until almost nine o'clock.

She watched Miss Bartley throughout their time with the children, admiring her ability to teach the girls in the midst of play. She gave every appearance of loving what she did and she did it well.

At length, Elizabeth turned to her. "Miss Bartley, you have been a governess for quite a long time. May I ask you a question?"

"Is there something about which you need advice? I would be more than happy to share from my years in this position."

Elizabeth breathed in deeply. "Yes, as a matter of fact, there is." She wrung her hands together as she formulated her question.

126

"Do you think… have you seen… any inappropriate behaviour on my part… in regards to Mr. Darcy or his sister?"

"Heavens, no!" she exclaimed. "What has brought this on?"

"I was informed that I have spoken with too much familiarity to them. It began, I believe, when I took Emily into the drawing room one evening to say goodnight. I soon found myself in a chess match with Mr. Darcy."

Miss Bartley's eyes widened. "Truly?" Her eyes crinkled as she leaned in. "Who won?"

Elizabeth laughed. "Needless to say, I have been strongly warned."

Miss Bartley narrowed her eyes. "It is an unfortunate position we are in, Miss Bennet. Oftentimes the servants will look down on us for being their superior, and those in upper classes look down on us as being their inferior." She looked at Elizabeth with understanding eyes. "It is an even greater misfortune when you once had the standing of society."

"I suppose it is something I have had a difficult time getting used to."

"May I say, Miss Bennet, that a governess must behave cautiously, for there have been far too many a naïve young lady who has gone into a household as governess, and allowed herself to be disgraced due to the prodigious attentions of a master."

"I hardly think Mr. Darcy would…"

Miss Bartley shook her head in denial. "No, I have never heard anything even remotely improper concerning the man. The Goldsmiths have been close acquaintances with him as long as I have been with them and they always speak of him in the highest regard."

Elizabeth remained thoughtfully silent.

"I understand you knew him before…"

Elizabeth looked up with an arched brow. A wry smile appeared. "Yes, but I fear our acquaintance was a rather contrary one. I believed him to be rather proud and unfriendly. I was not afraid to let him know how affronted I was by some of his behaviour… which, I now comprehend, was due more to reserve than pride."

"Oh, the lessons we sometimes learn too late."

"Far too late," Elizabeth added softly.

~~*

The rains persisted throughout the night, occasionally interspersed with a flash of lightning and boom of distant thunder. Sleep came sparingly for Elizabeth as her turbulent thoughts vied with the fierce rain to keep her from the sleep she so desired.

She found herself wondering what took place in the drawing room that evening. What conversations took place? What did Mr. Darcy talk about… and with whom did he speak? Did he even notice her absence?

The downpour also brought to her recollections of occasions at Longbourn when the rains pelted the roof so violently that it eventually worked its way in. Mary was the unfortunate one who needed to sleep with buckets on the floor in her room to catch the water until the roof could be repaired. Other times there were leaks in the kitchen and sitting room. While she felt safe and secure within the walls of Pemberley, her heart still ached for Longbourn and the life she had there.

That morning, after having slept very little, she awoke to the increasingly familiar sound of rain hitting the windows. She and Emily dressed and went downstairs. As they entered the dining room, Mr. Darcy greeted them; a raised eyebrow to Elizabeth the only indication that he may have wondered why she did not join them in the drawing room the night before.

During the meal, as everyone enjoyed the bountiful repast, there was much talk about the rains. Several commented on the growing rivulets of water they noticed cascading down the incline away from the house. Small ravines in the landscape were now pooled with water, creeks were now rivers, and the lake in front was continually increasing in length and width.

Elizabeth could see the strain of uncertainty on Miss Darcy's face as she was again faced with another day of entertaining everyone indoors. The men, who had hoped to spend the morning fishing, agreed that conditions were just not suitable.

As they were finishing up the meal, Mr. Darcy's steward, Mr. Barstow, came in and whispered something to him. He immediately stood up; his eyes narrowed in concern. He turned to his guests at the table, begging to be excused for a moment. He followed Mr. Barstow, walking out in haste.

Everyone turned to each other, wondering what may have occurred. Without bothering to make his own conjecture or ask to be excused, Mr. Hamilton promptly stood up and followed his cousin. Miss Darcy watched him leave and then looked back at her guests, uncertainty etched on her face. Mr. Goldsmith stood up and was also soon out of the room.

No one seemed to notice Miss Darcy's distress save Elizabeth, who finally said to the young girl, "Miss Darcy we will understand if you wish to join your brother."

A small smile appeared. "Thank you, Miss Bennet. I believe I shall." She looked to the others. "Please excuse me."

For several minutes they could hear hushed, but intense voices outside in the hall. At length, they returned.

Miss Darcy and Mr. Goldsmith took their seats while her brother and cousin remained standing. Miss Darcy looked noticeably troubled and the three men sombre. Everyone waited to hear what Mr. Darcy had to say.

"With all the rains we have had, in addition to heavier rains up north, the rivers have swollen considerably and are now overflowing their banks, threatening some of my tenants' homes. Those who were able to leave have fled and are taking refuge with family members or at inns in neighbouring villages.

128

Unfortunately, a few of my tenants are stranded; a bridge which crossed the river is now submerged. Several have attempted to cross it, but travel is treacherous. It is even thought that someone may have been swept away in the waters and there are people searching for him. These families are unable to make it safely anywhere... but here."

Elizabeth noticed several eyebrows rise at this announcement. "Hamilton, Goldsmith, and I will be setting out shortly with my steward to facilitate their move to Pemberley, while Georgiana works with the staff to prepare for them."

"You are to bring your tenants here?" asked Rosalyn in disbelief.

Darcy slowly turned to her, taking in a deep breath before answering. "Yes, there is no other alternative. It is only until the rains cease and the threat of flooding is over."

"But surely there is something else that can be done," Mrs. Willstone lamented. "These are merely common folk, are they not? Can you trust them walking these halls?" She gave a nervous laugh.

Mr. Darcy's jaw tightened and he spoke with more than a little agitation. "These are my tenants, Mrs. Willstone, and I cannot and will not allow them to risk their lives because I fear some menace from them. They will be in the north wing and you will likely not even see them. There is no reason for concern."

He reached down and picked up his cup, quickly downing its contents. "We will likely be gone for most of the day. As my sister will be otherwise occupied assisting Mrs. Reynolds and the servants in readying the wing and welcoming these guests, I invite you to spend today at your leisure. You may enjoy everything that Pemberley has to offer."

He looked down at his sister. "You will do fine, Georgie," he said reassuringly. "Mrs. Reynolds has done this on more than one occasion." He turned to his friend and cousin. "Come. There is much to do before we leave."

Everyone slowly rose from the table and the three men briskly stepped from the room. Miss Darcy left immediately to find Mrs. Reynolds. The Willstones and Rosalyn huddled together, conversing in hushed tones about this unfortunate arrangement. Elizabeth and Miss Bartley decided that for the duration of the morning, they would allow the three girls to play together.

Once in the playroom, Emily and her friends cheerfully found all kinds of amusements with which to entertain themselves. Elizabeth inquired of Miss Bartley if she would mind keeping watch on Emily while she retrieved something from her room. Elizabeth wanted to get the book of Cowper's poems and do some further reading. Miss Bartley told her she would gladly watch Emily as long as she needed.

When Elizabeth walked out, she heard voices coming from the entry hall. She stopped suddenly when she recognized Rosalyn's agonized voice.

"Mr. Darcy, you said yourself that travel is treacherous. Heavens! Someone has been swept away already and is likely killed! It is far too great a risk going yourself! You are Master of this place and surely have more than enough servants who ought to be the ones to take care of something like this."

"I appreciate your concern, Miss Mathews, but it is I who must go."

"But sir, there is flooding everywhere." An encouraging smile appeared. "Your tenants will be just as grateful and appreciative if you send someone else; you could easily send several servants to give them the assistance they require."

Elizabeth quietly stepped into the hall. Darcy looked up at her, exasperation and exhaustion etched in his features.

Looking back down to Rosalyn, he said, "While that may be true, my presence will speak more to them of my concern and give them more reassurance than any of my servants would give."

"But certainly…"

Elizabeth came alongside her and gently placed her hand on Miss Mathews' arm, giving it a soft squeeze. "We understand your concern for your tenants. Please be careful out there, Mr. Darcy."

His eyes met hers and he let out a soft sigh. "Thank you, Miss Bennet. I shall make every endeavour to keep life and limb – my own and those of my tenants – safe." With a quick bow, he quickly turned to the door and stepped out.

Rosalyn let out a soft huff, but before she could express her frustration to Elizabeth, Mr. Darcy's cousin and friend approached. Noticing the two young ladies, Mr. Hamilton looked at them with a playful smile. "Has old man Noah come this way, yet?"

Rosalyn narrowed her eyes at him. "Who?"

Elizabeth chuckled. "He means Mr. Darcy, I believe, who is going to lead his tenants two by two into the ark – Pemberley – to save them from the flood!"

Mr. Hamilton acknowledged her with a nod of his head. "You know your Bible stories, Miss Bennet."

"Yes," she replied. "Noah – Mr. Darcy just stepped out."

With the briefest of bows, the two men then left.

"I know the story of Noah's Ark," Rosalyn protested, her arms folded tightly in front of her. "I just did not know what he was talking about."

Elizabeth smiled. "Mr. Hamilton is one who enjoys making light of even a difficult situation."

"Whereas Mr. Darcy can be so very serious." Rosalyn let out a mournful sigh. "And so very stubborn!"

"About certain things I am sure he is."

"I do not understand what is taking him so long to give me assurances of his affection. He has certainly had sufficient opportunity. Goodness, we only have two weeks here. What is he waiting for? Certainly he cannot doubt my regard for him and my devotion to his sister."

"Roslyn, he is his own master as well as Pemberley's Master. If that is his design, he will do it in his own time."

"Well, I am getting quite impatient with the man."

Elizabeth suddenly had an image in her mind of Caroline Bingley and wondered if this was what always happened to a woman who pursued a man like Mr. Darcy. She could only hope it would not happen to her!

The two ladies each went their own separate ways. Elizabeth retrieved her book of Cowper's poems, bringing it back to the playroom. She looked forward to reading more of this great poet's verse.

Throughout the morning, Elizabeth stepped out from the playroom and looked down the hall. They were just down from the north wing, where the tenants were going to be housed. On several occasions she saw servants going through the large door that cordoned off that wing, carrying linens and supplies for the tenants who would be coming.

Elizabeth wondered how Miss Darcy was faring in the midst of this. On one of those occasions when she stepped out, she encountered the young girl herself, dissolved in a pool of tears.

"Miss Darcy!" Elizabeth rushed over to her and put her arm about her. "What has happened? What is wrong?"

Miss Darcy shook her head, unable to say anything.

"May I help you with something?" Elizabeth asked.

Miss Darcy took several deep breaths and finally, in a whimpering voice said, "I am trying to do my best, and I am making every attempt to like her for my brother's sake, but she is questioning everything I do."

"Who is?" asked Elizabeth.

Miss Darcy wiped her eyes. "I know she is only trying to help me, but I think I know what is best!"

Elizabeth shook her head in confusion. "Are you speaking of Mrs. Willstone?"

Miss Darcy waved her hand in the air. "No, no. It is Miss Matthews. I just came from the sitting room upstairs, telling her all that I… we… have done." A look of pained distress filled her eyes. "I am sorry. I should not have said anything."

Elizabeth closed her eyes in compassion at what the young girl must have experienced. Not only had Rosalyn challenged Mr. Darcy's decision to go himself to assist his tenants, she now had distressed his sister. "Miss Darcy, you know Pemberley and you know your tenants. Miss Matthews may be trying to be of assistance, but you must do what *you* believe is right."

After a few shaky breaths, Miss Darcy said, "I confess that I have a difficult time saying *no* to people. When Miss Matthews tells me what she thinks I ought to do, even though I know it is not right, I still cannot say *no* to her."

"Perhaps," Elizabeth gently suggested, "you can merely thank Miss Matthews for any advice she offers and tell her that you will consider it. Then, you may proceed in any manner you deem best. That way you do not have to actually say *no* to her."

Miss Darcy looked up at Elizabeth and said very softly, "That is very sound advice. Perhaps I will try it." She wiped her eyes with her handkerchief. "Many

131

times I feel as though I will hurt someone's feelings if I say no. I once found myself in a very… perilous situation because I could not say *no*."

Elizabeth's heart lurched in understanding, more than the young girl could even comprehend. She knew Miss Darcy likely was referring to the time she came so very close to eloping with George Wickham.

Elizabeth wrapped an arm about Miss Darcy's shoulders with tender affection. "We all learn from our mistakes, do we not? And hopefully our weaknesses will develop into positive strengths."

That prompted an appreciative smile from Miss Darcy.

"Is there anything I can do to help?" Elizabeth asked. She then laughed as she added, "And I promise not to give you any unwanted advice."

"You are very kind, Miss Bennet. I know that Mrs. Reynolds is working with our staff to address their physical needs, but many of these tenants are emotionally weary. Mrs. Goldsmith is down there now, but would you…"

She paused and nervously fingered the handkerchief she held, casting her eyes down. She then looked up and continued, "Would you be able to visit with some of our tenants later this afternoon?"

Elizabeth smiled. "I would be most happy to. I will come down when Emily naps later today."

"Thank you. I think you would be a good listener," Miss Darcy replied.

"I will do what I can," Elizabeth assured her.

Elizabeth began to walk away, but she stopped and turned to the girl. "To own the truth, Miss Darcy, I suffer from something very similar to what you have shared with me, although it is actually quite the opposite. You see, I have a tendency to say *no* to people far too readily, even when a *yes* would have been much more sensible and in my best interest." With a smile she added, "Perhaps we can learn from the other and find the perfect balance!"

Miss Darcy smiled. "I think I would like that very much."

Chapter 18

Later, Elizabeth and Emily went upstairs to the music room to allow the young girl some practice. Emily sat down at the pianoforte and Elizabeth pulled out the easy pieces of music that the young girl had been working on.

As Emily played, Elizabeth thought back to her conversation with Miss Darcy. In addition to all Miss Darcy shared about her difficulties with Rosalyn – her struggle saying *no* to people and her warm acceptance of Elizabeth's offer to be of assistance – Elizabeth also pondered Miss Darcy's statement that she was making every attempt to like Miss Matthews for her brother's sake. That meant that Miss Darcy was still under the impression that her brother had feelings of affection for Rosalyn. Elizabeth wondered whether it was founded on something more than just conjecture.

After a suitable length of time at practicing both the pianoforte and singing, Emily was ready for rest. Elizabeth took her to her room and then returned downstairs, going straight to the north wing. She opened one of the large double doors that separated it from the rest of the house and walked through.

As she walked down the hall, she followed the sound of the voices which brought her to a sitting room. It appeared this had become the gathering place for those who wished to visit with one another. Several children were scattered about reading or colouring or playing with a toy they brought along. There were several ladies and an older gentleman. Elizabeth surmised that all the able men were out trying to protect their homes from the rising waters. Everyone seemed to be acquainted, and from Elizabeth's viewpoint, they seemed fairly content in their circumstances. Who would not in a place such as this?

The sound of a child crying drew Elizabeth's attention, and she walked farther down the hall. She came to a large dining room and looked in, noticing a little girl at the window looking out.

Servants bustled in and out, readying the room for the evening meal. They scurried around the girl, occasionally patting her on the head or whispering something to her. The girl kept gazing out, her little fingers pressed against the pane. A few sniffles and short gasps accompanied her soft cries. Looking about the room, Elizabeth saw no one else there who would be her family, so she walked up to her.

"Hello, there. You are not very happy, are you?"

The little girl shook her head, keeping her eyes to the window. Elizabeth looked out with her to the courtyard.

"What is your name?"

The girl muttered a very soft, "Rachel."

"That is a very nice name," Elizabeth replied. "Is your family here?"

The girl nodded. "Mamma is feeding the baby, and Pappa is out there somewhere."

"It can be a little frightening when things like this happen. You have nothing to worry about. I am very certain your father will return shortly." Elizabeth stooped down so she could talk more easily with her. "I have been here all week and have been fed the most delicious food and have been very well taken care of. I am sure you will be, too."

Elizabeth placed her finger under Rachel's chin and turned her face to look at her. "Can I see a little smile?"

Rachel responded with sniffling and a fervent shaking of her head. "Misty is missing and I know she will drown!"

Elizabeth leaned in to her, concern gripping her. "Who is Misty?"

"My kitty. Misty cannot swim and will drown."

Elizabeth pursed her lips together and then asked, "Is Misty very special to you?"

With a nod, Rachel turned her eyes back out the window. "I wish we could have found her before we left. Mamma said we didn't have time to look for her."

"I would guess that if your father finds her, he will bring her back directly."

Tears filled Rachel's eyes as she said weakly, "He said Mr. Darcy would not allow us to bring a cat with us here."

Elizabeth's heart ached for the little girl. Of course he would likely have set down rules for their coming and staying at Pemberley. She turned her eyes out the window, knowing that there was little chance of Misty being found. She let out a quick breath. The men were most likely busy with other more important things.

She decided to let Rachel talk about her cat. "Rachel, tell me, what does Misty look like? What colour is she?"

"Grey," Rachel answered. "With just a little white above her nose." Her finger touched her nose as she said this.

"She must be very pretty."

Rachel nodded. They were silent for a few moments and then Rachel whispered, "And sweet."

Elizabeth smiled. "I imagine you know just how to make her purr."

Rachel turned and looked at Elizabeth. Her lower lip trembled as she said, "She likes to have the top of her head scratched."

Elizabeth reached out and took her hand. "You know, I saw some other children playing down the hall. Sometimes it helps me to think about other things when I am afraid or worried. I would guess that if you joined them, you would feel better directly."

Rachel quickly turned back to look again out the window. "But I would not want to miss Pappa in case he finds Misty."

"Why do you not go and play with your friends and I will come and get you as soon as he returns."

Rachel turned as if to do as Elizabeth suggested, but then stopped. Elizabeth gave her an encouraging nod. "I will let you know if Misty… or your father… returns."

Elizabeth guided Rachel to the door and then watched as she slowly walked away. One of the maids, who had been preparing the dining room, spoke up. "You sure have a way with the young 'uns. We tried everything to console her. She is terribly worried about her cat!"

Elizabeth smiled and began to walk back to the sitting room. When she came to the door, she peeked in. Rachel was sitting next to another young girl about her age and they were talking. She seemed distracted, at least for now. Chances were, however, that she would worry about her cat as long as they were here.

Elizabeth walked down the length of the hall, to see if there was anyone else who looked like they needed someone to talk to. There was no one in the hallway, and as most of the doors were closed, she did not feel that she should disturb the occupants. She reached the end of the hallway and was just about to turn around when the doors to the courtyard burst open. She stepped back quickly as a tall figure, drenched from the rain, strode in.

The man was looking down, holding his coat tightly about him, a cape covering his head. He glanced up just as he was about to collide into Elizabeth. "Miss Bennet!"

Elizabeth could not prevent a laugh from escaping as she found herself looking into Mr. Darcy's dark eyes. "Mr. Darcy?"

He pulled the cape down with one hand, keeping his other secured across the front of his coat. Water ran down his face and dripped from his hair. "How is everyone faring?" he asked.

"I have only just arrived, but I believe Mrs. Reynolds and the servants have everyone well settled."

At that moment, a sound came from underneath Mr. Darcy's coat.

"Why, Mr. Darcy!" Elizabeth laughed as she looked up at him with wide eyes. "I do believe your coat just meowed!"

The look of fatigue and concern melted into a smile. "And because of that, I need a little help," he said as he struggled to unbutton his coat with his free hand. As his coat fell open, Elizabeth saw that he held a cat, wrapped snugly in a scarf so she would not scratch him. The poor thing was frantically trying to wiggle out. "There is a little girl here, a Miss Weber…"

Without thinking, Elizabeth gently reached in to pet the cat's head. "Hello, Misty. Be still now, will you?" She looked up and smiled. "I spoke with little Rachel and she told me about Misty." She reached in and wrapped her hands around the cat, becoming suddenly mindful of what she was doing. Her cheeks warmed in a blush. For a brief moment she lost all ability to think what she ought to do, and allowed her hands to linger in the warmth of his chest.

A sharp intake of breath drew her eyes up to Mr. Darcy's face. Dark eyes and lowered brows met her.

She had to will her hands to leave their place of sanctuary in order to retrieve the cat. To disguise the feelings that his presence stirred within her, she looked back at the cat and asked with a nervous laugh, "Are you Misty? I certainly hope so!"

She could only see the cat's face, but readily saw that she was grey with a little white around his nose.

Casting her eyes down as she felt a blush stain her cheeks, she told him, "Rachel has been terribly worried."

"Well, this better be Misty," Darcy answered in a somewhat stilted voice. "Otherwise I climbed that tree for nothing!"

"You climbed a tree?" she asked incredulously, looking back up and meeting a contented grin. She was grateful that the awkward moment had passed. "Certainly you did no such thing!"

"I most certainly did! That girl practically refused to leave until we found the cat. The waters were rapidly approaching her house and they could delay no longer. After they departed, I was trying to keep my horse to higher, dry ground, and heard a meow. It was coming from a tree down an embankment whose base was about five inches in water. The poor thing would have been stranded until the waters receded. If she tried to come down, she would surely have drowned. So I jumped off my horse and climbed up to get her. I think she was more than anxious to get down, but in order to bring her back here, it was necessary for me to wrap her up securely in a scarf so she would not scratch me." He reached over and scratched the cat's head. "For reasons beyond my comprehension, she did not like being stuffed under my coat!"

Elizabeth tilted her head and laughed, not sure whether to believe him. It was so unlike what she would have expected from Mr. Darcy, yet his face revealed genuine sincerity.

He gave her a hopeful smile. "I certainly hope this is Misty."

Elizabeth was able to reassure him. "Rachel told me she is a grey cat with a white nose, just like this one. I do believe, Mr. Darcy, that you shall be her hero." She brought her hand up again to scratch the cat's forehead. Misty soon began purring. "Do you mind if I take her to Rachel? I promised her I would."

"Certainly, but do not let Mrs. Reynolds see you with it. She is terribly allergic and thinks it is an offence to even entertain the thought of keeping an animal in the house. Make sure Miss Weber keeps the cat locked in her room. I do not want it roaming the halls. I will see to it that they get what they need for the cat." He spoke with resolute brusqueness.

"Yes, sir," Elizabeth said. "Is there anything else?"

Darcy closed his eyes and shook his head. "Pray forgive me, Miss Bennet. I have been barking orders all morning to ensure a smooth transition. I did not mean to…"

"You have no need to apologize, sir. You have done so much."

She turned to leave, but Mr. Darcy called to her. "A moment, Miss Bennet. There is something else, if you would bear with me."

"Yes?"

His eyes darkened. "You did not come to the drawing room last night."

Elizabeth bit her lip as she determined what to say. "No, sir. I was unable to."

"Why?" His question was uttered with the same fervency as his earlier demands had been.

Elizabeth swallowed to moisten her mouth. She could not bring herself to look up at him. "I cannot say."

His brows lowered at this. "You will be there tonight?"

Elizabeth cast her eyes down, shaking her head slowly. "I am sorry, sir, but I cannot."

She heard him take several breaths. "Tell me why."

She looked up into pleading eyes. "I am... I am the Willstones' governess. They do not deem it proper." She saw his lips press tightly together and his jaw clench.

After a moment he said, "You are my guest and I have invited you to join us in the drawing room."

Elizabeth smiled, more out of unease than pleasure. "I beg to differ, sir. I am not your guest. The Willstones and Miss Matthews are your guests. I am employed as a governess to the Willstones' daughter and therefore I answer to them and their wishes."

Her quick curtsey was met with a scowl. Elizabeth turned to find Rachel and return her cat to her, her heart wishing fervently that her circumstances were different.

~~*

The rains continued for the remainder of the day and night, letting up only intermittently. The next day was spent as the others had been, allowing Emily time with the Goldsmith girls and then Elizabeth working with her on her studies and music.

Throughout the day, however, a fluttering deep within intruded as Elizabeth pondered whether she would see Mr. Darcy in the north wing when she went down again today. The Willstones may have forbidden her to join the others in the drawing room in the evening, but as they were not inclined to associate with Pemberley's tenants, she felt this was the one place she could encounter Mr. Darcy and not risk anyone's censure if she conversed with him. But would he be there?

At length while Emily napped, Elizabeth went down to the north wing and walked in to find very few people about. She greeted some that were in the sitting room, asking how they were faring. She looked for Rachel, but did not see her. She smiled as she assumed she was inside their room playing with her cat.

She spoke with a few more people, and upon discerning that there was nothing else she could do, reluctantly decided to leave. She saw neither Georgiana nor Mrs. Reynolds, but her greatest disappointment was that Mr. Darcy did not stop in.

She walked through the doors that took her to the main house and heard a commotion coming from the far end of the south hall. As she walked closer, she saw two men walk into the infirmary. Mr. Darcy walked toward her with a rather harried look upon his face. He stopped, breathing heavily from exertion.

"Mr. Darcy, is something wrong?" Elizabeth asked.

He placed his two hands firmly on her shoulders. Looking at her intently, he asked, "Do you faint at the sight of blood?"

She did not interpret his gesture as a sign of affection or his feelings. From the intense look on his face, she deemed it more a response to something that had happened. "I never have before," she answered. "What is it?"

"Come with me," he said, releasing her shoulders, but grasping one of her hands firmly in his as he turned toward the infirmary. She had no option but to follow.

As they walked down the hall, his strides were long and hurried. To keep up with him, Elizabeth took several steps to his one. "What happened?" she asked again.

At the sound of her voice, he seemed to relax slightly, his grip loosening and his stride slowing. Turning his head, he answered, "There has been an accident."

When they came to the infirmary door, he stopped. He glanced down at her hand and she thought he gave it a gentle squeeze, but kept it firmly in his. "Mr. Hamilton has been injured."

Her eyes widened in concern, but she found it difficult to tend to his words when she was aware solely of her hand enveloped in his. "Is it... serious?"

Mr. Darcy smiled. "He will survive. His arm and shoulder were cut by some rocks. It is messy. I have sent for a doctor, but I can use your help until he arrives." His eyes searched hers as he waited for an answer.

"I will do what I can."

"I know you will." He paused and pressed his lips tightly together before continuing. "Miss Bennet, I do not want word of this spreading. There is already *enough* concern about our being out there."

"I understand." Elizabeth felt a strong reference to Rosalyn in his admonition. Her fears had come to fruition, although it had not been Mr. Darcy who injured himself, but Mr. Hamilton.

"Good." He took in a deep breath. "Please do not think ill of me for asking you to help me with this. Many of our maidservants would not do well with this type of injury. In addition to having much more to do in caring for the tenants, I did not wish to impose on them, Mrs. Reynolds, or my sister."

"I do not mind."

He nodded slowly as he looked down briefly at their hands before finally releasing hers. He exhaled slowly. She felt he was going to say something and waited, looking at his face expectantly. She saw conflict in his face as he furrowed his brow and clenched his jaw. Finally, he said, "Then let us go in."

They waited no longer and entered the room. Mr. Hamilton was lying on the bed; a servant Elizabeth recognized from around Pemberley was pressing tightly

138

against a cloth that extended from his upper arm to his shoulder. The servant nodded at Darcy and Elizabeth.

Hamilton peered up at them, grimacing at the movement, but it was quickly replaced by a smile. "Miss Bennet, have you come to nurse me back to health?"

Elizabeth walked over to him, glancing briefly at his blood-stained shirt. "I assume this was not another struggle with a fish!"

Hamilton laughed. "Unfortunately it was another rock!"

Elizabeth turned to Darcy. "What shall I do?"

He pointed to some clean, dry cloths and a basin of water. "I will need you to clean the wound. Mr. Peyton, here, is applying pressure to help stop the flow."

As she walked over to soak some cloths, she asked what happened.

"I was probably taking my horse too quickly down an embankment and he tumbled, throwing me against some rocks."

"Probably?" Darcy said incredulously. "You *definitely* were taking your horse too quickly down a mud-filled, water-laden, unstable hillside."

"How did the horse fare?" Elizabeth asked with a smile.

"Better than me!" Hamilton said. He turned to his cousin. "I am grateful you are here, Miss Bennet, for Darcy shows me no sympathy."

Elizabeth returned with the cloths, lifting an eyebrow to Mr. Hamilton at his comment. The servant let up pressure to allow Elizabeth the ability to cleanse the area around the gash. When he did, an excessive flow of blood poured out, causing Elizabeth to sway unsteadily. Her head began to spin when strong hands suddenly gripped her shoulders… again.

"Miss Bennet?"

"I am sorry, Mr. Darcy," she said as she took in some deep breaths. "I did not expect it to be so…"

His face was close to hers, his eyes searching. "Pray forgive me, Miss Bennet. I should not have put you through this."

Elizabeth waved her hand in the air. "No, no, I am well. Now."

She took in another deep breath as she turned back to the wound and began to clean it. Her heart pounded so violently she wondered whether Mr. Darcy could hear it. He released her shoulders and walked over to a cupboard. As she saw the extent of the wound, she imagined that the doctor would be required to suture it to keep it closed.

Darcy brought over a bottle and held it over the wound. She looked up questioningly. "Alcohol," he said. "If you can wash away more of the blood, I will then pour this over the wound."

They worked together well, Elizabeth savouring the close, caring presence of Mr. Darcy. While his cousin teased about how *un*caring Darcy was, she knew that indeed he was caring and that his cousin truly appreciated him. Darcy often looked up at Elizabeth, and in quiet admiration nodded his thanks.

When she inquired about the condition of the tenants' homes, they told her that one home was in imminent danger of being flooded, but the men had been working tenaciously to divert the waters by digging trenches and building up barricades with mud and trees, which they hoped would hold as the waters approached. She also found out that the man who they presumed had been swept away was found unharmed.

When the doctor finally arrived, he ordered everyone out of the room except, of course, Mr. Hamilton and Mr. Darcy. Elizabeth walked to the door and just as she was about to step out, she heard the familiar sound of Mr. Darcy's voice call out her name.

"Miss Bennet," he said, softly.

She turned toward him. "Yes?"

"Thank you," he told her. "I could not have done it without you."

She smiled in acknowledgement of his words and walked out. For the first time since arriving here, she thought their day of departure would come too quickly.

Chapter 19

It had been two days since the families sought refuge at Pemberley, and the rains finally let up; the sun making a most welcomed appearance. Everyone was delighted that the prospect of returning home was near, but they would need to wait until the waters of the river receded a great deal before it was deemed safe enough.

Mr. Hamilton remained in his room healing nicely from his wounds. Everyone had been told he was merely not feeling well, but it was expected that he would be recovered soon. As Mr. Darcy had first relayed this news at the breakfast table the day following the accident, he stole a knowing glance at Elizabeth. She returned a sly smile at his pretence of an excuse for his cousin's absence.

That afternoon, as the sun poured its rays through the windows, Elizabeth felt a gaiety and a joy that she had not felt in quite a few days. Each time she passed a window, she gazed out, feeling the warmth of the sun on her face, and eagerly anticipated exploring Pemberley's magnificent grounds. They had less than a week remaining, and while she knew practically every inch of Pemberley's house, save for one very private hall, she still wished to explore the splendid grounds.

That day while Emily napped, Elizabeth made her daily visit to the families in the north wing. As she opened the doors to the wing, she stepped through and found everyone hustling about. There was much excitement.

It was joyous confusion, and someone mentioned to her that they had just received word they would likely be able to return to their homes tomorrow afternoon. Before she could even utter a word expressing her delight, she heard a shriek, and the sound of little footsteps racing down the hall captured Elizabeth's attention.

It was Rachel, and just as the little girl was about to collide into her, Elizabeth reached down and lovingly grasped her shoulders. "What is it, little one?" she asked.

"Look out!" she squealed. "There goes Misty!"

Elizabeth turned around abruptly, seeing the grey cat slither out the door through which she just entered. "Wait here, Rachel. I will go after her!"

Elizabeth stepped out the door and closed it behind her before moving into the hall. She turned, hoping to see where the cat went. She looked across the hall that led to the playroom and saw nothing. She turned her eyes down the main hall to her left. She caught a brief glimpse of Misty just as she scampered around the far corner. Elizabeth walked as quickly as she could, calling the cat's name. When she came to the corner, she turned and again looked around. Her heart pounded as she considered that the cat may have gone into any room, which would certainly cause more than a little disruption.

A slight movement caught her attention, and she looked up to see Misty going up the stairs. "Oh, no!" Elizabeth said softly and let out a frustrated sigh. She saw no one to ask for help, so she kept following the cat, calling her name softly.

"Misty, here kitty, here kitty!" The cat stopped at the top of the stairs and looked down as if to see whether she was still being followed. Elizabeth stopped her movement and gently called her. "Come here, Misty." Leaning over, she held out her hand, as if fingering some delectable morsel. Misty looked at her a brief moment, and then turned and ran off again. She watched in dismay as the cat disappeared around the corner that led to Mr. Darcy's private chambers.

"Oh, no!" Elizabeth's eyes widened as her heart pounded mercilessly.

When Elizabeth reached the top of the stairs, she was out of breath and quite distressed. She knew Mrs. Reynolds would not be happy about a cat loose in the house. She also knew that venturing down this hall was completely forbidden to her. She stood at the corner of the hall looking down, and debated what she ought to do.

When she spied Misty lying casually under a small table in the hallway, Elizabeth made a quick decision. She believed that she could easily catch the cat now if she approached her very calmly. At least all the doors along the hall were closed, and the worse that could happen was that the cat would run all the way to the end of the hall. Or... that someone would come up and find her here.

Her heart reminded her with every beat that she should stop and turn around. She deemed it prudent to call out for someone, just to alert anyone that might be up here that she needed help. "Hello? Is anyone here? Come here, Misty. Come here, kitty. Anyone?"

She walked slowly toward the cat, bending low and holding out her hand. How she wished she had thought to obtain a morsel of meat to entice the cat! "Here, Misty! Come to me!"

The cat eyed her from its reclined position, but Elizabeth could see by the look in Misty's eyes that if she felt threatened at all, she would be up and gone in an instant. Elizabeth paused, making an attempt to soothe and reassure the cat. "Misty, I mean you no harm. Please, allow me to come pick you up! You... we... do not belong here!"

The sound of a door opening just opposite her caused her to scramble to her feet. Her face whitened in dismay as she found herself staring into the face of Mr. Darcy. His hair was wet and dishevelled and his shirttails were loose. Her face displayed her great sense of mortification as his exhibited surprise. "Miss Bennet?"

"Please forgive me, Mr. Darcy. You must wonder... allow me to explain... you see ..."

At that moment, Misty, startled by the opening door and Mr. Darcy's presence, darted through the open door in which he stood.

Both pair of eyes widened as they watched the cat rush past Mr. Darcy, who made a futile attempt to snatch her up. In a shaky voice, Elizabeth blurted out.

"Misty escaped from the north wing and I was trying to retrieve her."

Darcy turned to look into the room for the cat, and then back at Elizabeth. He shook his head, the beginning of a smile slightly curving his lips. "Wait here. I believe she ran under the bed."

He walked back in, calling the cat.

Elizabeth hesitantly took some steps toward the room, letting her gaze take in its beauty. With each step she took toward the door, she was able to see more and more. It was a massive room with a definite masculine look. Two large windows were framed with dark green window coverings. It reminded her of the dark green of Pemberley's woods. She could see a plush chair in the corner of the room and a large bed covered with an intricately designed quilt in the same dark green, accented with navy blue, burgundy, and a milky white. Heavy wood furniture dotted the room, but did not overwhelm it.

She was no longer able to see Darcy, but could hear him trying to coax the cat out from under his bed. She assumed he was on the other side on the floor. She held back a giggle, but a nervous smile appeared as she waited for him to rescue the cat again.

At length, when he did not seem to have as much luck as he had getting her down from the tree, Elizabeth decided she had best leave before anyone came. He could always bring Misty downstairs once he retrieved her. Elizabeth was just about to suggest that when he stood up with cat in hand. As he turned and saw her at the door, he stopped and took in a sharp breath. His eyes darkened and did not leave her face.

He held Misty close to him, scratching the cat's head as he slowly began to walk toward Elizabeth. He stopped when he was standing in front of her just inside the room. He said nothing.

Elizabeth could not determine from his demeanour whether or not he was angry with her for coming to this part of the house or angry at the cat, but his silence unnerved her. She took a very small step forward, and with every attempt at keeping her voice calm said, "I will take her down."

As Darcy stepped forward to bridge the final distance between them and handed the cat to her, he said in an uneven voice, "Miss Bennet, we must talk."

As she wrapped her arms around Misty, she felt the warmth of his body and the strength of his arms. She knew she should not look up at him, for he would certainly see the strength of feeling she now had for him. But she could not help it, and soon found herself gazing up into his face.

"Yes," she said barely above a whisper, both their arms still wrapped around the cat. A noise at the end of the hall prompted Elizabeth to continue. "But not now... not *here*." Her voice shook.

"No, not here," he concurred, his voice gravelly. Reluctantly he pulled his arms from between her and the cat. "But soon."

"Yes, soon," Elizabeth answered, willing herself to turn her eyes from his.

"It would be best if you left before someone sees you and makes a wrong assumption."

Elizabeth turned, eager to flee from this wing before anyone saw her, yet desiring to linger and gaze a little longer into Mr. Darcy's eyes.

Elizabeth scurried toward the stairs tightly holding onto the cat; her heart only now beginning to still since first coming up here in her pursuit of the feline. Her mind raced with a myriad of thoughts as she considered how absurd this past week had been at Pemberley. She shook her head as she thought back to her first day when she encountered Mr. Darcy unexpectedly in his library. She had been mortified!

Now, when faced with a similar situation, she had all the assurance that Mr. Darcy thought no less of her, and possibly still had those feelings of love he once had for her. He wished to talk with her! The very thought evoked feelings of both heightened anticipation and solemn dread, depending on what it was she imagined he wished to say. There was always the possibility that he wished to set her in her place and discourage any expectations she may have in securing his affections anew.

When she returned to the north wing with Misty, she encountered not only the women and children, but saw that the men had returned. Since the immediate threat of flooding was over, they had returned to get some much needed rest. Apparently Mr. Darcy had just returned when she encountered him.

Elizabeth quickly found Rachel, who was anxiously waiting for her return, and handed Misty to her. She admonished her to keep the cat to their room so she would not escape again, although the thought crossed Elizabeth's mind that she would not mind chasing after her if she could encounter Mr. Darcy again. She surprised herself by giggling as she considered the state in which he had stepped from his room. She shook her head as she recalled how startled they both were.

She visited with Rachel and her mother for a while, holding the baby while they chatted. When Mr. Weber returned, she was happy to make his acquaintance. He told them how the rivers had receded sufficiently, and although still muddy, the road between Pemberley and their neighbourhood was well packed down and safe enough for the conveyance of the laden carriages.

That night at dinner, everyone was in the highest of spirits, confident that things would soon return to normal. The tenants would be leaving, and Mr. Darcy would no longer be occupied with the obligations that had been placed upon him.

While Rosalyn had disparaged it, Elizabeth appreciated how Mr. Darcy had taken it upon himself to ensure the safety of his tenants and their transition to Pemberley, and then took such prodigious measures to prevent damage to their homes. As Rosalyn had informed him – as inappropriate as her meddling was – he was certainly not required to go himself. But as Mrs. Reynolds had said, he was very good to his tenants, and this was a prime example – a tangible display – of his care and concern for his tenants. That his good friend and cousin accompanied him was an indication of their respect for this man and his ways.

The attitudes of Mr. Darcy and the other two men were a stark contrast to those of the Willstones, from their disapproving remarks to their avoidance of all association with "those people" who were brought – most unfortunately – to Pemberley. She found their response surprising, especially as they were actually being critical of Mr. Darcy himself. Almost everything she had heard them say about the man up until now had been laden with praise.

It was Elizabeth's recollection, however, of Rosalyn's very first remarks to her that had caused her the greatest astonishment. Her praise of Mr. Darcy had included his generosity, and she had also confided that her own father had married beneath him. Certainly her response to the tenants' plight and Mr. Darcy's actions should have been tempered with a little more compassion.

While she now felt a very real sense of coldness from the Willstones and Rosalyn, and was expected to continue to abide by Mrs. Willstone's admonition, she was encouraged by every glance and smile Mr. Darcy made in her direction. From across the table, he carried on conversations with his guests, but there were times when his eyes were solely directed at her.

At one point, they began discussing the possibility of an evening of musical entertainment by those who wished to perform. Elizabeth readily noticed the sparkle in Rosalyn's eyes. This was the type of diversion she had longed for. Elizabeth knew she wished to perform with the hopes of impressing Mr. Darcy with her voice and playing. She did play and sing well and Elizabeth knew she would likely be the star of the evening.

With a sly smile, Mr. Darcy asked, "Shall we anticipate the children's involvement? I do not believe a child is ever too young to perform before a small party of acquaintances."

Elizabeth looked first to Miss Bartley. She was eagerly nodding her head. "Gladys and Harriet have been practicing a duet on the pianoforte. I am sure they would be more than willing to exhibit."

Darcy directed his next statement to Elizabeth. "Having heard Miss Emily sing to Miss Bennet's playing, can we expect your participation, as well?"

Elizabeth smiled and looked at Emily. "Shall we oblige Mr. Darcy?"

Emily looked from Elizabeth and then back to Mr. Darcy. "We have been practicing several pieces," she said eagerly, nodding her head.

"Good!" he said, and then turned to Georgiana. "You shall pick the night, Georgie. Tomorrow night? The following night?"

Miss Darcy seemed to search her brother's face for reassurance, perhaps even strength. He smiled at her and she seemed to receive what it was she needed from him. Turning to the others at the table, she softly, yet decidedly told everyone that there would be an evening of music two nights from tonight.

Rosalyn's eyes suddenly lit up. "Would it be possible to have it in the ballroom? I noticed a pianoforte in there when Mrs. Reynolds showed it to us."

Miss Darcy looked to her brother again. He nodded.

"That is a very good idea, Miss Matthews."

Rosalyn smiled, and then added, "We could have our own private little ball... with dancing!"

The announcement was received with much delight and was considered the perfect diversion after all that had happened.

That evening, as Elizabeth spent the evening in the playroom with Emily, the anticipation of an evening of music – a ball of sorts – with the others gave her much to think upon with delight. She looked forward to performing with Emily, and decided she would practice with her as much as she could on the morrow and the following day.

She wondered whether Mr. Darcy played an instrument. Or would he sing? But more importantly, she wondered whether she would have the pleasure of dancing with him. Elizabeth shook her head and told herself she ought not to get her hopes up. The Willstones most likely would not permit it.

~~*

The following day, the pianofortes in the music room and the drawing room were occupied with those practicing for their performances. Elizabeth and Emily worked on a song in which they played a duet on the piano, and then sang together. After their practice, Elizabeth felt quite confident that they would do reasonably well.

In addition to practicing their music, Elizabeth worked with Emily on her studies. Then after much pleading from Emily, Elizabeth retrieved the illustrated bird book from her room. As they looked at the different pictures, Emily picked out the birds she knew by name and studied the ones she did not know.

Before going back to her room to rest, Elizabeth took Emily down to the dining room for a glass of water. While down there, she came upon Miss Darcy, who was sitting at the table having some tea. Elizabeth sat down with Emily while she drank her water and asked Miss Darcy if the tenants had all left.

"Yes," she replied. "I received word that they all were able to safely return to their homes."

"I am glad to hear that," Elizabeth said.

A look of anxiety crossed Miss Darcy's face. "Unfortunately there has been some damage elsewhere to some homes and my brother has gone out to assist them. He may not return until later this evening."

"I am so sorry," Elizabeth replied. "Was it some of Pemberley's tenants?"

"No, but one of the homes is a family member of one of our servants, so he wished to help out."

Elizabeth let out a slow breath. "Your brother is certainly generous of his time and prodigious in his care for others."

Miss Darcy wrapped her hands around her cup of tea and looked down into it. "He is too good. He feels a great sense of responsibility toward all that is his. That includes his tenants and servants."

Elizabeth smiled gently. "You are fortunate to have such a brother."

Miss Darcy lifted her eyes. "Unfortunately, I fear I will always measure any gentleman I meet against him. I fear there are few men like my brother."

Elizabeth now lowered her eyes. "No, I suppose not."

Emily finished her water, and Elizabeth thanked Miss Darcy for their visit. As she and Emily walked upstairs, Elizabeth reflected on Miss Darcy's words. At that moment she did not think she could have ever been more wrong about someone than she had about Mr. Darcy.

After leaving Emily in her room with instructions to rest if she could, but to play quietly if she could not, Elizabeth crossed the hall to her room. She encountered a maid coming out of her room.

Elizabeth greeted her, knowing that maids came in and out all day as they did their chores. This time, however, the maid stopped.

"I just left a package for you. Mr. Darcy said it was something you needed and to leave it in your room."

"Thank you," Elizabeth said, curious as to what it was she needed. She could not recall expressing any particular need to him.

When she walked in, she saw a wrapped parcel. She picked it up and her fingers nervously untied the string and pulled off the paper.

When the paper was removed, she slowly lifted the lid of the box. Looking in, what met her eyes brought a broad smile to her face. She lifted out a pair of mud boots.

Her heart beat excitedly as she anticipated what he meant by this gift – what he was suggesting. She readily recalled their conversation when she told him that she could not go out on her walks due to the mud, and she had no mud boots in which to walk. She brought the pair up to her heart and held them tightly there.

Her eyes widened as she considered the possibility of walking out tomorrow morning to the top of the ridge behind the house. She walked to the window and looked out at the grounds. While still wet and muddy in some places, the sun would likely dry quite a bit of it up today, and tomorrow if there was no rain, she ought to be able to have a very pleasant morning walk. And watch the sunrise. In her mud boots. With Mr. Darcy at her side.

A nervous excitement propelled her to walk about her room. She could not sit still. She tried several times, but just the anticipation of what the morning would bring – and the undeniable message the gift of these boots meant – were too much to allow her to rest. A smile and a true sense of contentment – she even allowed herself to admit it to be love – could not be denied. That he still loved her was something that, for the first time since arriving here, she could dwell upon with a compelling assurance.

Later that day, a smile graced Elizabeth's face as she brought Emily downstairs, encountering Rosalyn and the Willstones. Despite Mr. Darcy's absence, nothing could dispel her joy. There was still some time before dinner, and they retreated to the sitting room. Mrs. Willstone asked her daughter how her music practice went. Rosalyn appeared to be engrossed in a book, which Elizabeth surmised was only a pretence so she would not have to converse with her. She wondered whether her fervent feelings of love for Mr. Darcy could be discerned by the others. At the moment, she truly did not care.

The sound of footsteps drew everyone's attention. Heads turned with the expectation, Elizabeth was quite certain, of seeing Mr. Darcy return. Instead it was a servant holding a letter.

"Miss Bennet, a letter was just delivered for you. They said it was urgent."

"Thank you," she said as she took it from him, a feeling of unease coursing through her. Looking down, her forehead creased and she pursed her lips as she saw that it was from her sister, Jane.

She fingered the letter, not so much from an uncertainty about whether she should open it here, but from what its contents might contain.

All eyes were upon her, which added to her distress. "If you do not mind…" Her shaking fingers broke the seal of the letter and she opened it.

Her eyes widened as she read the first few lines of the missive. Her fingers covered her mouth as she shook her head. "Oh, no!" she cried. She stood up as she read as quickly as she could, hoping to find a resolution at the end of the letter, but matters only seemed to get worse.

"What is it, Miss Bennet?" Mrs. Willstone asked. "What has happened?"

Elizabeth found it difficult to even take a breath. As her mind comprehended all her sister had to say and how it would affect her, she said, "It is my younger sister, Lydia." Taking a much needed breath, Elizabeth choked out, "She is… she has left her friends and is missing."

Chapter 20

"Missing?" asked Mr. Willstone. "Your sister is missing?"

Elizabeth nodded her head repeatedly, her eyes moving feverishly through the letter. This was far worse than she could ever have imagined. "She was visiting a friend whose husband is a colonel of a militia and they were stationed at Stratford. Apparently…" Elizabeth looked up, wondering how much she should say. "She is gone. It is thought she may have eloped with one of the officers."

Mrs. Willstone raised an eyebrow at this. "She *may* have eloped?"

Elizabeth looked back down at the letter. Jane, while not wishing to distress Elizabeth, truthfully wrote that marriage between them was not likely. It was the officer with whom she ran off, however, that caused her much distress. Lydia had run off with George Wickham! Lydia's actions alone would bring disgrace to her family, but being that it was with George Wickham would certainly bring an end to any feelings Mr. Darcy still had for her.

Tears began to fall freely as she made an attempt to answer Mrs. Willstone. "It says that Lydia left a letter and it is assumed they are in London."

"And not married?" Mrs. Willstone said, as she motioned for Rosalyn to remove Emily from the room.

"It is… not known."

A look of abhorrence plainly coloured Mrs. Willstone's features. In a soft, low voice she said, "Miss Bennet, this is grave, indeed."

Elizabeth looked up. "Jane has asked for me to come."

Mrs. Willstone's eyes narrowed for a brief moment, but then she smiled, a cold, rather forced smile. "Yes, dear. You must go to London. It is only right."

Elizabeth looked at her with surprise. "But my duties to Emily…"

Mrs. Willstone waved her hand in the air. "We shall manage. But how shall you get there? We cannot loan you a carriage and we certainly cannot expect Mr. Darcy to loan you one of his to take you all that way."

"I suppose I shall have to hire a post chaise. Perhaps I can get one from Lambton."

Mr. Willstone made a suggestion. "Your friends in Lambton might be of assistance."

"Yes!" exclaimed Mrs. Willstone. "Certainly they will help."

Elizabeth slowly looked up. "They did tell me if I needed anything…"

"You must send them a note," interrupted Mrs. Willstone. "Inform them that you need to leave for London as soon as can be arranged. Inquire whether they will allow you to come tonight. We can certainly loan you our carriage to convey you to Lambton."

Mrs. Willstone stood up and walked over to a desk. "Come, Miss Bennet. The sooner you send off a note to them, the sooner you will be on your way."

Elizabeth stood up and slowly walked over. She could not deny that she was pleased Mrs. Willstone was being so obliging, but she could not help feeling she was merely trying to rid the home of her. Her feelings warred within, as she greatly wished to be with Jane, yet she did not want to leave Pemberley and Mr. Darcy.

She sat down at the desk and began writing, her hand shaking. Mrs. Willstone hovered over her. "Be sure to let them know that you are quite in need of their assistance... that you would greatly appreciate any help they can give. Do not give them too many details... they may not offer their help if they know the unfortunate particulars."

Elizabeth scribbled a short missive, only briefly detailing the situation, but expressing her need for their help. A servant was summoned and asked that someone deliver the note as soon as possible and to wait for a response.

Mrs. Willstone stood up, holding herself erect. Elizabeth thought how tall and imposing she now suddenly appeared. "Now, Miss Bennet, it would be best to pack your belongings so you will be ready to leave as soon as we hear back from your friends. If you like, I shall have one of our maids come and assist you."

Elizabeth took a deep breath. Everything was happening faster than she wished. "I do not have many things. I can manage."

"Good. We would not want to bother the Pemberley staff with this. We must try to keep this as quiet as possible."

Elizabeth turned to look at her employer. "But I should like to say goodbye to Mr. Darcy and his sister... to thank them for their kindness and generous hospitality..."

Mrs. Willstone shook her head. "Tsk. Tsk. They will likely not even notice your absence. Besides, I understand that Miss Darcy left just a short while ago pay a call on someone. You will likely be already gone by the time either of them returns."

Elizabeth's heart sank and her shoulders sagged with the weight of these past few minutes. She could barely take a breath and her mind scarcely allowed her to comprehend all the consequences her youngest sister's actions would have on her... and her family. She was already being shunned by the Willstones because of the possible disgrace to her family, and she would now likely be dismissed by the man who once sought her hand, and now had secured her heart.

Back in her room, she was grateful for the solitude. Pulling out her travelling bag, she opened it and placed it on the bed. She went to open the drawers, pulling out some books and the stack of letters she had placed beneath them. She then went to the closet and retrieved her dresses and folded them as carefully as possible to prevent them from wrinkling.

She looked down at the two books she had in her possession. One was Cowper's book of poems, and the other was the illustrated bird book. She would have to return them to the library. As she picked them up, there was a knock at the door. Elizabeth answered it and found a young servant girl standing there. "I have a letter for ye that just arrived." She handed it to Elizabeth. "Can I be of any help? Do ye need some help with your packing?"

"I am just about finished, but please, I would like a few moments to read this first."

The maid nodded and waited while Elizabeth opened the letter and read the words from the Ketterlings. They were more than happy to make any arrangements for her to journey to London, and welcomed her to stay with them as long as she needed. She looked up at the maid. "I will need my things to be brought down. I will be leaving to go to my friends in Lambton. The Willstones offered me their carriage if you would be so kind as to inform them that…" Elizabeth took in a shaky breath. "…that I will be leaving."

The maid curtseyed. "Yes, ma'am. I will notify them and send a manservant for your parcel."

She turned to leave, but Elizabeth stopped her. "Excuse me, but do you know if Mr. or Miss Darcy have returned?"

The maid shook her head. "Not that I have heard."

"Thank you," Elizabeth said softly. "Would you also be so kind as to return these books to Mr. Darcy's library?"

"Yes ma'am," the maid said as she picked up the books and turned to leave.

Elizabeth walked over to the window and looked out over the beautiful grounds. She turned her head to look at the ridge behind the house. Her heart lurched as she thought about how much she longed to join Mr. Darcy up there in the morning to watch the sunrise. The very last thing she placed in her bag was the pair of boots.

With a sadness and grief that pervaded her whole body, she stepped from the room, and for one last time walked down Pemberley's grand staircase.

Upon meeting Mrs. Willstone downstairs, Elizabeth was informed that their carriage was being readied, and she would send one of their maidservants along with Elizabeth to Lambton. Emily stood at her side, her eyes stained red from tears.

"Emily wished to say goodbye, but we would prefer that you make it brief," Mrs. Willstone said icily.

Elizabeth stooped down and wrapped the little girl in her arms. "I will miss you, Emily," she told her. "You keep practicing your playing and singing. Will you do that for me?"

Emily nodded. "Do you have to go, Miss Bennet? Why do you have to go?"

Mrs. Willstone placed her hands on Emily's shoulders and gently pulled her away. "There, you have said your goodbye. Now, Emily, be off with your friends."

A look passed between Elizabeth and Emily that spoke of the love and affection they had for one another. Elizabeth fought to keep back her tears.

"Where is Rosalyn?" Elizabeth asked. "I should like to say goodbye to her."

Mrs. Willstone let out a long sigh. "She is spending some much wanted time with Mrs. Goldsmith. I would not wish to interrupt them. They are becoming good friends, and we know how important that will be in Mr. Darcy's eyes."

Mr. Willstone then walked in. "The carriage is ready, Miss Bennet."

"Thank you, Mr. Willstone. Goodbye. Goodbye, Mrs. Willstone."

As she walked away, she felt as though her fate was already settled in their minds and she most likely would never see them again. She could live with that.

She stepped outside and as she walked down the front steps, turned to look down the length of Pemberley from one end to the other. It was this place and its Master that she would miss so terribly. How she wished she could at least have said goodbye. How she wished she could at least have had a morning walk with him. She reminded herself that it no longer mattered. A tear fell freely down her face, which she neglected to wipe away.

As she approached the carriage, she nodded at the maidservant who waited there. It took all of her strength to step up into it. She felt as though everything within her fought leaving. When she was finally in and seated, she kept her head to the window, longing to see Mr. Darcy hurrying out to prevent her departure. As the carriage began to pull away, she imagined him coming out and rushing after it, his hand reaching out to her.

She inhaled deeply, her breath shaky. She knew that once he learned what happened – including all the particulars – he would be grateful she left. She gazed toward the magnificent house as the carriage drove around the circular lane and then away from it. She wished to see Pemberley and all its grandeur as long as she could. She had a sombre conviction that she would never see it again.

When she arrived in Lambton, the Ketterlings welcomed Elizabeth graciously. They were only acquainted with the fact that there had been a family crisis and Elizabeth needed their help. They offered her their home for as long as she needed to stay and assured her that they would secure transportation for her to London as soon as possible. Mr. Ketterling informed her that he would inquire first thing in the morning whether a conveyance would be leaving some time tomorrow.

They did not press her for information, but allowed her some privacy in the room that would be hers during her stay. Once left to herself, Elizabeth collapsed onto the bed and allowed the tears to fall. She convulsed with sobs that came from the depths of her very soul. She closed her eyes, trying to wipe away the images of Mr. Darcy that intruded. But more than that, she wished to still those ardent feelings that had developed over the past week. She did not leave the room for nearly an hour.

Alone there, she imagined with dread all that this would mean for Lydia, Jane, herself, and her whole family. The worst for Lydia would be if Wickham took advantage of her with no intention of marrying her. He had no reason to marry her – she had no fortune. Elizabeth wondered how long Lydia would remain with him after she discovered the truth. The longer she stayed, the worse her reputation would be ruined.

She thought with alarm how Mr. Bingley might choose to end his engagement with Jane if their family was tarnished by Lydia's actions. It certainly would be a true test of his love and devotion to Jane. Elizabeth could only hope it was strong enough to weather this storm.

Then her thoughts went to Mr. Darcy. She could not pull up one ounce of hope that he would overlook this offence. Even if his love for her had remained constant this past year, this was certainly a disaster of the worst kind. To consider marrying someone whose family reputation was now tainted by the thoughtless and dissolute actions of the youngest sister would be damaging to his name as well as his sister's. Add to that the fact that George Wickham was involved was even more devastating.

Mr. Darcy had every reason to despise the man and would assuredly do anything to protect his sister and keep her from him. If Wickham did marry Lydia, as unlikely as Elizabeth felt that would be, Mr. Darcy would put as much distance as he could between her, her family, and himself.

Elizabeth dried her eyes and dabbed her face with a moistened cloth, steeling herself to leave the shelter of her room. She knew dinner would be served soon and she felt obligated to tell the Ketterlings everything that had occurred. She would not reveal all, particularly Wickham's involvement, but she would be forthright about Lydia. She was fairly confident that she could trust them to be understanding.

They were served a delicious meal, but Elizabeth ate and drank very little as she relayed to them the news she had received. She picked and poked at her food, only occasionally taking a bite. The Ketterlings were, as she expected, very sympathetic and offered her kind words of consolation. While she expressed her appreciation for their words, in truth they did little to soothe her pain.

Mr. Ketterling assured Elizabeth that he would check with the livery station on carriages that could convey Elizabeth to London. He warned her, however, that due to the recent rains and flooding, nothing had been able to leave in several days. There may be no space available for her tomorrow, but he would secure her passage on the first one available. He assured her that she was welcomed to stay with them as long as she needed.

The conversation soon turned to other things. The Ketterlings were more than eager to express their admiration for Mr. Darcy and how he opened up Pemberley to those families who were stranded and whose homes were threatened by flooding water. With each word of praise they uttered for him, Elizabeth felt a greater sense of loss. She returned to her room early, hoping sleep would come and relieve her of her anguish.

~~*

Elizabeth tossed and turned throughout the night, granting her with very little sleep. While she lay awake in her bed, her thoughts presented her with every conceivable outcome of Lydia's actions, most of which were injurious to all. The few times she did fall asleep, her dreams tormented her with images of Mr.

Darcy in all his warranted anger. His dark eyes flashed before her, speaking volumes more than any words could. While he said nothing, his tall, commanding figure issued her orders to leave Pemberley, as she lay curled up at his feet sobbing.

Elizabeth wakened early, even more distressed than the previous day. The passing of one night did nothing to ease her misery, fears, and pain. Her only hope was that Lydia had already been found and perhaps Jane had sent off another missive alerting her to a respectable resolution. She hoped whatever the outcome, it would somehow appease Mr. Darcy as far as Wickham was concerned. The pain within, however, reaffirmed to her that no resolution would suffice.

She crawled out of bed and walked over to her window. As she peered out, she saw the bright colours of the eastern sky announcing the sun's arrival. Her heart skipped a beat as she considered that she ought to be out on the ridge behind Pemberley, watching the sunrise with Mr. Darcy. She wondered if he had indeed taken a walk and what he was thinking as he watched the myriad of colours paint the sky.

Tears filled her eyes as she felt her heart truly breaking. How she wished that she had not received such encouragement from Mr. Darcy this past week. How much better it would have been if she had received his censure for the way she had refused him. How much easier it would have been to leave Pemberley if she had not come to love him.

Elizabeth remained in her room until she heard the sounds of others moving about the household. Once she was assured people in the household were stirring, she dressed and walked out to the drawing room. She found Mrs. Ketterling in the sitting room drinking tea.

"Good morning, Miss Bennet," she said. "Did you sleep well?"

"Yes," she lied. "It was most comfortable."

"Good. Would you like some tea?"

"I would like that very much."

Mrs. Ketterling had her maid bring out a cup of tea for Elizabeth. She took it from her and wrapped her fingers about the warm cup, took a sip, and closed her eyes for a brief moment. Behind her closed lids, she saw Darcy's eyes flash at her again. She opened her eyes quickly, looking away from Mrs. Ketterling, fearing she might see the distress etched on her face.

Fortunately for Elizabeth, Mrs. Ketterling was looking down at a sampler she was embroidering. Elizabeth breathed in slowly as she sipped the calming tea, hoping it would still her heart and diminish her anguish.

Breakfast was served shortly after Mr. Ketterling joined them. Elizabeth was fairly certain they perceived her lingering grief, for they ate in relative silence. She was grateful that they did not press her with unwanted conversation.

Once they had finished, Mr. Ketterling announced that he would be leaving to see what he could find to insure a prompt, safe passage to London. He apologized for not having the means himself to provide for her journey.

Once he left, Elizabeth found it difficult to sit calmly. She was eager to be gone; to return to her family. She walked several times to the window and gazed out, wishing to fill her mind with anything but that which pressed heavily upon her.

Mrs. Ketterling studied her furtively, raising her eyes occasionally from her needlework. At length, she lifted her face to her and smiled. "It appears to be a very pleasant morning, Miss Bennet. Would you care to join me in a walk about the neighbourhood?"

Elizabeth turned and her face lit up with a smile. "I would enjoy that very much," she said.

They each took a light shawl with them as the cool morning air had not yet fully yielded to the warmth of the rising sun. They walked in silence for a while, greeting the occasional neighbour they met, and Mrs. Ketterling only speaking when Elizabeth spoke to her first.

Once Elizabeth appeared to be more inclined to talk, Mrs. Ketterling asked her about Pemberley... and Mr. Darcy.

"Miss Bennet, I know your visit to Pemberley was cut short, but did you enjoy the time spent there? Was Mr. Darcy as accommodating to everyone as he was to us that day we came to fetch you?"

Elizabeth swallowed, her mouth going dry at merely the mention of his name. Now, as she contemplated how to answer Mrs. Ketterling's questions, all her feelings – which she had been trying to bury – rose and threatened to overwhelm her.

She blinked her eyes several times to clear her eyes from the moisture that filled them. "He is... he was always very kind," she assured her new friend.

Mrs. Ketterling beamed a smile of satisfaction. "I always believed he was. He is so admired here, but people know so little about him. It is good to know he is truly a gentleman."

Suddenly the words of Elizabeth's refusal assaulted her. *Had you behaved in a more gentleman like manner...*

They came back to the house, and Elizabeth had to admit that despite their one conversation that caused her unease, it had been precisely what she needed. They waited in the sitting room for the arrival of Mr. Ketterling. He returned about an hour later and came directly to them.

"It is as I expected. The carriages for hire are completely booked today and tomorrow morning. While a morning departure would be more favourable, I have arranged for you to take an early afternoon carriage. It will have one overnight stop and will get you to London the following day. Does that sound suitable?"

Elizabeth nodded. "Yes, if you can put up with me for another day."

Mrs. Ketterling assured her again that they would be happy to keep her as long as necessary.

They settled into easy conversation, Elizabeth grateful for all they had done. At length, Mrs. Ketterling picked up her sampler and Elizabeth perused a few books in a small bookcase, selecting one she thought she could finish before she left, eager to set her mind on other things.

It was about an hour later that a knock was heard at the door. Shortly after, their housekeeper stepped into the room and announced that Mr. Darcy from Pemberley wished to speak to Miss Bennet.

Chapter 21

Mr. and Mrs. Ketterling stood up immediately as Mr. Darcy stepped into the room. Initially too stunned to respond in like manner, Elizabeth felt her cheeks warm with colour. She was grateful that the Ketterlings had the presence of mind to warmly welcome their esteemed guest.

"Mr. Darcy!" exclaimed Mr. Ketterling. "It is good to see you again. Welcome to our home."

"Thank you, sir. I hope I have not come at an inconvenient time." He stole a look at Elizabeth, whose face overtly exhibited her astonishment at his coming.

"Not at all. Would you care for something to drink?" Mrs. Ketterling's eyes shone with admiration.

Darcy stepped into the room, waving his hand slightly. "No thank you. I need nothing."

Silence filled the room and Darcy shifted from one foot to another in apparent discomfiture. His fingers wrestled with each other as he looked at Mrs. Ketterling, her husband, and then back to Elizabeth.

"Please have a seat, Mr. Darcy," Mrs. Ketterling offered.

"Thank you." As he walked over and sat down, the others did the same. Elizabeth sat stiffly, bringing her hands together and holding them tightly in her lap. She could not imagine what prompted him to come all this way; certainly he had been told about her sister's actions.

Mr. and Mrs. Ketterling looked at him expectantly; Elizabeth could barely breathe. He finally spoke, looking directly at Elizabeth.

"I only discovered this morning about your departure, Miss Bennet. I returned home too late last night and as I saw no one, went straight to my room." His fingers began to tap lightly against the armrest of the chair. Pursing his lips tightly together, he continued, in a slow, deliberate manner. "This morning when I returned from my morning walk," he paused for a moment and searched her face. "I inquired about your absence when you did not come down for breakfast."

Elizabeth looked down when he first mentioned his morning walk. She knew his veiled meaning. This should have given her hope that he had been eagerly expecting her to join him, but she realized that once he knew all, his opinion of her – if it had been at all favourable – would certainly change.

He ran his fingers brusquely through his hair and then stood up. He began to walk about the room. "I understand you wish to travel to London to be with your family in this… time of crisis."

Elizabeth mutely nodded.

Darcy took a few ragged breaths and then rubbed his jaw with his hand. "There will be no need for you to take a carriage for hire. I shall provide you with one of my carriages along with a travelling companion from my staff. I shall ensure one of my most reliable maidservants will accompany you for the full length of your journey as well as one of my most trustworthy drivers."

Elizabeth's eyes widened as the Ketterlings looked on in high regard.

"How kind of you, sir," Mr. Ketterling exclaimed. "I already have made arrangements for her to travel post, but this will…"

"Mr. Darcy!" Elizabeth interrupted, angst filling her voice. "You are under no obligation to go out of your way for me in this manner. I cannot allow you to do such a thing! I do not expect it of you and it is unquestionably unnecessary!"

He clasped his hands behind his back and began to pace slowly about the room. "I quite expected you to protest, Miss Bennet, but I will brook no opposition to what I have stated." He stopped and turned his face to her, his jaw firmly set and brows narrowed. "It has already been arranged."

While grateful for his consideration, she wondered how much he had been told. Perhaps he did not know the particulars of what her younger sister had done. News of this most certainly would colour his treatment of her.

"Mr. Darcy," Elizabeth said, her voice soft, yet determined. "You may not be aware of the full extent of my family's crisis. My younger sister, Lydia…"

"I am fully aware, Miss Bennet, and it is unfortunate. We can only hope that once you arrive in London you will find that all has been resolved."

Elizabeth looked down, a feeling of resignation coursing through her. He knew, but he did not know *all*.

"There is one matter, however, on which I must insist."

All eyes turned to him.

"I will be sending a rider to London first thing in the morning to ascertain whether the roads are yet passable. While I have every confidence in my carriage and driver, there might still be roads that are washed out and bridges that are unsafe due to the recent rains. My rider will travel to London, determining the best possible route, and then will return with a report. It is only then that I will send my carriage for you, Miss Bennet."

"Mr. Darcy, you are too generous," Mrs. Ketterling gushed. She was not protesting; she was bestowing praise upon him.

Elizabeth shook her head, fully aware that if he knew about Wickham, he would not be so generous. She needed to acquaint him with all the details. She was surprised, then, to hear his next request.

"Would you be so kind, Mr. Ketterling… Mrs. Ketterling… to allow Miss Bennet to step out with me? There are a few matters I need to discuss with her."

Elizabeth's eyes shot up and she looked over to her hosts. They both nodded with understanding and gratitude for all this man had ever done and was now doing. "Certainly, certainly," Mr. Ketterling consented. Elizabeth did not believe they would deny this man any request.

Elizabeth stood up as Darcy beckoned to her. As they walked toward the door, he said to the Ketterlings, "I do appreciate all you have done for Miss Bennet."

Mr. Ketterling waved a hand in the air. "No, Mr. Darcy, it is *you* who have done so much for her."

They walked out slowly and quietly. Mr. Darcy finally broke the silence.

"Miss Bennet, as I was unaware of your departure yesterday, when I walked up to the ridge this morning and you did not show up, I questioned why. I pondered the strong possibility that you may have judged me completely devoid of good manners and breeding by giving you that pair of mud boots, because of what you may have alleged my meaning was in doing so."

"Oh, no, sir, I…"

Darcy put up a hand. "Still, while I was up there waiting, I berated myself for *again* acting completely without propriety." He let out a long sigh. "I imagined that you thought me a rake!"

Elizabeth let out a soft chuckle. "I did not, sir."

He looked down at her and smiled. "At breakfast, when I first heard you had left Pemberley, my initial thought again was that I had been the reason for your departure. You wanted nothing but to be out of my presence."

"I am sorry to have caused you concern."

"Miss Bennet," Darcy stopped and turned to her. "There are a few things I need to relate to you. Some things occurred after you left that might distress you."

Elizabeth looked up at him questioningly. Now she wondered whether he *did* somehow come to learn of Wickham's involvement.

Darcy breathed in deeply and combed his fingers through his hair. "Apparently, after you left, Miss Willstone went into your room looking for that book of birds the two of you had so enjoyed."

"Oh," Elizabeth exclaimed. "I gave it to one of the maids to return to the library.

Darcy nodded. "Miss Willstone believed it to be somewhere in your room, so she searched for it." He paused. "Fairly extensively."

Elizabeth lifted her brows, encouraging him to finish.

"She did not find the book, but she did find…" He reached into a pocket and pulled out a piece of paper. "…This."

As he held it out, Elizabeth gasped as her eyes recognized the meticulous handwriting of Mr. Darcy. It was the first page of the letter he had had written to her at Rosings. Red flushes of mortification spread across her face; her stomach suddenly growing queasy. "Oh, no!" Her hands went up to her cheeks. "I am so sorry, Mr. Darcy. I thought I had packed it away!"

"She claimed to have found it on the floor under your bed."

Elizabeth shook her head as she tried to think. She remembered reading it one night on her bed and when Rosalyn came in, she quickly stuffed it under her pillow. It must have fallen to the floor, and she put the remaining pages in her drawer without ensuring all the pages were accounted for.

"Did they all come to know about it?" she asked, looking warily up at him.

"Not right away. Apparently Miss Willstone put it in one of her pockets and forgot about it until the evening meal. She pulled it out at dinner."

Elizabeth felt as though she could not take a breath; she felt so much shame and distress. To have that letter come into the hands of everyone was one thing, but for Mr. Darcy to know that she had kept it all this time was another. "This is terrible!" she said.

"Well, it is not so much to you."

She looked up warily and asked, "What do you mean?"

"As you know, I was not there. When Miss Willstone pulled it out, announcing that she had found it in your room, Miss Matthews snatched it out of her niece's hand and began to read it. My sister recognized my handwriting and protested that we ought not be reading someone else's personal letter. My good cousin, Hamilton, promptly liberated it from Miss Matthews' hands."

Very softly, Elizabeth asked, "How much did they read?"

Darcy shifted from one foot to another, Elizabeth recognizing this as a sign of his unease. "Basically just the first sentence of the letter. At least the Willstones and Miss Matthews only read the first sentence, but I believe my cousin has now apprised himself of the whole page."

Elizabeth let out a frustrated huff. "They must wonder about the propriety of a letter written by you to me."

Darcy nodded. "There has actually been a great deal of speculation, especially as to the nature of the first sentence."

Elizabeth tried to recollect what that first sentence said. She ought to know the whole letter by heart, but with all that had happened, and with Mr. Darcy's close presence, she could not recall. "May I have the letter?"

He promptly handed it to her. As her eyes read the missive, she took in the words. *Be not alarmed, Madam, on receiving this letter, by the apprehension of its containing any repetition of those sentiments, or renewal of those offers, which were last night so disgusting to you.*

Elizabeth looked up at him and saw that his face appeared grim. "You said earlier that it was not so horrible to me. What did you mean?"

Darcy's jaw tightened and his brows pinched tightly together. "Most of the conjecture last night was based on what type of offer I would have made to you that would have been so disgusting to you."

Elizabeth's heart quickened as he spoke. She wished to hear, and yet at the same time did not want to hear, what it was they believed.

Darcy's voice softened. "Someone said they thought they saw you in the private hall to my chambers yesterday. That led to the consensus that I... that I made a most dishonourable request of you."

Elizabeth stomped her foot and spun around, bringing her arms up and folding them in front of her. Her eyes filled with tears and she could not prevent one from spilling down her face. She took in a shaky breath. "I am so sorry, Mr. Darcy."

Darcy looked down, wishing to console her, but knowing the Ketterlings were likely watching them through the window. "Miss Bennet, I want you to be assured that you have come through this shining like a star, for according to this letter, you were disgusted by my offer."

"I am so sorry, Mr. Darcy." Elizabeth could not imagine he was pleased with these rumours. "What about your friends and cousin. What about your sister?" Elizabeth wondered with true concern that those who truly cared for him would not be under the wrong impression.

"I had an obligation to confide in them the reason for the letter. Besides, Hamilton would not leave it. He pressed me unremittingly to justify my actions."

"I am so sorry," Elizabeth could think of nothing else to say.

My good cousin is getting quite a laugh about it, particularly when he recollected his comments the day of the picnic."

Elizabeth looked up at him with appreciation. He was not angry at her; he seemed to not even be angry at the rumours that were swirling about.

She suddenly thought of Rosalyn, and wondered if there was anything to the conjectures about his feelings of regard for her. "I am quite certain," she began, "that you will be able to explain the letter and its contents to Miss Matthews and all will be well with her. She will certainly forgive you."

His eyes narrowed and he expelled a short breath. "Miss Matthews? What is she to me?"

Elizabeth glanced down at her hands, which she rubbed briskly together. "I was under the impression, in fact several have been under the impression, that the invitation to Pemberley was to further your acquaintance with her."

Darcy's head dropped and he let out a long breath. He was silent for a moment before saying to her, "No, Miss Bennet. If that has been what everyone believed, I have been a fool. It was all for…"

"Mr. Darcy, please!" Elizabeth stopped him. "There is something I must tell you."

She could not bear to have him express his admiration for her, if that was what he was about to do, and then withdraw it once he heard about Wickham.

"What is it?" he asked.

Elizabeth clasped her hands together and looked down at them as she proceeded. "You said you knew about the contents of the letter I received from Jane, that my youngest sister Lydia has run off with an officer?"

He nodded. "That is precisely what I was told."

"You know my sister, Mr. Darcy. She may have no qualms about not marrying, and if she does not, it will bring disgrace to my family."

"We cannot be sure of that, yet."

"No," Elizabeth answered, turning her head and looking off into the distance. "But there are particulars about this whole situation with which you are not acquainted." She turned back and looked at him, tears now freely falling down her face. "The officer she ran off with is… is George Wickham."

Elizabeth saw it immediately. His eyes widened in shock and then slowly narrowed in anger. She saw in him the recognition of all the consequences of her sister's actions. She saw the calculations in his mind as he battled what he now knew with what he possibly felt. She saw the resignation and the determined set of his jaw when he had made his decision.

He looked down at her. She saw him swallow and take a few short breaths. "This is grave, indeed," he said slowly. "This alters everything."

Darcy made a quick bow, his eyes searching Elizabeth's face. "I must go. I will keep you no longer."

He walked to his horse, adeptly bringing himself up onto the saddle. He turned and looked at her one last time, his eyes dark with anger, his breathing ragged. "I will send my carriage and maidservant for you once I know the route to London is safe. Good day, Miss Bennet. May God be with you." He then nodded at her and gave the horse a few short kicks, bringing it to a gallop as he rode off down the street.

Elizabeth's eyes blurred with tears as she watched him disappear around a corner, prompting her to release a sob of anguish. She realized she may never see him again.

Chapter 22

Elizabeth stood gravely still, unable to move. Mr. Darcy was gone. She could no longer see him; no longer hear the sound of the galloping horse's hooves. The picture of him as the anger spread across his features would remain with her forever. She knew not whether she would ever see him again.

She fisted her hands and breathed in deeply. Presently she felt unequal to the task of putting on a smiling face for the Ketterlings, pretending that she was grateful to Mr. Darcy for his generous offer as she listened to their continued words of praise for the man. It would only cause her heart to ache even more.

She finally turned and walked slowly to the house. The window coverings moved slightly, confirming her suspicion that her hosts had observed her interaction with Mr. Darcy. She hoped if they detected either hers or Mr. Darcy's discomfiture, their good manners would prevent them from speaking about it.

Elizabeth was grateful that they appeared oblivious to her distress. After only minimal discourse, Mr. Ketterling excused himself to cancel her journey on the carriage for hire. Elizabeth and Mrs. Ketterling returned to the sitting room, just as they had been prior to Mr. Darcy's unexpected arrival. Mrs. Ketterling picked up her needlework and Elizabeth opened her book. Mrs. Ketterling appeared to make steady progress on her stitches, whereas Elizabeth could barely grasp a single word on the page in front of her. Her mind was in turmoil; her eyes continually filled with tears.

~~*

It was two very long days before Elizabeth heard anything from Pemberley concerning her journey to London. While the Ketterlings ensured her comfort as much as possible, Elizabeth was eager to leave. At times she wished she had taken the hired carriage, but knew her hosts would protest, as Mr. Darcy's offer had been so much more superior. Their praise for Mr. Darcy's prodigious care for her was profuse.

It was in the late afternoon that a message arrived from Pemberley. Elizabeth eagerly opened it, hoping she could now travel to London.

Miss Elizabeth Bennet,

Please be advised that I will be sending one of my carriages for you at first light tomorrow. One of the maidservants from Pemberley will accompany you. She will be staying on at my town home in London, so fret not that she is making this journey unnecessarily. I have arranged for an afternoon and evening meal for you and a room at an inn will be provided as needed. My wishes are for a pleasant journey and a suitable outcome of your family situation.

Mr. Fitzwilliam Darcy

The note was brief and to the point. As her eyes perused the missive written in Mr. Darcy's very meticulous handwriting, her thoughts went back to the *other* letter. Each recollection of that letter coming into the hands of the others at Pemberley brought with it spasms of mortification for what he must have endured at everyone's conjectures. Yes, she had come through it fairly unscathed. She could only hope that he had been able to smooth over any rough and turbulent waters that the Willstones and Rosalyn had stirred up.

That evening, once her things were packed, save for what she would need in the morning, she sat down upon her bed. Disappointment swept through her. She had fervently hoped that Mr. Darcy would have paid another visit in the two days she had continued here. She knew in her heart, however, that it would have been highly unlikely.

The news Elizabeth had relayed to him about Wickham's involvement in her sister's running away was bad enough, but what her misplaced letter had cost him was another. That was her fault and he now had to admit to his close friends, his cousin, and most likely his sister, what he had hoped to always keep from them. She was quite certain it would be terribly humiliating for a man of his standing to have to admit to being refused in marriage.

Elizabeth spent her final evening with the Ketterlings in their sitting room, as they had done every evening. Elizabeth was finally able to attend to the words of the book, but this evening Mrs. Ketterling seemed more inclined to talk than focus on her stitches. She anticipated Elizabeth seeing her aunt again, and wished her to convey a message to her. Initially, she only wished her to know how much they had enjoyed the company of her niece. In the course of the evening, however, she kept thinking of additional things she would like to tell her. At length, Elizabeth suggested that she write her aunt a letter. Mrs. Ketterling agreed that would be the best thing to do, and promptly sat down at a small desk and penned a missive. Elizabeth was relieved, as she would have felt awkward passing on to her aunt the praises Mrs. Ketterling had bestowed on herself.

Even before the clock struck nine o'clock, Elizabeth excused herself. Although she would not be waking much earlier than was the norm for her, she expressed to them a wish to retire early to allow a good night's sleep. In truth, she hoped to have some time to herself as she anticipated her departure on the morrow. Now that the time had drawn near, she felt almost completely consumed by grief, as deep as when she lost her father.

When she finally climbed into bed and rested her head upon her pillow, she knew sleep would elude her. Her heart ached, her eyes burned from the tears she had shed, and her mind would not relinquish the images of Mr. Darcy from appearing before her. She wondered how long it would be before she could ever forget him. Perhaps never!

~~*

164

Elizabeth woke when the hall clock struck five o'clock. Having had mere fragments of sleep, she awoke with a heaviness that proclaimed to her the distress of her heart even before her mind clearly recollected it. She lay in bed briefly, and then sat up and stretched, touching her toes to the floor. She walked over to pick up her shawl which lay folded on a nearby chair and tossed it over her shoulders to take off the slight chill of early morning.

Stepping to the window, Elizabeth peered out and noticed a faint slice of light hovering over the tips of the hills in the distance. She knew the carriage from Pemberley would arrive soon.

There was a light tap at the door, and a maid announced herself. Elizabeth bid her come in, and she entered with a kettle of warm water, which she poured into the basin. Elizabeth thanked her and told her she would be downstairs shortly.

Elizabeth walked over to the basin and dipped a cloth in the water. Bringing it to her face, she pressed it to her eyes, hoping to diminish the redness. If the Ketterlings noticed, perhaps they would attribute it to lack of sleep or sadness over her youngest sister's situation. Once dressed, she came downstairs and found Mrs. Ketterling waiting for her.

"Good morning, Mrs. Ketterling," Elizabeth said. "There was no need for you to rise and see me off. We said our goodbyes last night."

Mrs. Ketterling shook her head. "I had every intention of seeing you off, Miss Bennet. I will see you into the carriage and make sure you are properly tended. It is the least I can do for my good friend."

"You are too kind," Elizabeth replied.

They were served a light meal. Elizabeth, however, ate sparingly as she did not find herself particularly hungry. She did enjoy a cup of tea, and as she was taking the last sip, there was a tap at the door.

"You carriage has arrived, I do believe," Mrs. Ketterling said with a wink.

Elizabeth's heart sputtered at the glimmer of hope that Mr. Darcy would have accompanied it.

A servant soon appeared announcing the arrival of Pemberley's carriage. If Mr. Darcy had been present, he would have certainly been announced, as well. Elizabeth's heart sank.

Elizabeth and Mrs. Ketterling walked out as her baggage was taken to the carriage. She saw that the only ones who had come from Pemberley were the driver, a maidservant, and a manservant. The manservant easily hoisted Elizabeth's baggage onto the carriage and secured it. The maidservant approached Elizabeth, curtseyed, and introduced herself. Elizabeth remembered seeing this young lady, who was about her own age or a little older, while at Pemberley. Her name was Anna.

Once everything was loaded on the carriage, Elizabeth turned and wrapped her arms around Mrs. Ketterling. She had much to thank her for, and she wanted to make certain she knew she had appreciated all they had done for her. Tears filled her eyes, and this time Elizabeth was not so inclined to hide them from her, for Mrs. Ketterling would understand the reason for them.

The sun was now peaking over the tops of the distant hills. The few clouds that dotted the sky were filled with reds and yellows against the dark blue. A few stars could still be seen in the early morning dawn. This would likely be the last Derbyshire sunrise she would ever see. It would have been beautiful from atop the ridge.

After a tearful goodbye, Elizabeth stepped into the carriage. As she sat down, its plush cushion startled her. She was not used to riding in such luxury. Anna handed her a blanket and a pillow, which Elizabeth accepted gratefully. As the carriage pulled away, Elizabeth gave a final wave of her hand to Mrs. Ketterling, and then leaned her head toward the window, gazing out. She found each breath difficult to take as they made their way through Lambton, down the dirt road. It veered to the right, taking her in a southerly direction; each turn taking her farther away from Pemberley.

Her eyes turned upward to the sky as the sun climbed higher. She closed her eyes and wondered whether Mr. Darcy had taken his customary walk up the ridge to watch the sunrise. Had he waited to see the carriage off this morning? Was he grateful she was finally out of his life? A tear escaped through her closed lids as she reasoned that he certainly had to be.

~~*

The two ladies rode in silence for the first part of the trip. Elizabeth was grateful that Anna seemed to respect her wish for quiet and rest. The young girl likely assumed she was sleeping, as she kept her face away from her, her eyes closed except for those few times she opened them to see the scenery through which they passed. When she finally felt equal to it, she turned to Anna, stretching out her arms as if just awakening.

Anna smiled at her. "I hope you were able to get some sleep. I know it was an early departure."

Elizabeth smiled. "Fortunately, I am an early riser. I did not sleep well last night, however, so it has been good to get a little more rest."

Anna nodded and then leaned forward, pulling up a large parcel. "If you are at all hungry, I have some things the kitchen sent along for us."

"Thank you, but I have no need of anything right now."

The girl continued to look in the parcel and pulled something out. "Mr. Darcy thought you might enjoy some reading material." She held two books in her hand and extended them to Elizabeth.

Elizabeth's eyes widened as she recognized the book of Cowper's poems that she had spent a good amount of time reading while at Pemberley. If he had not been aware of that, he may have recollected her mentioning the fondness she had for Cowper from their conversation at the top of the ridge. The other book was a compilation of short stories.

"I shall enjoy these very much," she told Anna. She looked down at the

166

books, her fingers stroking the supple leather of the covers. She then lifted her eyes to Anna. "Do you enjoy reading?"

"I do not have the time to read much." She let out a nervous giggle. "Although I must confess that I often crawl into bed with a gothic novel." Her shoulders shivered. "Sometimes I become so dreadfully frightened by those stories that I find it impossible to sleep."

Elizabeth laughed. "I have read my share of them. *Udolpho* can have you imagining all sorts of things! The normal sounds a house makes at night suddenly become something ominous!"

Anna chuckled. "Hearing footsteps approaching down the hall is my greatest fear. I always imagine it is someone who has evil intent."

Elizabeth's hand remained resting on the books. "How long have you worked at Pemberley?" she asked.

The young lady smiled. "How long have I not? My grandmother was the late Mrs. Darcy's personal maid. When my mother was young, she shadowed Mrs. Reynolds and recently became the housekeeper in the Darcys' London home. My father is the butler and one of my brothers is apprenticing as a steward."

"Is that why you are going to London – to see your family?"

The young girl nodded. "Yes, as well as the fact that I frequently go back and forth as needed." Anna turned to look out the window. "When I was younger, I had a secret hope to someday become Miss Darcy's personal maid. My grandmother taught me everything she knew about being the personal maid of a Mistress, but so far I have not had the opportunity. I was too young when Miss Darcy began to require one, and she has been very happy with Ellen."

"So you go where you are needed and do what is needed?"

Anna nodded. "I am frequently allowed to serve as a personal maid to guests who for one reason or other are without one while at Pemberley or in Town. I truly enjoy tending to the ladies, helping them look pretty."

"If you enjoy that so much, could you find employment elsewhere being someone's maid? Certainly you have good experience and would likely get a good recommendation."

Anna shrugged her shoulders. "I suppose I could, but working for the Darcys has been too good. I have heard too many stories about Masters who treat their help harshly and with very little respect. I could not bear that. I would prefer to work for the Darcys doing what they need, rather than work for someone else, even if it was doing what I enjoy doing. I am still young and hope that one day there will be a position for me."

She gave Elizabeth a sly smile. "I have always hoped that Mr. Darcy would consider me for his wife's personal maid…" she let out a chuckle. "…if he ever decides to take a wife." She shook her head and narrowed her brows. "There are so many women who have made fools of themselves over the man. He sometimes seems oblivious to it all, but then I think there are times he does see it and finds it appalling. Some wonder if he will ever find a woman who will love him for himself and not merely for his fortune, his estate, and his standing in society."

Elizabeth pursed her lips as she listened. She wondered if the young girl had heard any of the speculation about her and Mr. Darcy in regards to the letter that was found. By her words, Anna did not seem to have any knowledge of it. Elizabeth hoped that word had not spread amongst the servants.

The time in the carriage that first day passed quickly. Elizabeth and Anna commented on the passing scenery, a poem Elizabeth read, or the food they enjoyed that had been sent along. They made two stops before making a stop at an inn for the night. Elizabeth was grateful for Anna's company. They ate their evening meal together in the inn, and Elizabeth was adamant that they share a room. As they prepared for bed, Anna found herself doing those things a personal maid would do, and Elizabeth kept reminding her that she was solely required to accompany her to London, nothing else. She did concede, however, to allow her to arrange her hair the next morning. Elizabeth thought to herself that she would very much enjoy having someone like Anna attend her.

They continued on their journey early the next morning after a hearty breakfast. Elizabeth was more inclined to eat, as she was enjoying Anna's company and was very well pleased with the way in which the young lady arranged her hair. She also knew that some time this afternoon she would be home – at least at her aunt and uncle's home. She would see Jane, and nothing could diminish her anticipation of that.

Elizabeth became more reflective the closer they came to London. Anna seemed to sense that and left her to her thoughts. Those thoughts prompted her to consider the possible scenarios she would encounter when she arrived. The most likely of these were that Lydia had not been found and no one knew anything more than what had been initially conveyed in the letter. There was also the possibility that she and Wickham had been found in a disgraceful situation and her family would already be suffering the dire consequences of that. Elizabeth found it difficult to hope that Lydia had returned home on her own volition, leaving Wickham before anything happened. She knew both her sister and Wickham too well to hope for that.

As Elizabeth nervously rubbed her hands together in contemplation, she knew her own chances of marrying for love were now lost. The man she loved would never consider an alliance with someone having such family members as those two. She would somehow recover, but it was Jane for whom she had the greatest concern. She wondered how loyal Mr. Bingley would remain toward her. A disgrace such as this would surely give him the right to break off their engagement. What he would do in this situation would certainly signify whether he put his love for her above all else.

At length, Elizabeth observed they had reached the outskirts of London. They passed by an increasing number of houses, and they encountered more carriages travelling on the road. Her heart quickened its pace, seeming to mimic the busyness upon which they came. It was now only a matter of time before she would know which of her conjectures were true.

As she kept her eyes to the window, she began to see sights that she recognized. Looking at Anna, she asked, "Will you be going directly to the Darcys' town home after leaving me at my aunt and uncle's?"

Anna nodded. "Yes. I have been at Pemberley over a month now, so I am eager to see my family." She smiled and folded her hands, placing them in her lap. "I have nowhere else I would rather go."

Elizabeth soon saw the park in which she often walked when visiting her aunt and uncle. Then they passed the row of homes that lined the street around the corner from their residence. The carriage made a final turn and stopped in front of their home.

A broad smile appeared on Elizabeth's face. It was good to finally be at a place she could call home! She would soon see her family, and no matter Lydia's outcome, she would have Jane and her aunt and uncle to help her bear it!

The door opened and the driver helped her out as the manservant retrieved her luggage. Before turning to walk up to the house, she looked back in at Anna. "I do hope to see you again. Thank you for making the journey here pleasant. I appreciated your company and everything you did."

"I did nothing out of the ordinary. But thank you for your kind words."

Elizabeth started for the house, but stopped. Looking back at Anna, she said, "Please thank Mr. Darcy for me. Tell him I am most grateful."

Anna smiled. "I certainly shall."

Elizabeth turned, and her chest briefly tightened at the mere mention of his name. Her eyes took in the modest house the Gardiners called home. It was nothing to Pemberley, but it had all the warmth and love one could ever want. Her heart swelled with the anticipation of seeing those she loved, despite whatever had befallen them.

The manservant, having deposited her bag on the step of the Gardiner home, knocked. Just as Elizabeth stepped up to the door, it opened. "Miss Bennet!" cried Nichols. "It is good to see you!"

"It is good to see you, too Nichols." She stepped in and handed her light shawl to him. "How goes things? How is everyone?"

Before answering, he gave directions to the manservant as to where he could take Elizabeth's things, and then turned to Elizabeth. "I believe you will find them all in good spirits. They are in the drawing room, Miss Bennet."

"Thank you, Nichols," she said with a smile. "There is no need to announce me. I shall see myself in."

"Yes, ma'am."

Elizabeth could hear voices as she walked briskly toward the door, but the one she readily recognized, despite the fact that she had not seen her in almost a twelvemonth, was that of her mother. Her raised, high-pitched exclamations caused Elizabeth to inwardly shudder, knowing they could mean just about anything.

As Elizabeth stepped through the door, her mother sat directly in front of her. Spotting her daughter, Mrs. Bennet brought her hands together in a loud clap. "Look here! Lizzy has arrived!"

Elizabeth walked directly over to her, taking her hands in hers. "Hello, Mama. It is so good to see you." She leaned over and kissed her mother on the cheek. Her aunt and Jane were seated on either side of her mother, and as she reached out to grasp each of their hands, Mrs. Bennet continued.

"It is good to see you, too, Lizzy, but what news we have to tell! We are all quite delighted with all that has transpired. It has all turned out so splendidly!"

Elizabeth looked at her mother, relief flooding her. Waiting for an explanation, she then looked questioningly at her aunt and sister. Mrs. Bennet answered her unasked question with, "Lydia is to be married! Is that not the most wonderful news?"

Elizabeth's eyes widened as she released Jane's and her aunt's hands. The contrast between her mother's joyous expression and the more sombre expressions of Jane and her aunt spoke volumes to her.

Elizabeth shook her head as she slowly asked the dreaded question, "To *whom* is she to be married?"

"Why, Mr. Wickham, of course! And it was arranged so handsomely by Mr. Darcy." Mrs. Bennet waved her handkerchief excitedly in the air. "He even provided them with their own home in Hertfordshire, a very easy distance from Meryton!"

"Mr. Darcy?" exclaimed Elizabeth. "How could that be? He would not have…" Suddenly she saw it all in their eyes. They were not looking at her, but beyond her. At once she knew that someone was standing behind her.

She swallowed hard, trying to moisten her suddenly dry mouth. Taking a deep breath, she slowly turned. She found herself face to face with the two gentlemen who had apparently been seated across the room all this time. They were now standing, as they must have stood as soon as she entered, but they had been out of her view. Her mind made every attempt to comprehend what she saw, but she could not.

The two gentlemen bowed, and Elizabeth made an awkward attempt at a curtsey. "Good afternoon, Mr. Bingley," Elizabeth said. Her eyes then turned to the other, confusion sweeping across her face. "Good afternoon, Mr. Darcy."

Chapter 23

Elizabeth had so many questions; unfortunately the only one forefront in her mind was 'Why is Mr. Darcy here?' But she could not ask that now. She turned back to her mother, struggling to formulate a question, let alone a thought.

"Where is Lydia now?"

"Lydia and Kitty are upstairs," her mother answered with a wide smile. "Most likely they are talking about the wedding!" Mrs. Bennet pursed her lips. "Mary is with them."

Mrs. Gardiner smiled. "I am quite certain Mary wants to ensure there is a little decorum in their plans."

Mrs. Bennet waved her handkerchief again. "Oh, she will only lecture and moralize. Poor Lydia! You know how Mary can be so tiresome in her opinions."

Elizabeth sighed. "When is the wedding to be?"

"Two weeks. There is so much to do!"

"She is to be married before…" Elizabeth paused, not knowing whether there even would be a wedding between Jane and Mr. Bingley. She bit her lip, deciding what to ask next. "Is my uncle here? My cousins?" Her questions only served to give her time to think.

Her aunt answered, "My husband had some business dealings today. He ought to be home soon. The children have been spending these days with my sister, who agreed to take them for a time." She gave her a knowing look. "We thought it would be best."

Elizabeth wanted answers – needed answers – and she desperately searched for some way to get them. Her mother then conveniently answered one, as Elizabeth had questions concerning Mr. Wickham. As Mrs. Bennet spoke, her eyes were again directed behind Elizabeth. Tilting her head toward the gentlemen and nodding in approval she said, "Mr. Darcy has graciously allowed Mr. Wickham to remain in his town home until the wedding."

Elizabeth turned abruptly and stared incredulously at Mr. Darcy. She felt as though she were in a dream where nothing made sense.

Mrs. Bennet's eyes narrowed as she looked at Elizabeth and continued in her discourse, shaking her head in displeasure. "My brother has insisted upon some excessive rules that keep Mr. Wickham from seeing his Lydia as much as they would wish. They…"

Before Mrs. Bennet could finish her thought, an idea came to Elizabeth. Without thinking, she interrupted her mother by looking to her sister and saying, "Jane, I am desperately in need of some fresh air and a walk. I have been confined in a carriage for two days and would *very much* enjoy a stroll about the neighbourhood."

She reached over and grasped Jane's arm, startling her somewhat as she pulled her to her feet. "Perhaps Mr. Bingley and his friend would accompany us." It was not a question. "Will you excuse us, please?"

She ushered Jane quickly through the room, eyeing Mr. Darcy as she walked past in a way that meant she wished to talk with him. The two men gave short bows to Mrs. Gardiner and Mrs. Bennet, and then silently followed Elizabeth and Jane as they walked out of the house.

After taking several impatient steps away from the house, Elizabeth heard Mr. Darcy whisper something to Mr. Bingley, who immediately stepped up alongside Jane.

"May I?" he asked, extending his arm. Jane willingly took it, prompting Elizabeth to pause and wait for Mr. Darcy to draw up alongside her.

In two steps he was at her side, but she remained where she was, bringing him to a halt. Once Jane and Mr. Bingley were a sufficient distance ahead, she turned and began to walk, Darcy following her lead.

"What are you doing here?" she asked in a whispered voice fraught with bewilderment.

"What kind of greeting is that?" he asked. "You spend almost two weeks at Pemberley and you greet me with, 'What are you doing here?'"

Elizabeth looked up at him, trying to read the expression on his face. His eyes betrayed his fatigue, and his creased brow revealed the days of frustration he must have experienced dealing with Wickham. But when his eyes turned to meet Elizabeth's, his lips curved up in a slight smile. The sight stirred her deeply and her heart responded with an ardent pulsing.

"I trust you understand my meaning," she answered quickly. Turning her eyes back to the path before them, she continued, "The last I saw you, I had just informed you about Wickham's involvement in my sister's dreadful behaviour. I believed you to be quite... incensed at the news. You departed immediately to return to Pemberley... and your guests!"

"True," he said solemnly. "I *was* greatly incensed. And I did return to Pemberley, but only briefly. I knew that if anyone could find Wickham and your sister in London quickly, it would be me. I determined to set off immediately."

Elizabeth opened her mouth but words did not come. She slowly shook her head as a myriad of thoughts and more questions assaulted her. She was finally able to utter, "But why would you do this? You had guests at Pemberley! You despise the man!"

"Hmmm, yes, on both counts," he murmured. "Georgiana is likely entertaining the Goldsmiths and Hamilton as we speak. I suspect that by now, the Willstones have departed."

Elizabeth lowered her head. "Their premature departure is due to the letter, is it not? I am terribly grieved over the... misunderstanding and mortification that letter must have caused," Elizabeth said softly, feeling deep regret for her carelessness.

"It was not just the matter of the letter that prompted their departure. That misunderstanding merely gave them a convenient excuse to leave." He stopped and let out a huff, combing his fingers roughly through his hair. "If ever I gave them… gave *Miss Matthews*… the impression that I…" He clenched his jaw and looked down. Softly and repentantly, he said, "It was not my intention to mislead or deceive anyone. I fear I do not always see these things clearly."

A smile touched Elizabeth's lips at his admission. It revealed a side of him that she found rather engaging. Here was a man who was so eligible, yet oblivious to the ladies who set their sights on him. It was very possible that he was unaware of even Caroline Bingley's profuse admiration. Elizabeth sensed his discomfiture, however, and deemed it prudent to quickly change the subject.

"You departed Pemberley, yet the letter I received while at the Ketterlings informing me that the carriage would come the following day… it was written by you."

His smile was tinged with guilt. "I wrote it before I departed for London and I advised those who accompanied you not to inform you that I had been away."

"But why?" Elizabeth asked as she stood looking up to him.

Darcy turned and began to walk again. He took a few steps away from her in silence, obviously weighing his words. Coming to a stop, he turned to look back at Elizabeth, who remained at a standstill. "I knew you would discourage any assistance from me if you knew my plans. It was my decision to keep you uninformed of my coming to London to find Wickham and your sister."

"You had no reason to do all this. You were under no obligation to me, my family, and most of all, Mr. Wickham. What you have done for him… for my sister…" Elizabeth let out a disgusted sigh. "We both know how little Wickham deserves any such generosity."

Darcy gazed down at her with a single brow raised. "*That* is why I did not wish for you to know. I have already acted and yet still you state your argument for why I should not." A smile appeared, giving Elizabeth the assurance that he knew her well.

His smile disarmed Elizabeth. She looked down and shook her head. "But why would you do all this?"

"I had my reasons."

He was obviously not going to explain. With questions still swirling in her head, she debated which one to ask next. She was grateful that Jane and Mr. Bingley were quite a distance ahead of them, but her voice softened as she asked her next question. "What are Mr. Bingley's views on Lydia's actions? Certainly he must have considered that if our family was tainted with disgrace, it would not be in his best interest to marry Jane."

Darcy chuckled lightly under his breath. "My good friend Bingley is of a most peculiar nature. He is so easy going and good natured that he hardly ever anticipates any wrong occurring." His voice became reflective and he tilted his head at Elizabeth as he said, "I believe your sister is very much like him in that regard."

Elizabeth murmured an assent.

Darcy turned and began walking again; this time Elizabeth followed. "When

I arrived at your aunt and uncle's house, Bingley and your sister were both overly confident that Wickham and Lydia would be found and the situation would not be as dire as first thought." He looked down at Elizabeth and smiled. "On this occasion, I did not interfere with my own conjectures, hoping – yet doubtful – it would progress as they both anticipated."

"How soon did you find them?"

Darcy drew in a breath. "It was not until the following afternoon. I will spare you the details of how I came to find them. Suffice it to say that marriage was the only viable option."

"So they are to marry, then." In frustration, she kicked a large pebble that lay in the path. "And allowing Wickham to stay at your London home? I cannot believe you would do so much for that man."

He pursed his lips slightly before answering. "Right now, he is tied up and gagged in one of draughtiest rooms of the house. I allow him only bread and water and will keep him there until the day of the wedding."

Now Elizabeth chuckled, but only briefly. "While I highly doubt that, it certainly would be what he deserves."

Darcy shrugged.

"Pray, forgive me, Mr. Darcy, but I must inquire about the house. How can you justify it? They are far too undeserving!"

Darcy let out a long breath. "While what I did may sound generous, I have implemented some very strict imperatives. As a matter of fact, the house does not belong to them and will never belong to them. It is in my name and even if Wickham gambles away everything he owns, the house cannot be taken away. It sits on enough land with sufficient crops and several tenants who will supply a modest income for them. I have hired a reliable associate to be steward and he will handle all the finances. Your sister will be safe."

"But still, neither of them deserves this."

Darcy halted his steps and turned to Elizabeth. "They deserve each other and they will certainly get what they deserve."

Elizabeth's breath faltered and she stopped and looked up at him as she realized his meaning. "Yes, I suppose they will…"

Darcy continued, "The home is large enough to accommodate the Wickhams, as well as your mother and two younger sisters if they choose to live there. They will no longer need to be at the mercy of your aunt and uncle in Meryton. This will improve their situation."

"I hope they have expressed their gratitude."

"Abundantly."

"And Wickham has agreed to this?"

"It was the only way I would untie him."

Elizabeth readily noticed the curl of his lips. "It pleases me – yet perplexes me – that you can jest after all that man has done. He ought to be locked up and the key thrown into the Thames!"

"We are of like mind in that," Darcy offered. "Wickham agreed because he had no other recourse. He had far too many debts – most from gambling – and was about to be dismissed from his regiment for disciplinary reasons."

"And this man Lydia wants as her husband?" Elizabeth cried out in frustration, pounding her fists through the air. She was not really expecting an answer.

His silence was answer enough.

Finally, Darcy asked, "Do you mind if we speak of other, more pleasant things?"

"Oh, yes!" Elizabeth exclaimed, and the two continued walking. "Please allow me to tell you how much I appreciate you arranging for my travels to London in your carriage. It was most comfortable and I truly enjoyed Anna's company on the journey."

"I am pleased. Georgiana knows her well and thought she would make a good travelling companion for you."

"Thank you also for the books. We enjoyed reading from them as we journeyed, helping the time to pass more quickly. That was very kind of you. I really did not expect…"

He nodded and waved his hand through the air. "It was nothing."

When Elizabeth glanced up at him, she noticed his pinched brow and tightly pursed lips, a sure indication of the awkwardness he was feeling, likely due to all her praise. She decided to leave the topic of their next discourse to him.

He finally spoke. "The first morning you were at the Ketterlings, I had no knowledge of your departure. I thought… I had hoped you might walk up to the ridge…"

"In my mud boots?" she said with a mischievous smile, hoping to ease his discomfiture.

"Yes, in your mud boots," he replied as he brought his hands together and nervously rubbed his fingers. "I wished to show you something."

"The sunrise? I remember."

He shook his head. "There was something else."

Elizabeth stopped and turned to look at him. "What was that?"

Darcy looked toward Jane and Bingley, who were now slowly walking back towards them. "There is a house and some land that is for sale. It is on the other side of the ridge. When you encountered me that first morning, I had just come from viewing it from up there." He moistened his lips and paused. "I thought it would be a good home for Bingley and his new bride. I wished to know your opinion of it."

Elizabeth's brows rose as high as her jaw dropped. "You wished to know my opinion?"

"I know the view of the estate from up there was somewhat limited; however, I believed you would have had an idea whether your sister would be pleased with it."

"Have you mentioned it to Mr. Bingley?"

"Yes, we leave first thing in the morning for Derbyshire. He wishes to see it."

"And he will make his decision on his own?"

Darcy skewered his mouth. "You mean without my interference?"

Elizabeth laughed. "Perhaps I wondered whether he would seek my sister's input."

"I promise you the decision will be totally, completely in his hands, but…" Darcy took a deep breath and Elizabeth waited for him to let it out. "If he asks for my advice, I will certainly give it."

Elizabeth smiled. "Indeed, I am quite certain *he* will… as will *you*."

Darcy's demeanour grew serious. "I wondered whether you… I mean, I thought you might… reside with them once they are settled. You no longer have a need to be a governess."

"This is not something Jane and I have even discussed. Perhaps Lydia would want me to live with *them*." A twinkle in her eye as she glanced up at Mr. Darcy was met by the darkening of his own. "Then again, perhaps not," she quickly added.

He was silent for a moment and Elizabeth wondered if her teasing had angered him. She promptly reassured him, "If Mr. Bingley and Jane did invite me to live with them, *that* would certainly be my preference."

"I thought so. I hoped so." Darcy fisted and then opened his hands, stretching his fingers taut. After a brief moment of silence, he stopped walking and turned toward Elizabeth. "I wished to know your opinion… how you felt… about them living so close to Pemberley… given the prospect of you living with them."

Elizabeth searched his eyes. Her heart pounded as she contemplated what he wished to know. Was he concerned that she would not wish to live so close to him? Or did he hope she did?

She could not immediately think of an appropriate answer, so she asked a question. "Just how close is it to Pemberley?"

"Well, that is no easy answer. If you wish it to be close, it is merely a three mile walk from the top of the ridge down to the edge of their property. If you would prefer it to be far, it is a gruelling fifteen miles by carriage as you have to drive out through the woods, cross a river, and then proceed around the ridge."

Elizabeth laughed, her heart still pounding. The deliberations of her answer, however, were interrupted by the return of Charles and Jane.

Jane's arm was tucked so intimately through Bingley's that Elizabeth felt a tinge of jealousy. How she would love to wrap her arm through Mr. Darcy's in similar fashion.

"Have you heard about the house, Lizzy? Has Mr. Darcy told you?"

"Only the barest of details. I know it resides either three miles or fifteen miles from Pemberley, depending upon your mode of transportation."

"I think it sounds wonderful, Lizzy. You will come and live with us, I hope. It is a big enough home. You can have your own apartment."

Elizabeth cast her eyes to Mr. Bingley, who seemed to be in hearty agreement. "I can barely contain myself with this news Darcy brought. Imagine him being our neighbour! I am inclined to take the house sight unseen, based on Darcy's encouragement!"

Elizabeth glanced at Mr. Darcy, who displayed an awkward smile. He put up his hands in protest. "Now, Bingley, I have merely told you what I thought. You must decide for yourself!"

"Have you ever steered me wrong, good friend?" Bingley asked.

To Elizabeth, the silence was deafening. She was quite certain Darcy's thoughts – as hers – went to the advice he had once given his friend about Jane. That seemed so very long ago.

Elizabeth saw the admiration in both Jane's and Bingley's faces as they looked at Mr. Darcy. He, however, had paled, his eyes cast down in remorse. Elizabeth was convinced he was about to confess his grievous fault in front of them all. There was no need to announce it now!

Without thinking, she slipped her arm through Mr. Darcy's and before he could utter a word said, "Tell us about the house as we walk back, Mr. Darcy. I should like to hear all about it." She encouraged him with a nod of her head.

Darcy tenderly took her hand and gave it a gentle tug, pulling her arm further through his, securing it against him. He then placed his other hand over hers. It was then that she became aware of what she had done. How often had she taken a gentleman's arm, but this time it prompted a warm flush to sweep across her face, sending a shiver that reached all the way to her toes. Nothing had ever felt as right as this; her arm nicely tucked in his. He held onto her hand as if he feared she would be snatched away.

She lifted her eyes and met his. All trace of the fatigue and frustration she had seen earlier in his features had been replaced by a look of tenderness. She rewarded him with a smile.

"Come, now!" exclaimed Bingley. "We are waiting."

Darcy looked over to his friend. "Waiting?" he said, apparently unmindful of the previous discussion.

A nudge from Elizabeth, and a soft, "You were about to tell us about the house," brought him to his senses.

They began to walk and he proceeded to tell them all about Braedenthorn Manor, at least as he recollected it. He had made inquiries about the house and it was shown to him one of the days he had been gone from Pemberley. It was of moderate size, in very good condition; the living quarters were all quite spacious, the downstairs sitting room and library were small, but the dining room and kitchen were recently remodelled and expansive. The gardens had not been maintained, but the roads leading into it were.

It required much concentration for Elizabeth to tend to his words, particularly when she felt his fingers entwine with hers. Jane and Mr. Bingley conveniently walked ahead of them, and when they looked back to better hear Mr. Darcy's words, they were so enthralled with his descriptions that they did not notice how tenderly he held her hand, nor did they notice the warm blush upon Elizabeth's cheeks.

As they came to the house, the sun was just beginning to set. Jane and Mr. Bingley took the steps quickly, but Mr. Darcy stopped, pulling back gently on Elizabeth's arm. He looked down at her hand in his, giving it a tender stroke with his fingertips. He glanced up and searched her face. "You have yet to answer my last question, Miss Elizabeth."

"Your last question?" she asked breathlessly. "Which one was that?" She truly could not comprehend anything beyond the touch of his hand.

"If you choose to reside with your sister, your *elder* sister, that is, what are your feelings about living in such close proximity to Pemberley?"

Elizabeth pinched her brows down in contemplation. "Pemberley is a fine house," she said, making a vain attempt at concealing a smile. "One could not ask for a finer estate to have in one's neighbourhood."

He lay her hand flat against his open hand and stroked it with his other hand. "I believe you know my point was that *I* would be *your* neighbour."

Elizabeth felt her heart would burst, it beat so fervently. He stood so close; her small hand now pressed between both of his and his eyes searched her face. "I think…" she said slowly as she forced herself to breathe and think clearly. "I would very much like it."

Mr. Darcy must have been holding his breath as well, for as soon as the words were out of her mouth, he released a long puff of air. "I am very glad to hear that."

He reluctantly released her hand, but not before giving it a gentle squeeze, and the two proceeded into the house. Once they crossed the threshold, he released her arm, but her heart he would not relinquish.

Chapter 24

When Elizabeth and her companions entered the house, they greeted her uncle, who had just returned. From the sound of the raised voices they heard as they approached the drawing room, she was certain that Lydia and her sisters had come downstairs and joined the others. Just as Elizabeth was about to step in, she heard the voice of George Wickham.

She was surprised by the anger that swept through her at the mere sound of his voice. It brought back memories of how greatly she had been deceived by his cunning charm, and how deeply he had wounded Mr. Darcy and his sister. As she followed Jane and Mr. Bingley in, she steeled herself for her – and Mr. Darcy's – encounter with him.

When they stepped into the drawing room, Elizabeth not only saw – but felt – the glare Wickham levelled at Darcy as he lifted his gaze beyond her to him. Wickham immediately looked back at Elizabeth and a forced smile appeared as he walked over to greet her. "Good afternoon, Miss Elizabeth." Despite his air of self-assurance, his voice faltered. "It is good to see you again."

"Hello, Mr. Wickham," Elizabeth uttered through a clenched jaw, followed by a mumbled wish for felicity in his marriage to her sister. He expressed an appreciation for her kind wishes, but she paid little heed to his words.

She abruptly excused herself to go over and greet her sisters, but kept her eye on Mr. Darcy to see how he would proceed. He turned away from Wickham immediately, forgoing any sort of greeting, and walked to the far side of the room. He lowered himself into a chair near her aunt and they began to converse. Elizabeth felt a gripping pain as she realized how difficult it must be for him to be in Wickham's presence. When Darcy turned to Elizabeth, she gave him a heartening smile. He acknowledged her with a smile of his own, and she then turned her full attention to her sisters.

She greeted each of them with a hug, truly pleased to see them, yet saddened for the attitude both Lydia and Kitty displayed. While they talked excitedly of the wedding, in whispers they derided the admonitions their uncle had placed upon the newly engaged couple. To Elizabeth's discerning eye, Lydia appeared even more immature than her sixteen years. The manner in which Lydia talked about her upcoming marriage made it appear she was more interested in the fact that she was to be married before any of her sisters than she was in the person whom she was marrying. Elizabeth was angered, but not surprised.

The Gardiners' home, being only of modest size, had a dining room that would comfortably accommodate eight. For that reason, Mrs. Gardiner asked Elizabeth, Jane, Mr. Bingley, and Mr. Darcy to dine together in the smaller breakfast room while the others gathered in the dining room. Elizabeth wondered whether her aunt had any suspicions regarding the feelings she harboured for Mr. Darcy or that he might possibly have for her, but reasoned she would have no reason to suspect.

Elizabeth was grateful for the separate, more intimate arrangement. When they sat down to dine, the voices from the other room were often raised and excitable, particularly those of Lydia and her mother. Elizabeth rarely heard her aunt or uncle, or even Mr. Wickham. She wondered with spiteful curiosity how much *he* was enjoying these people who were to become his own family. That thought, however, made her shudder as she considered how Mr. Darcy would expend just as much effort tolerating certain members of her family.

Despite the occasional discomfiture brought on by the outbursts coming from the dining room, Elizabeth truly enjoyed the camaraderie that the foursome shared as they dined. Jane and Mr. Bingley were exceptionally happy – she could almost tangibly feel the love they had for one another. It was also apparent that Mr. Bingley and Mr. Darcy had a deep, abiding friendship. As Elizabeth watched their interactions, she readily noticed the respect the two had for one another.

Much of their conversation was about the estate in Derbyshire. Excitement brightened the engaged couple's eyes as they began to imagine what life would hold for them once they were married and had a country home of their own. Jane proclaimed that she loved the estate even before seeing it. Mr. Bingley, while just as eager to claim the house as their own, guardedly reminded her that he would only make a decision after seeing it for himself and determining whether it would suit them. In the very next breath, however, he spoke as if he had already taken possession of it.

In the course of the evening, Jane and Mr. Bingley repeatedly thanked Mr. Darcy for all he had done for them. Bingley often expressed how much he valued his friend's guidance. With each utterance of praise, another look of discomfiture spread across Mr. Darcy's features. Elizabeth readily surmised that he felt awkward not solely for the profuse praises being heaped upon him, but due to his awareness that she had questioned how much influence he exerted over his friend. She smiled, however, in the realization of just how much Bingley looked to his friend and respected his advice.

Later, when everyone gathered together in the drawing room, Elizabeth felt again the lack of decorum that several family members exhibited. She often found herself recoiling at something one of them did or said. Save for Jane and her aunt and uncle, her family obligingly gave hearty confirmation to Elizabeth of their ill-manners. Mr. Bingley never seemed to notice; his eyes and thoughts were solely on his beloved Jane, her face continually serene, her smile soothing. Mr. Darcy, however, stiffened at every outburst or reckless deed, seeking, it appeared, solace from these disturbances by turning his eyes upon Elizabeth's face. While she could not return the same expression of serenity as Jane, she gave him an encouraging smile that she hoped would blot out the disorderly commotion occasionally exhibited.

Elizabeth was inclined to believe that Mr. Darcy and Mr. Wickham had made a pact of some sort to keep their distance from one another. Perhaps Mr. Darcy had threatened Mr. Wickham that if he came within arm's reach of him, all he had offered would be revoked. She wondered just how the arrangement of Wickham residing at his town home taxed him and she assumed Mr. Darcy was more than happy to return to Pemberley on the morrow if only to be out of Wickham's presence.

Elizabeth would miss him dearly, but she had sufficient assurances in her heart that he still loved her. While he had not explicitly communicated his affection, his actions had revealed how much he still cared for her. He certainly had withheld nothing.

Later that evening when Mr. Bingley and Mr. Darcy were about to take their leave, Jane opportunely asked Elizabeth to step out with her to say goodbye to the gentlemen. Elizabeth was delighted to oblige her. At the least, she might be able to leave Mr. Darcy with a final memory of the evening that was more agreeable than what he endured during the last few hours.

When they stepped out into the cool evening air, the engaged couple walked ahead toward the waiting carriage. Mr. Darcy stopped and turned to Elizabeth.

"Bingley and I shall be gone for three or four days," he said. "I shall return in time for the wedding."

Elizabeth's eyes saddened and she let out a long sigh. "Yes, the wedding." She looked up at him. "You are confident Mr. Wickham will not flee in your absence?"

Darcy smiled, hoping to lighten her mood. "Did I not tell you that I keep him bound and gagged?"

Elizabeth let out a soft chuckle, appreciating Darcy's humour in such a dreadful situation. "Yes, you did, sir. I must have forgotten."

"May I... when I return, may I call on you here?"

The only light came from inside the home, but Elizabeth readily could see the intensity of Mr. Darcy's gaze. He searched her face as he awaited her answer.

She nodded slowly and smiled. "I should like that very much. I look forward to your return."

He let out a long breath of air and smiled in return. "I am glad."

He turned to leave, but Elizabeth reached out her hand and wrapped her fingers about his arm, bringing him to a halt. He turned to look at her and then very slowly covered her hand with his. A smile appeared, one of many that Elizabeth had seen directed at her tonight. "Miss Bennet?" he said. "Ought we not join your sister and Bingley? I cannot vouch for his behaviour. We may need to serve as their chaperones."

"In due time. There is a matter of great import to me which requires an answer."

He tilted his head. "And what would that be?"

"I asked you earlier, but you never answered directly." Elizabeth pursed her lips tightly together, and then released them, taking in a short breath. "Why did you do all this for Mr. Wickham... for my family?"

He brought her hand forward, holding it in front of him and placed his other hand on top of hers, tapping it lightly with his fingers. He looked down at their joined hands for a moment and then glanced up, his eyes boring into hers. "Do you truly not know?"

Her heart pounded so strongly she wondered whether he could hear it. She was grateful for the darkness that surrounded them, for he would not see her flushed cheeks. She moistened her lips and answered with a single raised brow, "We have had a history of misunderstanding each other whenever we conversed, Mr. Darcy. I do not wish to be under any misapprehension because of something that was not explicitly communicated."

"Hmmm," Darcy murmured, now stroking her hand with his fingers. "You see, Miss Bennet, I…" he spoke slowly, taking great care to articulate what he wished to say in a manner that would not be misunderstood. "I find that my regard for you has endured… and has grown… since its inception. It endured an initial four months of self-imposed banishment from your presence, when I convinced Bingley not to return to Netherfield. I had determined to rid myself of all my feelings for you; feelings which I had deemed… unreasonable." He gently pressed his hands against Elizabeth's and smiled. "I now know it was anything but unreasonable."

As he spoke, Elizabeth felt her heart pound so that it almost constricted her throat. She was very careful, however, not to move, so as not to distract Mr. Darcy's declaration.

He continued, "When I encountered you at Rosings, I was rather surprised to discover that my feelings for you had not diminished as I had intended, but were more fervent than they had been in Hertfordshire. While it was inexcusable, I believe that was the reason why my words to you in my… when I… came to you that afternoon were so filled with how great my struggle had been."

Elizabeth listened quietly, knowing this was not easy for him. She placed her other hand on top of his, to encourage him to continue.

"Consequently, my regard endured another year of separation as a result of…" Darcy took in a deep breath and let it out slowly. "As a result of the outcome of that afternoon at Rosings."

Elizabeth cast her face and eyes down, feeling a sense of regret for all she had said to him. He pulled his hand out from under hers and lifted her chin up with his fingers.

"It taught me things that I never had considered about myself." Very softly he said, "As much as it put me under a weight of despair, I was eventually able to examine what you said to me, see the truth in it, and make an attempt to alter my ways. In the course of that year, I could only hope that one day I would have another occasion to show you I had heeded your grievances against me."

Elizabeth shook her head in protest. "But so much of what I said was horribly wrong!"

"And yet much of what you said was painfully accurate." Darcy again covered Elizabeth's hands with his. "This past Easter, while visiting my aunt, I learned from her of your father's death and how Mr. Collins had taken ownership of Longbourn through the entail. While her sole concern was finding a new clergyman, I was consumed with concern about *you*. I could not stop wondering where you were… what you were doing… *how* you were doing."

He must have shuddered, for she felt it course through his hands. "Then you found me at the Willstones," she said softly.

"Georgiana and Bingley told me about their encounter with you. When I heard from them that you were a governess to the Willstones' daughter, it was all I could do to keep myself away. It was convenient that I knew the family, and I soon found myself plotting to attend functions I knew they would likely attend. I hoped that in conversing with them, I would, at the least, hear about you and how you were faring."

Elizabeth smiled. "So you found an obliging and willing participant in Rosalyn."

Darcy skewed his mouth. "Little did I know that the attentions I paid to her, which were solely founded on my desire to hear word of you, she attributed as regard."

"As did her family," Elizabeth reminded him.

He let out a groan and shook his head briskly. "I am ashamed of my behaviour. I was so foolish."

"I suppose we both can admit to behaving foolishly at one time or another."

There was silence between them except for a slight breeze that rustled the leaves about them. Darcy lifted his gaze toward Bingley and Jane. He looked back down at Elizabeth with resolve in his eyes.

His weight shifted from one foot to another. "I wish you to know, however, that I do not consider my actions regarding Wickham and your sister at all foolish. When I tell you my regard for you has endured, that was one occasion when I had no inclination whatsoever to try and diminish what I felt for you. I determined as soon as you informed me of his complicity that I would do whatever I could to remedy the situation because…" His chest heaved with a breath. His voice was deep and low as he continued, "Because for a very long time I lived with the belief that I would never have another opportunity to declare my love to you. I love you, Elizabeth. I love you more than anything." He took a step closer to her.

Her breath caught at his words, and before she could respond with any coherent thought, he brought her hands up and quickly kissed the back of each of them. She was convinced the ground shook beneath them at that moment. She looked up at him, her head swimming in a wonderful dizziness. Even if she had wanted to, she could not respond with any words.

"I look forward to seeing you when I return," Darcy said softly.

He turned to leave, reluctantly releasing her hands. "Mr. Darcy, please wait!" Elizabeth's voice did not sound natural. The pulsing of her heart from her head to her toes made it difficult to even think.

Darcy stopped. "Yes?"

Her voice was almost a whisper. "Please allow me… there is something that I wish to tell you… I *must* tell you… before you leave."

He paused, his brows lowering in apprehensive anticipation of her words.

She gave him a reassuring smile and chuckled softly. "You expect some dreadful proclamation. I assure you it is not." Her heart beat wildly as she said, "Fitzwilliam, I love you, too."

His head tilted and he smiled, but at the same time his eyes glistened. "I have often dreamt of hearing you say those words." His voice broke in the midst of his admission. "You have made me the happiest of men."

They stood for several minutes in silence, staring into each other's faces. Darcy reached out and took Elizabeth's hand, squeezing it gently. He lifted it up slowly and pressed his lips to it, allowing the contact to linger slightly longer than he had before. His breath brushed against it as he softly whispered, "I shall count the days until I see you again."

Darcy released her hand and looked over at his friend. "I fear Bingley is ready to leave. Shall we?"

They walked over and joined the couple at the carriage. Jane came and stood next to Elizabeth, taking hold of her arm as the two men stepped up into the carriage. Elizabeth was grateful for the support Jane unwittingly gave her. She felt such euphoria that she was certain she would topple over at any minute. As the carriage began to pull away, Bingley's and Jane's eyes were locked together, as were Darcy's and Elizabeth's.

Jane still held tightly to Elizabeth's arm as they returned to the house. When they joined the others in the sitting room, they again encountered a boisterous Lydia, who was pleading with their uncle to allow Mr. Wickham to call the following morning. His visits had been limited to dining with the family at supper and spending the evening with them. While Lydia was protesting, Wickham looked as though he would rather be at an inquisition.

Elizabeth chuckled. The two certainly deserved one another.

It was not too much later that Wickham announced he had best leave. Elizabeth thought it was interesting how Mr. Darcy and Mr. Wickham kept their distance from each other. While Wickham was staying at Mr. Darcy's town home, he was obviously not given the privilege of even riding in the same carriage with him.

When he took his leave, Elizabeth and Jane eagerly retreated to Jane's room, which they would share for the duration of Elizabeth's stay. They looked forward to their time alone to enlighten each other about the past few months.

Once they had readied themselves for the night, they climbed into the bed. They sat with their backs leaning up against the headboard, a single candle lighting the room. Jane grasped Elizabeth's hand. "Lizzy! You must tell me everything that happened at Pemberley! With Mr. Darcy's most prodigious actions and singular attentions, I can only attribute it to an understanding between the two of you!"

Elizabeth squeezed her sister's hand. "Up until today, I fear we suffered only from *mis*understandings."

"I do not believe it!" Jane declared.

Elizabeth let out a laugh. "Mostly on my part. When he invited the Willstones to Pemberley, I was under the impression he did it because of a fondness he felt for Rosalyn. She had confided in me the strong regard she held for him. When I first arrived at Pemberley, I naturally felt awkward around him because I had turned down his offer of marriage. It was not long, however, that I began to see a side of him that I had not seen before… or at least one that I had not allowed myself to see. It was very difficult for me when I realized I loved him."

"And yet you believed him to return Miss Matthews' regard?"

"Initially I did, yes. At length, however, I began to suspect that he did not, but I still could not imagine that he would have any remnant of those feelings he once held for me."

"Certainly he must have eventually declared his intentions to you whilst in his home."

Elizabeth turned to her sister. She pulled a loose lock of hair that had fallen down across Jane's face and brushed it to the side. With a smile, she said, "When I took leave of Pemberley, I had no assurances from him."

"He spoke nothing to you of his feelings before you left?"

Elizabeth let out a reflective chuckle. "I left Pemberley at the strong urging of the Willstones. They were quite displeased with the news your letter brought, and I believe they had also come to suspect the feelings I harboured for Mr. Darcy or that he harboured for me. Unfortunately, both he and his sister were away from home the afternoon I left. Neither he nor his sister knew I left to stay with the Ketterlings in Lambton until the next morning."

"Oh, Lizzy! I am certain Mr. Darcy would have allowed you to remain on at Pemberley."

Elizabeth shook her head. "Unfortunately, in my position, I answered to the Willstones. However, Mr. Darcy did call on me at the Ketterlings the following day. He had been informed about Lydia running off with an officer and my departure. It was then that I told him the officer involved was George Wickham."

"What did he do? What did he say?"

Elizabeth let out a long, drawn out sigh. "He was very polite, but said the situation was very grave and that it altered everything." She looked up into Jane's face. "Even though he had never clearly spoken to me of his continued affection, I believed with those words he was informing me that he could no longer afford to hold me in regard." Elizabeth gave a shrug of her shoulders. "He abruptly left. I believed I would never see him again.

"But think of it! He must have departed immediately to come here!"

"It appears he did."

"And?"

Elizabeth turned to look at Jane, her smile reaching her eyes. "Tonight, my dear Jane, he declared that he still loves me."

Jane wrapped her sister in a hug. "I knew it! I just knew it!" Jane released her arms, but tugged at the sleeve of Elizabeth's nightdress. "Just think of it, Lizzy! We may soon be neighbours!"

Elizabeth began to laugh, and then promptly covered her mouth with her hand to stifle it. "Jane," she said. "He has not yet proposed to me. The poor man is likely to wait quite a long time before he does that again!"

Jane slid down in the bed, pulling the coverlet up to her chin. Elizabeth blew out the candle and joined her.

"I think he is very eager to ask for your hand again."

In a whisper, Elizabeth continued, "I cannot help but wonder, Jane, if Wickham had not agreed to marry Lydia, would he have still declared his love for me. He would have been a fool to do so. He is the type of man who cannot afford to marry a woman whose family has been disgraced in this manner, for his own standing in society as well as his sister's." She let out a long sigh. "It is serious enough that his affections lay toward one who was a governess."

"Certainly it is a good indication that Mr. Darcy has declared his love for you before they have even taken their vows."

Elizabeth nodded pensively. "Perhaps, but consider how determined Mr. Darcy was to get Mr. Wickham to agree to marry Lydia. Did Wickham force him to augment his offer to what it is now by continually saying 'no' until he had procured all he wanted?"

"If he did, it is a strong confirmation of Mr. Darcy's love for you!"

With a sigh of resignation, Elizabeth added, "And a strong confirmation of Wickham's lack of character and reluctance to marry our sister."

Jane sighed. "He cannot be as bad as that, can he?"

"Only time will tell whether he deserved such generosity as Mr. Darcy has bestowed on him."

"I only hope it will not be at Lydia's expense," Jane said with concern in her voice. She rolled onto her side and took Elizabeth's hand again. "But certainly Mr. Darcy has every intention of renewing his offer. I am convinced of it!"

"Perhaps," Elizabeth replied with a soft chuckle. "We can only wait and see."

In the darkness, Elizabeth pondered whether she had as much confidence as her sister. Yet it was something she desired more than anything.

When she dwelt on the fact that for the past two days Mr. Darcy had been in the midst of the chaos and cacophony her family produced, had been reacquainted with all their idiosyncrasies, and would be irrevocably tied to his worst enemy by aligning himself with her, she marvelled that he still loved her. She was overcome with love and a greater appreciation for this man.

Chapter 25

With their favourite men away, Elizabeth and Jane occupied themselves by helping with the preparations for Lydia's wedding. Their willing assistance in tending to the details was more to facilitate the swift passing of the next three days than in any joyous anticipation they felt for this union. There was much to do, including several visits to the linen drapers, millinery, and final fittings for dresses and the trousseau.

Between Mrs. Bennet and Lydia, there never seemed to be an end to the proceedings. Lydia could not be satisfied; she continually wanted more satin, more lace, more ribbon, more of anything that she did not already have. Her greatest disappointment seemed to be that Mr. Wickham would not stand up at the ceremony wearing his regimentals. Mrs. Bennet fretted that nothing seemed good enough for her favourite daughter and lamented at his not being dressed in his fine red coat, as well.

If there was boisterous excitement about the upcoming nuptials, it could all be attributed to their mother and youngest sister. The demeanours of the Gardiners, Elizabeth, and Jane were subdued. Mary was not hesitant to voice her contrary opinion on the subject. Even Kitty had begun to see the folly in her sister's actions. Whereas she had always looked with envy toward Lydia – who more easily attracted the eye of men because of her flirtatious behaviour – Kitty now saw things differently. Elizabeth and Jane had made a concerted effort to point out to her the error of their sister's ways, and eventually Kitty was persuaded that Lydia had not behaved prudently at all.

Mrs. Bennet's sister and her husband, Mr. and Mrs. Phillips, arrived in Town the day after the men departed for Pemberley, thus removing the burden from the Gardiners of housing Elizabeth's family. Mrs. Bennet, Mary, and Kitty stayed with them in their modest London home.

Mr. Gardiner insisted, however, that Lydia remain in his household – *under his excessive domination*, as Lydia claimed – so that he could keep her under his guard until the wedding. In the same manner, Elizabeth began to wonder whether Mr. Wickham was actually under lock and key in Mr. Darcy's town home. He appeared promptly at six o'clock each evening and departed by eleven, always accompanied by one of Mr. Darcy's manservants.

The evenings proved to be the most tiresome for Elizabeth, for she found it increasingly difficult to tolerate Wickham's pretentious charms. His actions were as agreeable and civil as one would expect in a gentleman. She hoped he had improved in character, but in truth doubted that he had.

The wedding was to take place in a church in the Phillips' neighbourhood. A special license had been obtained which allowed the marriage to take place in a swift manner at any church as long as it was available. Elizabeth wondered which of her uncles had made those arrangements – it could easily have been Mr. Darcy's idea, as well – but it allowed Jane and Mr. Bingley to be wed in the church she had been attending with the Gardiners without there being any memory of a less dignified wedding performed there earlier.

If there were any doubts about Mr. Wickham's suitability, Mrs. Bennet silenced them with her words of approbation. She repeatedly congratulated herself on such a fine son-in-law.

One evening, Elizabeth's mother had been excessively diverted about all the prospects that presented themselves, so much so that Elizabeth cringed with each new outburst. Mrs. Bennet seemed unable to respond in a refined manner to any subject at hand; she was exasperatingly boisterous, whether it was in delight or agitation. Having been in more civilized society for more than a year and away from her mother for that length of time, Elizabeth found herself more easily annoyed. If she knew herself at all, she knew it would be difficult for her to have to live again with her mother.

Later that evening, after Wickham had taken his leave, Mrs. Bennet was still in lively spirits as she prepared to depart to the Phillips' home. "Just think!" she continued in her exclamations. "Such a fine home in Hertfordshire! And so close to our old neighbours! Those Collinses will have nothing to us! Why, we have twice as many tenants and a good portion more land. What a grand thing for my son-in-law! He shall take such prodigiously good care of us and I shall no longer have to live with my sister in her small house in Meryton, or move to some unknown county with Jane!"

At first, Elizabeth listened to her mother's words with tried patience. But a sly smile slowly lit her face as a thought came to her. She wondered whether part of Mr. Darcy's profuse generosity had been governed by his desire that Wickham be the one to provide a home for Mrs. Bennet. Punishment for Wickham and a reprieve for Mr. Bingley in having to do the same. And *him*, she mused, if he indeed renewed his offer to her.

On the third day, when the men were expected to return from Derbyshire, Elizabeth and Jane waited anxiously for word of their arrival. Whereas they appeared to concentrate on their needlework or reading that occupied them throughout the day when wedding details did not, both were easily distracted by the sound of a knock at the door or a carriage coming to a stop out front. By evening, they had heard nothing from the gentlemen, and their hopes then turned to the following day.

It was just after noon the next day that Elizabeth, Jane, and Mrs. Gardiner were visiting in the drawing room. Lydia was with her mother and uncle meeting with the curate of the church. A fervent smile crept across Jane's face as the servant stepped in and announced Mr. Bingley. Elizabeth felt an immediate surge of disappointment when Mr. Darcy did not step in with him, but she was still as eager as Jane was to hear about the journey to Pemberley to see the manor that might become theirs.

After their initial greeting, he was invited to sit down and join them. A few pleasantries were exchanged and then Jane asked the question that was foremost in her thoughts. She wished to know what he thought about the estate.

"Braedenthorn manor is everything I could want!" Bingley cried out, and then looking at Jane, corrected himself. "That *we* could want! I do not believe I have ever seen one more suitable. The view of the peaks in the distance is magnificent, and there is abundant space and more rooms than I can even try to recall!" He looked at Jane and smiled. "I know we will be most happy there."

"Is everything settled, then?" Jane asked softly.

"Both Darcy and my solicitor are looking over the papers. Once everything is negotiated in a way they deem prudent, I will sign!" He turned to Jane and grasped her hand fervently. "Braedenthorn will then be ours! I cannot wait for you to see it! I know you will be delighted!"

Jane smiled. "If you are delighted with it, I shall be, as well!"

Elizabeth wore a steady smile as she observed her elder sister and Mr. Bingley. He spoke with enthusiasm as he gave them particular details about the house and grounds. The excitement in his voice and the receptive brightness in Jane's eyes were a greater indication of love than anything Elizabeth had witnessed the past few days between Lydia and Mr. Wickham.

After allowing Mr. Bingley sufficient time to convince Jane of the manor's suitability and splendour, Elizabeth asked Mr. Bingley if he had travelled back to London with his friend.

"Oh! Yes! Darcy! I mean no! He remained back for a few days! But I do have a letter for you, Miss Elizabeth!"

Elizabeth's eyes widened, turning immediately to her aunt, who met her gaze with raised eyebrows. She looked back at Mr. Bingley.

"From Mr. Darcy?" Elizabeth tentatively asked, knowing it would not be construed as the most prudent thing for him to do.

"Oh, no," Bingley laughed. "The letter is from Miss Darcy. Darcy will be travelling back with her in a few days."

Mr. Bingley handed the letter to Elizabeth. "I understand Miss Darcy wishes to invite you to their town home after church services on Sunday."

"Thank you," Elizabeth said as she took the letter. Sunday would be after the wedding. George Wickham would no longer be residing at their home. She looked down at the letter, eagerness prompting her to excuse herself to read it. She was able to slip away easily, as Mr. Bingley and Jane had begun another discussion on the favourite subject of theirs – Braedenthorn.

As Elizabeth walked briskly to Jane's bedroom, she fingered the envelope, noticing for the first time its bulk. It certainly held several sheets of stationery. Her eyes widened as she pondered whether Miss Darcy was an avid writer, or perhaps had large handwriting.

She pulled out several pieces of fine linen paper and slowly unfolded them. Her eyes looked down onto a letter written in a decidedly feminine style. She smiled as she began reading.

Dear Miss Bennet,

It is with great pleasure that I write to express my appreciation and gratitude to you for all you did during your recent stay at Pemberley. There were times when I needed a reassuring smile or someone to talk to, and I found that person in you. You may not even be aware of the encouragement I received from you, but I truly consider it a privilege to count you as a friend.

I do regret your sudden departure and that I did not have the opportunity to properly see you off when you left Pemberley.

Needless to say, the gaiety we had at Pemberley was much diminished with your departure. I have it on good authority that there was one at Pemberley, in addition to my brother and me, who grieved your loss. Emily did not understand the reason for your leaving and, unfortunately, I am quite certain she will not fully comprehend it as the Willstones relay to her their opinion on the matter.

I would have you know that I did all I could to reassure Emily that you still love her and care for her deeply. She asked that I send you a letter from her. She dictated it to me and it is enclosed.

Miss Bennet, I so look forward to renewing and deepening our acquaintance. This brings me to the purpose of my letter. My brother and I will be travelling to London in a few days and I would like to invite you to join me at our town home on Sunday. If you have no other plans, I would enjoy having you for tea after services. Would one o'clock be suitable?

I will arrange a carriage for you if one is needed. My brother will be in contact with you to ensure you have directions to the home if you are conveyed in your family's own carriage.

I do hope I will see you in London on Sunday. When my brother and I arrive, I will be spending the first few days at the de Bourgh home. My cousin, Anne, whom I believe you met in Kent, is in Town for a short while and I look forward to seeing her. Please give word to my brother when you see him on Saturday whether you will be able to visit and if you require a carriage.

Sincerely,
Miss Georgiana Darcy

Elizabeth smiled as she read Miss Darcy's words. She was surprised by the words of appreciation she expressed. While Elizabeth enjoyed their brief and infrequent conversations, she had little idea Miss Darcy took them so to heart.

She placed the letter Miss Darcy had written behind the others and noticed the same handwriting on the next letter. Looking at the bottom of the page, she saw that this was the letter Emily had dictated to her.

Dear Miss Bennet

I want you to know how much I miss you. We will be leaving here soon, and Miss Darcy kindly wrote down what I wanted to say to you. I love you and hope you can come back and be my governess again. I hope that what happened is not terribly bad. I hope you can find your way back to our country home or that when we come back to London you will visit me. I will always remember you.

Love, Emily

Elizabeth's heart tightened within her as she read Emily's words. She missed her, too, but was certain that if she wrote her back, Emily would not receive her letter. Most likely, her family would not allow her letter to be read to her.

She slowly moved Emily's letter to the back and found another letter tucked behind it. Her heart leapt as she recognized Mr. Darcy's meticulous handwriting and she smiled as she recollected Mr. Bingley's words. Mr. Darcy *had* written to her! Her eyes feasted on his words, not able to devour them as quickly as she would have liked.

Miss Bennet,

I do hope you will forgive me a second time for presenting you with a letter, this time even more surreptitiously than the first. My intentions when I left London were to return promptly. Those plans have changed, and my sister and I will depart in a day or two. When I first arrive, unfortunately another pressing matter will occupy my time. I will, of course, attend the wedding of your sister and Wickham, if only to make sure he is there and to stand up for him. As well as to see you.

When we first arrive, Georgiana will not, as you would likely surmise, be in residence at our home while Wickham remains. She will stay with our cousin, Anne, who only just recently arrived in Town. My sister much prefers Anne's company without her mother's overbearing presence, and it is not often that Anne finds herself without our aunt. It is all very convenient.

I have every hope that you will be able to visit my sister on Sunday. She looks forward very much to your company and seeing you again. As do I.

There is much I would like to say to you, but I shall wait until I can speak those things face to face. I hope that an opportunity to do so will be forthcoming.

Until then, I remain yours,
Fitzwilliam Darcy

Elizabeth reread his words, running her fingers over them. Her eyes continually returned to his words, *As well as to see you, As do I,* and *Until then, I remain yours*. Reading them over and over prompted her heart to skip a beat. She pressed his letter over her heart, and even through the fine stationery, she could easily feel the fluttering deep from within. While she would have to wait longer to see him, his words to her would ease the waiting.

~~*

On the day of the wedding, Elizabeth had rather expected the skies to be grey and cloudy, with a heavy drizzle leaving everything cold and wet. But the day dawned bright and beautiful; a warm, sunny day with a deep blue sky dotted with puffs of white clouds.

Elizabeth could not be more anxious for it to be over. As the day had grown closer, her mother displayed more agitation, Lydia became more demanding, and Mr. Wickham grew more silent. Elizabeth wondered with increased concern whether he would truly go through with it.

In addition to the apprehension she felt about the upcoming nuptials, Elizabeth fought a swelling tide of impatience to see Mr. Darcy again. It was apparent that she would not see him until the ceremony. She understood that he was going to accompany Mr. Wickham to the church.

It was to be a small ceremony with only their family in attendance. Despite her protestations against the strict treatment by the Gardiners, Lydia requested that Mr. Gardiner give her away. They arrived at the church and Elizabeth sat beside Jane in one of the front pews in the church. Mr. Bingley sat on the other side of Jane.

As the ceremony began, the reverend stepped out to the front. Elizabeth watched as Wickham followed him. Her heart leapt as she finally caught sight of Mr. Darcy. He strode in rigid and erect, not looking in the least bit as though he was enjoying himself. He rather looked like he would wish to be anywhere but here. As his eyes swept the church, they settled on Elizabeth's face. His countenance relaxed somewhat as she gave him a smile. A slight smile was returned.

When Lydia strolled down the aisle toward Wickham, she seemed to thoroughly enjoy being the centre of attention. All eyes were on her, except Elizabeth's and Darcy's. It appeared he forbade himself from looking at either the bride or the groom. As long as he kept his eyes on Elizabeth, he managed well.

It was difficult for Elizabeth to heed the words of the ceremony; she was so sceptical of Wickham and mindful of Mr. Darcy. At length, the ceremony ended, and everyone rose to proceed the short two blocks to the Phillips' home for the wedding breakfast.

As Elizabeth's family walked toward the carriages, Mr. Darcy approached Elizabeth. "Miss Bennet, do you not think it is very fine walking weather? It is a short distance to the Phillips' home. Would you care to walk with me?"

A genuine smile lit Elizabeth's face. If Darcy had been at all in doubt of her feelings for him, this was all the assurance he needed.

"I would like that very much."

Elizabeth told Jane she would meet them at the house, and joined Mr. Darcy. As he extended his arm, they began slowly walking. "I shall be making only a brief appearance at the wedding breakfast this morning," he told her.

She certainly understood his wish to distance himself from Wickham; she wished she could do the same. She still experienced disappointment, however. "There is no need to explain," she reassured him.

Darcy shook his head. "It is not just Wickham. My cousin is in Town and he requires my assistance."

"Mr. Hamilton?" Elizabeth asked.

"No," Darcy let out a soft laugh. "Colonel Fitzwilliam."

"Ahh," Elizabeth smiled. "How is the Colonel?"

"Doing well, I believe." He reached over with his free hand and placed it over Elizabeth's fingers, which were closed around his arm. "He hopes to see you again. Do you plan to visit my sister on the morrow?"

"Yes, indeed I do. Please inform Miss Darcy that my uncle is providing me with his carriage and I shall be there promptly at one o'clock."

"He and I will likely stop by after you and Georgiana have had some time together." Darcy let out a deep sigh of contentment. His fingers wrapped around Elizabeth's and he gave them a gentle squeeze.

She looked up at him appreciatively. "You have done so much. How can I ever thank you?"

Darcy shook his head. "You have no need to thank me. I did nothing out of the ordinary."

Elizabeth let out a laugh. "Nothing out of the ordinary?" Elizabeth shook her head. "You somehow managed to convince Mr. Wickham to marry my sister when he truly had no inclination to do so. I saw him over the course of this past week and I can most assuredly tell you there is no love on his part. She has no fortune… nothing to offer him." She cast a sideways glance at him. "I was actually convinced you truly did have him under lock and key." She let out a soft laugh. "How is it that he agreed?"

Darcy took a few steps in silence and then stopped. Turning to Elizabeth he said, "I know Wickham well enough to know that he has a weakness."

"Only one weakness?" Elizabeth asked incredulously. "I believed I witnessed many!"

"One that I could use to my advantage." Darcy grew serious. "Pemberley."

Elizabeth's eyes widened in surprise. "Pemberley?"

Darcy nodded. "He has an ardent fondness for Pemberley due to having grown up there. He has been prohibited from coming anywhere near it for several years." Darcy took in a deep breath and again squeezed Elizabeth's hand. He seemed reluctant to continue.

"And how did you use this weakness?"

"He learned of your coming to Pemberley, most likely from…" he paused, as if unable to speak her name. "…Mrs. Wickham herself. I imagine someone in your family had informed her and she innocently enough told Wickham. He began to make some assumptions based on what he had observed when we were in Hertfordshire."

Darcy's eyes grew warm, his voice soft. "Those assumptions – that I harboured a strong regard for you – led him to believe that if he and your sister married, he would naturally be welcomed back there. There was also most likely some conjecture on his part that he would receive financial benefits."

Elizabeth's heart beat wildly. While she wished to divert this conversation to only speak about this regard he felt for her, she needed to know more. "Do you mean he intended to marry her all along?"

Darcy nodded. "He knew that if he compromised her, it would help his situation in attaining his goal. Unfortunately, he had more than a willing participant."

Those words were difficult for Elizabeth to hear, and she bit her lip and cast her eyes down. "She was such a fool!"

Darcy continued, "When I showed up at the doorstep where Wickham and your sister were staying, his assumptions concerning how I felt about you were confirmed."

Elizabeth's heart skipped a beat, her breath caught. The two walked again in silence, letting Darcy's last words linger between them. A part of Elizabeth wished to burst with joy, while yet another part recoiled at all he told her.

"He was…" Darcy spoke with forcefulness. "…and still is convinced that this will grant him permission to return to Pemberley. But it will not!"

Elizabeth was taken aback at her complete comprehension of his meaning. If they were to marry, her sister would not be allowed either. "I see," she said softly.

Darcy saw at once the regret that shaded her features. "It is only Wickham I will prohibit… unless he can prove to me that he has changed. I shall amend my decision only if he alters his dissolute ways."

Elizabeth extended to him a nod of her approval. "And how long shall you require this changed behaviour to be displayed? Six months? One year? Will five years be long enough?"

"You know him as well as I do. He can act very agreeably when he wants. But the gentleman I have set in place as his steward, Mr. Atkins, will know precisely how his behaviour weighs up in every area of his life." Darcy cast a sly glance down at Elizabeth. "Do you think ten years will suffice?"

"Perhaps twenty," Elizabeth replied with a resigned laugh.

When they reached the Phillips' home, Elizabeth could not recall seeing one house, one tree, one carriage pass them along the way. Before they stepped in to join the others, Darcy paused. "I know the past few weeks have been difficult. This situation with Wickham and your sister has been unfortunate, indeed, and I imagine it has taken its toll on you. It has on me. I look forward to a new day tomorrow with all this behind us."

They stepped into the Phillips' home to a celebration that was truly not a celebration at all. Darcy stayed only briefly, taking his leave within the first half an hour.

Before leaving, Mr. Darcy gave Mr. Gardiner directions to his town home and to Elizabeth he gave all the assurances that he would see her at his home when she came to visit his sister. For that, Elizabeth was grateful.

194

Chapter 26

After sending the newly married couple off to their new life together – which Elizabeth hoped would not end in a terribly disastrous way for her sister – Elizabeth and Jane returned home with the Gardiners. Mr. Darcy's words had rung true. This whole incident had taken a toll on her, yet now she could look with joyous anticipation toward a new day tomorrow.

With thoughts filling her mind and a myriad of feelings flooding through her, Elizabeth slept only fitfully that night. Not wishing to keep Jane awake by her tossing and turning, she slipped out of bed and walked over to the chair by the window. Sitting down, she draped a light coverlet across her lap.

In the early morn, as the dawning light began to permeate the skies, Elizabeth awoke, still in the chair. At some point, she must have finally fallen asleep. Her view of the sunrise was not as expansive as at Pemberley, being partially obscured by the homes, buildings, and trees surrounding them, but the reds and oranges stretched out their hues high above the horizon.

She watched until the colours faded, the clouds returning to shades of whites and greys, and the sky taking on an array of blues. Jane still slept soundly and the only evidence that anyone else was awake in the house was the aroma of baking bread.

It seemed to Elizabeth, as she sat and observed London awaken outside the window, that with the tumult of Lydia's marriage behind her, the sky was a deeper blue, the birds sang more cheerfully, and an indescribable warmth settled within her. She took in a contented breath and let it out slowly. She would see Mr. Darcy today and now had the assurance that he held an equal affection for her as she did for him.

Later that morning after returning from church services, Elizabeth visited briefly with everyone until it was time for her to take her leave. She had not felt such nervous anticipation since that day she first arrived at Pemberley. If only she could calm her heart's vigorous beating. Her aunt teased her about her beaming smile that had not once disappeared from her face all morning.

The carriage ride to Mr. Darcy's home took her from the unfashionable Cheapside neighbourhood into a more fashionable district. The duration of the journey took approximately twenty minutes, providing her with ample time to calm her heart and collect her nerves. When the carriage came to a stop in front of a fairly large stately home, any success she previously had vanished, for her heart quickly returned to its fervent pulsing.

While the house itself was not as large as some of the others in the neighbourhood, its grounds covered a greater expanse. Several large trees were interspersed about the lawn with small flower gardens surrounding their bases and bordering the house. When the carriage door opened, Elizabeth stepped out, smoothing out her dress with one hand and nervously fingering her necklace with the other.

She walked to the house slowly, her eyes taking in everything about her. When she knocked on the massive wooden door, it was opened directly. She introduced herself to the gentleman that stood before her and informed him that she had come to see Miss Darcy.

"Come in, Miss Bennet. We are expecting you. I am Mr. Harrington. Unfortunately, Miss Darcy has been delayed, but she should return directly." He looked down the main hall, a trace of agitation on his face, as a woman hurried toward him. "This is Miss Bennet," he told her as she approached. Turning back to Elizabeth, he said, "This is my wife, Mrs. Harrington, who is the housekeeper."

Elizabeth readily noticed the same harried look on her face, but dismissed it when she saw the striking resemblance to Anna, the young servant girl who had ridden with her to London. Of course! She said her mother was the housekeeper and her father the butler!

"I am so pleased to make both your acquaintances. I met Anna, who I understand is your daughter, on my journey from Pemberley. I truly enjoyed her company."

They both expressed their appreciation for her kind words and then Mrs. Harrington gently took Elizabeth's arm, guiding her down the hall.

"I know Anna will be delighted to see you. Unfortunately, we have had an unexpected guest arrive who has thrown everyone into fits. I shall inform Anna you are here. Come, you can wait for Miss Darcy in the parlour."

Elizabeth put out her hand to bring her to a halt. "Mrs. Harrington, if this is an inconvenient time, I can certainly make arrangements to visit another day."

The housekeeper shook her head. "I would not think of sending you away without hearing first from Miss Darcy. It is only a minor difficulty."

The look on her face told Elizabeth otherwise, but she dutifully followed her through the house to the back parlour. She heard a commotion coming down one of the halls, and saw two maids rushing toward her, their faces pinched with exasperation. This was not like anything she witnessed at Pemberley and she wondered *who* caused such turmoil.

Mrs. Harrington invited her to make herself comfortable and inquired whether she would care for some refreshment. Elizabeth sat down and replied that perhaps some tea was all she required. The housekeeper nodded and told her she would bring her some directly.

As she walked out, Elizabeth leaned back in the chair and cast her eyes about the parlour. In addition to the few pieces of furniture that dotted the room, several large paintings were hung on the wall, and a cabinet with wood and glass doors housed a myriad of crystal, china, marble, and wooden accessories. Curiosity prompted Elizabeth to walk over and take a closer look at them.

As she eyed figurines and vases, hand-painted plates, and framed miniature portraits, she again heard the sound of hushed, but troubled voices and hurried footsteps. When she glanced toward the door, she saw Anna carrying a tray with her tea.

"Oh, Anna! It is good to see you again!"

"Miss Bennet, I am pleased you were able to come." She walked toward Elizabeth and set the tray down on a table. She poured the tea and handed the teacup to her. A worried glance cast unwittingly toward the door alerted Elizabeth to her distress.

"Anna, tell me, has something happened? I feel as though this is the most inopportune time for me to be here."

Anna took in a sharp breath, but shook her head fervently. "I know Miss Darcy would not want you to leave before seeing her. Unfortunately, she is not here and neither is Mr. Darcy. That is why everyone is in an uproar." Her eyes turned to the door. "She will just *not* see reason."

Elizabeth looked confused. "Miss Darcy?"

"Oh, no! Not Miss Darcy!" Her nervous laugh was accompanied by a creased brow.

The sound of strident footsteps approaching grew louder and Anna's eyes widened. A singular pounding of one foot signalled that someone had stopped. Elizabeth turned to see who had prompted such a look of fear on Anna's face.

Elizabeth's jaw dropped as she beheld the woman before her. A look of anger mixed with great suspicion swept across her features as she noticed Elizabeth. In a loud voice directed at no one in particular, she exclaimed, "What, may I ask, is *she* doing here?"

Elizabeth politely curtseyed, and when she lifted her head, she pursed her lips and swallowed to moisten her suddenly dry mouth. "Good afternoon, Lady Catherine. It is an honour to see you again."

Lady Catherine's eyes narrowed and her lips puckered tightly together before saying, "You are Miss Elizabeth Bennet!"

"Yes, madam, you are correct." Elizabeth replied, a slight chuckle inadvertently escaping. *As if I needed her to inform me of that!* she thought to herself.

Lady Catherine's eyes almost appeared closed save for the glint that peered through. She took several steps forward, bringing her into the room. Looking at Anna, she told her, "You may go. We have no need for you here."

Anna looked at Elizabeth as if waiting to be excused. Elizabeth gave her a resigned nod.

Lady Catherine turned back to Elizabeth with a stern look etched on her face. "I come expecting to find my nephew or my niece, and instead I find *you*!"

"I have also come to see Miss Darcy." Elizabeth tried to smile, but knew it was a futile attempt. "I understand she has not yet returned from an unexpected errand."

"What business have *you* with my niece?"

With a start, Elizabeth readily recollected the insolence this woman exhibited when she met her at Rosings. "This is a social call. She invited me for tea."

197

Lady Catherine let out a disgusted huff. "This is insupportable!" The cane Lady Catherine held tightly in her fist pounded to the floor. "My niece has no reason to take notice of a mere governess! Yes, I know that is what you are. Why would she invite *you* to tea?"

Elizabeth's eyes widened, appalled at her words. "I beg your pardon, Lady Catherine, but my father was a gentleman, and therefore I was and always will be a gentleman's daughter. My vocation as a governess was only prompted by my good father's death, and…"

"That does not signify!" Her words were unleashed in fury. "I am well aware who you are… and who you are *not*! The Darcy family is esteemed well above your insignificant family. The associations of my niece and nephew must be kept to those of distinction of rank or fortune! Your family has not even the slightest connections worthy of anyone's notice."

Elizabeth's jaw dropped at the accusation levelled against her, but only briefly. If Lady Catherine meant to intimidate Elizabeth, the words she spewed out only served to bolster Elizabeth's courage.

"Perhaps Miss Darcy's choice of associations is something you ought to allow her to make herself."

Lady Catherine shook her head for emphasis. "Headstrong girl! I cannot believe that my niece, for no other purpose than a social call, invited someone so far beneath her to her home for tea!"

"I am aware of no other purpose that Miss Darcy may have had in inviting me," Elizabeth replied coolly.

Lady Catherine studied Elizabeth silently for a brief moment, and then began wagging her finger at her. "Do not think that I do not know what you are about, Miss Bennet! I am not unaware of your recent stay at Pemberley." In a severe tone, she voiced her dreaded suspicion, "Was it your design to use your arts to draw my nephew in whilst you were there?"

Elizabeth coloured as she listened with increasing astonishment. "I had no part in the decision to go to Pemberley. The family for whom I worked was invited. I knew nothing of it until it was a settled matter!"

"You expect me to believe that you journeyed to Pemberley without any thought of how you might secure my nephew's notice?"

Elizabeth let out a breath, almost a chuckle, and shook her head. "When I departed for Pemberley, I had no reason to believe, no designs or even *hopes*, that he would harbour even the slightest regard for me. I went dutifully and solely as Miss Emily Willstone's governess."

"Then you must know that any aspirations you may have to secure his regard, any arts you employ, would be futile."

"You assume that I intended to use feminine wiles to secure Mr. Darcy's regard. You cannot be further from the truth."

"Do not trifle with me, Miss Bennet! You know you can never marry him!"

While the sound of muffled footsteps and hushed voices outside the door suggested to Elizabeth that some of the servants were perhaps listening, she steeled herself to reply. "Lady Catherine, whether or not I marry your nephew will solely be determined by whether or not he asks me, not from your empty threats!"

"You are an insolent girl!" she cried out. "Have you no respect for our family? He has been promised in marriage to my daughter since their birth! Both his mother and I wished it!" Lady Catherine's body shook with the fervency of her words. Her eyes widened with one sharply arched brow as she watched Elizabeth to see how she would respond to this.

"I came to know of that even before my visit to Rosings," she answered, her voice steady. "If Mr. Darcy chooses to honour that wish, then you ought to have nothing to worry about." Elizabeth paused, "If his understanding is compatible with yours, I wonder why you feel so inclined to caution me."

Lady Catherine again pounded her cane sharply against the floor. "Tell me, Miss Bennet, whether or not *you* harbour any designs on my nephew! Do you seek to become engaged to him?"

Elizabeth felt her ire rise, but made a concerted effort to suppress it. "You claim that to be an impossibility. If he is engaged to your daughter, how can he become engaged to someone else?"

Lady Catherine threw her shoulders back and lifted her chin in the air. "You must promise me this, Miss Bennet! If my nephew asks for your hand, you must not accept him!"

The pounding of footsteps coming toward the room abruptly stopped. Elizabeth hoped it would be someone coming to rescue her from Lady Catherine's abuse. But it apparently was not, as no one stepped in.

Elizabeth swallowed and straightened her shoulders. She lifted her head and looked directly into Lady Catherine's eyes. "I may be insupportable and headstrong, but one thing I am definitely not is easily intimidated. You insist that I refuse an offer of marriage from your nephew. I cannot promise anything of the sort. I will only reply that I would be more than delighted to accept an offer if he were ever to make one."

"This is not to be borne! I have never met with one so devoid of propriety! Do you not know who my nephew is? Do you not comprehend that it would be beneath his dignity to marry one such as you! Do you not know…?"

"That is enough!"

The voice boomed across the room with such force that even Lady Catherine started. They both turned to see Mr. Darcy stride with determined steps toward them. He came to a halt at Elizabeth's side, his breathing ragged, his eyes glaring.

"I will hear no more of your tirade against Miss Bennet. What right have you to treat her – a guest in my household – in such a rude, disparaging manner?"

Without waiting for his aunt to answer, he turned to Elizabeth. "Pray, forgive me for the reception you received here."

His aunt seemed momentarily stunned by his unexpected appearance, but just as suddenly she relaxed. A forced smile appeared as she said, "As one of your closest relatives, you know the high regard of your family name is of utmost importance to me. I am glad for your arrival and I do not regret my conversation with this woman."

Lady Catherine's nose flared as her upper lip curled under. She directed an accusatory glare toward Elizabeth. "Miss Bennet is a pretentious woman with no connections, rank, or fortune. You would be wise, Nephew, to stay as far away from her as possible. She has aspirations that would ruin you and dishonour your family name. You *must* have no further contact with her!"

Darcy's eyes narrowed and he took a moment to compose himself. Elizabeth readily saw the turmoil in his face, the tension in his body. Suddenly his features softened and he seemed to relax slightly.

"I fear that is impossible," he said slowly.

"Impossible?" his aunt asked. "Why?"

Darcy turned to Elizabeth. "It is very simple. She made a promise to me and has yet to keep it."

Both Lady Catherine's and Elizabeth's eyes widened and their brows were raised in surprise at his statement. Lady Catherine boldly asked, "What promise? Whatever do you mean?"

He smiled softly, reassuringly, at Elizabeth. "She promised to watch the sunrise with me from the ridge behind Pemberley." He cast his eyes down and shook his head. "I fear that I must hold her to it."

Elizabeth's heart beat relentlessly as she tried to conceal a smile, much like she believed Mr. Darcy was doing, while Lady Catherine did not make any attempt to conceal her anger. "View the sunrise with you? I have never heard anything more disgraceful! This woman ought to be ashamed! *You* ought to be ashamed! You are to marry my Anne and this sort of behaviour…"

"I fear *that* will be impossible," another strong voice interjected.

Lady Catherine and Elizabeth turned toward the door to see Colonel Fitzwilliam walk in, followed by Miss Darcy and Miss de Bourgh.

As he walked in, he greeted his aunt with a brief kiss and turned to Elizabeth. "Miss Bennet, it is a delight to see you again."

Elizabeth nodded and softly replied, "It is good to see you, as well."

"Whatever do you mean?" his aunt insisted upon knowing. "Why is his marrying my Anne impossible?" She turned to look at Anne and asked, "Where have you been? You know how much I dislike not knowing where you are!"

Elizabeth watched as Anne slightly shielded herself behind Colonel Fitzwilliam. "She has been with me!" the Colonel announced. He drew in a breath and took a rigid soldier's stance. "And the reason my good cousin cannot marry Anne is because… *I* intend to marry her!"

The colour drained from Lady Catherine's face and her body was wracked with tremors as she came to understand his words. Her voice cracked as she said,

"You? You cannot marry Anne!"

"And why not? We care deeply for one another. We love each other!"

Lady Catherine shook her head violently. "No! This cannot be! You have nothing to offer her!"

"He loves me, Mother," Anne's voice, although weak, was firm. "And what is more important is that I love him."

"I have never heard anything more absurd in my life! You have no idea of what you speak!"

As Lady Catherine continued her tirade now aimed at Colonel Fitzwilliam, Mr. Darcy drew Elizabeth quietly out of the room. Miss Darcy followed, tucking her hand through Elizabeth's arm.

In a hushed, fervent voice, she said as they walked out, "I shall never forgive myself for not being here to welcome you when you arrived. This whole affair between my two cousins came about so suddenly. Anne asked me to help her run an errand before her mother returned to Town today. The errand unfortunately took longer and my aunt arrived sooner than we expected. When we heard she was on her way here, we hurried over, hoping to arrive before she did. I am so sorry!"

"Think nothing of it," Elizabeth replied reassuringly as she gently patted the back of Miss Darcy's hand.

"I know how my aunt can be. I cannot imagine what she must have said to you."

At that moment Mr. Darcy stopped and turned around. "Whatever she said, it will all be forgotten now. She has a greater concern that is going to occupy her thoughts for quite some time."

"The Colonel marrying her daughter?" Elizabeth asked.

Darcy nodded. "While she will require considerable time getting accustomed to the idea, I am convinced she will come to see the good in it." Darcy stopped at the door to a spacious room. "As your visit today was an invitation from Georgiana, I shall leave you two here and send for some refreshments." With a slight shrug of his shoulders, he added, "Then I shall be off to ensure my cousin does not have to resort to some military manoeuvre to subdue our aunt." With a wink at Georgiana, he added as he walked toward the door, "Please refrain from revealing to Miss Bennet too many of our family secrets."

Once Mr. Darcy stepped from the room, Georgiana eagerly turned to Elizabeth and gave her a charming smile. They began talking at first about very general subjects. To Elizabeth's discerning eye, it appeared as though Miss Darcy exhibited a bit less shyness than she had witnessed at Pemberley. She hoped that it was an indication the young lady felt at ease in her company.

The time passed quickly as they talked about their families. Elizabeth sensed that Georgiana felt a bond with her in that they had both lost their father. They shared with each other what they remembered most and how much they missed them.

At length, the conversation returned to the incident with Georgiana's aunt and cousins. Elizabeth could not help but wonder what was currently transpiring. She could not hear a thing.

"Again, I must beg your forgiveness for my aunt's behaviour earlier. When we arrived at the house, Mr. Harrington informed us of the encounter taking place between the two of you. My brother immediately set off at a very rapid pace down the hall; I suppose to intervene."

"It is not at all your fault, Miss Darcy; however, I am glad you arrived when you did."

"You must have been standing up fairly well against her," she laughed softly. "When the rest of us reached Fitzwilliam, we found him stopped just outside the door, listening, with a slight smile on his face."

Elizabeth's eyes widened. "Did he? I cannot imagine what he heard, for I cannot recall one word I said to your aunt. I hope it was nothing terribly dreadful!"

"I am quite certain it was not. To own the truth, we often speak amongst ourselves how we wish more people would stand up to her. Besides, he was more concerned for any abuse my aunt was heaping onto you, than any you would return to her. While we could not clearly hear what she was saying, we all heard her tirade."

"I doubt that what I said to her would be considered standing up to her." Elizabeth laughed as she tried to recall what she had said. "I was only saying…" She paused as she suddenly recollected the very last thing she had said to Lady Catherine before Mr. Darcy walked in. Her fingers covered her mouth and her cheeks flushed slightly, wondering whether he did indeed hear her. Georgiana looked at her curiously.

Elizabeth turned her head and her heart trembled when she saw that Darcy was standing in the doorway to the room, casually leaning against it. She quietly wondered just how long he had been there.

"All is well," he said softly, giving no indication that he overheard anything. "They have returned to my aunt's home to discuss that which both my cousins wish and that which my aunt will fight for several more days. She will eventually concede and all will be well."

Georgiana reached over and grasped Elizabeth's hand. "I am so sorry you had to witness such a mêlée in our family. Since they are now gone and all is quiet again, would you care for a tour of the house?"

Elizabeth heartily agreed. She was accompanied throughout the house by Mr. and Miss Darcy. Each contributed to what the other had to say and gave her a history that proved quite interesting. She was of the opinion that this tour was much more in depth than one that might be given to just any person coming to their London home.

When they finished, Miss Darcy made a suggestion. "The day is very pleasant. Would you enjoy taking a turn about the grounds behind the house?"

"I would love to," Elizabeth softly answered.

They walked to the back of the house and stepped out. The grounds were lush, with a lawn that stretched out before them and trees that formed a barrier to the outside world. They walked toward a bench that was covered with a lattice canopy filled with wisteria blossoms. The scent was heavenly. Mr. Darcy gestured toward the bench, inviting Elizabeth to sit down.

Elizabeth took a seat, and when she looked up, she was startled to see Miss Darcy gone. Only Mr. Darcy stood next to her. His brown eyes were warm and his smile tender.

Elizabeth's heart pounded and her mind began to spin as he sat down on the bench beside her.

Chapter 27

In the relative seclusion of the bench, Mr. Darcy turned toward Elizabeth. "Miss Bennet, I had hoped your visit here today would have been a pleasant one. I am deeply grieved over the behaviour of my aunt."

"As I told your sister, it was not her fault; neither is it yours."

He reached out and took Elizabeth's hand, cradling it in his own. He lightly stroked the back of it with his fingers. "My sister truly enjoyed your company. You have been very kind to her."

His gentle touch and close proximity produced such light-headedness in Elizabeth that it made it difficult to even think. Her heart pounded so strongly, she felt it up in her throat, making words difficult to express. She took in a deep breath and let it out slowly. "She is a wonderfully sweet young lady whose company I truly enjoy."

"For that, I am most grateful." He looked down at their hands. "It is apparent she feels equally toward you."

"I could not be happier," Elizabeth reassured him.

Mr. Darcy pressed his other hand upon hers. "As am I, but to own the truth, I do not wish to talk about my sister." His eyes searched hers and grew warm.

"Miss Bennet…" he began. His voice was noticeably unsteady, but he turned and looked at her with a demeanour of hopefulness. "Elizabeth, there is much I would say to you today, but being a man of few words, any that come to mind seem inadequate." He took both of her hands in his. "I have acknowledged to you that my feelings and wishes over the duration of the past year and a half have not diminished or changed. They have remained constantly with me, despite attempts over the course of the past year to push them away or talk myself out of them." He paused and gave her a slight smile. "Not because I felt they were wrong, but due to how things were left between us when we parted at Rosings."

Elizabeth broke in, "I am so sorry for my words that day. If I had known what I know now…"

Darcy lifted one hand and pressed it briefly to her lips to silence her. "No. I needed to hear what you said to me. It pained me at the time, but as I reflected upon it, even that first night, I knew that you spoke the truth about both my behaviour in Hertfordshire and my actions regarding your sister."

"I have often regretted how I spoke to you that day…"

A crooked smile appeared and he swallowed, taking in a deep breath. "I do not wish to speak about Rosings, either." He pursed his lips and closed his eyes briefly. "Elizabeth," he said as his eyes opened and gazed intently at hers. "My love and regard for you is so fervent that at times I can hardly bear it. I am convinced that life without you would be painfully empty and hopeless."

He paused and studied her face. Very slowly he said, "I would be honoured if you would consent to become my wife." He reached out and stroked her cheek with the back of his hand. "There is none other with whom I want to share the sunrises or explore the many paths at Pemberley. There is none other with whom I want to read Cowper's poems and Shakespeare's sonnets." Taking her hand again in his, he asked, "Will you marry me, my dearest, loveliest, Elizabeth?"

Elizabeth fought back the tears of joy that threatened. She bit her lip as she considered that despite all they had been through, he still wished to marry her. She thought for a moment before answering.

She whispered his name. "Fitzwilliam, you know my heart, but I cannot help but consider the truth of what your aunt said to me earlier. Marrying someone in my position... one who is merely a governess, could readily cause a great deal of gossip. Your standing in society..."

His face drained of all colour and she felt his hands tighten about hers. "Elizabeth, you must know that I do not care about any of those things. I..."

With her hands enclosed in his, she brought them up to her lips and kissed each one, bringing a halt to his words. "You may not care what it means to *you,* but there is your sister you must consider. She may have a more difficult time in Society due to your marriage to one so beneath you." She looked down briefly, and then looked up into his eyes. "Therefore, while I *do* agree to your offer and desire most heartily to become your wife, I ask that we not announce our engagement until after I have spent sufficient time living with my sister and Mr. Bingley in their home. Perhaps in a relatively short amount of time, I will become known as the esteemed Mrs. Bingley's sister, rather than a mere governess, and consequently, more worthy of your hand."

Darcy let out a sigh of relief, but the look of apprehension still remained. "There is truly no need for this."

"Perhaps, but I must insist upon it all the same."

Darcy eyed her curiously. "What do you consider to be a relatively *short* amount of time?" he asked. "A week? Two weeks?"

Elizabeth chuckled and tilted her head as she paused to consider her answer. "Hmmm. Since it is entirely out of our hands, we shall have to wait and see."

Darcy drew nearer to Elizabeth. "I have waited this long; if you adamantly insist upon it, I suppose I can wait a little longer." He leaned in close to her face and whispered, "But I will do everything in my power to introduce you to everyone I know as the finest young lady in my acquaintance. I am convinced that word will spread throughout London directly that a very fine, eligible woman has finally captured the notice of Fitzwilliam Darcy of Pemberley!"

Elizabeth smiled as Darcy grasped her fingers and brought them close to his lips. As he spoke, his warm breath poured over them. "I regret that I will be occupied for the next several days with my cousins and their wedding. It is going to be a small ceremony in Rosings church, which I would be delighted for you to attend as my guest, but..."

Elizabeth shook her head firmly. "The last person you need at their wedding is me. Your aunt will have enough to contend with without my presence." She smiled and her eyes displayed a mischievous sparkle. "Besides, we would not want people to speculate about us. Heavens! What would people say if I attended the wedding as your guest? We are not even engaged, yet!"

Darcy smiled at her humour, but then earnestly said, "In my heart, we *are* engaged. I am as committed to you now as I ever will be." He looked down at her slender fingers encased in his. "If there *are* speculations, let them suppose that there is no one else for me, then I shall not care a whit what anyone thinks!"

Elizabeth's breath caught and she closed her eyes as she felt his lips touch her fingertips. When she opened them, she saw that he had drawn closer to her, his eyes level with hers. "I am an exceedingly fortunate man. It is not often that one is granted a second chance when one behaved so reprehensibly the first time."

Elizabeth met his intense gaze. "And I am an exceedingly fortunate woman," she replied, her voice trembling, "indeed, for very much the same reason."

His eyes searched her face, and slowly he leaned in and kissed her forehead. Drawing back only slightly, he whispered, "Forgive me for this, Elizabeth …"

His lips touched hers before she could object or give her willing consent. Her eyes immediately closed again as his arms wrapped about her, pulling her even closer. Elizabeth's heart beat thunderously and she was certain Darcy was just as aware of it as she was. In truth, their hearts beat as one, with the same fervour.

Very reluctantly and slowly he pulled slightly away.

"Elizabeth," Darcy said, his voice raspy, "my staff is very discreet; however, I would not wish for your reputation to be compromised." With a slightly raised brow and crooked smile, he added, "Although it would serve to expedite my wishes if one did raise an objection to my behaviour just now and insist we marry without delay."

He removed his arms from about her and took her hand again. She wrapped her fingers tightly around his and looked up into his face. "Trust me when I say, Fitzwilliam, that I would marry you tomorrow if it were not for my concerns." She looked down and shook her head slowly. "Waiting until I am well settled with Mr. Bingley and my sister may do nothing to improve the manner in which I am received, but I feel we must at least make an attempt, particularly for your sister's sake."

With a sly smile, Darcy said. "It is fortunate, then, that Bingley is talking with your sister this very day about moving the wedding to an earlier date. With the matter of his estate settled, he sees no reason to delay."

Tilting her head at him, Elizabeth smiled. "The more I come to know Mr. Bingley, the more I feel he is a very wise man." A single raised brow revealed her suspicions that Mr. Darcy had been the one to suggest that idea to his friend. Darcy's awkward glance down at the ground and a sharp intake of breath confirmed her thoughts.

She gave his hand a fervent squeeze to reassure him. "Do you know how soon he hopes to marry?"

"As soon as the church is available. Perhaps two weeks. Three at the most."

"Then we shall have much to do!" Elizabeth exclaimed. "Another wedding!"

His voice now grave, he spoke softly. "It is opportune, then, that I shall be occupied with both of my cousins while you are in the midst of the plans for your sister." He looked steadfastly into Elizabeth's eyes. "I leave again on the morrow for Kent with Colonel Fitzwilliam. I shall miss you."

"I shall miss you, too." She studied him pensively. "It is regrettable, is it not, that whilst I was at Pemberley, we were together almost every day and knew not how the other felt. When our feelings have finally been voiced, we have not spent even two consecutive days together. This is lamentable, indeed!"

Elizabeth reached up and stroked his cheek with the back of her hand. It took her by surprise how smooth his face was. As she studied his face, he clasped his hand over hers and brought it to his lips again, kissing it before he said, "We ought to return inside. I would not wish to set a poor example for my sister."

"Heavens!" Elizabeth exclaimed. "How ill-mannered of me! How could I have neglected her as I did?"

Darcy looked at her with a sly gaze. "Could it possibly be the effect I have on you?"

Elizabeth stood up abruptly and folded her arms in front of her. "Mr. Darcy," she softly laughed, a tremble in her voice acknowledging the truth of his words. "Fitzwilliam, if you *have that effect* on me, as you suggest, then I fear that I shall be repeatedly apologizing to Miss Darcy for my neglect of her."

Darcy rose and took her arm. "Shall we go in, then, and make the first of what will likely be many apologies to Georgiana?"

Elizabeth smiled and tucked her arm further into his. "We might as well get it over with."

~~*

It was apparent that Miss Darcy was well aware of her brother's intentions, for when they told her of their engagement – along with the extenuating circumstances requiring it to be kept a secret – she feigned surprise and exhibited true delight. While she wished, as did her brother, to announce it to the world, she promised to keep the news to herself.

Both Mr. Darcy and his sister accompanied Elizabeth back to the Gardiners later that day. Elizabeth invited them inside, knowing everyone wished to be introduced to Miss Darcy.

The Gardiners and Jane and Bingley enjoyed the added company of the young lady. Elizabeth detected no awkwardness at all between her and Mr. Bingley, and was grateful that theirs had been a good friendship. Mr. Bingley informed them with utter delight that he and Jane would now be marrying in only two weeks.

Knowing it would be safe with them, Mr. Darcy and Elizabeth announced their engagement to everyone, along with the news that it was to be kept a secret until a later date. The announcement was received with great delight.

The two gentlemen and Miss Darcy took their leave close to midnight. As Elizabeth sat with her aunt and uncle and Jane in their small sitting room, they talked excitedly amongst themselves about two forthcoming weddings.

As conversation slowed, Elizabeth looked up at her family with concern in her eyes. "I am truly happy," she said slowly, "but I wonder what would have happened had Mr. Darcy not been able to persuade Mr. Wickham to marry Lydia." She took in a deep breath. "He most likely would not have felt it prudent to make me an offer of marriage."

Her uncle let out a hearty chuckle. "If you truly believe that, Elizabeth, then I fear you do not know Mr. Darcy very well!"

Elizabeth tilted her head toward her uncle. "Why do you say that, Uncle?" she asked him.

He slapped his hands down upon his knees. "When he first came to Town, he met with me. I assumed it was to discuss how we would find Wickham and Lydia and what to do when we did."

"And it was not?"

Mr. Gardiner rocked his head back and forth playfully. "Well, partially. He also came seeking my permission to ask for your hand. That was before those two had even been found!" He leaned his head back against the chair. "Yes, my dear. I believe he was planning to marry you whatever the outcome!"

Elizabeth treasured that revelation in her heart for the duration of the time Mr. Darcy was in Kent.

~~*

The next week passed with wedding plans made and finalized. The banns would be read for the following two weeks at their churches, and their wedding would take place the Saturday following.

Mr. Darcy and his sister spent a little over a week in Kent, as the wedding of their cousins took place. Elizabeth was delighted to receive several letters, always addressed from Georgiana, but one hidden inside from her brother. From their words, Elizabeth came to understand that their aunt was becoming more inclined to accept this first marriage with the passing of each day, but occasionally bemoaned how unfortunate it was that the Colonel had not been the firstborn. Elizabeth laughed when she read Mr. Darcy's words that if that had been the case, it was highly unlikely that he would have remained unwed for as long as he had. He assured her, however, that the Colonel did have a fond regard for Anne. Elizabeth pondered whether Lady Catherine would accept the marriage of her *other* nephew as readily.

In one of the letters, Mr. Darcy informed her it had only been at Easter that he realized the affection his cousins had for one another. Patrick, while often teasing Darcy about *his* having to marry Anne, kept those feelings to himself. He felt it would have gone against both cousins' wishes, as well as his aunt's. During that visit, Darcy had made it perfectly clear to his cousin that he had no intention of ever marrying Anne merely to keep some vain hope expressed long ago by his own mother and aunt. It was likely something the two women planned in the dreams that come along with motherhood. It was after Darcy made his resolve known that Patrick declared his feelings to Anne, which were joyously returned by her. Apparently she had always, but hopelessly, preferred him over Mr. Darcy.

~~*

As the day of Charles' and Jane's wedding approached, all their family and friends descended upon London for this celebration. Households were crowded and there was a constant flurry of activity. Despite all this, Jane remained her calm and serene self throughout.

The day of the wedding broke bright and warm. The excitement was palpable, very different than what was felt the day of the Wickhams' wedding. Elizabeth and Jane spent a good amount of time up in their room readying themselves for this momentous day. Elizabeth did not think she had ever seen a bride more beautiful and told Jane that Mr. Bingley was a very fortunate man. Jane corrected her sister saying that *she* was the one who was most fortunate.

As they rode to the church, Jane grasped Elizabeth's hand tightly. It was the only visible display Elizabeth saw of her sister's feelings. She was never one to show any nervousness or excitement. As Elizabeth gazed out the window watching the neighbourhood pass by, she thought of Mr. Darcy's initial interference. While Elizabeth had been able to easily discern the fond regard her sister had for Mr. Bingley, Mr. Darcy had not. Jane, always so serene and composed, had never appeared to him as one fervently and passionately enamoured with Mr. Bingley.

Even now, Jane chose to exhibit that sweet, gentle spirit that everyone associated with her. Elizabeth hoped with a sly smile that at least Mr. Bingley was privy to more demonstrative displays of her affection and would have no doubt of her love for him.

As the time for the ceremony drew near, Elizabeth and Jane waited in a small room in the back of the church. Jane took Elizabeth's hand in hers. "Oh, Lizzy! Do you truly know how happy I am?"

Elizabeth gave her a reassuring smile. "I certainly do."

"And you know how happy I am for you and Mr. Darcy. While I look forward with great delight to your residing with us at Braedenthorn, I cannot wait until you marry and become Mistress of Pemberley!"

The mere thought of that flooded Elizabeth with a sense of eager anticipation. Before she could reply to Jane, their uncle poked his head into the room. "It is time, ladies. Are you ready?"

Elizabeth nodded and looked at Jane. "Are you ready, Jane? This is *your* wedding!"

"I am."

Elizabeth preceded Jane down the aisle, keeping her eye on the gentleman who stood beside the groom. Mr. Darcy had never looked finer, and her heart skipped a beat when she realized that the next time she walked toward him down the aisle of a church, it would be as his bride. From the look on his face, he had also come to that realization.

During the service, Bingley and Jane could not take their eyes off each other. Darcy and Elizabeth suffered from the same curious symptom. The first couple gazed unabashedly at one another; the latter couple, however, was forced to do it covertly. At present, they could only look forward to *their* day to stand at the front of the church. They each hoped it would be soon.

~~*

Elizabeth did not leave for Braedenthorn immediately following the wedding. She wished to give Charles and Jane some time alone and allow Jane to learn her way around the new estate and establish herself as its Mistress. She would need to make many decisions, and while Elizabeth would love to be by her side as she made them, it would be best for her to learn her duties as much as she could on her own.

While Elizabeth remained in London, she and the Gardiners were repeatedly the guests of Mr. and Miss Darcy. He did not wait until Elizabeth was settled at Braedenthorn to begin acquainting her with his circle of intimate friends. While many had returned to their country homes for the summer, the ones he encountered were enthusiastically introduced to Elizabeth. He made a point of introducing her as the *esteemed Miss Elizabeth Bennet, sister of Mrs. Charles Bingley of Braedenthorn, Derbyshire*. She was also, however, introduced as the particular guest of Miss Darcy, which served to thwart any premature speculation about her and the esteemed Master of Pemberley.

The fervency with which Mr. Darcy made these introductions may have appeared to reveal his concern about her lesser station becoming known. In truth, however, it was his conviction that the sooner Elizabeth felt she was being received well, the sooner she would agree to make the formal announcement of their engagement.

The two weeks in Town were unlike any she had ever experienced. She watched with rapt delight a Shakespearean play performed on stage. Darcy enjoyed seeing her fascination as she enjoyed a ballet and an opera for the very first time. The music that filled her ears, both in voice and instrument, was far superior to anything she had ever heard in all her years in Hertfordshire.

At length she received a missive from her sister expressing her wish for her to join them. Plans were made for the journey that Elizabeth and the Gardiners would take. Mr. Darcy and his sister made immediate plans, as well, to return to Pemberley. They all looked forward to reuniting in a few days.

Chapter 28

Jane was delighted when Elizabeth and the Gardiners arrived at Braedenthorn and she rushed out to greet them when she happened to pass a window and saw the carriage approach. Elizabeth readily noticed the glow of happiness that lit her sister's face. She seemed truly happy, and for that, Elizabeth was grateful.

Mr. Bingley was away when they arrived, which gave Jane the opportunity to give them a leisurely tour of the house. While not as large as Pemberley, it suited them well.

After seeing the house, Elizabeth was anxious to walk about the grounds to get a little fresh air and exercise, or so she told the others. When she stepped out, she immediately walked over to a clearing, where she could readily see the ridge off in the distance – the ridge that was situated behind Pemberley.

The sight of it brought a thrill to her heart. She knew Mr. Darcy was just on the other side. From Braedenthorn it would be a long walk up the ridge, and it was unlikely she would ever make it to the top to see a sunrise without leaving long before daylight even began to touch the skies. But she knew it would be a tolerably easy walk to the top, about as far as Oakham Mount was to Longbourn, and she could make the trip during daylight without any difficulty.

Coming to a tree which offered both shade and an unobstructed view of the ridge, she sat down and leaned against it. Her hands lightly skimmed over the grass at her side, and she stopped to pick a few blades, bringing them up to her face and twirling them against her nose.

"Do you plan to eat those or merely inhale them?"

Elizabeth gasped at the sound of Mr. Darcy's voice, and she struggled to turn around and rise to her feet. He stepped around and held out his hands to her. She reached out and he took each one in his, easily pulling her up. As she came to her feet, she leant into him, wrapping her arms about his neck.

"I am so glad to see you; to finally be here!"

Darcy returned her embrace by drawing her even closer, his arms encircling her waist. "I am delighted you are here, as well." He kissed the top of her head and pulled back with a smile. "It has only been three days, however, since we last saw each other."

"It seems like forever!" she countered, nuzzling her head against his chest.

Darcy let out a hearty chuckle. "Yes, I suppose it does." He released one hand and lifted her face toward him. "Is this the kind of reception I can expect now that we are neighbours?"

Elizabeth skewered her mouth. "Was my behaviour terribly shocking?" She began to pull away, but Darcy held her tight.

Darcy lifted his eyes toward Braedenthorn. "Do you not fear that someone might see us?"

She reached up tentatively and fingered his neck cloth. "You know they already know."

He smiled down at her. "The Bingleys know, but what of the servants? They are the ones who talk more than anyone else."

A look of comprehension coloured her features and again when she tried to pull away, his arms held tighter.

"Not yet." His gaze held her fast, and she watched as his face drew near. When his lips pressed against hers, all thoughts were swept away and she experienced a wave of light-headedness, prompting her to grasp onto him more tightly. The blades of grass she held in her fingers fell to the ground.

There was something so right in his kiss that she did not want it to end. She was pleased that he seemed just as inclined to keep her in his arms, his lips pressed to hers. At length, he pulled away, but only slightly.

He touched his forehead to hers, and took several slow breaths. He seemed unable to speak.

Elizabeth casually ran her hand down her dress to smooth it out and to settle her senses. She was the first to regain command of her voice. "Do you think we truly need to worry about the servants talking?"

Darcy chuckled. "Ah, now you are concerned." He drew back and smiled. "Most of those that Bingley hired have worked at Pemberley at one time or another. They know what is expected of them and that it could cost them their job if they gossip about what goes on inside and out of the house. Unfortunately, it does not always guarantee their silence."

They began to walk back toward the house and Darcy turned to her. "Speaking of servants, you will require your own personal maid while you are here. I am sending a young lady over for you from Pemberley."

"My own maid?" she asked with surprise. "Goodness, I used to have to share one with my four sisters at Longbourn."

"The decision whether you want to keep her is yours, but I think you will like her. Her name is Anna Harrington."

Elizabeth instantly turned to him at the mention of her name. "Anna!" she said excitedly and clasped her hands together. "I think she and I will get along admirably!"

A satisfied smile appeared. "I thought she would be good for you."

~~*

The Bingleys hosted their first dinner party for the Gardiners, Elizabeth, and Mr. Darcy and his sister. The newly wedded couple were grateful it was a small party made up of people they loved and cared about. At the end of the evening everyone complimented them for the delicious meal their cooks prepared and for a very enjoyable time.

They were all invited to Pemberley the following evening for what would be a slightly larger dinner party. Invitations were also extended to people in the neighbourhood whom Mr. Darcy highly esteemed. He believed it beneficial for the Bingleys and Elizabeth that he introduce them directly.

212

For the next few days, Charles made visits with his friend to some of the neighbouring homes. Some visits were in reciprocation for a visit paid at Braedenthorn, others were to allow Mr. Darcy to make an introduction or promote an acquaintance. Quite soon thereafter, invitations to small parties, larger gatherings, and even a ball were received and accepted.

During that first week Elizabeth was there, she had been invited, along with the Bingleys and the Gardiners, to three small dinner parties. The hosts all appeared to be on quite intimate terms with Mr. Darcy and they received their new acquaintances warmly. Jane won them over by her kind-heartedness and Elizabeth by her liveliness and intelligent conversation.

The Gardiners returned to London after having spent a pleasant fortnight at Braedenthorn. They had enjoyed their stay, visited friends in Lambton, including the Ketterlings, and reassured Elizabeth that they would return in a day's notice for another wedding.

The following week was the ball to which they had been invited. While Elizabeth was still adamant that no one should suspect any attachment between her and Mr. Darcy, she did allow him two dances, and then watched in delight as he kept a rigid eye on her as she danced with several other available gentlemen.

Two weeks later, Caroline Bingley and Mr. and Mrs. Hurst arrived. Elizabeth had not seen Charles' sisters since his and Jane's wedding. A small dinner party was held to welcome them.

Elizabeth was well aware of the lack of enthusiasm the two sisters exhibited for their brother's choice of his bride. The few brief times she saw them before the wedding, Elizabeth readily noticed the looks they stole between each other and knew exactly what they were thinking. Several times she spied the two sisters in fervent conversation and suspected from their hushed voices and pinched brows that they were discussing their brother's intended… and her family.

Elizabeth was quite certain that Caroline must have been highly disappointed that things did not go as she expected – or at least as she hoped – between her brother and Miss Darcy. While those hopes were now dashed, Elizabeth wondered whether Caroline still clung to hopes regarding Mr. Darcy and *herself*.

During the course of the evening, Elizabeth was far too dutiful in her neglect of Mr. Darcy, which allowed Caroline Bingley to make a complete fool of herself in regards to him. Elizabeth rather enjoyed seeing how her affianced carefully, politely, and repeatedly put Caroline in her place. A desperate look he cast at Elizabeth was interpreted by her as a plea to announce this engagement soon!

Later, when the men had joined Bingley in his study, Elizabeth found herself alone with Caroline, who took the opportunity to speak her mind.

"Tell me, Miss Bennet," Caroline said, "whatever happened with your ward? Will you be returning any time soon as her *governess*?" She emphasized the last word in a vulgar tone.

"I do not believe so. I am confident the Willstones will find another."

Caroline leaned in, as if wanting to share with Elizabeth some secret between them. Instead, her voice was accusatory. "Do not expect, Miss Bennet, to overcome your standing in society by merely residing with my brother at his estate. You are a governess and that shall always be before you. If you suppose to attract the eye of some man of distinction and fortune, I would kindly offer you a word of advice. Do not get your hopes up. Most gentlemen of noble birth will not take notice of you. Do not imagine that this arrangement will change anything. Especially concerning *one* particular gentleman!"

Elizabeth remained silent while she collected herself. She would love to announce to her that indeed, *one* particular gentleman had *already* taken notice of her, but she could not. Not yet. "There is doubtless some truth in your words, Miss Bingley. I would imagine *most* gentlemen would not pay me notice and I have no intention of seeking *them* out."

Caroline smiled. "It is good you understand your place."

Elizabeth smiled knowingly back at her. "Oh, I understand. Believe me, I truly do."

Bingley's home had a small courtyard in the back of the house, and Elizabeth immediately sought it out. It angered her that Caroline felt it was within her rights to attack her – a member of her own family – in that way. She had not improved in her essentials in the slightest! Elizabeth stepped out, grateful that it was Jane who had married Mr. Bingley. Jane would give his sisters all the benefit of the doubt and inevitably they would be won over by her sweet goodness. Jane could overlook any fault, while Elizabeth invariably had to bite her tongue to prevent herself from saying something harsh in someone's defence.

Elizabeth crossed her arms in front of her and leant on the railing of the staircase that led down to the courtyard. Her life had certainly altered drastically this past year. Her mind could barely comprehend the changes, the ups and downs, the doubts and fears, and the hopes and joys that permeated it.

She closed her eyes and took in a deep breath. A cool breeze swept over her and the fragrance from a night-blooming jasmine sent its sweet fragrance in her direction. She walked down the few remaining steps and let out a long, drawn out huff.

"That sounded like a sigh of great frustration, Miss Bennet."

Elizabeth's heart lurched at the voice and she turned to see Mr. Darcy quietly step out from the house.

"Fitzwill…" With a finger to his own lips, he reminded her that she ought not call him that. Not yet, at least. With a smile, she acknowledged him with a nod of her head. "Mr. Darcy, I merely required some fresh air."

He came down the steps to her side and gazed down at her. "Are you unwell?"

She turned to him with a wide smile. "Now that you are here, I am quite well."

He directed his eyes out to the courtyard, while he reached over and furtively took her fingers in his. "You do realize that if we announced our engagement to everyone, we would have no need for stealing moments to ourselves."

Elizabeth's head shook and her lips pursed tightly together. In a forceful whisper she said, "There have been a few times this evening I have been very tempted to blurt it out!"

Mr. Darcy chuckled. "Any time you wish to will be fine with me."

They talked a few minutes longer, Elizabeth revelling in his closeness.

At length, Mr. Darcy gave her fingers a slight squeeze, saying, "If it were not for Bingley's sisters, I would most boldly remain out here with you for the duration of the evening, but as such, I best return. Perhaps you will follow me shortly?"

Elizabeth nodded. "Yes. I shall stay out here a few minutes more."

Darcy returned to the house and after several minutes, Elizabeth did the same. When she stepped inside, she heard Miss Bingley's excited voice. It was apparent that she had encountered Mr. Darcy.

"You see the futility in it, do you not? She wants to pass herself off as an esteemed lady, when she is not! You must be aware of this and alert my brother, so he will not earn the scorn of those in the neighbourhood!"

"I fail to see your point, Miss Bingley. Miss Elizabeth's father was a gentleman, as you well know. Why should she not be received with the respect she deserves?"

"Because she cannot change the fact that she was a lowly governess! That will always be what people see! Certainly you can see that she has aspirations that are completely unreasonable!"

There was silence for a moment and Elizabeth felt her ire again rise. Finally, in a somewhat stern voice, Mr. Darcy said, "I see. Do you speak from your own personal experience, Miss Bingley, due to the fact that your father merely made his fortune in trade? Do you encounter people who have blocked your *own* aspirations to rise from the standing in which you were born?"

There was more silence, and Elizabeth stepped toward them. She walked up to Mr. Darcy and unflinchingly slipped her hand through his arm. Elizabeth's smile was returned by Caroline's look of bewilderment and shock. Darcy, seeing Elizabeth's bold action, had somewhat the same look on his face.

"Has he told you the good news yet, Miss Bingley?" she asked, looking intently at her. "Has he told you that we have recently become betrothed? Shall you now wish us joy?"

Caroline sputtered something unintelligible. She looked at Mr. Darcy and her eyes pleaded with him for a repudiation of Elizabeth's absurd announcement. Instead, he said, "It is true, Miss Bingley. You may have not heard, as we have not yet made a formal announcement. But indeed, we are to marry!"

For a brief moment, Elizabeth noticed a look of grief and resignation pass over her features, but just as quickly, she threw back her shoulders and lifted her head high. "May I offer you my congratulations? I hope you will be happy." She then turned and walked stiffly, and quickly away.

Elizabeth waited a few moments before turning to Darcy, who was shaking his head in Caroline's direction. Elizabeth smiled and gave his hand a furtive squeeze. "I thought I would truly enjoy seeing the look on her face when I told her, but instead, I feel rather sorry for her."

"It is because you are not like her. You are compassionate, not mean spirited." He turned and looked at Elizabeth. His hand cradled her chin, tilting her face up toward him. "I believe, Elizabeth, that we ought to announce our engagement soon."

Elizabeth had begun to feel the same way. At the end of the evening, Mr. Darcy invited everyone to Pemberley the next evening. There was only one thing Elizabeth wished to do before they formally announced their engagement, but she was not sure how to bring it about. Upon talking with Georgiana, she asked her if she had any ideas.

Georgiana thought a moment and then smiled. "Yes," she said. "I think I do."

~~*

The next evening at Pemberley was enjoyed by everyone, particularly Elizabeth. It was not merely due to Caroline's restrained behaviour, but the thought that their engagement would soon be known by all!

At the end of the evening, the Braedenthorn party took their leave. A light mist had begun to fall, prompting Mr. and Mrs. Hurst and Caroline to hurriedly thank the Darcys, bid them goodnight, and hasten into their carriage. It was already half-way around the circular drive when the others walked up to their waiting carriage.

Charles and Jane thanked Mr. Darcy and his sister before stepping up into it. As Elizabeth stepped toward the carriage, Darcy stopped her, taking her hand and pressing it to his lips. The unspoken words that were written across his face begged her to consider that sufficient time had passed and she was highly esteemed by those in the neighbourhood – at least by those who mattered.

Once inside the carriage, the footman shut the carriage door, and both Darcy and his sister expressed their enjoyment of the evening. After expressions of gratitude to the Darcys for the evening, the carriage began to pull away. Elizabeth watched Georgiana excuse herself and quickly return to the house. Darcy stood and watched, giving a final wave goodbye.

Inside the carriage, Elizabeth retrieved her parcel as the carriage veered far to the right along the circular drive, so that for a moment, it was out of view of the front of the house. The door opened and she quickly stepped down. Charles and Jane waved goodnight to her and the door was then quickly and quietly closed. The carriage continued on. It was only a brief moment before Georgiana appeared.

"I think that went well!" she said. "He will not suspect a thing, as long as we can sneak you up to your room. I do not think that will be difficult, as he will likely watch the carriage as long as he can see it!"

"Do you think he wondered why we pulled so far to the right?"

"Not enough to give him pause for concern. Once he sees the carriage continue on, I am quite certain he will think no more about it!" Georgiana let out a soft chuckle. "But the weather... will that make a difference in the morn?"

Elizabeth answered her with a hearty, "No, it most certainly will not!"

Georgiana hurried with Elizabeth to the room she had the last time she was here. As they walked in, a flood of memories swept over her. This was where she had been when she realized she loved him. This was also where she had been when she thought all hope was gone.

Anna appeared, having come to Pemberley earlier in the evening. She helped ready Elizabeth for bed and told her she would waken her before sunrise. There was really no need, as Elizabeth barely slept at all!

~~*

The following morning, Elizabeth was already sitting up in the bed when Anna tapped at the door. She bid her come in, and Anna quietly, and most efficiently, helped Elizabeth dress. She was proving to be an exceptional personal maid. Elizabeth not only appreciated her friendliness, but her excellence at all she did.

Once Elizabeth was dressed, the last thing she put on was her pair of mud boots. Then she and Anna quietly took the back staircase down and walked out through Pemberley's courtyard, to avoid encountering Darcy. Georgiana had taken measures with Mr. Grant, her brother's valet, to ensure that he would indeed take a hike up the ridge that morning. Mr. Grant was to have given him assurances that the sunrise 'looked to be spectacular,' but he also conveniently delayed him somewhat until he heard the 'all is clear' tap. That meant Elizabeth had already preceded him down.

The morning was only just beginning to dawn as she began her climb up the ridge. It was darker than when she walked up here that first morning, but enough light permeated the skies to allow her eyes to grow accustomed to the dimness and keep to the path. Fortunately, the sky had cleared, and while the path was slightly damp, it was not terribly muddy. When she reached the summit, it seemed as though nothing, in all directions, was yet awake.

She walked over to the bench that sat atop the ridge and took a seat. Her heart raced relentlessly as she waited. It was but a moment later that she heard the sound of twigs cracking from the path. She clasped her hands in excitement, but then for a moment feared it would not be Fitzwilliam, but some animal. She sat very still, however, keeping her eyes to the place at the summit where the path would bring him up.

She turned her head slightly when he appeared a short distance away. He immediately stepped toward the edge of the ridge and looked down the other side. She could see that he looked toward Braedenthorn. It even appeared as though he looked down toward the paths that came up from there. She smiled quietly as she wondered whether he thought she would actually hike up all that way in the darkness.

He seemed so riveted as he looked out at the valley that Elizabeth wondered whether he would ever notice her. She finally decided to take matters into her own hands. "Ahem," she cleared her throat, prompting Mr. Darcy to spin around.

He did not take the time to greet her or even ask what she was doing there or how she got up there. In a few long strides he came to stand in front of her and took her hands, pulling her to her feet. He wrapped his arms about her in a firm embrace and fervently pressed his lips to hers.

Elizabeth was so completely astonished by his fervour, so enthralled by his ardent display, that she felt she would collapse to the ground if she did not grasp onto him more firmly. He must have sensed this, for his grip tightened about her.

At last, reluctantly, he slowly drew away. "Pray, forgive me, Elizabeth." He took in two deep breaths. "I have come up here so often, thinking of sharing the view and the sunrise…" He lifted her chin with two of his fingers, "… with you. Consequently, when I saw you, I could not even utter a polite 'Good morning,' or 'I am pleased you have come!'"

He leant over and briefly kissed her lips again. He drew back with a smile and said, "I am delighted to see you here, but heavens! You must have hiked up here in the complete dark!"

"I wished to keep my promise." Elizabeth smiled and lifted her fingers tentatively to push back some strands of hair that had fallen across his forehead. "However, I did not climb up from Braedenthorn. I stayed at Pemberley last night. Your sister helped me with the plan."

"You spent the night at Pemberley?" he asked as he studied her face in the predawn morn.

"I did. Now, come, sit down. I thought we could sit on the bench and wait for the sun to rise."

He grasped her hand. "Certainly."

She cast a sidelong glance at him. "Just as we did at your town home."

"My town home? We did not wait for the sunrise. Not only would it have been impossible to see, it was the wrong time of day!"

Elizabeth nodded at him and smiled. "Yes, that is true, but I meant while we wait for the sun to rise this morning, we can sit *exactly* as we did there."

Darcy narrowed his eyes at her, pondering her meaning. They sat down and Darcy took her hand.

"Good," Elizabeth said. "You remembered."

Darcy's brows rose. "Ah, yes. I took your hand." He smiled. "Are we to talk of apologies for my aunt's behaviour and then Georgiana?"

Elizabeth shook her head. "I think not."

Darcy pursed his lips. "Rosings?"

"Definitely not!" she laughed.

Darcy smiled. While it appeared he was trying to subdue the elation he felt, in case he was in error, Elizabeth knew that he had comprehended what her words and her joining him meant.

He grasped her hand tightly and looked at her. Their eyes remained fixed on each other. "Elizabeth," he said softly. "I fear I cannot do all things *exactly* as we did in London!"

With wide eyes, Elizabeth looked up at him. "You cannot?" she asked, her heart suddenly lurching with alarm.

He cradled her hands in his. "Not precisely." After a pause he added, "Because I neglected to do this."

He slid off the bench and knelt before her on one knee. "Elizabeth…" He looked down to reach for her hands when he suddenly stopped and began to chuckle. "Elizabeth, what is this?" He pulled the hem of her dress up slightly to reveal her mud boots.

"You know precisely what they are! Now… what were you about to say?" she asked coyly.

Taking her hands, he lifted them up and kissed each one, a smile still displayed on his lips. "My dearest Elizabeth, I would be the most honoured man of all Derbyshire, of all England, of the entire world, if you would consent to be my wife. Will you marry me?"

Elizabeth grinned and nodded, leaning toward Darcy to kiss both of his hands. "With all my heart I accept your offer… to watch the sunrises, to explore the paths around Pemberley…"

"In your mud boots," Darcy interjected.

"Yes, in my mud boots… and to read Cowper's poems and Shakespeare's sonnets… with you."

Darcy chuckled. "Yes, all those things." Very softly he added as he gazed intently at her, "And more."

Elizabeth's heart stirred within.

Raising a single brow he asked, "May I finally announce it to whole the world?"

Elizabeth nodded. "You certainly may, Fitzwilliam."

At that moment the top edge of the sun appeared, shining its light upon the couple. They both turned and watched as it made its slow ascent over the dark silhouette of the mountain, painting the sky in reds, oranges, and yellows. There was not a sound heard as they watched the first of many sunrises unfold before them.

Once the sun had risen and the sky brightened, Darcy stood up. He turned to Elizabeth with his hand extended. When she rose to her feet, he asked, "Are you quite sure I can announce this to the world?"

"Oh, yes!" she said. "I want everyone to know!"

Darcy gave his head a nod and then walked over to the edge of the ridge looking down on Pemberley. He cupped his hands around his mouth and began to shout, "I AM GOING TO MARRY ELIZABETH BENNET!"

Elizabeth let out a hearty laugh. "Fitzwilliam Darcy! What will everyone think?"

He walked over and lifted her face to his. "I truly care not what anyone thinks!" He took her hand. "Come, we shall make sure everyone at Pemberley is awake and tell them the news. Then we shall go to Braedenthorn and inform *everyone* there!"

The staff at Pemberley was called together for an important announcement. Speculation rose, but it was kept to a minimum because of Mr. Darcy's dislike of gossip of any kind. The news about his engagement to Miss Elizabeth Bennet was received with elation.

After sharing breakfast with Georgiana, the three departed for Braedenthorn to share the news with everyone there. Charles and Jane were delighted that the engagement was now official. Caroline had already informed the Hursts about the engagement and how her hopes were now crushed forever, so they all received the news with polite indifference. It was very exciting news, however, to the staff that had come to know Elizabeth in the few weeks she had been residing there. Since they all were from neighbouring villages, they were also acquainted with Mr. Darcy, either by reputation or having worked at Pemberley. Most were pleasantly surprised by the news, having secretly wondered amongst themselves whether he would ever find a suitable woman to marry. They all extended heartfelt congratulations to the couple.

Darcy was prompt in attaining the marriage license and securing Pemberley church for their wedding. It would be but a few short weeks before he and Elizabeth would at last become husband and wife.

Chapter 29

The bells in the steeple at Pemberley church sent their chimes tolling across the countryside. Darcy paced back and forth in his chambers. He had been ready for more than an hour, but another hour still remained before he needed to set out for the church. For the third time in as many minutes, he stood in front of the full-length mirror, fingering his neck cloth and tugging at his coattails to straighten them. Both actions were unnecessary and only served to calm his frustratingly heightened nerves.

His valet entered. "Is there anything further I can do for you, Mr. Darcy? Do you wish me to bring you something to drink?"

Darcy shook his head. "Thank you, no." He filled his lungs with a breath and then in a soft whisper said, "I just wish this was over with!"

"It shall be, sir. Very shortly." Mr. Grant smoothed Darcy's coat with his hand. "Just keep your eyes on Miss Bennet, sir. I guarantee everyone will have their eyes on her, as well." With a smile, he added, "The groom is never as appealing as the bride."

"This is most reassuring, Grant," Darcy muttered.

"I wish you to know, sir, that we are all very pleased with Miss Bennet and believe she will be a delightful Mistress of Pemberley."

"Thank you, Grant."

The dependable valet reached up to Darcy's neck cloth and tightened it in one place and straightened it in another. "And may I add, sir, that I am quite certain she will make you a most delightful wife!"

Darcy smiled and gave a tug on his coat. "Of that, I am most persuaded." He then turned to Grant. "You may go. I should like some time to myself."

"Yes, sir."

Upon his valet's departure, Darcy walked to the window and gazed out. Bracing his arms on the window sill, he looked out over the front grounds of Pemberley and smiled. He had to admit the grounds and home were beautiful, but up until this day, he always felt there was something lacking. When Elizabeth graced the halls at Pemberley with her presence, everything seemed so right and complete. He let out an audible sigh and gave another tug on his coat.

Without bothering to knock, Colonel Fitzwilliam barged in. "Darcy!" he exclaimed. "We are all waiting for you downstairs. The least you can do is join your family before the nuptials. Come, you have spoken barely two words to my mother-in-law since we arrived. I have spent a great deal of energy since your engagement was announced making her see the good in it. And *that*," the Colonel gave a tug to his cousin's neck cloth, "after doing everything in my power to convince her to see the good in *my* marriage to Anne!"

"You are correct. I have neglected everyone far too long. I am just... I have not felt inclined to participate in idle talk, as they will be of a mind to do." Darcy paused as words escaped him as to the violence of his feelings. In a soft voice, he looked to his cousin and said, "My heart is so full. I am happier than I can even believe myself to be."

The Colonel gave him a sly smile. "Shall you be happy with such a mother-in-law as Mrs. Bennet?"

"Are you happy with *yours*?" Darcy truly wished to know.

Patrick laughed. "I have always been able to brush aside our aunt's idiosyncrasies far better than you. However, from what I have seen of Mrs. Bennet's behaviour these past few days, I would garner a suspicion that she, much like our aunt, is one who easily tries your patience."

Darcy returned a satisfied look. "I shall fare quite admirably."

"Hah!" Darcy's cousin laughed. "Mrs. Bennet is conveniently ensconced four full counties away in Hertfordshire, whereas I must live at Rosings with mine."

"Only when you are on leave from your regiment. But I will give you credit in that regard, my good cousin. You are a much better man than I." Darcy gave his cousin a slap on the back and turned to walk out.

~~*

It was but a short while later that Fitzwilliam Darcy stood with an immaculately dignified posture at the front of Pemberley church. His arms hung loosely at his side, his fingers alternately fisted and stretched open. Occasionally he slipped one hand into his coat pocket to take hold of the diamond and sapphire ring he would place on his beloved's finger. It had once graced the finger of his mother, and soon it would be on the finger of his wife. The mere feel of it in his hands brought a stirring to his heart. Elizabeth had not yet seen the ring, as his wish was that she would set her eyes upon it for the first time when he placed it on her finger in the ceremony.

Darcy shifted from one foot to the other as he looked out at all the eyes presently upon him. Fortunately for him, they were all family and intimate friends, so he was able to endure it moderately well. He waited eagerly for the moment he would see Elizabeth walk toward him, knowing that at that moment, all would be well.

His cousin stood at his side, more relaxed and much more able to enjoy these moments before the wedding. Truth be told, he was rather enjoying the discomfiture Darcy was experiencing. It was not often that he witnessed his cousin, who rarely exhibited lack of control, experiencing such tremors of nervousness. He whispered words to his cousin intended to help him relax, but instead they only served to prolong Darcy's impatient agony.

Darcy could do nothing more, in those torturous moments of waiting, but to allow his eyes to gaze out at the guests. They came to rest upon his cousin Anne and her mother. Now that Anne was married to Patrick, she seemed a different woman. Marriage to their cousin had been good for her and seemed to enliven and embolden her. Darcy hoped the frailty that had consumed her life would fade and she would find in her husband the strength she had always lacked.

Darcy then glanced at his aunt, who sat proudly and rigidly at her daughter's side. He was quite certain her pride was in none other than herself. Darcy was truly grateful his cousin had persuaded her to accept both marriages. It had merely taken a veiled threat that while he and Anne would be making numerous journeys to Pemberley, she would not be accepted there if she did not accept Elizabeth as Darcy's wife. While she spoke not a disparaging word against Elizabeth when they came for the wedding, she did comment to Darcy that very morning how unfortunate it was that he did not look as fine as the Colonel did at his wedding to Anne, for Patrick was dressed in his regimentals.

Darcy's eyes turned to the Hamiltons and his cousin, Peter. He had been indispensable when things had grown chaotic at Pemberley. When Darcy abruptly left, leaving the Willstones and Miss Matthews with unanswered questions and mild accusations, Hamilton stepped in to assist Miss Darcy in tactfully making excuses for her brother and gently addressing their concerns. He also unwittingly became the shoulder upon which Miss Matthews cried.

From what Hamilton told his cousin, however, Miss Matthews was more disappointed than grieved upon learning that while Darcy was fond of her, he had never formed any sort of attachment toward her. Hamilton effortlessly consoled her, reassuring her that it had never been Darcy's intention to deceive her. By the time they departed Pemberley, Rosalyn was quite convinced that Hamilton himself had formed an ardent regard for her and she hoped to see him in Town next season.

Darcy's fists tightened and held their grip when he noticed Wickham and Lydia. He could hardly ban him from the wedding of his sister-in-law. While they had not been invited to Pemberley in the days before the wedding, he had no choice but to allow him to come to the wedding breakfast there following the wedding. Wickham was given, however, a strict admonition that he was not to walk liberally about the place as he was once accustomed to doing.

His eyes drifted to Mrs. Bennet and he wondered, with an honest measure of dread, how often she would expect to be a guest in their home. With an involuntary twitch of his mouth, he deliberated how difficult it would be to persuade Bingley and his wife to keep her at Braedenthorn when she came to visit her two eldest daughters. He readily assured himself that Bingley would cheerfully and most graciously expect Mrs. Bennet to reside with them.

Darcy's musings were interrupted when the doors at the back of the church swung open. He was the first to turn his eyes to the back, his heart quickening its pace. He watched as Jane walked slowly down the aisle, glancing at her husband and smiling as she passed him in the pew. When at last Elizabeth stepped out with her uncle by her side and began to walk toward him, he took in a sharp breath. He had never seen a bride more beautiful. He let out his breath in a long sigh of contentment.

As Elizabeth walked toward him with her gloved fingers tucked through Mr. Gardiner's arm, she saw only him, the man who would be her husband, her companion, her love, her protector and provider. In the course of the hour, she would no longer be Miss Elizabeth Bennet, but Mrs. Fitzwilliam Darcy.

As she came near, it took every ounce of control for Darcy not to step forward to take her from her uncle's arm. Quite believing he would, the Colonel gently reached out to stay him with his hand.

When Elizabeth finally reached him, they turned together to face Reverend Grierson. He began to speak the traditional words of the ceremony; words that had been spoken thousands of times before and would be spoken many more times in the years to come. The words were familiar to Darcy, having attended too many weddings to count; several, in fact, over the course of the past month. But this time they were being spoken to him and his beloved Elizabeth. He never imagined his feelings would be so violent.

He often imagined how he would feel as he stood with his bride at the altar. He had witnessed far too many grooms in states ranging from stark terror to dutiful obligation to casual indifference. There had been only a few who stood with unabashed devotion. He was certain the love and devotion he felt for Elizabeth could clearly be seen on his face.

Elizabeth and Jane had often dreamt of their wedding day. As young girls they had talked and planned and envisioned the man they would each marry. While Elizabeth was determined to only marry a man she loved, she had never considered living in a home as splendid as Pemberley. She turned and stole a glance at the man at her side and her heart pounded within. She was grateful she had come to see the good in him and love him. He certainly exceeded by far every daydream she and Jane ever conceived. And while she could not dismiss the beauty and splendour of his Pemberley, she was convinced that she would have married him if he was the mere caretaker of an inn!

Darcy and Elizabeth spoke their vows and responded to the reverend's questions with heartfelt earnestness. There was no doubt in each of their minds that they would love and honour, serve and obey… in sickness and in health, for richer or for poorer, till death did part them.

As a sign of their covenant and commitment, Darcy gently took her hand and slid the ring upon Elizabeth's finger. She gasped as she caught the sparkle and brilliance of the centre diamond flanked on either side by two sapphires. She lifted her eyes and her lips parted, wishing to express her wonder at such a gift. She spoke not a word, but her face told him the extent of her feelings.

Darcy knew he must wait, but every fibre in his body wished to draw Elizabeth to him and kiss those beguiling lips. He merely had to wait until that pronouncement that they were now man and wife. *I can do that…* he told himself. *I can do that… I …*

In the midst of his silent resolution, he heard a voice, "I now pronounce you man and wife. You shall no longer be known as you were, but from this day forward you shall be known as Mr. and Mrs. Fitzwilliam Darcy."

At long last the moment Fitzwilliam Darcy had been waiting for was here.

Elizabeth was now his wife! He looked at her first and smiled, and then leant down and kissed the lips that had earlier beckoned him and now smiled back at him. He savoured their sweetness. He wrapped his arms about her, delighting in her soft touch. If it were not for the multitude of eyes upon him, he would have been tempted to prolong the kiss. He slowly and reluctantly pulled away.

The newly wedded couple turned to face their guests and walked back up the aisle as man and wife.

~~*

Pemberley's staff had worked throughout the night to transform the ballroom into a room worthy of the celebration of their Master and his new bride. The foods they prepared and musicians that played were the finest in the county. Flowers filled every corner, topped every table, and were even placed in small vases along the wall. Candles were lit even though it was daylight, providing a warm and magical atmosphere.

While the guests had nothing but praise for the lavish affair, the couple noticed very little save for each other. Darcy wanted nothing but for this obligatory celebration to be finished. He wished to be away from the crowds of people and be alone with his wife.

After the breakfast, Darcy and Elizabeth were expected to begin the dancing. As Elizabeth faced her husband, waiting for the piece to begin, she thought back to their dance together at the Netherfield Ball. She thought pensively how they had argued during the one and only dance that they shared together. She had little to like about him then and much to dislike. Yet she had been blind to the fact that he had begun to hold her in high regard.

As the dance began, she was able to truly appreciate his proficiency. Previously, she had been so prejudiced against him that she hardly noticed anything about him – on the dance floor and elsewhere – that would have evoked her appreciation. This time as they danced, they refrained from talking. All that was needed was a glance, a smile, and a squeeze of the hand to know what the other was thinking.

It was mid-afternoon when finally the couple began to say their farewells and thank everyone for coming. After receiving a celebratory send-off, the couple departed Pemberley, eager to begin their life together.

~~*

Darcy had made plans to spend the first few days of married life away from Pemberley. He made arrangements to stay at a small cottage on a lake about an hour's carriage ride away.

As they sat together in the carriage, Elizabeth gently stroked her husband's hand. "I have been doing much thinking of late, Fitzwilliam, and am quite of the opinion it was best for the two of us that I had such strong feelings of dislike for you initially."

Darcy raised an eyebrow and looked at her. "Truly? Why is this?"

A smug smile swept her face. "In my study of the character of ladies such as Caroline Bingley and Rosalyn Matthews, I believe that they once had been quite amiable. I knew for a fact that Rosalyn was. We got along quite nicely while in London. But something changed once we were at Pemberley."

"What changed?"

Elizabeth slipped her hand through Darcy's arm and leaned back in the carriage, her eyes turned forward. "She became quite unreasonable, suspicious, even scheming." Elizabeth shook her head. "I can only assume that this is what has happened to every young lady who set her eyes upon you as an excellent prospect for marriage."

Darcy shook his head. "This is preposterous!"

"Is it?" Elizabeth asked slyly. "Consider the fact that you could find no suitable lady in Town. The only reason for that is they all knew who you were and what you were worth. It was already too late for them. Their behaviour around you was altered beyond anything suitable for you."

Darcy rolled his eyes. "And you?"

She rolled out a long, soft sigh and tightened her grasp about him. "Due to the fact that I initially found you quite objectionable, I was spared any character transformation."

Darcy turned his eyes to her. "Your reasoning is flawed, my dear, for you did soon come to view me with strong regard."

Elizabeth nodded. "Yes, but that was after becoming acquainted with the real Fitzwilliam Darcy. I do not wish to grieve you, my love, but I fell in love with you, and not your fortune or your estate or your standing in society."

Darcy feigned disappointment. "That is a heavy lot, indeed. I had hoped that at least one of those would have worked in my behalf."

Laughing at his humour, she leant over and kissed his cheek. "Perhaps when I saw Pemberley I was quite moved to change my opinion of you." She pursed her lips and cast a sly glance at him. "I believe, my dear husband, *that* is why you were initially attracted to me."

"You claim to know what attracted me to you? Please, I wish to hear your opinion!"

Elizabeth laughed. "It was due to the fact that I was *not* impressed with such things. I did not swoon or fawn over you or cater to your every whim. I argued with you and clashed with you. What woman in her right mind would do such a thing if she wished to win over a man?"

Darcy raised an eyebrow and studied his wife. "Are you saying it was merely because you presented a challenge to me that I was not used to facing?"

Elizabeth rubbed her chin and pondered this. "A challenge? I had not considered that." Then she shook her head. "No, I do not believe you saw me as a challenge, for you would have improved your behaviour much sooner on my behalf. I prefer to think that I was merely not what you were used to. My indifference toward you was… perhaps you found it a pleasant change."

"Hmmm," Darcy murmured. "You seem to know *me* so well, tell me about yourself. When did *your* feelings toward me improve?"

Snuggling against him, she said softly, "It was before I came to Pemberley."

"Truly?" Darcy asked. "Might I inquire how this came to be?"

Elizabeth smiled. "Rosalyn was your greatest advocate." She lifted her brow and smiled when she heard him groan. Continuing on, she said, "The things she said about you made me realize your goodness. Your letter, of course, helped me to see things more clearly, but what she and others said of you were things I could not dismiss. By the time we departed for Pemberley, I was bound to love you, even though I did not know it at the time."

Darcy cupped Elizabeth's face with his hand, bringing it toward him. "I had so wanted another opportunity to show you who I truly was. I realized at Rosings that I had become someone I did not wish to be. I saw in you someone who did not cater to the trappings of society, and yet I was guilty of that very thing. When I began to socialize in the same circles as the Willstones and knew you to be the governess of their daughter, I formulated a plan to bring you to Pemberley. I am still grieved over the part I played in misleading Miss Matthews."

"They shall be fine. I received a letter of congratulations from Emily just the other day. Her new governess wrote it for her. I would assume her parents gave her permission. I would like to think that we shall be on friendly terms when we see them again."

"I hope so, as long as Hamilton does not break Miss Matthews' heart anew."

"Is she fond of him?"

"She seems to have formed an attachment to him. He has a gift of humour that helped her during that difficult time at Pemberley. He was able to make her laugh."

Elizabeth nodded. "Yes, she did seem to like that in him."

The carriage came to a stop and the door opened.

"Well, my dear. If all our journeys pass this quickly with such stimulating conversation, I shall be willing to travel with you anywhere, for I usually find travelling most tedious."

They walked up to a small cottage that was situated by itself on a small lake. An inn was located just at the end of the lane.

"This is where we shall spend our first few days, Elizabeth. I hope it will please you."

"It looks delightful, Fitzwilliam."

"Our staff will reside at the inn and we will either take our meals there or have them brought to us. I felt we could have some enjoyable time alone here. As they got an earlier start, they most likely have the cottage ready for us. Shall we go in?"

Elizabeth nodded just as Mr. Grant opened the door. She gasped as she peered inside. Although small, it had a simple elegance. Mr. Grant and Anna, as well as two additional servants, welcomed them and stepped aside as they walked in. A meal was waiting and a small table was set for just the two of them. Flowers and candles added to the ambiance.

Elizabeth looked around her and walked over to a window overlooking the lake. "Shall we be able to see the sunrise from here, do you think?" she asked.

"As a matter of fact, yes," Darcy joined her at the window and pointed to some hills on the far side of the lake. "It ought to rise just over that ridge."

Elizabeth turned and clasped her hands in joy. "This is delightful!"

Darcy pulled her close to him and gave her a gentle kiss atop her head. "I am pleased you like it."

"Are there paths to walk?" she asked.

Darcy nodded. "Several."

"Did you bring your books of Cowper's poems and Shakespeare's sonnets?"

"I most certainly did."

Her head burrowed contentedly against his chest, and she wrapped her arms tightly about his waist, latching her fingers together at his back. Closing her eyes, she breathed in his manly scent. When she opened her eyes, she noticed something placed on a small table in the corner of the room. She lifted her head so her chin rested against his chest and cast her eyes up at him.

"Is that your chess set, Fitzwilliam?"

He turned his eyes toward the object in question. "So it seems," he replied.

"And do you intend to add chess playing to the aforementioned diversions?"

"If it is acceptable to you."

"Then we shall have not an idle moment as we watch the sunrise, explore the paths, read Cowper's poems and Shakespeare's sonnets, play chess..." Elizabeth paused and looked up into his eyes with a teasing smile. She stood on her toes, wrapped her arms about his neck, and brought her lips to his ear. In an uneven voice she whispered softly, "And *more*?"

Darcy's breath caught and he placed his hands on either side of Elizabeth's face, combing his fingers slightly into her hair. He looked deeply into her eyes, his own smouldering. "And *much* more," he whispered, as he slowly lowered his lips to meet hers. She rose up on her toes again to meet his lips, and the two remained captured in a fervent, passionate kiss. The servants discreetly turned their attention to small chores that in truth needed no tending.

Mr. and Mrs. Darcy did not seem inclined to end the kiss, prompting Mr. Grant to silently lead Anna and the other servants back past the otherwise occupied couple and out the front door, quietly closing it behind them. Turning to the now overtly grinning servants, he said with a smile of his own, "I believe it would be prudent of us to adjourn to our chambers at the inn and wait until we are summoned." Assuming a manner of authority and tact, he added, "I trust it will be some time before our services will be required."

Epilogue

One year later

Darcy stood atop the ridge behind Pemberley looking down toward Braedenthorn. He had climbed to the summit with the hope that he would see Elizabeth returning from a visit with her sister. The warmth of the late afternoon sun pressed against his back and a slight breeze rustled his coattails. He took in a deep breath as he gazed at the view in silent wonder. How could he be so angry at a woman he loved so overpoweringly?

He paced back and forth, as if his fierce strides would bring her into view. She knew he did not want her making that long, strenuous walk in her condition! Not alone and especially not when she was carrying their child!

He gazed out at the valley below, his eyes taking in the verdant greens that would soon give way to the reds and browns of autumn. He watched the path that wound its way down the hill toward Braedenthorn. He did not see her.

He had just returned from three days in London and was disappointed that she had not been home to greet him. When inquiring of Mrs. Reynolds as to her whereabouts, she informed him that Mrs. Darcy was visiting her sister and would return in time for dinner. The look of apprehension on her face prompted him to press her for the particulars on her means of transportation.

"She has walked, Mr. Darcy," she said nervously, knowing well his feelings on the matter. "But I am quite confident she is still able bodied enough to do so."

Concern for her safety and the welfare of their baby battled with the anger that rose as he realized in his absence, she had gone against his bidding. He had returned home a day early with a burgeoning desire to see her and hold her. He had so much to tell her, and coming home to the news that she had walked to Braedenthorn did not sit well with him.

Darcy immediately left the house and climbed up the ridge himself, his anger and concern propelling him.

He remained at the top and watched, hoping she would appear from around some curve in the path or out from behind a hedgerow. He chose not to walk down himself, for there was always the possibility that she may have taken the Bingleys' carriage home and then he would miss her.

As he waited, pacing back and forth, he allowed his thoughts to drift to Elizabeth and the baby she would have by mid spring. This was something he found himself doing often since she gave him the exciting news. The Bingleys had been more fortunate in producing an heir within a twelvemonth of their wedding. It was just prior to the birth of their baby that Elizabeth determined she was with child. Joy flooded him at the news that he would be a father.

Darcy feared that walking the three miles to Braedenthorn would in some way harm her or their unborn child, and insisted from the onset that she take the carriage. Whereas she and her husband frequently chose to walk up the ridge behind Pemberley and then down to the Bingleys' home – an easy distance of three miles – he now looked upon it as treacherous!

If Elizabeth planned to be back by supper, as Mrs. Reynolds claimed, she ought to already be on her way, so all he could do was wait. At length, he saw her coming from around a curve in the path. She was oblivious to him and seemed to take each stride effortlessly as if there was no alteration in her condition. Immediate relief swept through him, but he kept watch until he saw that she was almost to the top. Then he walked over to the bench and sat down.

Leaning back and crossing his arms, he waited – rather impatiently. Now that his concern for her welfare was satisfied, his ire again began to rise. His foot tapped on the ground mercilessly as he kept his eyes on the spot where she would come up from the path. It was but a few minutes before Elizabeth reached the top. She was looking down at a blade of grass twirling between her fingers. He smiled, much as he always did, whenever he had the opportunity to watch her when she was oblivious of his scrutiny. The mere sight of her diminished his anger. He had to remember that he was very displeased with her actions and quickly donned an air of disapproval as she neared.

When she glanced up and noticed him sitting there, she abruptly stopped. Her jaw dropped and her eyes widened in comprehension at his presence. Just as quickly, however, she ran up to her husband and sat down on his lap, wrapping her arms about his neck.

"When did you arrive home, my dearest? I thought you were not to return until tomorrow." She leaned over and kissed his forehead.

"I returned a day early. I thought I would surprise you. Are you surprised?" he asked with playful sarcasm.

Reaching up and combing her fingers through his hair, she answered, "I am surprised, but delighted!"

Darcy pulled her closer, enclosing her tightly within his arms. He pursed his lips as if pondering his next words, then asked, "Can I always expect you to defy my directives when I am away? Dare I ask how many times you have walked to Braedenthorn on your own?"

Elizabeth leaned her head against his shoulder. "Now, my dear Fitzwilliam, this was truly the only time… save for the day two weeks ago when the weather was so pleasant. I can barely restrain myself when the sky is so blue and the air is so warm. I simply must go outside and take a stroll for the cooler days of autumn and winter, as well as my condition, shall soon keep me housebound!"

"Elizabeth!" Darcy exclaimed. "Braedenthorn is not a stroll; it is a three mile hike! I will not allow it as long as you are carrying our child!" He took in a deep breath and let it out slowly. "Besides, you should not be walking about without an escort. If something happened to you…"

Elizabeth cupped his face with her hands and turned it to face her. She leaned in with a smile on her lips and a sparkle in her eyes and kissed him, rendering him silent. His arms tightened about her even more, and his hands pressed lightly against her back.

230

"Nothing has happened to me and nothing shall. It is a very easy walk, as you have declared many times yourself."

"That was before…" Darcy looked down at her dress, which only had a barely discernable bulge. "What would have happened had you been too tired to return?"

Elizabeth laughed. "The Bingleys do have a very nice carriage that I am sure they would allow me to take. Although it is not as nice as yours…"

"Ours!" Darcy corrected her.

Elizabeth nodded her head and smiled. After a year of marriage she still had a difficult time believing all this was hers. "Ours." She leaned her head on his shoulder and sighed. "I regret causing you concern. I will not set out for Braedenthorn again unless someone accompanies me."

"Unless *I* accompany you!"

"If you insist."

"Do you promise?" he asked, wanting reassurance.

Elizabeth breathed in deeply. "Yes, I promise." She fingered the collar on her husband's coat. "Tell me, how was your time in London?"

"All transpired well. Fortunately there were no surprises." He leaned over and kissed the top of Elizabeth's head. "You will not believe who I came upon while stopping in at my solicitor's office."

"Who?" Elizabeth asked.

"Mr. and Mrs. Willstone and Emily."

Elizabeth pulled back in surprise to study her husband's face. She knew not what kind of reception he would have received. "And how were they?" she asked.

"They are all doing well. Emily is about to have a new brother or sister. She has grown considerably in the past year. I am also told that Miss Matthews has a fairly strong attachment to a young man from Bristol."

"Truly? Was the meeting between you awkward? Did you sense any ill feelings?"

"I felt awkward at first, not knowing how they perceived me. I did apologize, however, for the misunderstanding and hoped they would understand."

"And?"

Darcy smiled. "Mrs. Willstone was very gracious and attributed my actions to secure your regard as romantic in the least. They expressed a wish to dine with us when we come to Town for the season."

"I should like that very much. I so look forward to seeing Emily again."

"As she also wishes to see you."

Elizabeth sighed. "Any other news?"

"Your aunt and uncle are well. Kitty is doing much better living with them and caring for the children. Since Mary wed Reverend Flourand and moved to Birmingham, Kitty found living with the Wickhams and your mother not especially palatable. I am certain that being the only Bennet daughter unmarried

231

proved to be quite distressing to her. I understood your mother and Lydia both had much to say to her about it."

A twinkle appeared in Elizabeth's eyes and she grasped Darcy's coat sleeve, giving it a tug. "Then we must introduce her to someone."

Darcy looked down with a sly grin. When he looked up, he said, "I already have."

"You have? Who?" Elizabeth asked with eager, yet incredulous interest.

"Hamilton was with me when I stopped by to visit them. He was in port for a few weeks. He certainly had a captive audience in Kitty who laughed at every one of his jokes and who was enthralled by his stories of being at sea."

Elizabeth chuckled. "But certainly he cannot afford to marry someone like Kitty. She has nothing to contribute to the marriage."

"I am not saying that they will, but Hamilton will do well in the navy and he does have a fairly substantial inheritance. He merely likes people to *think* he is destitute."

"He is a good man. I think they would be good for each other." Elizabeth bit her lip as she pondered whether to ask her next question.

"Go ahead and ask," Darcy said. "I know you want to know."

"Has there been any news of Wickham's whereabouts?" Elizabeth asked, fearful however, of the answer.

"None. Your aunt said that Lydia is convinced he will return shortly and she most likely will take him back." Darcy paused, his face clouding over. "But if he returns and the creditors come looking for him, his steward will send him packing."

Elizabeth let out a melancholy sigh and again rested her head against her husband's shoulder. The two sat in silence enjoying each other's presence. There was nothing she could do to stave off the heartache that Wickham might inflict on her family. She knew, however, she could trust the measures her husband had taken in providing for Lydia and her mother in the event of Wickham behaving as they strongly suspected he might. That very thought allowed her to relax in her husband's warm embrace, almost to the point of slumbering.

"Oooh!" Elizabeth suddenly exclaimed, jolting up out of her serenity. She lifted her head and placed her hand across her waist. "Butterflies!"

Darcy shook his head, looking from her to the area around them. "I see no butterflies, Elizabeth."

"No, I felt them! That is how Jane described the first indications of movement! It is as if there is a butterfly fluttering about inside!"

Darcy placed his hand in the same area. "You felt the baby? Can I feel it?"

"I do not think you will be able to now. In due time, though, the poking arms and kicking legs will be sufficiently strong for you to detect." She giggled and said, "There it is, again."

Darcy let out a deep sigh of contentment. Still holding Elizabeth on his lap and keeping his hand firmly against her stomach, he leaned his head against hers.

"Do you mind if we stay up here a little while longer?"

Elizabeth tilted her head up and kissed the tip of his chin. Very softly Elizabeth whispered, "I will stay here with you as long as you wish – forever, if that is your bidding."

Darcy looked down at her, his eyes piercing through to her very soul. His fingers went up and gently stroked her face, and she leaned into them, keeping her eyes upon him. He loved her. He loved her eyes. They had transfixed him ever since the very first time he saw her. They still had the power to stir him. Very gently he pulled her face closer and claimed her lips with his. Their kiss deepened, evidence of the ever growing love they each had for the other. Their embrace tightened as if to ensure nothing would ever come between them.

Fitzwilliam and Elizabeth Darcy would never take their love for granted. They were far too mindful of the fact that had either one not given the other a second chance, their lives would now be dramatically altered. Instead of the abiding love that filled them, they would be consumed with something else… something far more unbearable than regret.

The End

Kara Louise lives in Kansas with her husband.
They share their 10 acres with
an ever changing menagerie of animals.

Other books by Kara Louise ~

Pemberley's Promise

Drive and Determination

Assumed Engagement

Assumed Obligation

and

Master Under Good Regulation

www.ahhhs.net.

Made in the USA
Lexington, KY
19 January 2010